FIRST STRIKE

A PROSECUTION FORCE THRILLER

LOGAN RYLES

SEVERN RIVER
PUBLISHING

Severn River Publishing
SevernRiverBooks.com

This is a work of fiction. Names, characters, businesses, places, events and incidents are either the products of the author's imagination or used in a fictitious manner. Any resemblance to actual persons, living or dead, or actual events is purely coincidental.

ISBN: 978-1-64875-474-6 (Paperback)

ALSO BY LOGAN RYLES

The Prosecution Force Series

Brink of War

First Strike

Election Day

Failed State

The Reed Montgomery Series

Overwatch

Hunt to Kill

Total War

Smoke and Mirrors

Survivor

Death Cycle

Sundown

To find out more about Logan Ryles and his books, visit

severnriverbooks.com/authors/logan-ryles

To Isaac and Emily

For all the good times...
And all those to come.

1

Kangwŏn Province
Democratic People's Republic of Korea

Gok Chin-ho could feel the cold in his bones. Not just seeping in off the mountains and cutting through his threadbare coat, but also radiating from within. Creeping out from his lungs and saturating his blood, it was a cold that transcended the early April frost and spoke of a much more chilling factor.

Fear.

He left the car next to the pothole-infested highway and started into the trees on the lower half of a hillside. Frozen leaves crunched under his feet, and he clutched the folder to his side. Breath misted in front of him, and for a split second, his exhausted vision blurred and the shadows around him merged into a figure—a tall man in an olive drab uniform with a sneer on his lips and armed with an AKM rifle.

Gok stopped, blinking hard and sucking down icy air. The figure vanished—just another illusion of his paranoid mind stretched to a perilous level of strain. He glanced sideways amid the trees and almost stepped back. He could make it to the car and return to the research facility northeast of Pyongyang within a couple hours. He could use his keycard and a crafted excuse to slip past the ironclad security, back into his research office.

Before it was ever missed, he could return the file, lock the drawer, and hurry home. Then he could hold his wife and kiss his daughter on the head, forgetting any of this ever happened.

But long before he cemented his intentions to back out, another thought came to mind. He saw the weapon again, gleaming under fluorescent lights. Sleek, shiny, and even elegant, it was a masterpiece of unthinkable destructive capacity.

A weapon to end the world.

No. He couldn't go back. It was now or never.

Gok pulled his coat closer around his stomach and crept forward, choosing a path between the fallen limbs and away from shallow trenches. A snow flurry drifted past his face, and he looked up to a full moon blazing down amid scattered clouds.

He thought about Sinju, his twenty-year-old daughter. He thought about her future and her freedom. He thought about what would happen to her if he failed.

And he pressed on.

Another hundred meters into the steepening incline, Gok saw the gnarled camphor tree rising above the forest, its evergreen leaves collecting the gathering snowfall. The tree dominated the space like one of the supreme leader's intercontinental ballistic missiles. Its limbs swayed and rustled in the wind, but all else around it was silent.

Gok stopped a few yards away, looking impulsively over his shoulder, then checked his watch. The American should've been there by now, waiting for him next to the landmark tree. Gok clutched the file folder to his stomach and huddled over, feeling the bite of the wind through the myriad of little holes in his threadbare coat.

He risked a whisper into the forest. "John?"

Gok wasn't sure if the name was real or not. The man who called himself "John" was Korean-American by birth, born to a Korean mother and an American Army officer during the seventies—or so he claimed. He looked more Korean than Western, which was probably why he could sneak through the restricted borders of the hermit kingdom without detection. But Gok believed John was from the West. He saw the boldness in his shoulders, symbolizing his fearless efforts to undermine the regime in Pyongyang. This man wasn't cowed by communist abuse. He breathed free air in America, and Gok longed to breathe the same.

"John?" Gok whispered again.

No answer.

Gok started around the tree, choosing his steps carefully. He'd met the American there twice before, once for an initial orientation to his duties, and the second time to report on the presence of the supreme leader's new weapon. John was interested in the weapon—distressed by it, obviously. He wanted proof. He wanted details. He wanted anything and everything Gok could bring him, and in exchange, he was willing to help Gok and his little family flee North Korea.

It was the offer of a lifetime and the gamble of a millennium. Gok knew all too well what the consequences of failure could look like, but he also knew what the consequences of the new weapon could look like, and that second mental image was far worse.

"John?" Gok repeated one last time, raising his voice.

"Chin-ho?" John used Gok's given name, appearing like an apparition out of the shadows ten meters away.

Gok froze, at once relieved and then instantly on guard again. Something was wrong—he could see it in John's strained features. The American's cheeks were pale, and he looked impulsively over his shoulder.

"Did you bring it?" John hissed.

Gok looked into the trees. He couldn't see anything except deepening shadows, but something in his spine began to tingle.

"It's here," Gok said, still clutching the file. His English was weak, but he knew enough to get by. "Did you bring soldiers?"

John stepped forward, holding out his hand. Gok saw his lip twitch, and once again, the American glanced over his shoulder.

Gok stepped back. "What is wrong?"

John snapped his fingers. "Give me the file."

Then Gok heard a click in the distance, barely perceptible but deathly familiar to him. He recalled the sound perfectly from his years in the

Korean People's Army—the snap of an AKM assault rifle switching from safety to fire.

John heard it too, and his face washed pale.

"Run!"

Gok didn't need a second warning. He turned and dashed back down the hill just as the AKM opened fire, joined almost instantly by the voices of two or three of its twins. Gok glanced back to see John hurl himself to one side, then fall to the ground amid a spray of blood, his face blown away by successive thirty-caliber rounds.

The icy fear Gok felt all night turned boiling hot, and he sprinted back to the highway. Bullets snapped through the limbs overhead, and he ducked low, his heart pounding and his lungs burning. The edge of the forest appeared just ahead, the fields beyond now obscured by gathering snowfall. The moonlight had vanished, leaving everything murky dark. He broke through the trees and stumbled over a fallen log, landing face-first in the snow.

More bullets whizzed overhead, joined by shouts in harsh Korean for him to stop. But Gok didn't stop. He clawed his way forward through the ditch and back to his car. One window was shot out, but none of the reckless gunfire had found its way to the tires yet. Gok scrabbled to his feet and rushed around the front bumper, slinging the file in ahead of him. The motor turned over with a lazy cough, and more bullets slammed against the fender.

Gok jerked the car into drive and slammed on the gas. He could see the men streaming out of the trees now. They weren't soldiers of the KPA. No, these men wore the dark uniforms of the Ministry of State Security.

North Korean secret police.

Muzzle flash lit the hillside as another barrage of gunfire ripped toward the car, but now the tires grabbed the busted highway, and the little sedan rocketed forward. In mere seconds, the pops of the AKMs were obscured by the roar of wind ripping through the blown-out glass, and both Gok and his file faded into the night.

2

The pound of the overblown bass was deafening, surging past Reed's earplugs and building into a headache-inducing crescendo inside his skull. Dull lights flashed amid smoke, and the crowd screamed like fifth graders on a field trip to Disney World. He could smell marijuana on the air—mixed with sweet and bitter undertones of whatever else the kids smoked these days—and the constant press of bodies crammed toward the stage twisted and surged back and forth like waves in a hurricane.

Chaos. Anarchy. The worst possible place to conduct security.

Reed stood in the shadows behind the band as America's newest rising superstar, Carmen Rain, danced across the stage and screamed into the mic. She wore almost nothing, which Reed at first interpreted as a stylistic choice, or perhaps a shameless use of her admittedly noteworthy body. After enduring the first sixty minutes of the show, however, he better understood. The stage was brutally hot. Each strobe of the lights sent fresh waves of heat radiating across the band and a new wash of sweat trickling down his back.

He was so ready for this to be over.

Reed adjusted his hand on the grip of the Glock 19 strapped to his hip. His black uniform was now saturated and clung to his skin like a wetsuit, leaving him dreaming of stepping back into the sixty-degree weather outside.

"Birmingham, you're amazing! Thank you!"

Carmen conducted an elaborate twirl, followed by a split right on the stage. Then she ducked her head and dropped the mic, and the stage went black.

Finally.

Reed started forward, joining his cohort as the crowd roared and another surge of weed smoke rolled across the stage. Carmen was already on her feet, stripping the earpiece out and accepting a water bottle from an aide. She led the band off the stage, Reed hanging close to her left side while his colleague took the right. The pound of her latest radio hit was now replaced with a Justin Bieber song from five years before, but the crowd continued to chant her name.

Lights again flooded Reed's face as he accompanied the singer into the back room, then turned his back while she stepped behind a curtain to change. This was his first time working security for a pop star this significant, but the routine was generally the same. Keep close enough to make them feel safe while remaining invisible enough to let them feel superior.

Reed was fine with that. He wasn't interested in fraternizing with a half-naked girl ten years his junior anyway.

Carmen took less than five minutes, reappearing in skin-tight leggings and a brown leather jacket with a fur collar. It was a designer piece Reed had seen before on one of her posters. Apparently, Carmen had signed some kind of endorsement deal with a boutique fur-and-leather brand, and probably received extra money for wearing the outfits as often as possible.

Reed was neither impressed nor impulsively compelled to purchase an overpriced leather jacket.

The singer stopped in the hallway to straighten her hair in front of the mirror, shooting Reed a sideways look as she flicked a lock behind one ear. The glance was followed by a coy wink, and Reed looked away.

They headed down the hallway, through two metal detectors that buzzed as Reed and his colleague passed through with their jet-black handguns still strapped on. They pressed through twin glass doors, back into the glisten of midnight, and Reed greedily sucked down cold air.

Carmen's SUV waited just a few yards away, exhaust gathering beneath the bumper while the driver waited for them. Ten more paces and Carmen would be safe inside, rushed back to the airport for her next set in some other city.

Somebody else's problem.

Reed saw the small crowd rushing toward them out of the corner of his eye, and he picked up his pace. They were fans, mostly, waving poster board signs and squealing for autographs. But sprinkled amongst them, his trained eye caught the hard edge of different expressions—anger and indignation. A quick survey of the signs produced messages of outrage over Carmen's endorsement deal, each etched in harsh, bold letters.

Losers wear fur!

Wear your own skin!

Carmen turned toward the crowd, offering a cutesy wave and reaching out for a Sharpie thrust at her by the nearest maddened fan. Reed shoved in front of her, stiff-arming the kid as the protestors hurried to break free from the pack.

"Ma'am! Get in the vehicle!"

Carmen cursed him and tried to reach around. Maybe she couldn't see the bucket of fake blood swinging from the arm of the skinny white girl with hellfire in her eyes. Maybe Carmen was simply too stupid to know what it meant.

Reed shoved himself sideways, catching the majority of the deluge as crimson rained down like a waterfall. Carmen screamed as Reed's colleague grabbed her by the arm and dragged her toward the SUV.

"Go to hell!" the protestor screamed, hurling the bucket.

It missed Carmen by inches, bouncing off the SUV instead. Then the skinny girl cocked her fist and launched forward.

She never stood a chance. Before she left the pack, Reed was on her, sweeping her knees and ratcheting her arm behind her back. The girl's shoulder popped as her chin smacked the ground, and before he even knew what he was doing, Reed was straddling her with the Glock pressed to the base of her skull.

Everybody screamed. The SUV door slammed shut, and tires squealed. The girl on the ground jerked, and Reed pressed harder with the Glock, forcing her neck down and immobilizing her. He smelled burnt rubber and fake blood, and his vision turned red as his finger slipped off the frame of the pistol, dropping toward the trigger.

Neutralize the threat.

His finger depressed the safety blade, and then he began to squeeze, every molecule of his body ordering him to fire.

"Reed! Let her go!"

He recognized the voice and looked up to see his colleague standing two feet away, his face washed pale, his hands shaking. Reed was suddenly aware of the screams around him evaporating in an instant, leaving everything still and silent.

Then he looked down to see the skinny girl pinned between his knees, her cheek pressed into the rough concrete. She wasn't fighting anymore and had fallen completely limp, the anger in her face replaced by terror.

She no longer looked like a threat. She looked like a terrified kid in over her head. About to be blown away.

Reed lifted his finger and lurched back, his hand shaking as he holstered the weapon. His colleague hurried to help the kid up, while everyone else stood back in a semicircle of horrified silence.

"Get out of my office, and never come back!"

The envelope spun across the desk, landing in Reed's lap. He fingered the smooth paper and stared dumbly at the Glock in front of him, next to his uniform shirt. The fat man sitting across from him was red-faced and sweaty, his shirt unbuttoned to expose a tangled mass of salt-and-pepper chest hair.

"Are you serious?" Reed said.

The fat guy spluttered, then burst into a harsh laugh. "Am I serious? Are *you* serious?" His question exploded into a near-shout, and Reed's back stiffened.

"I did my *job*. You hired me to protect people."

"From psycho murderers and terrorists, jackass! Not from nineteen-year-old college kids with buckets of paint."

"She charged her! What was I supposed to do? Watch it happen?"

"You were *supposed* to step between them. You were *supposed* to deescalate the situation. Does that word mean anything to you?"

Reed looked down at the envelope in his hand. He could see his name printed on the check nestled behind the clear plastic windowpane. He hadn't checked the dollar amount, but the math was simple. Twelve bucks an hour times thirty hours this week.

His first week on the job. His only week.

Reed stood and kicked the chair back. He clenched his fist, crushing the envelope, and leaned over the desk.

The fat guy recoiled, fear playing across his face. His mouth moved but no words came out, sweat dripping from his nose.

Reed just turned and left, not bothering to shut the door. In moments, he was back outside, feeling the sting of the wind biting through his undershirt as he stomped to the 1969 Camaro parked in the back corner of the lot. The old car was battered and in desperate need of new paint, and bullet holes from violent encounters of years gone past were now filled with body putty and sanded smooth. The door creaked as he slid inside, then he slammed it and sat in the perfect stillness. Reed tore the check open and checked the amount, noting that it was at least a hundred bucks short. He jammed it into the glove box and cranked his window down.

The aggressive rumble of the motor flooded his veins with adrenaline—not that he needed any—and Reed slid the shifter into first gear. In seconds, he was rumbling out of downtown Birmingham, headed southeast back into the old neighborhood district of Mountain Brook.

It was a classy place full of homes ranging in size from barely over a thousand square feet to well over ten thousand, all built among the tangled foothills of the Appalachian Mountains. Reed grew up there years before when it was a much more affordable area to live in. After returning to Birmingham six months previously in an effort to settle down, he rented a little house and paid in advance from his savings account.

It was a mistake. Eighteen hundred bucks a month seemed reasonable at the time, calculating based on his previous multi six-figure income as an elite operator. Now that he'd put that life behind him in an effort to become an average Joe, the bills were quickly piling up. He couldn't afford Mountain Brook on twelve bucks an hour. Not even close. When the lease expired, he'd have to move his little family someplace a lot cheaper, and the thought made his stomach churn. Not because he was too good to live simply. Reed had always preferred the simple life, despite his previous wealth. The revulsion in his mind was brought on by a feeling of failure.

This wasn't the life he promised Banks, his beautiful young bride of eighteen months. And it wasn't just Banks anymore, either. It was also little Davy, his newborn son. David Montgomery II was due to be born the next week, but Banks gave birth prematurely. Davy was just four pounds when he was born—so frail he spent the first week of his life at the hospital.

Five weeks later, he'd gained three pounds but was still terrifyingly little and fragile. He still required extensive medical care, also. More bills Reed couldn't hope to pay.

The Camaro squeaked and rumbled as he pulled into the narrow driveway. There was only room for one car, but that was okay. They only had one car. Reed cut the motor off and sat for a minute, listening to the muffler tick as it cooled and thinking about every moment in his life he'd felt helpless.

There weren't many. Reed hadn't lived a life indulging in self-pity or excuses. His chaotic career began with a tour in the United States Marine Corps, which hadn't ended as anybody may have hoped, but no matter the adversity, Reed carried himself through with a relentless belief in his own ability to overcome.

To outlast.

To muscle his way through, no matter the pain.

That relentless strength served him well in the years that followed, full of their own pain and suffering. Sometimes he really believed he'd come to the end of his rope.

But nothing felt like this. Nothing made him feel as incompetent and worthless as watching the bills stack on the end of the counter and knowing he was helpless to pay them. He couldn't obliterate debt with a blast from an M4A1, or snipe bill collectors with a precision shot from a thousand yards.

That wasn't how this new world he found himself in worked, and despite his bleached criminal record, compliments of the White House, Reed didn't have much in the way of a civilian résumé. Actually, he had nothing in the way of a civilian résumé.

All he was good at was neutralizing threats. Corporate America ran from people like him.

Reed dragged himself out of the car, leaving the check in the glove box. Banks would ask about his payroll. She managed all the finances. He would have to explain why it was such a pitiful, worthless amount. He'd have to tell her how they were going to buy diapers for Davy the following month, and how that guy who kept calling from the hospital was going to get paid, and what they were going to do for housing when the pre-payment expired later that year.

Answers he didn't have and didn't want to think about. Right then, he wouldn't even try.

Reed unlocked the door and went inside, noting the sticky note pressed next to the key rack as he hung up his car keys.

Dinner in the oven. Love you.

Banks had drawn a tiny heart next to the note, and it made his stomach twist with guilt. Reed ignored the kitchen, moving down the hallway and into the bedroom without a sound.

Davy slept in the cradle on Banks's side of the bed. Reed knelt next to it and watched his infant son breathing gently, swaddled up in a soft blanket with a blue hat pulled down over his ears. Pudgy cheeks glistened in the nightlight, making Reed feel a little better about Davy's health. At least for now.

He crept back to his feet and walked around the cradle, leaning over to kiss Banks on the cheek. His beautiful wife slept wound up in a blanket, her head resting on a pillow, a cloud of tangled blonde hair surrounding her scalp. When his lips touched her skin, her eyes fluttered open, and she sat up in a rush.

"What is it? Is Davy okay?"

Reed put a gentle hand on her shoulder and whispered to her. "He's fine . . . he's good. I was just letting you know I'm home."

"Oh."

Reed kissed Banks on the forehead and tucked her in. By the time he made it to the bedroom door, she was already fast asleep again—an anxious new mother worn down by long days stressing about her child.

Reed left the bedroom and retrieved a beer from the fridge. The family bulldog snored like a dragon as Reed passed through the living room, pausing to scratch Baxter behind the ears. The dog pretended to still be asleep, but the ripple of pleasure passing up his spine gave him away.

Reed rolled the sliding glass door open and stepped onto the back patio, cracking the beer open and tossing the cap carelessly to one side. He drained half of it, then slumped into the waiting patio chair, looking up through the trees to the black sky and thinking about life. Thinking about days when he didn't feel like a washed-up failure.

He closed his eyes and imagined how it felt to press a trigger—the surge of adrenaline in his blood as he rushed from cover to cover, engaging the enemy and watching as they melted away before him like ice on a griddle.

Not worried about bills or bank account balances or being fired. Just worried about the next shot. Staying alive. Breathing longer than the man he was shooting at.

He imagined what it felt like to live in that moment, with no thought for any future beyond the next five seconds, and more than anything, he longed to feel it again.

Reed drained the beer and rubbed the bottle, his mind blurry with exhaustion. He dug his cell phone from his pocket and thumbed a favorite contact, shooting off a quick text.

FREE TOMORROW NIGHT?

3

"What about purify? Like, purify Washington!"

Jill Easterling, Maggie's brand-new chief of staff, wrinkled her nose at the political strategist sitting across from her. "Purify? Are you serious? What is she, a Brita filter?"

Maggie might have laughed if she wasn't so exhausted. She sipped coffee, simultaneously wondering what coffee tasted like. She drank so much of it these days, she couldn't remember flavor profiles anymore. She only remembered the moderate energy boost each cup promised, and she kept them coming to power through the fourteen-hour days that lined her calendar like a mile of dominos, each one toppling into the next.

This wasn't what she imagined when she dreamed of becoming president. Not even close. And sitting in endless meetings, listening to political analysts and campaign advisors debate which slogan should be printed beneath her name on bumper stickers made her want to jump off the Washington Monument.

"You told me you wanted an anti-corruption message," the strategist spluttered. "I'm telling you that's too narrow. Especially when you're facing off against *two* parties!"

Ah, yes. The party argument again. Ever since Maggie announced her intention to run for office after completing the term of her predecessor, pundits and advisors from every political persuasion clamored for her to "pick a side." Maggie assumed the office of vice president as an independent, something of a unicorn in Washington. She was proud of her lack of political affiliation and didn't see a need to change. She enjoyed the ability to pick and choose policy from both sides of the aisle, depending on what seemed truly best for each individual circumstance.

That was the ideal, anyway. The closer she ground toward Election Day, the more impossible that ideal felt.

"Look," the strategist said, laying his hands flat across the table in an obvious effort to both condescend and humor Jill.

Bad idea, Maggie thought.

"I'm not saying you can't make this thing work straddling the fence. What I'm saying is that we're two hundred and six days away from Election Day, and both the Democrats and the Republicans are gearing up to primary. Ten weeks from now, you'll be battling two *massive* ad campaigns, and both of them will be pointed dead at you. If you don't do something to differentiate your message and get ahead *now*, you won't stand a chance."

"The Trousdale campaign is outraising both parties by a factor of three," Jill said, pushing her gold-rimmed glasses up her button nose.

Oops, Maggie thought. When Jill adjusted her glasses, trouble was on the way.

The strategist smiled. The expression dripped with arrogance. "Look. Jilly. The funding is impressive, I won't lie. But this is a two-party country, okay? Independents don't win. I'm here to make a miracle happen!"

The room fell deathly quiet. Jill didn't so much as blink. Maggie suppressed a grin.

And three, two . . .

"What did you call me?" Jill said.

The strategist frowned. "Huh?"

"*What* did you call me?"

Her voice dropped an octave, still a relative squeak from her five-foot-nothing frame, but carrying an edge nonetheless.

"I . . . uh . . ." the strategist scrambled.

Jill rocketed her chair back with all the force of a fighter jet leaving an aircraft carrier. She slammed her hand against the table, and water jostled out of a pitcher two feet away. The strategist's face flushed as Jill grabbed his notebook and flung it at him like a football.

"Get out! Take your crappy slogans and empty vision, and get the hell out of here!"

He spluttered and looked to Maggie, who said nothing and simply raised an eyebrow. Jill started around the table. She moved like a bowling ball, her petite frame seeming to roll on top of short legs.

The strategist never gave her a chance to reach him. He dashed through the door before she made it to the end of the table, leaving his notebook behind in a flutter of crushed pages.

"Well, that went well," Maggie said, sipping coffee.

Jill's face was crimson as she returned to her chair, smoothing her dress and brushing platinum-blonde hair behind one ear. She took an elegant sip of water and sat straight-backed. "My apologies, ma'am. I should never have brought him in. The man has the imagination of an Easter Island head."

Maggie suppressed a chuckle, watching as Jill poured herself a cup of tea and elegantly stirred honey into it.

She had selected her new chief of staff six weeks after the bloody demise of her last chief of staff. In the context of an administration rife with corruption, her number one priority was to find an outsider. Somebody who could be trusted not to have a closetful of skeletons and an army of patrons pulling his or her strings.

The quest was difficult, mostly because Maggie had no idea where to look or who to trust. But a few whispered conferences and insider tips soon led her to Jillian Easterling—aka "The Cannonball."

Jill was from Pennsylvania and began her career as an intern for one of the state's congressional representatives, eventually working her way up to become his chief of staff, and then dropping him like a rock when rumors of sexual misconduct surfaced.

"I don't tolerate hanky-panky," Jill explained when Maggie asked about the incident. "Married men should keep their junk to themselves."

Maggie tended to agree, but it was the remainder of Jill's explosive résumé that most impressed her. Jill moved on from her role as chief of staff to assume an advisory position for a senator from Ohio, and then she jumped ship to become chief of staff to his rival from across the aisle— Ohio's second senator.

Everywhere she went, Jill left a reputation for relentless hard work, unbendable ethics, and a feisty temper known to strike terror into the hearts of politicians, lobbyists, and journalists alike. That temper, coupled with her unusual rolling style of running, birthed the nickname *Cannonball*.

Jill liked the nickname, sometimes introducing herself by it whenever she felt the need to put somebody on notice. She did not, however, like being called *Jilly*. Not by anyone.

Maggie had no idea why.

"He may be right, you know," Maggie said, fingering the handle of her coffee cup.

"About which part?"

"The party thing. Running Independent gives us twice as many people to defeat. If we picked a side, we could neutralize half the opposition."

Jill shook her head. "You're looking at it backwards, ma'am. Running Independent hurts the establishment more than it hinders you. Most Independents fail for lack of exposure, but you've got plenty of that. You've got plenty of funding, also, which is an indicator that Americans are dissatisfied with their options. Plenty of people who vote one way or the other don't fully align with the political ideology of their chosen party. They just have to pick a side. You'll split the vote, poaching support from both sides and consuming the middle. Trust me. Both the Dems and the Republicans are shaking in their boots right now."

Maggie offered a tired smile. She enjoyed Jill's blunt optimism. She just wasn't sure she shared it. "You really think we can win?"

"With respect, ma'am. I wouldn't have taken the job if I felt otherwise. But you need a campaign manager, pronto. You need a full team. Should have had one months ago."

"I thought you were my campaign manager."

"I'm your chief of staff. When you're on the national level, roles don't overlap. I'm happy to assist your reelection effort, but it's not my area of expertise."

"Do you have any recommendations? I don't know where to look."

Jill nodded. "Of course. I'll make some calls and see who's available. We need somebody who believes in your independence as much as you do, which won't be easy to find. But I know where to start."

Maggie checked her watch. It was nearing noon, which meant the relative peace of sitting in the Roosevelt Room watching the Cannonball roll through strategists was coming to a close. Duty called.

"I do have a question," Jill said, her voice softening.

"Stratton?" Maggie said. "Look, we've been over this. I know he's a Republican, but I trust his judgment. He's been a good VP. I don't see a reason to take him off the ticket."

Jordan Stratton, formerly Senator Jordan Stratton of Illinois, was Maggie's nominee to fill the vice presidency after she vacated the role herself, almost ten months previously. Stratton was a lifelong Republican, which left Maggie somewhat at odds with portions of his political associations. But he was hardworking, deeply honest, and relentlessly loyal. She valued those things more than she worried about party affiliation.

"It's not about Stratton, ma'am. I agree with you. He looks good on the ticket."

"Okay. So . . . ?"

Jill looked away and flushed. Maggie cocked her head, watching as her chief of staff fidgeted with a pen. She'd never seen Jill this way before. She'd never seen her abashed, even for a second.

"What?" Maggie said.

"I'm sorry to ask, ma'am. Please understand I respect your privacy, but . . ."

"What?"

"Are you gay?"

Maggie sat frozen, feeling suddenly very uncomfortable with the temperature in the room.

"Why would you ask me that?"

Her words carried more sting than she intended. Jill flushed a little deeper and slid an iPad across the table. Maggie scanned the screen and felt her own cheeks flush.

"Maggie and Jill—A White House Item?"

It was a tabloid headline, flashy yellow, and matched with a picture of Maggie giving Jill a side hug after introducing her at a press conference. At the time, Maggie thought the image looked comical. Jill never wore heels, and these days, Maggie almost always did, further highlighting the extreme difference in height.

The hug hadn't meant anything. It was just a warm gesture.

"What the hell, Jill?"

Jill cleared her throat, seeming to regain some of her grit. "I'm not trying to pry, ma'am. This story will probably fade into the muck, but leading into an election . . . well . . . people have questions."

"Questions?"

"Questions about, you know. Your love life."

Maggie switched the iPad off. "I'm not gay, Jill. And regardless, my love life is nobody's business."

Jill nodded a couple times as though she were trying to calculate a tactful response. In the end, she chose a blunt answer, per usual. "Except it is, ma'am. Americans are used to their president having a spouse. A family. It's about stability. For a young single woman to run for office with no attachments . . . It's not fair, but the press will eat you alive."

Maggie rested her forehead between a thumb and forefinger. She felt a headache coming on and thought about the half-empty bottle of Excedrin in her desk. She couldn't remember the last day she hadn't popped pain meds to manage the strain in her skull. She needed a break.

Jill got up, collecting her things. "I'll make some calls about the campaign manager. Thank you for your time, ma'am."

She left the room quietly, leaving Maggie in a rare moment of stillness. It felt good, regardless of how temporary it was.

Protect the country. Maintain the economy. Juggle international interests and social norms. Manage Congress. Pass meaningful legislation. Oh, and don't forget a little public romance.

Wow. She needed a break.

A soft tap rang against the polished wooden door.

Maggie sat up. "Come in."

The door swung back, and a tall man in a jet-black suit stepped in. Heavy eyebrows accentuated an iron face and the stern jaw of a cop or soldier.

Or, in this case, her personal bodyguard. James O'Dell served as her chief of security while Maggie was Governor of Louisiana. Since her ascent to Washington, O'Dell had become something of a Secret Service agent, but not really. He carried a gun and underwent extensive training alongside the other agents, but O'Dell served a closer, more personal role.

The past August, when the Air Force One fiasco ended with two dead traitors bleeding out in the presidential bunker, it was O'Dell who cleaned up the mess. It was O'Dell who "took care of things" on her behalf. Made the bodies go away. Arranged meaningful explanations for the disappearances. Made sure nobody would ask questions.

While the rest of America was told that President Brandt's plane went down due to pilot error, O'Dell was one of the precious few who knew the truth about internal sabotage. One of the few who would take that secret to his grave.

Yes, O'Dell was more than a bodyguard. Closer than a friend. He was a right-hand man as near to the core of her administration as one could get.

"Hey, James. What's up?"

O'Dell offered her a respectful smile. "I've got a message for you, ma'am."

Maggie squinted. O'Dell wasn't in the habit of playing message boy. There were aides and emails for that. She could think of only one reason why he would deliver a message himself, in person.

It was off the books.

"Who?" Maggie asked.

O'Dell shut the door gently.

"Director O'Brien, ma'am. He needs to meet with you, off the record, and as soon as possible."

4

Birmingham, Alabama

Reed parked the Camaro in the back of a Dollar General parking lot and lit up a cigarette. The smoke tasted good on his tongue but didn't ease the strain in the back of his mind.

That was the thing about urban stress. Civilian stress. In a combat zone, nicotine worked wonders to relax his body. There was something about being shot at that was so immediate and present.

I was just shot at. I almost died. But I didn't, so now I'm gonna smoke this cigarette and feel good.

The stress Reed felt now wasn't like that. He could smoke a pack a day, and nothing would ease the strain of too many bills and not enough money. Too many needs and not enough answers. That strain was perpetual. Never-ending. It hung like a cloud over his head wherever he went—asleep or awake, day or night.

But he still smoked. Because it was all he knew to do.

He finished the cigarette and flicked it out the window, reaching for another as the Jeep appeared in the parking lot. It was a Gladiator, one of Jeep's new truck models, equipped with heavy mud tires and a moderate muffler just loud enough to growl when the driver hit the gas. The Gladiator pulled next to the Camaro, and Reed got out, not bothering to lock the car as he hopped into the passenger seat.

The man behind the wheel was taller than Reed—a feat, to be sure. At six-foot-six, Rufus "Turk" Turkman was one of the most imposing men Reed had ever known. A born Tennessean with a thick accent and a penchant for lousy jokes, Turk was Reed's oldest—and maybe *only*—friend. They met in the Marines, and many roadblocks and catastrophes later, the relationship they enjoyed felt a lot more like brotherhood than anything else. It was a relaxed, comfortable thing. A dependable thing.

"You're late," Reed muttered, slamming the door.

"Didn't know I was on a schedule."

Turk spun the Gladiator around and back onto the highway, buzzing his window down and hanging one arm out. He drove slouched back, his knees poking up near the steering wheel, his head only an inch from the ceiling.

Reed followed suit with his window, then lit another smoke. "You know. They make bigger trucks."

"Jeep don't."

Reed chuckled, blowing smoke out of the side of his mouth. The wind sucked it out into the night, and he passed the cigarette to Turk.

"Banks at the house?" Turk asked between drags.

"Yeah."

Turk said nothing, but Reed detected the question on the air. He slouched into his seat, feeling the tremble of the Gladiator's tight suspension shooting up his spine. The feeling reminded him of Iraq and riding in Humvees. Maybe that was why Turk insisted on buying Jeeps, even though they were much too small for him. They reminded him of good times, maybe. Times when they both had a purpose in life.

"She thinks I'm working," Reed said, answering the unspoken question.

"Night off?" Turk asked.

Reed grunted. "You might say I was recently allocated unlimited nights off."

Turk took a long pull on the smoke, holding it for a while before he tilted his face to breathe out the window. He rested the smoke against his leg, twisting it like a pencil.

"Sorry to hear it," he said at last.

Reed shrugged. "It is what it is."

They rode in silence for a while, the county roads around them leading into progressively rural landscapes with nothing but occasional houses and rolling hills to break the monotony.

"You need some money?" Turk asked awkwardly.

Reed flicked his hand. "Nah, man. We're good. Still got some cash from before."

It was a lie, but Reed wasn't about to divulge his financial stress. That was his problem, and he'd solve it. One way or another.

Turk grunted and popped a stick of gum into his mouth, leaning back again. "How's my nephew?"

Reed smiled, thinking about little Davy. He'd spent most of that morning playing with his infant son, tickling him gently until Davy's chubby cheeks lifted into a toothless grin. It was still far too easy to feel Davy's ribs, but he was slowly gaining weight.

The simple joy in his eyes was . . . priceless. Reed never thought he'd see anything as beautiful as Banks smiling up at him. But with Davy, it was different. It was deeper, somehow. More primal.

Davy had his mother's eyes. Reed thanked God for that.

"He's great," Reed said. "Looks more like his mom every day."

Turk grinned. "Well, there's a stroke of luck."

They both laughed as Turk turned off the paved county road and onto a dirt drive. Trees overhung the Gladiator on both sides, their spider-like limbs scraping against the roof as they bounced over potholes and through shallow ruts. Up ahead, Reed saw a ten-foot chain-link fence, lined with barbed wire and wrapped in a thick chain. "Private property" and "No trespassing" signs lined the fence alongside the bold logo for a prominent local TV station.

Turk stopped the Jeep, and Reed slid out, jogging to the fence and dropping to his knees. He slipped the lockpicks out of his pocket and made short work of the padlock, unwrapping the chains and pushing the gates back to allow Turk to pass. Then he hopped back in, and they bounced another hundred yards into a wide clearing, surrounded on all sides by the chain-link fence.

Rising from the middle of the clearing was a TV tower reaching nearly fifteen hundred feet high, with distant red lights marking it all the way to the top. Guide wires were strung from the tower down to the packed Alabama dirt on all sides, holding it in place as sparse clouds passed slowly overhead.

Turk cut the Jeep off and tilted his head to peer upward. They sat quietly, enjoying the stillness.

Turk shot Reed a sideways look. "Hoorah?"

Reed smashed his knuckles against Turk's. "Hoorah, Jarhead. Let's roll."

They piled out of the truck and hurried around back. Turk had a tonneau cover stretched across the Gladiator's bed, latched down. As he moved to unlock it, Reed detected the faintest hint of a limp in his right leg —residual effects of a gunshot wound to the thigh the previous August. Turk was ninety-five percent recovered from that injury, but he still moved stiffly sometimes.

The undersized cabin of the Jeep wasn't helping.

Turk lifted the cover and dug through the bed, towing out twin harnesses strapped to parachute packs. Reed slipped his legs through the harness, locking the straps across his chest. He adjusted everything to make sure it fit correctly, then double-checked his access to the parachute's pull cord.

Everything was in place.

He moved to Turk's pack, and they took turns inspecting each other's gear.

"Good?" Turk said.

"Good."

Turk shut the tailgate, then they started toward the tower. Another ten-foot fence lined with barbed wire surrounded its base. Reed defeated the lock, and they moved inside, ducking through the support struts and inside the metal superstructure. A ladder waited, leading straight up the core of the tower.

Reed's stomach tightened as he looked up. The shifting clouds overhead gave the illusion that the tower was slowly falling to one side, already making his head spin before he even left the ground.

He ignored the growing nausea and placed one foot on the bottom rung, then began to climb.

All his life, Reed had been afraid of heights. As a Force Recon Marine, parachuting was a mandatory activity, and Reed eventually developed a comfort with it, repeating numerous high- and low-altitude jumps in both training and combat.

But he never *liked* it, and after he left the Marines, he did whatever it took to avoid encounters with high places.

That was, until he settled down with Banks. Until the gunshots stopped and life was littered with more overdraft fees than adrenaline boosts.

That was when Reed developed a new relationship with his fear of heights. A relationship that made that fear the target of his every aggressive instinct. The fear was his enemy, now—his only enemy—and he'd vanquish it, one way or another.

With each passing rung of the ladder, the ground below faded away, and the wind whistling through the tower's bars felt colder on Reed's cheeks. Turk climbed just below him, hauling himself up with easy pulls of his muscular arms. Together they crossed the halfway point, and Reed tilted his head back to view the bottom side of the service platform still another seven hundred feet up. The clouds moving by seemed to rush now, and his head swam. He almost let go of the ladder as an overwhelming sensation of plummeting sideways to his death overcame his mind.

Reed clamped his eye shut and stopped, clinging to the ladder a long moment and waiting for the dizziness to pass.

"Don't look at the clouds," Turk drawled. "You do this every time."

Reed muttered a curse and started climbing again. The rungs bit into his hands and felt narrow under his boots, but the angrier he felt, the easier each step became. This wasn't about fear anymore. This was about over-coming. Vanquishing.

It was no different than ten months earlier when he and Turk flew to Turkey at the behest of President Maggie Trousdale. No different than when they fought their way out of an Iranian firefight, only barely escaping with their lives.

This was just another form of war.

They eventually reached the platform, and Reed crawled through the narrow hatch first. He avoided looking down as he used the superstructure to steady himself, then slowly stood up. It felt so much colder up there than it did fifteen hundred feet below. The wind howled, too, battering against his face.

Reed wished he'd brought goggles to block out the wind, but no, he wasn't going to need those. This would be over too soon.

Turk reached the platform behind him and stood a minute, adjusting his parachute straps. Reed busied himself, stretching and hopping on the balls of his feet and listening to the creak of the platform beneath him. He let the prospect of an impending fall flood his veins with adrenaline, blocking out the fear.

It's time.

"Hey, look." Turk pointed through the bars, back down the drive toward the road.

Reed followed his gaze and saw headlights pointing toward the gate. The vehicle was motionless for a moment, then it turned off the county road and started down the track, toward the tower. Reed couldn't make out much between the tangled tree limbs, but he thought he saw a shadowy bar stretched across the roof of the SUV.

Cops.

"Go!" Turk hissed, pushing him toward the edge of the platform. Reed moved, ducking his head to slide through the bars, then followed with his legs until he stood on the outside of the tower, his legs curled back to grab the edge of the platform. His stomach conducted perpetual somersaults. Everything inside of him, down to the molecular level, screamed at him to get back inside the protective barrier of the bars. To hurry back down to the ladder. To *not* do what he was about to do.

Reed grinned, enjoying the sting of the wind in the cold of night. And then he simply let go.

The air that rushed by his face was supercharged with a dump of adrenaline, flooding his mind and bringing his body to life with electric energy. The first half of the tower rushed by in a blur—flashing by so quickly that Reed couldn't really see it—and then he was only five hundred feet off the ground.

Reed pulled the chute, feeling the snap of wind against the cloth snatching him upright and sending his feet rocketing downward. His arms shook, but none of the fear remained. Now all he felt was unmatched elation. Perfected freedom.

No stress. No bills. Just a glorious brush with death.

His feet hit the ground, and Reed rolled, dropping to his knees to absorb the shock and then landing on his feet again. His body shook, and he clenched a fist, shooting it toward the sky as Turk plummeted down just behind him. Another chute snapped in the air, and then Turk was swinging down, returning the fist pump as his boots made contact.

Blue lights flashed, and a siren chirped. Reed clawed his harness off and quickly moved to wrap the parachute into a bundle.

"Leave it!" Turk shouted, ripping his own off and breaking into a run toward the Gladiator.

Reed didn't need to be told twice. The Chevrolet Tahoe bolting out of the drive bore the yellow stripes of a county sheriff's deputy, and the spotlight flashed on. Turk threw himself into the driver's seat and hit the ignition as Reed slammed his door. The tires spun, and Turk jerked the wheel to the right.

"Stop! Get out of the vehicle!" the cop barked through a loudspeaker.

But Turk wasn't about to stop. Reed clung to the overhead handlebar as the Gladiator completed its spin and made a beeline for the gap between the trees and the rear bumper of the Tahoe.

The cop saw what they were doing and shifted into reverse. White lights joined the taillights of the SUV.

Reed gripped the dash, holding his breath as Turk planted his foot on the gas. Trees flashed by, and the Tahoe shot backwards.

Then they were through. Turk's right rear fender scraped against the Tahoe's bumper, but it wasn't enough to stop them. They hit the track again and bounced over ruts, rocketing through the open gates and back onto the county road. Turk flipped his headlights off and turned left, stomping the gas and flying over the next hill.

In mere moments, they were lost in the winding foothills, Reed's mind a mess of flashing trees and overwhelming, glorious thrill. He slumped back into the seat, still grinning and panting to catch his breath as Turk slowed and glanced into the rearview mirrors.

Then Turk laughed, and Reed reached for the cigarettes.

"Hoorah?" Turk said.

"Hoorah, Jarhead."

5

After sharing half a pack of cigarettes, Turk returned him to his car, then headed back north. Reed's old battle buddy lived in East Tennessee, someplace about three hours northeast of Birmingham. It was a long drive, but it was Friday night, and Turk had the weekend off.

It was worth it.

The Camaro rolled to a stop at the end of the driveway, and Reed flicked the ignition off. His body was battered and sore and still tense with the strain and thrill of the last two hours, but it was good not to think about anything for a while. Even if it was temporary.

He slid his key into the front door and gently turned the lock, thinking about taking a shower before bed—something to wash the smell of cigarettes away and prevent Banks from questioning how he smoked at a non-smoking job. He didn't want to lie to her.

The door slipped shut, and Reed kicked his boots off, then stretched and headed for the kitchen. Beer first. Then shower.

He dug a Yuengling from the back of the fridge, then popped the top off against the counter's edge and drank half of it, the refrigerator door still open.

It burned on the way down, and his muscles relaxed.

"Where the hell have you been?"

Reed almost jumped out of his skin. He stumbled back, pivoting toward the voice. Banks stood in the shadows, dressed in an elegant white nightgown, her arms crossed and eyes blazing.

Reed wiped his mouth and lowered the beer, hesitating. "Work," he said at last, wincing as the lie left his mouth. He hated lying to her.

Banks pursed her lips. "You sure about that?"

Reed didn't answer.

She took a step forward, glaring up at him, her blonde bangs trailing into her face.

"I called the office, jackass. I told them we hadn't received your direct deposit. Know what they said?"

Reed didn't answer. There wasn't much to say.

"They said they cut you a check when they *fired* you." She punched him in the chest, hard enough to sting.

Reed stumbled back, allowing the refrigerator door to swing shut.

A tear slipped down Banks's cheek. "Why did you lie to me? Where did you go?"

Reed looked at his feet and suddenly wished he could crawl into a hole. He'd never felt like that in his life. Not once. Not until he let Banks down.

"Is there somebody else?" Banks whispered, her voice hoarse.

Reed's gaze snapped up. "No. No, it's not like that."

She spoke through clenched teeth. "Then *what* is it?"

"I . . . I met Turk."

"You met Turk. You went drinking?" Her voice softened, and he wondered if she was giving him a way out. He wondered if she wanted him to take it.

But he couldn't lie to her again.

"No."

"Where did you go?"

"We went jumping."

Banks's bottom lip trembled. Everything was still, like the eye of a hurricane, then she slapped him hard enough to rattle teeth.

Reed's head snapped back, and she leaned in, driving her hand as though she were trying to take his jaw off.

"Damn you, Reed. You *promised* to stop that!"

Reed fell against the counter, disoriented. His face stung.

"What's wrong with you?" Banks screamed, tears rushing down her face. "You're a father, Reed! A father! Does that word mean anything to you?"

It was the second time in as many days somebody had asked him that question. Reed still didn't have an answer.

"It's not like that, Banks." Reed rubbed his cheek. "I just . . . You don't . . ."

"Don't what, Reed? Don't understand?" She pointed toward the bedroom. "Davy is my son. You hear me? My *son*. I won't let him grow up fatherless. Not like I did. Not like *you* did!"

Those final words sank in like bullets, ripping right through him. Reed felt primal rage explode in his chest, and he clenched his fist, standing tall over her.

"Don't you *dare* use that against me! My son will *never* be without a father."

"You sure about that? Because I'm waking up in the middle of the night, and I can't find you."

Reed turned away. He clamped his eyes shut and breathed slowly, trying to cage the monster within. Trying to shut down the blazing rage that surged through his blood like poison.

"You have no idea what this is like for me," he whispered through gritted teeth. "I spent *years* mattering. Years with a purpose, a job . . . Something to be good at." He wheeled around, snapping in a millisecond. "Now I can't even feed my family!"

Banks's cheeks were streaked with tear stains. She stood in the dim light, looking frail and fragile, like she was a breath away from just curling up and dying.

Reed felt the anger inside grow cold, leaving instead an emptiness hallmarked by the pain in her face.

What kind of man am I?

"Those are *our* problems, Reed. Not yours. Ours. But we can't be *us* if you lie to me."

She walked out of the kitchen, storming down the hall. He heard the bedroom door shut and the lock click. Then everything was still, leaving him with nothing but a silent kitchen and a half-empty beer resting on the counter.

6

Oval Office
The White House

The man sitting across from Maggie was of average height, but his spindly frame, bald head, and eagle-like nose made him look taller than he was.

Victor O'Brien, Director of the Central Intelligence Agency, was relatively young for his position—only forty-eight. But he fit the role as well as his suit fit him, matching the stereotype of a cold, calculating spook so naturally he appeared born for the role.

Maggie liked him. She felt he was good at his job, and he never wasted her time. But she wasn't sure she trusted him. That was impossible to say.

The woman sitting next to O'Brien looked nothing like him. She was short, a bit overweight, and wore a cheaper suit that didn't fit as well. An underling, Maggie figured. An analyst, advisor, or some nature of specialist. She was good at her job, certainly, or else O'Brien wouldn't have brought her, but not sporting a high enough salary to justify a better wardrobe.

"Thank you for meeting with me, Madam President," O'Brien said. His voice was calm and neutral, but Maggie could tell something was on his mind—not just because he requested to meet with her. That was rare, but not strange. She could tell because he requested to meet with her "off the record."

That could only mean bad news. News she might want to disavow later.

"Of course, Mr. Director. What can I do for you?"

"I'm afraid we have a situation. It's quite delicate. Top secret, actually. I must insist it doesn't leave this room."

Maggie glanced from O'Brien to the woman. He'd never spoken to her this way before—not with so much authority. She didn't mind it so much, but it put her on edge.

"What's going on?"

O'Brien motioned to the woman. She dug into the briefcase and produced a file, laying it across the table between them and flipping it open. Inside were several high-gloss pictures of a long, sleek rocket. Well, more likely a missile, complete with sharp fins projecting from either side and tipped with a white warhead.

"Are you familiar with missile technology?" O'Brien asked.

"Assume not."

"What you're looking at is a Chinese-made DF-ZF hypersonic glide vehicle. Somewhat similar to a missile, but not the same."

"A nuclear weapon?"

"A nuclear weapon delivery system, similar to an ICBM."

"Intercontinental ballistic missile. I'm familiar."

O'Brien flipped the image over, exposing a blank back side, and clicked a pen open from his pocket. The woman still hadn't spoken. She watched quietly from the chair next to O'Brien, adding to Maggie's discomfort.

O'Brien drew a large circle on the paper. "ICBMs are pre-targeted launch vehicles. This means when they leave the silo, they launch into a preordained flight path that is both predictable and unmodifiable. Pretend this circle is Earth, and on the left side we have Russia. The right side is Los Angeles . . ." He marked an X on each side, then drew an elongated curve up, over the top of the globe, and back down to the other side. The shape resembled the Gateway Arch in St. Louis.

"If the Russians launch an ICBM from Moscow, the weapon breaches the atmosphere and hurtles through outer space, crossing the ice cap and plummeting back through the atmosphere to hit its target. It's like playing tennis. The server hits the ball up, it arches over the net and lands. You can see it coming and predict both its flight path and target, which allows you to intervene prior to impact."

"Anti-missile defense systems?" Maggie said.

O'Brien nodded. "Exactly. ICBM flight paths can't be altered post-launch, which allows us to knock them out of the sky en route. In theory, anyway. Like hitting a tennis ball before it lands."

Maggie tapped the sheet. "But this weapon is different?"

"Very different. A hypersonic glide vehicle—sometimes called a hypersonic missile—never leaves the atmosphere, and it can be steered en route, like a drone or a jet. A very fast jet. Our intel on China's DF-ZF is limited, but we estimate it is capable of flight speeds in excess of Mach Five, or about one mile per second."

O'Brien returned to the circle and drew another line from Russia to Los Angeles, but this time, it wasn't a parabola arching into outer space and crossing the North Pole. This time, the line cut straight across the planet, zigging up and then dropping back down at random before making impact.

"We can't predict the flight path. That's the bottom line. The weapon could head for Los Angeles but reroute for San Francisco or Seattle mid-flight, drastically inhibiting our ability to shoot it down. At Mach Five, we would have little to no warning."

The room went silent, and Maggie thought about old eighties movies like *War Games* and *The Day After*. Those films were made during a period where the entire world waited in breathless fear at the prospect of total nuclear holocaust, only moments away at any given point.

The world had moved on, she thought. Sure, she knew nuclear weapons were still an integral part of international diplomacy. A theoretical threat.

But this . . .

"We don't have anything like it?" Maggie asked.

"We're working on our own prototypes. Neither ours, nor the Chinese version, is truly weapons capable, but we're both getting closer every day. Unfortunately, that's not the problem."

Feeling a sudden chill, Maggie looked up from the sheet. "What's the problem?"

O'Brien shuffled through the papers and exposed a new image. Unlike the first, this one was grainy and dark. Shadows played across it, making it difficult to make out the focal point of the image.

Maggie lifted the sheet and squinted, studying the shapes. At first, she saw nothing, but then it jumped out at her like one of those trick photos with something blatantly obvious hidden in plain sight.

It was the weapon, she was sure of it. The Chinese DF-ZF hypersonic missile lay across giant steel sawhorses in a warehouse, semi-covered by a tarpaulin. In the background, she thought she saw people, too, dressed in radiation suits and moving amid the shadows, but the image was too grainy to be sure.

"Where is this?"

O'Brien cleared his throat. "That photo was taken three days ago, inside the Yongbyon Nuclear Scientific Research Center. In North Korea."

Maggie's blood ran cold. She held the image and looked from O'Brien to the woman who still hadn't spoken. She dropped the image on the table. "The North Koreans have this?"

O'Brien blinked behind his glasses and nodded once. "It seems so, ma'am."

"Why am I just now hearing about it?"

O'Brien gathered the images back into the folder, then flipped out a new page and tapped on the heading. It was a personnel file, with another grainy black-and-white image printed in the top corner.

"Gok Chin-ho, ma'am. Korean nuclear physicist and weapons engineer. We've been slowly grooming him as an interior asset for the last eighteen months, hoping to mine details of Pyongyang's nuclear weapons program. He was the one who photographed the weapon inside Yongbyon and notified the Agency of its presence. Our intentions were to trade schematics of the weapon for assistance in getting both him and his family out of North Korea."

"Your intentions *were*?" Maggie pressed.

"Two nights ago, our interior agent, a Korean-American asset code-named Monk, was scheduled to rendezvous with Gok and retrieve the schematics. Monk went offline shortly before the scheduled rendezvous, and we haven't heard from him since. We're getting nothing out of Korea."

"What does that mean?" Maggie said. "And again, why am I just now hearing about this?"

O'Brien twitched. "At any given time, the Agency is running dozens of highly covert, top-secret operations. We read you in the moment any operation becomes worthy of your attention."

"You mean the moment you have no other choice."

O'Brien didn't answer.

Maggie turned to the woman, suddenly annoyed by her perpetual presence and prolonged silence. "Who are you?"

The woman straightened. "Dr. Janet Strickland, ma'am. I specialize in the study and analysis of the Democratic People's Republic of Korea and the Cho Regime."

"You mean North Korea?"

"North Korea is a Western term, but yes, ma'am. That's what I mean."

"So, why are you here?"

O'Brien stepped in. "Dr. Strickland is the unchallenged authority on politics and culture inside the DPRK. She knows more about Cho Jong than Cho himself, and she monitors the entire nation on a micro-level. If somebody sneezes in Pyongyang, Dr. Strickland finds out why."

"Is somebody sneezing in Pyongyang, Doctor?" Maggie asked.

Strickland nodded. "I'm afraid so, ma'am."

She flicked through the sheets and produced yet another image, this one grainy again. It was of a Korean man, maybe fifty or fifty-five years old, dressed in an olive drab military uniform.

"General Jang Bon-hwa, a senior military official inside the Korean People's Army. He's climbed the ranks quickly, especially in the last five years, but intel from some of our interior assets indicates he's not as enchanted with the supreme leader as the rest of the nation."

"Enchanted?"

"It's an accurate word. To understand the DPRK, you have to understand the way the North Korean people view the Cho family, and Cho Jong specifically. He's more than a dictator to them . . . much more. He's closer to a god. The Cho family has remained in power over the last seven decades by leveraging extreme isolation and propaganda. North Korea is a truly brutal place to live, consumed by poverty and human rights abuses unrivaled by most places in the world. But the people don't revolt because half of them are brainwashed into believing they actually live in a worker's paradise, and the other half are too afraid to speak out against the regime."

Maggie tapped the photo of General Jang. "But you said this guy is different?"

"He is. Early in his career, Pyongyang appointed him as a liaison to Beijing and Moscow. Jang has traveled extensively on behalf of North Korea, and he's seen the truth about the outside world. More than that, however, Jang is a true radical. We don't know a lot about his personal life, but intercepted correspondence between Jang and some of his trusted associates indicate dissatisfaction with the Cho regime."

"He opposes dictatorship?"

"Quite the contrary. He doesn't feel Cho has gone far enough. North Koreans are fed an endless stream of anti-Western, and specifically anti-American, propaganda. They are taught from an early age that we are the enemy, and only the infinite wisdom of their supreme leader can save them. Jang believes the propaganda about the West, but he doesn't believe Cho is doing enough to confront us. Jang wants open war—nuclear war, preferably, and we believe he may be ready to take matters into his own hands."

O'Brien stepped back in. "We believe General Jang may be plotting a coup, ma'am. Our assets in Pyongyang are signaling increased tension between military officials and party leaders inside the government. It's likely that Jang will be displaced and executed in the near future, but in the short term, there's still a risk he influences Cho in the wrong direction or seizes power altogether. Pyongyang's existing nuclear arsenal is a problem, but we're confident we could deflect any attack they launched, given enough notice."

"But not with a hypersonic missile," Maggie said, pointing back to the stack of photographs.

"Exactly. We really don't know how Pyongyang got their hands on this. It could be a fake. It could be a gift from China, or stolen from China. It could be something they cooked up on their own based on a stolen Chinese or Russian design. Regardless, the risks are far too great to ignore. We *need* Gok's schematics, now more than ever. We need to get him out."

"Why are you coming to me with this off the record?" Maggie asked.

"Why aren't we in the Situation Room with a full panel of military advisors?"

O'Brien shifted, but Maggie already knew the obvious answer.

"The details of our operation with Gok are highly classified," he said. "Details of what we know about China's hypersonic programs, North Korea's nuclear programs . . . It's not something we want to advertise. But more importantly, we can't send traditional assets into the DPRK to retrieve Gok. The Agency doesn't have the available manpower, and it would be illegal anyway."

Maggie connected the dots. "You need me to authorize somebody off the books. A black ops team."

"That would be ideal."

Maggie crossed her arms. She didn't like this position. She didn't like being off the books, in the shadows, talking to one half of her government and cutting out the other. Everything about it put her on edge, and for good reason.

She'd been here before, and it rarely ended well.

"I don't keep spooks in my back pocket, Mr. Director. That's not how the White House works."

O'Brien exchanged a glance with Dr. Strickland, then he smoothed his pants over his knees and leaned forward. "With respect, Madam President. We both know that's not true."

7

Minsu Jeong knew something was wrong the second he stepped out of his shabby, fifteen-story apartment. The city was dark and not yet stirring in the pre-dawn hours of early morning, but there was a tension in the air that defied the stillness.

Pyongyang wasn't a busy city. Workers arose at sunrise to usher skinny kids off to school before boarding busses of their own to ride to state-assigned jobs. In spite of six- and eight-lane-wide highways, traffic was light to the point of being sparse. Only government officials and the very elite owned cars. Everybody else used trains and busses—dated contraptions gifted from the USSR.

Even by eight or nine in the morning, there wouldn't be a lot to listen to in Pyongyang—the clatter of a passing train, the occasional shout of one neighbor calling a greeting to another, some foot traffic.

It was calm, in a dead or dying kind of way. At four a.m. it should've been almost silent, but it wasn't.

Minsu heard the shouts from four blocks away, carrying easily down the wide highways as they were joined by the bark of a loudspeaker, and then there were successive handgun shots.

He ducked low into the shadows alongside the towering apartment blocks, easily dodging the spotty pools cast by occasional streetlights. It was dark in Pyongyang, not just because the sun had yet to rise but because electricity was restricted.

The closer Minsu drew to the clamor, the more difficult each step became. A warning deep in his mind alerted him that he was headed down a dangerous path. That he would be better off returning to his apartment, crawling back onto his creaking mattress and sleeping until sunrise like everyone else.

But Minsu couldn't turn back. It was his job to be on the street when nobody else dared leave their homes. The Americans counted on it.

Two hundred yards passed beneath his worn shoes, and then Minsu rounded a corner, remaining in the shadows as he peered toward the source of the noise.

It was a laundromat—another state-sponsored affair, worn, with dirty windows and a crooked sign. Minsu knew the place and had frequently employed its services when the laundry center in his aging apartment block failed. He immediately noticed the shattered front door and detected the oily odor of a gasoline fire on the air.

Minsu crouched in the darkness, sifting through his pocket for the camera. It didn't look like a camera. It looked like an asthma inhaler. A gift supplied by the Americans. He wasn't sure if they would care about a laundromat fire, but they might take interest in the knot of Korean People's Army officers gathered around the front door, beating the piss out of a scrawny Korean man.

Minsu took pictures, squeezing the inhaler to trigger each snapshot. There were eight KPA officers standing in front of the laundromat, highlighted by the slow flash of a protection department fire truck's red lights and the more rapid blue flash of security department police cars.

The man on the ground screamed, holding up his hands and pleading for mercy. Minsu recognized him as the laundromat's manager, an old man named Dak-ho. The KPA officers were busy bludgeoning him with short clubs, striking his legs and chest as he desperately attempted to shield his face.

"Where are they?" one officer shouted. "Who are you working with?"

Dak-ho screamed and tried to scrabble backward. The KPA officers followed him, boots joining the clubs in a perpetual shower of abuse. Minsu subconsciously shrank into the shadows, but then he noticed the other faces leaning out of the darkness on the far side of the street—more Koreans, leaving their apartments to see what the fuss was about.

"Tell us, you dog!"

Dak-ho curled into a ball, sobbing on the concrete. The next boot landed on his ear, crushing down and twisting. The old man cried out but didn't answer the question.

Minsu lowered the camera and surveyed the edges of the streets. He no longer needed to conceal himself in the shadows; he wasn't alone. Dozens of Koreans now crept out of the darkness, watching in muted terror as the beating continued. Two of the KPA officers broke from the pack to threaten the growing crowd, swinging bloodied clubs at them.

The people didn't move.

Then a long black sedan with no license plates arrived. It rushed down the street from the direction of the government district and was accompanied by twin motorcycles driven by men in matching black uniforms. Secret police.

Minsu's stomach churned, and he crammed the camera back into his pocket. It was time to leave now. He didn't need to stay. The Americans would be happy with the pictures.

The sedan ground to a halt, and the secret police parked their bikes, hurrying off and shouting at the KPA officers. The knot around Dak-ho loosened, and then the driver of the black car rushed out to open the back door.

The man who exited the back seat was short and slight. If he were a woman, he might have been called petite, with narrow shoulders and a round head crested in greying hair. As he left the car, he swept a gloved hand through his hair and deposited an olive drab hat over his scalp, topping off his KPA officer's uniform.

At first, Minsu didn't recognize him. He was just another officer of the bloated People's Army who'd come to see the show. But then a dim street-light glinted over the three stars pinned to each of his shoulders, and Minsu reached for the camera again.

The little man pushed past the secret police and looked down at Dak-ho. The forty-odd onlookers who watched from the shadows shrank back at the sight of the general, but nobody left.

Everyone waited for the inevitable.

The general crouched next to Dak-ho and twisted his jaw around. Minsu saw his lips move, but he couldn't make out the words. Dak-ho shook his head and muttered a plea.

The general's gloved hand tightened, and he repeated his demand, loud enough this time for the entire square to hear. "Where are the Americans?"

Minsu's blood ran cold. He crammed the camera into his pocket and stumbled back, but there was nowhere to go. The sidewalk behind him was now crowded with other Koreans, standing in horror as they watched.

Dak-ho sobbed and shook his head. The general released his jaw, rifling instead through the old man's threadbare jacket. He found a small flag, about the size of a napkin, folded up inside an interior pocket. An *American* flag.

The general stood up, his face twisting into a semi-gleeful sneer. "Traitor!"

Dak-ho screamed and clawed his way back, shaking his head and sputtering. He never got the chance to flee. The general dropped his hand into a wide coat pocket and produced a pistol. The safety clicked, then a flame blasted from the muzzle.

Dak-ho went down, but the general kept firing, emptying the gun into the dead body. A horrified gasp rang around the small crowd. Another episode of the Pyongyang theater.

The general jammed the gun into his pocket and snapped an order at one of the secret police officers. They thrust a bullhorn into his free hand, and he held up the little flag.

"Comrades! A traitor has been found in our midst. The Americans have sent agents into our city to poison the minds of our neighbors and incite them to commit acts of terror!"

Still clutching the flag, the general thrust his fist toward the burned-out laundromat. "They are here to bomb our city!"

Minsu could feel the ripple of palpable fear passing through the crowd behind him.

"We will run these rats from their holes and gun them down in the name of our dear leader!" the general screamed, saliva spraying from his lips. "Return to your homes! Anyone found on the streets will be suspected of treason."

Minsu joined the surge of bustling men and women hurrying back toward apartment blocks like a river of bodies, crushing in on every side as a universal undertone of panic rippled among them. Minsu kept up easily, pulling his coat tight around his chest.

He was just as afraid as anyone around him, but not for the same reasons. Unlike the others, Minsu knew the Americans.

And he knew they hadn't bombed a laundromat.

8

Maggie leaned over the Resolute Desk, sifting through the documents O'Brien had left for her. Thoughts of her impending campaign for reelection and the dozens of pressing decisions that needed to be made were long gone as images of nuclear holocaust took their place. She focused on the grainy photo of the hypersonic missile and tried to envision a weapon like that racing through the sky five times faster than the speed of sound, beelining for a major American city.

Even with a small warhead, hundreds of thousands would die. Millions, maybe. O'Brien left her a list of probable targets, alongside estimated casualties for each city. She wasn't sure how accurate the numbers were or if O'Brien simply invented the data in an effort to manipulate a green light for his planned mission.

It didn't matter, really. After the smoke cleared, a nuclear detonation in the middle of Kansas with only a thousand casualties would be just as deadly as a blast in the middle of Times Square. Both options would necessitate a full, strategic nuclear response from Washington.

Both options would result in full, global nuclear war. And at that point, tens of millions would die. Hundreds of millions.

What kind of brain-dead quack could *possibly* want that?

Of all the things she dreamed of doing as president, preventing nuclear Armageddon wasn't high on the list. From her first day in office, Maggie's presidency was chaos. The demise of her predecessor, President William Brandt, was a violent and terrifying affair that brought the entire globe closer to World War III than any event post–Cold War. Thanks in no small part to the black ops team Maggie illegally deployed into Turkey—the team she denied ever existed—such disaster was averted.

For a while, anyway. She had lied to the American people about Brandt's death, knowing that the truth was too dangerous to reveal. After calling the White House "home" for only nine months, one thing she knew with conviction was that another crisis was *always* just around the corner. The best she could hope for was to maintain calm. Maintain control.

Sometimes that required bending the truth. Spinning the story. But the reality O'Brien had laid out for her was something she couldn't spin. It was an ultimate threat.

The phone on Maggie's desk rang, and she hit the speaker button, not bothering to check the caller ID.

"Yes?"

"Ma'am, it's General Yellin. We have an evolving situation that requires your attention. Could you make time to meet us in the Situation Room this afternoon?"

Maggie checked her watch. After lunch she was due to meet with activists from Pennsylvania—a battleground state—to discuss corporate corruption and the protection of blue-collar jobs. Not the highlight of her day, but it promised to be less stressful than whatever problem the chairman of the Joint Chiefs was about to dump in her lap.

"Is it pressing, General?"

Yellin didn't hesitate. "I'm afraid so, ma'am."

"Okay. Let's do it at one thirty."

Maggie hit the end call button, then bumped the shortcut for her secretary's desk.

"Yes, ma'am?"

"Clear my afternoon, please. I'll be tied up."

―――――

The Situation Room was far from Maggie's favorite spot in the sprawling White House complex. Nestled on the ground floor of the West Wing, the conference-style room was barricaded by Secret Service agents and secured from digital intrusion with state-of-the-art, noise-isolating walls, hardwired video and internet feeds, and enough coffee to keep Maggie's cabinet running until the end of time.

Stratton, Maggie's vice president, used to joke that the Situation Room was like a nuclear aircraft carrier—capable of sustaining life and missions until the ice caps melted and the world became a swimming pool.

Maggie guessed Stratton was being funny, but she'd spent far too many stress-filled hours in this darkened room to find it charming. Maybe she'd commission a redecorator to come in and brighten the place up. As long as she would have to sit in there, saving the world from itself, it couldn't hurt.

O'Dell met her just outside the Oval Office, offering a tight smile and a cup of coffee.

"Fast morning, ma'am?"

She grunted. "Any other kind?"

He followed her all the way to the entrance of the Situation Room but hung back as she entered. The conference room table on the other side was already surrounded by the bulk of her National Security Council, with Jill sitting at her right-hand side and Stratton on her left. From there, the chairs were occupied in no particular order by her secretaries of State, Defense, Treasury, Energy, Homeland Security, her attorney general, and General Yellin. There were a couple people missing, most notably her ambassador to the United Nations and National Security advisor, but Maggie wasn't perturbed. On short notice, it was next to impossible to get the entire NSC around this table in under an hour.

Everybody stood as Maggie entered, and she offered a polite greeting, moving directly to her chair at the head of the table.

As everybody settled in, Maggie took a sip of water from the glass waiting for her, then glanced around the table. Her gaze stopped on O'Brien.

The CIA director's bald head gleamed under fluorescent lights near the end of the table, his owl eyes staring at her behind polished glasses.

Maggie sat with the glass halfway between her lips and the table, a question on her face. O'Brien was not part of the NSC and would only be there by special invite of a ranking member. She glanced at Jill. Her chief of staff only shook her head.

"Thank you for joining us on short notice, ma'am," Yellin said. The chairman of the Joint Chiefs was big, stuffed inside an Army dress uniform like the Michelin Tire Man. Bulging shoulders were lined with four gleaming gold stars, while his chest was decorated with enough medals to set off a metal detector across the room.

Maggie didn't know the general all that well, but his performance during the Brandt crisis was admirable, if a bit hotheaded at times. She felt he was good at his job, and in her mind, competence was a priceless commodity.

"What's going on, General?"

Yellin tilted his head toward O'Brien. The director of the CIA sat stiff-backed and attentive. "I invited Director O'Brien to join us. This morning, he told my department about concerning events in the DPRK. I've asked him to brief the NSC as a whole."

O'Brien got up and cleared his throat. "Madam President. Ladies and gentlemen . . ." He lifted a remote from the table and clicked a button. The eighty-inch screen at the end of the room flickered on, displaying a satellite map of North Korea.

"Last night, the Agency received encrypted messages from an asset deep inside Pyongyang, the capital of the DPRK. The photographs you're about to see were taken first on street level, and then from the windows of an apartment complex near the southeastern corner of the city."

O'Brien clicked the remote, and grainy photos played across the screen. The first appeared to display a small group of North Korean soldiers beating a man on a darkened sidewalk, just outside a laundromat. People were gathered to watch, and as the images progressed, Maggie noticed a growing pool of blood on the sidewalk.

She winced, and O'Brien turned to address the table.

"We're not confident of the identity of the victim. Shakedowns and beatings such as this are common in North Korea. Anyone suspected of treason, espionage, opposition to the state, or defamatory remarks against the regime is brutally punished. But what happened next is altogether unusual."

O'Brien clicked the remote, and images cycled ahead to display a black car pulling up next to the curb. A short man got out, his face obscured as he pulled a hat over greying hair. The next several images were blurred, and Maggie could only make out vague shapes, but the last photo was as crisp as a yearbook mugshot. The short man in the olive drab uniform leaned over the victim on the sidewalk, a pistol pointed downward, his face lifted into a sneer.

Maggie's stomach twisted. She recognized the man.

"You're looking at General Jang Bon-hwa, a senior-ranking officer of the Korean People's Army and a suspected direct advisor of Cho Jong. He's served as Pyongyang's primary defense officer for the last three years, with direct responsibility for state security in the event of an invasion or insurrection."

O'Brien clicked the remote again. The next image showed Jang screaming at the surrounding crowds with the aid of a bullhorn, his left fist clenched and held toward the sky. There was something wrapped between his fingers, tangled and difficult to make out in the grainy photo. O'Brien clicked the remote again, exposing a zoomed and enhanced image of the item in Jang's grip.

A soft gasp rang around the room, and Maggie felt the twist in her stomach again. The item was a small American flag.

"Jang is a known radical," O'Brien continued. "Intercepted correspondence between the general and some of his trusted associates include calls for the annihilation of the West, specifically the United States. He's a passionate advocate of the DPRK's nuclear program and is suspected of serving as a liaison between Pyongyang and Beijing to negotiate the sale of nuclear components for the construction of more developed weapons. The Agency is unclear how much influence Jang holds over Cho, but we know he regularly interacts with the dictator and probably reports to him directly."

O'Brien looked to the table. "Questions?"

Nobody spoke, although Maggie noted several people, including Jill, taking notes. O'Brien sipped coffee and hit the remote again. This time, the screen flipped from a photograph to a satellite image of a sprawling city. It was far clearer than anything Maggie had ever seen taken from Google Earth or a mapping software. She could make out people standing on random street corners and a dog lifting its leg over a fire hydrant. The city looked grey and desolate, with the shabby roofs of apartment blocks lined by clotheslines and potted plants.

"This is Pyongyang about five days ago," O'Brien said. "Note the empty streets and sparse foot traffic. Very few North Koreans own private vehicles, and many use trains and busses for transportation. At the time this photograph was taken, mid-morning, there's almost nobody on the streets. Most are either working at state-sponsored jobs or otherwise sheltering inside from cold weather."

O'Brien clicked the remote, and everything changed. The image was the same, displaying the same wide swath of aged buildings and grey streets, but now those streets were *packed* with traffic. Funny little green vehicles, surrounded by men carrying rifles, lined the streets, with further parties of armed personnel standing at the entrances of various apartment blocks. On the roofs of some towers, more soldiers were visible, kicking over the potted plants and holding citizens at gunpoint.

Maggie leaned forward impulsively.

O'Brien used the laser pointer built into the remote to mark spots on the screen. "You're looking at detachments of the KPA—the Korean People's Army. The men you see here, in olive drab, are KPA infantry. These figures here, in black, are officers of the DPRK's Ministry of State Security. Secret police, essentially."

He clicked through more satellite photos of different parts of the city, all displaying mass troop movements among businesses, factories, residential districts, and parks.

"The Agency has monitored Pyongyang for the past twelve hours," O'Brien continued. "It's unclear exactly what is happening, but the asset who photographed General Jang informed us that prior to sending everyone home, Jang blamed a gasoline fire at the laundromat on American terrorism and promised to root out those responsible. We believe that the troop movements you see in Pyongyang are an escalation of that effort and may be a preemptive effort of General Jang to trigger instability in the city while pointing blame at the United States."

O'Brien set the remote down and settled into his chair as though he'd just delivered a sales pitch on a new type of printer.

Secretary of State Lisa Gorman was the first to speak. "Wait a minute. Are you suggesting this guy is trying to trigger a war?"

O'Brien didn't answer immediately. He looked dead at Maggie, then folded his hands. "All I can tell you is that we didn't bomb that laundromat, but Jang is saying we did. He's placed the city on lockdown and is systematically searching every building for signs of Western terrorism. I can't be sure what he expects to find, and I can't prevent him from finding it."

"What does that mean?" Stratton asked. Maggie's vice president stat straight-backed next to her, his thick black hair neatly combed as ever, an impeccable deep blue suit matched with a royal blue tie and an American flag pin. "Are you saying we've got something to hide?"

O'Brien shook his head. "Absolutely not, Mr. Vice President. I'm saying that I can't prevent him from manufacturing whatever evidence he's looking for."

The usual flurry of questions filled the room. Maggie was accustomed to the routine at this point. The NSC usually took a moment to assimilate an intelligence report, but given enough time, they all had questions.

Maggie didn't have questions. She heard the subtext beneath O'Brien's message loud and clear, and it both frustrated and chilled her. It frustrated her because she felt like O'Brien was leaning on her, manipulating her in public to enable his black ops mission. It chilled her because deep down, she wondered if he was right. If this was as serious as it looked.

"Can I have the room, please?" Maggie asked.

Everybody fell suddenly quiet, swiveling toward her in confusion.

Maggie gestured to the door. "Please."

The NSC reluctantly stood and began to shuffle toward the door, making a show of checking phones and watches.

"Director O'Brien, stay. You too, General."

The doors shut behind the NSC, and Maggie waited for O'Brien and Yellin to resume their seats. O'Brien settled into his chair, making a show of smoothing his tie.

Maggie folded her arms. "Are you screwing with me, Mr. Director?"

"No, ma'am. Not in the least."

Maggie evaluated him, then tilted her head toward Yellin. O'Brien took the hint and dove right into a repeat of the brief he'd given Maggie the previous day, outlining the general details of the hypersonic missile discovered in North Korea, along with basics on its capabilities.

Yellin didn't ask a lot of questions. Maggie guessed the general was already pretty familiar with hypersonic weapons. She could tell by how his face turned grey that O'Brien hadn't been exaggerating the risks, either.

"As I said before . . . Jang is a radical," O'Brien said, wrapping up his spiel. "We can't be sure how much, but if there's even a chance he's staging a domestic emergency in order to trigger a standoff with the United States, we can't leave that unanswered. We need details of that weapon. We need to get Gok out."

O'Brien hadn't mentioned his request for a black ops team, but Maggie knew he didn't need to. The general was a smart man, capable of complex political and military math conducted in his head and on the fly. By the time O'Brien finished the speech, Yellin had already evaluated options of special forces and strategic recovery teams.

None of that would work. Maggie knew it, and Yellin knew it.

The general looked at her and simply nodded. "He's right, ma'am. If there's even a chance Pyongyang has their hands on a weapon like this, we can't afford to waste time. We need all the intel we can get."

"You mentioned assets," Maggie said, turning back to O'Brien. "You have people in Pyongyang?"

The director seemed hesitant to answer. "We have intelligence assets. Not operators."

"So, they can't find Gok themselves?"

O'Brien shook his head. "No. North Korea isn't a very diverse place. All our people on the inside are Koreans, able to blend in with the local population. But that also means they're highly restricted in their ability to move throughout the country, especially under Jang's lockdowns. And even if they could find Gok, they wouldn't be able to help him. They don't have the training or the equipment."

Frustration boiled within Maggie. She thought about her campaign and Election Day only a couple hundred sunrises away.

This wasn't what she needed to be worried about right now. The last thing she wanted to be doing on the cusp of the most important political race of her life was green-lighting an illegal black ops mission in the heart of the world's most secretive and corrupt nation.

Yet...

She thought about that missile again and what it would mean for the lives of millions to be at risk if America didn't step in. Winning an election wouldn't matter if she couldn't do her job *today*.

Maggie hit zero on her phone. "Send in O'Dell, please."

She hung up and looked from O'Brien to Yellin. It was obvious they were both thinking the same thing she was.

"I'll reach out," she said. "But I can't promise he'll take the job. Reed Montgomery is in retirement."

O'Brien leaned forward. "Then pay him, ma'am. Whatever it takes. We can't lose this one."

9

Birmingham, Alabama

The dull lights of the Sonic drive-in gleamed over the hood of the Camaro, barely illuminating the interior as Reed sat slouched back, a cheeseburger in one hand and a Coke cradled between his knees. Banks sat next to him, the remnants of a chili dog resting in her lap and a milkshake in one hand. She wore her hair in a ponytail, and without a speck of makeup on her smooth cheeks, Reed thought she'd never looked more beautiful.

He remembered the first time he saw Banks back in a bar in Atlanta. It hadn't been that long ago, really. About a year. But the memory felt enshrined in some sacred vault of his mind—a hallmark of his life.

Like the moment his father first let him sit behind the wheel of this very car. Or when the Eagle, Globe, and Anchor was slipped onto his chest and he officially became a United States Marine. Or years later, when he found Private Jeanie O'Conner lying dead in the Iraqi sand, beaten and bloody, raped and abandoned—the moment he tracked down her murderers and gunned them down like the dogs they were.

The moment The Prosecutor was born.

That night cost him his career, his freedom, and everything he ever loved or called home. It set him on a path of self-destruction that led through organized crime and more bloodshed than he cared to remember. But even though it required a presidential pardon to set things right in the end, Reed didn't regret it.

Because in a strange way, all those moments led him here, to a run-down fast-food restaurant east of town, sitting next to the love of his life, with his infant son nestled into a car seat behind them.

Reed sipped his Coke and looked over his shoulder, watching as little Davy slept, a tiny trail of drool slipping over his dimpled chin. He'd been right before when he told Turk that Davy looked like his mother. It gave him two beautiful faces to lose himself in every day.

Banks slurped her milkshake, then scraped whipped cream from the bottom of the cup and sucked it off the tip of the straw.

"Want another?" Reed asked.

Banks chuckled softly. "I think we're out of change."

Reed looked into the cupholder beneath the gear shifter. Three or four nickels, a quarter, and an insignificant number of pennies remained. It was all that was left of the spare change he'd scrounged to take Banks on this date.

Not for the first time, Reed felt like the biggest failure in the state. Counting those coins, he couldn't help but think about the dollars remaining in their bank account. It was enough to buy groceries for next week and pay the power bill, but not much more.

"Hey . . ." Banks put a gentle hand over his, her blue eyes shining with a hint of the old sparkle he loved so much. "Don't worry about it. I'm fat anyway."

Reed tried to laugh. Banks was the furthest thing from fat. She'd gained weight since returning to the States, but he would've been a lot happier if she'd put on a few more pounds.

He crammed the trash back into the bag and tossed it through the window and into a nearby trash can, then started the motor. "Let's take a drive."

They left the Sonic and took back roads outside of town, weaving through low hills fragrant with spring growth. Reed kept an eye on the fuel gauge, conscious of his need to refill the tank before beginning a job search the next day, but he decided not to overthink it.

Right now, he just wanted to be with Banks.

After a long cruise away from the city, Reed pulled into a county park and stopped the car in front of a wide-open field. It was dimly lit by security lights mounted high on telephone poles, and a hundred yards away, a small group of kids were tossing a Frisbee.

The engine cooled, and Reed leaned back, watching the kids play. He imagined what Davy would look like when he got to be their age and wondered if he would enjoy things like Frisbee and the outdoors. Or would he be nerdy? Would he like video games and computers?

Reed hoped he liked the outdoors. He hoped Davy saw value in the world sprawled out around him.

"This is nice," Banks whispered.

Reed took her hand and felt her fingers slip between his. He leaned close, kissing her softly. The kids shouted and laughed in the distance, and the muffler ticked, but it was all just background noise.

Reed settled into his seat again, gently stroking the back of Banks's hand with one thumb. "I could sell the car," he said at last. "That would give us enough to pay off some medical bills and buy some time."

"No," Banks said almost immediately. "You're not selling the car. It's the only thing David left you."

Reed looked out his window, rubbing his lip and longing for a cigarette. He'd been trying to cut back lately because of the expense and because Banks was worried about his health. He never smoked around Davy anyway, but right then, a cigarette would have really taken the edge off. "We're running short on options," he said. "When the lease runs out, we'll need to move."

"We'll figure it out." Banks gave his hand a squeeze. "I'll find a job. We'll make it work."

"You can't work. Who's gonna take care of Davy?"

"Maybe I can find one of those work-from-home jobs. Do something on a computer."

Reed smiled. The gentle strength in Banks's voice was like a levee. Waves pounded against it, and thunder rolled . . . but Banks couldn't be broken. Reed loved that about her.

"You're not getting a computer job," Reed said. "I'm going to figure this out. There are still some security firms in town. I'll make some calls."

They lapsed back into silence, watching the kids fight over the Frisbee. It seemed to be some kind of organized game, similar to football. They surged back and forth across the field, occasionally reaching a goal line and cheering. It looked fun.

"Wanna go home and get naked?" Banks said suddenly.

Reed reached for the keys. "Do I ever."

The drive home lasted half as long as the drive out. Reed pushed the old muscle car, and Banks turned up the radio. She sang along in the same soft, melodic voice Reed first fell in love with. It made him think of times gone by when Banks used to play her ukulele and write songs.

He wanted to buy her a new ukulele. It wasn't a memory he was ready to let die.

They were still five miles from the house when Reed first saw the car. It was grey and boring, with glistening LED headlamps and nothing in the way of stickers or modifications. He could tell from even a hundred yards away that it was a rental. As the car wound closer, his suspicions were confirmed by the presence of a branded license plate on the front bumper, advertising the rental company.

A tall man wearing sunglasses was seated behind the wheel of the small Ford. At each turn and traffic light, the vehicle followed the Camaro, hanging one or two cars back, but remaining close enough for Reed to track it in his rearview mirror.

Banks caught him fixated on the mirror and looked over her shoulder, peering through the back glass and then becoming distracted as Davy woke up.

"What is it?" she asked.

Reed shrugged casually. "Nothing. Cool car."

He switched his attention to the side-view mirror, turning off the highway and into Birmingham's Mountain Brook subdivision. The Ford followed at a distance but pulled to the side of the street half a mile before Reed reached his house. At the next intersection, Reed turned right instead of left, making a wide circle up the mountainside and then down a steep hill before passing the car again.

"What are you doing?" Banks asked, still bent over the seat to watch Davy.

"I like this hill," Reed said with a shrug.

"Well, get me home, Cowboy. The moment might pass."

Reed turned back into Mountain Brook, stealing a quick glance at the Ford. The driver lay back in his seat, still wearing sunglasses despite the time of day. As Reed passed, the man twisted, lifting the glasses and making eye contact.

Reed looked ahead, feeling a rush of adrenaline in his chest. He turned left at the stop sign and pulled into his driveway, switching the Camaro off and helping Banks unlatch Davy's car seat. The little guy had woken and began to cry, but as soon as Banks cradled him over one shoulder and caressed his back, he calmed.

"Don't worry," she whispered. "He'll be out in a minute."

Reed unlocked the door, then paused in the doorway, fumbling with the keys.

"We're . . . I think . . ." He looked back to the street.

"What?" Banks whispered, still caressing Davy's back.

"We're out of protection," Reed said. "I better run and grab something. Unless"—he pointed to Davy and shot her a cheeky wink—"you want another."

Banks rolled her eyes. "No way. Hurry!"

She shut the door, and Reed slid back into the Camaro, thoughts of Banks and a romp between the sheets already fading as he made his way down the street to the intersection. He rolled through the stop sign and checked for the Ford as he reached the bottom of the hill, but it was gone.

Reed expected that. He stopped at the light and thought quickly, putting himself in the shoes of the man behind the wheel—evaluating what his next move might be.

Reed flicked his blinker on and turned right.

10

The Vulcan statue was the largest cast-iron statue in the world, fifty-six feet tall and set on a stone pedestal atop a mountain ridge just south of downtown Birmingham. Crafted to depict the Roman god, Vulcan, deity of fire and forge, the statue was originally cast in the early twentieth century as a symbol of Birmingham's heritage in the ironworks industry.

Reed remembered visiting the statue with his father, and he also remembered a concrete trail carved into the mountainside just beneath the statue, with a clear view of the Birmingham skyline spilled beneath it. It was a quiet place, almost always empty at this time of night, and only ten minutes away from Mountain Brook. If the man behind the wheel of the Ford wanted to talk, the Vulcan Trail was as good a place as any.

Reed made it to the statue in seven minutes and parked at the head of the trail, slipping a SIG P226 from the glovebox and tucking it into his pants before leaving the car. He didn't see the Ford, but that didn't necessarily mean anything. The driver could've parked higher up the mountain and walked down.

The trail was quiet, overhung by hardwoods and nestled against the mountainside with the city spilling off to Reed's right. Only his footfalls rang off the concrete, with the gentle whisper of wind drifting past his face.

Reed kept his hands at his sides, free and ready for action, but he wasn't really expecting a fight.

Not from this man.

Reed reached the overlook and stopped, turning away from the continued trail and looking out over the city below. It spread beneath him like a tapestry of lights and sounds, the bulk of the downtown towers rising out of the valley in a concentrated knot, with hospitals and the University of Alabama at Birmingham clustered closer to the mountain.

It was beautiful and had always been one of Reed's favorite places in the world.

A footstep tapped the ground to Reed's left, but he didn't look up. He kept the man in his peripheral vision as he dug a cigarette out of his pocket and cupped his hand to light it. The man stopped ten feet to his right, giving Reed enough room to remain comfortable, and then he turned to take in the skyline.

"Hello, O'Dell," Reed said.

The man next to Reed shook a cigarette out of his own pack and lit it up. He stared at the city as though it were an art piece and then took a long drag before answering. "Hello, asshole."

Reed snorted and blew smoke through his nostrils. It had been over a year since he first met James O'Dell, personal bodyguard to Governor Maggie Trousdale. Their first encounters hadn't been pleasant, and as the months faded and Trousdale ascended to the vice presidency and then the White House, O'Dell hadn't forgotten.

Reed didn't care. He wasn't O'Dell's biggest fan, either.

"I saw a campaign ad the other day," Reed said. "Trousdale's gonna need to put an *R* beside her name if she wants to win Alabama."

O'Dell grunted. "Polls say otherwise. But we both know you don't care about politics."

"I really don't. So, why are you here?"

O'Dell reached beneath his jacket and produced a narrow file folder.

Reed accepted it, noting the "TOP SECRET" stamped across the face. He didn't comment as he flipped it open, exposing grainy images of some type of missile, followed by mug shots of an ugly Korean man in full dress uniform.

"General Jang Bon-hwa," O'Dell drawled. "Korean People's Army."

"DPRK?"

"Right."

"What's with the missile?"

"Hypersonic nuclear delivery vehicle," O'Dell said. "You familiar?"

"No."

"If an ICBM is a moped, that thing's a Corvette."

Reed peered at the missile, noting the fins built along one side near the nose. He shut the file and handed it back. "What do you want, O'Dell?"

"Not to be here talking to you, I assure you."

"Trousdale sent you?"

"Yes."

"I thought I made it clear the last time I talked to your boss. That business in Turkey was a one-time deal. I'm not an on-call ass-kicker. I don't work for the White House."

O'Dell replaced the folder in his jacket and lifted the cigarette from his lips. "There's a man named Gok Chin-ho inside North Korea. He's the one who slipped us the images of that missile. It's a Chinese weapon, and the Koreans aren't supposed to have it. But apparently, they do, and we really need to talk to this Gok guy about where they got it and if it's operational. There's some BS going down in Pyongyang right now, and it's possible a coup could be underway. General Jang is a radical. We need to make sure he's not a radical with a superweapon."

"And you think I can help with that?" Reed laughed, lighting another cigarette and blowing a cloud of grey toward the skyline.

"I think you're unemployed, behind on medical bills, and have three hundred and eighty-two dollars in your checking account. I think you've been fired from three jobs in the past six weeks, and you have a real problem settling into the real world. I think you've got a bad habit of jumping off tall things that weren't made to be jumped off, and I think your buddy Turk likes to jump with you." O'Dell faced him for the first time. "I think you're a loose cannon and a real SOB. But I'm not paid to think. I'm paid to make job offers."

Reed felt something between anger and defeat boiling inside of him. He wanted to hit O'Dell, and he wasn't sure why. Nothing Trousdale's Cajun bodyguard said was untrue, and Reed wasn't particularly ashamed or embarrassed by any of it. But hearing it all shoved in his face in one giant wad, like a crap sandwich packed with condescension and a side of the pathetic, made him realize just how bad it all was.

Reed looked away. "I don't work for the government anymore. I made a promise."

"That's nice, Reed. But take it from another guy who screwed without a condom. You don't get to keep promises anymore. Only commitments."

Reed sucked on the cigarette, enjoying the dull aftertaste. He let the space between them grow quiet, then he lowered the smoke. "How old?"

"Fourteen," O'Dell said. "She lives with her mom in Shreveport. Won't talk to me."

"I'm sorry."

O'Dell grunted, flicking his smoke down the mountainside. "That's life, Montgomery. Just because she won't talk to me doesn't mean the checks stop coming. You can keep scrabbling from job to job, getting fired and racking up debt, or you can take an all-expenses-paid vacation to Asia and forget about bills for a while. Better yet, you can scratch that insanity itch that's got you jumping off of TV towers like a brain-dead moron. Just name your price."

Reed avoided his gaze, thinking about little Davy again. Thinking about those bills and the clothes he needed. Thinking about the medical care Banks really should be receiving to help manage an ongoing fight with Lyme disease. Thinking about rent and the fact that a fifty-plus-year-old muscle car was no kind of family vehicle.

He held out his hand. "Let me see the folder again."

The house lay quiet when Reed switched the Camaro off. He sat, surveying the flower beds and thinking about how Banks planned to plant tulips when they first moved in. There hadn't been money for that, but he'd never forgotten.

Banks loved flowers. He kind of liked them himself.

Reed exited the car and stretched, feeling the weight of the SIG pressed against his spine. He unlocked the front door and slipped inside, still thinking about those tulips. Somehow, the empty flower beds around the porch felt like a metaphor for his entire life.

Reed eased the door shut, listening to Baxter snore from the living room. He turned and found Banks standing in the kitchen, dressed in elegant lingerie that barely reached her hips, a lacy neckline diving low, suspended by narrow straps.

She stood with her arms crossed, her bangs tucked behind one ear, her eyes cold. "Make it to the drug store?"

Reed pocketed his hands as he stood in the hallway, unsure of what to say and so sick of lying. "No."

"That's okay. Turns out we've got a whole box of protection."

Reed nodded, dropping his gaze across her elegant shoulders, then a little farther south. She looked so good. She always did. Every man in love thought his woman was an angel, but Banks . . . Banks was something special. One in a billion.

"Trousdale?" Banks asked, holding her head up.

Reed nodded.

She swallowed but didn't drop her eyes. A proud woman. A *strong* woman. "Can you tell me where?"

Reed shook his head.

For a while, they just stood there, the house still, save for Baxter's incessant snoring. Then Banks nodded softly, and she stepped forward, wrapping her arms around his back and running her hands up to his neck. She pulled him in and they kissed, long and slow, her tongue touching his and her fingers slipping through his hair. He cradled her back and pulled her close, smelling her skin and thinking about how perfect she felt in his arms.

Banks broke the kiss and looked up at him. She was crying, but there was a soft smile on her lips. "You'll always be my soldier," she whispered. "That's never going to change."

She pulled him into a hug, her chin resting against his shoulder. "Just promise me you'll come home."

He lifted her off her feet, sliding one powerful arm beneath her hips. She wrapped her legs around his torso, and they stumbled into the bedroom.

Reed whispered as he kissed her neck, "I promise."

11

By now, Reed was familiar with the dance. Whenever Trousdale needed to move people off the books, she employed aircraft operated by SAC, the CIA's Special Activities Center. A Gulfstream jet, piloted by two reclusive men in plain clothes, waited for him and O'Dell at a private airport outside the city. Within hours of his meeting on the Vulcan Trail, Reed was streaking north into Tennessee to pick up Turk.

Reed's old battle buddy had received a similar invite from Trousdale, and he was waiting on the tarmac with a worn backpack and a giant cheeseburger. His Gladiator sat parked in a long-term lot, and he greeted Reed with a short nod before settling into a seat and chowing down on the burger.

Once they were back in the air and headed toward Washington, O'Dell appeared from the aft cabin and walked them each through a series of mission briefs from the CIA, detailing the man named Gok Chin-ho and his involvement with North Korean nuclear programs. The more Reed read, the more chilled he became. O'Dell's association of a hypersonic missile as the Corvette of the tactical-weapons world was the understatement of the year. China's hypersonic guide vehicle wasn't a sports car, it was a stunt jet—literally.

And there was almost nothing America could do to shoot it down.

"We should launch first," Turk muttered, sifting through documents across from Reed. "Wipe these jerks off the map before they get cute with us."

O'Dell sat back in his seat and covered his face with a New Orleans Pelicans hat. "If you can't get Gok out of there, that may be our only option."

Reed locked eyes with Turk and saw a reflection of the tension he felt in his stomach. He looked out the window and watched the darkened Virginia countryside roll by, a field of black and grey with clusters of lights around small towns and airports. He wondered what that countryside would look like after a hypersonic weapon made impact in DC, just a hundred miles north.

What would any of the country look like? Chaos. Panic. A complete unraveling of fragile social fabric.

The Gulfstream circled west of Joint Base Andrews once, then landed quickly, diving in and turning toward an open hangar without any interaction with ground crew. Reed felt the plane grind to a halt and the engines wind down, then he looked out his window to see steel doors rolling shut behind them.

It was the same routine as the last time he visited Washington. Except this time, he wasn't an international fugitive. This time, things were a little more under his control.

"You'll have to check your weapons," O'Dell said, standing.

Reed shot him a look but chose not to argue, handing over the SIG. Turk produced a Glock 22 from his backpack, along with two spare mags and a knife. O'Dell took it all and dumped it into a seat, then nodded toward the cockpit. The air lock hissed, then the airstair swung outward.

"This way, gentlemen."

Reed and Turk followed, and the moment Reed's boots hit the concrete floor of the hangar, he knew something *was* different this time. An army of men in black suits guarded the perimeter of the building, their gazes locked on the three men leaving the aircraft. None of them looked military to Reed —more like Secret Service—and that made him wonder.

"This way," O'Dell muttered, leading them away from the plane toward a large office built into one corner of the hangar. It was guarded by two more men in suits, and long before Reed or Turk reached it, they were surrounded by agents carrying handheld metal detectors.

"Arms up, please."

Reed lifted his arms, spreading his legs and submitting to an invasive pat-down. The guys at the office door stepped aside, and then O'Dell led the way in.

The interior of the office was all one room, lined with desks, file cabinets, and computers, with a section in the middle cleared to leave room for a circle of office chairs situated around a table. Sitting at the far side of that table, dressed in a simple blouse with her dirty blonde hair pinned back, was President Maggie Trousdale.

Reed stopped, his hands in his pockets. He offered a deferential nod. "Good evening, Madam President."

Maggie rose and stepped around the table, offering her hand. "Hello, Reed. Thank you for coming."

Reed gave her hand a perfunctory shake, then returned his hands to his pockets. After greeting Turk, Maggie invited them to take a seat.

There were two other men at the table. Reed recognized one as General John David Yellin, chairman of the Joint Chiefs. He was a bulldog of a man, restrained by a subdued uniform. The stars were there, though—four of them on each shoulder.

The second man was short and mousy, with a bald head and round glasses. He eyeballed Reed the moment they entered the room, and Reed thought he recognized him, but he couldn't recall his name.

O'Dell retrieved a round of water bottles from a case and passed them out, then stood behind Maggie with his arms crossed, like some kind of tough guy.

Reed shot him a wink, then drained half the bottle.

"O'Dell briefed you on the flight?" Maggie said.

Reed nodded. "We know the situation. We don't know the plan."

Maggie gestured to the bald guy with the glasses. "This is CIA Director Victor O'Brien. He's got an idea where you can start."

O'Brien took his time joining the conversation, looking from Reed to

Turk and then back again, as if he expected one of them to suddenly leap across the table and eat him.

"As you know, your target is Gok Chin-ho, a North Korean physicist and nuclear weapons expert. He went offline two days ago during a rendezvous with his handler, during which he was supposed to produce schematics and details of the weapon. The handler also went offline, and we've been unable to reestablish contact."

"So, we're just supposed to waltz over there and . . . poke around?" Turk said.

"Of course not," O'Brien snapped, visibly irritated. "The best strategy would be for you to connect with his family. They live in a small village nine miles inland from North Korea's eastern coast. By the time you reach them, we should have better intel from inside Pyongyang about other places he could be hiding, so if they don't know where he is, we'll direct you from there."

Turk shot Reed a sideways look. Reed knew they were both thinking the same thing: *So, you want us to waltz over there and poke around.*

"How do we get there?" Reed asked.

Yellin answered this time. "We can't HALO jump like before. The DPRK runs far too tight a radar network for us to get anywhere close to their borders. But their coastal defense technology is pretty weak."

"SEAL Delivery Vehicle?" Reed asked.

Yellin nodded. "We've got a detachment of SEAL Team Five stationed in Japan and attached to the Seventh Fleet. They can get you in."

"What about extraction? Same plan?" Turk asked.

"We'll keep the SEALs on standby. As soon as you find Gok, you'll make contact, then meet us at the coast. We'll put Gok in a wetsuit and pull him out using the SDV."

"How are we supposed to communicate with you guys during all this?" Reed asked.

"My people are loading the plane as we speak," O'Brien said. "You'll be equipped with full tactical gear, including a compact satellite messaging device connected directly to Langley. Anything you need, you just buzz us up on that."

"Weapons?" Turk said.

"We're loading you out with Type 98 AK variants. They're similar to AK-74s, but with top-folding stocks. We've also got you set up with CZ-75 handguns chambered in nine millimeter, some Russian-built hand grenades, plastic explosives, and Chinese tactical knives."

Reed and Turk exchanged a glance.

"You kidding me?" Turk said.

O'Brien didn't blink. "It's imperative that no part of this operation link back to the United States. Ideally, you won't have to open fire at all, but if you do—"

"You don't want us leaving NATO brass all over North Korea," Reed finished.

"Exactly."

Great.

Reed folded his arms. He looked from O'Brien to Maggie to Yellin. None of them seemed to have anything further to say. Then he looked to Turk. His battle buddy appeared disgruntled, but nodded.

"Three things," Reed said. "And they're all nonnegotiable."

"We're listening," Maggie said.

"First, payment. We're not doing this for free."

O'Brien reached into his briefcase and pushed a document across the table. It was one page, topped with a sprawling letterhead that read "Hughe, Long and Crawly. Attorneys at Law."

"We've already opened a phony law firm and contracted with them to provide personal legal services to high-ranking members of the Agency," O'Brien said. "It'll glide through congressional oversight like greased lightning. We'll pay the firm for services rendered, and the firm will pay you. Then you file taxes like any other American."

Reed flipped to the next sheet and checked the amounts. They were generous, which gave him some relief. But the money wasn't in the bank yet.

He passed the documents to Turk, then looked back to Maggie. "Second. We're not messaging you, we're messaging Wolfgang. I'm not flying halfway around the world without somebody on this side to watch my back. Don't take it personally."

This time, it was Maggie's turn to exchange a glance with O'Brien and Yellin. O'Brien looked confused, but Yellin knew who Wolfgang was.

During the Turkish operation the previous year, Reed similarly employed Wolfgang to watch his back and help him run a private investigation separate from the Trousdale administration. Maggie wasn't a great fan of Wolfgang, and Reed couldn't blame her. An ex-assassin with a missing leg and a wall of diplomas six feet long, Dr. Wolfgang Pierce was a fascinating mix of a person—and more than a bit unsettling. He was lethal in the field, or had been anyway, before he lost his leg.

These days, he wasn't jumping any high buildings, but his mind was sharper than ever, and most importantly, Reed trusted him. If he was going to fly around the world and drop uninvited into one of the most inhospitable places on the planet, he wanted somebody he could depend on to watch his back.

"Wolfgang isn't cleared for top secret," Maggie said.

Reed shrugged. "Nonnegotiable. I'm happy to find my own way home."

"We prefer to communicate with you *directly*," O'Brien said. "Any delay could be deadly."

Reed actually laughed. "Don't talk to me about deadly, Mr. Director. I'm the one sneaking into North Korea uninvited, remember? You want me to go, you deal with Wolfgang. And you pay him, same as us. Period."

O'Brien sniffed but ducked his head once in surrender.

"Third thing?" Maggie asked.

Reed twisted his lips and stared at the table a long time, drumming his fingers. When he spoke again, his tone softened. "Third thing. If something happens to us, our families get cared for." Reed looked up. "*Well* cared for. They never have to worry about another thing. Ever."

Maggie nodded once. "You have my word."

12

Zushi Beach
Kanagawa, Japan

Lieutenant Joshua Gagliardi never wanted to be a Navy SEAL. He just wanted to be the baddest SOB on the planet, and some recruiting officer back in Lincoln, Nebraska, told him that "The baddest SOB on the planet is a Navy SEAL . . . but you aren't tough enough to be a SEAL."

Gag—nobody actually called him Gagliardi, and he couldn't blame them—set out to prove that recruiter wrong, signing on the dotted line and only realizing weeks later that the recruiter had probably been baiting him.

By the time Gag graduated the Naval Academy in Annapolis, Maryland, and commissioned as an ensign, it didn't really matter. He was in love with the Navy on a molecular level. Everything about pushing his mind and body to the extreme limits of their capacity brought him to life in a spiritual way, and he thrived on the abuse of the famed Basic Underwater Demolition school, or BUD/S training—the initial phase of becoming a SEAL.

One hundred and forty-eight men lined up next to him on day one of BUD/S. Thirty-two graduated. With every ear-splitting ring of the quitter's bell at the Naval Amphibious Base in Coronado, California, another man left the team, and Gag grinned wider. Because he was one man closer to being the baddest SOB on the planet.

Three years later, Gag had calmed down a little. He'd learned slowly that always trying to one-up every man around you—especially when those men were every bit as dedicated to being bulletproof as he was—didn't pay off. As an officer, he was expected to lead, and that was a different kind of challenge. Expecting great things out of himself was easy. Leading others to accomplish great things and allowing them to take credit for them could be difficult, but Gag embraced that, also. After all, it was a lot easier to be the baddest SOB on the planet with an army of Navy Frogmen for friends.

The Japanese sun beat down on him as he slogged along the beach, running in combat boots right at the surf line. With each passing wave, water washed as high as his knees and glistened on his shirtless torso, but Gag didn't mind the salty cold or the burn in his thighs. As he jogged past a couple of Japanese women sunbathing on the sand, he caught them eyeballing him, and he couldn't resist shooting them a wink. One blushed, and the other waved him off with faux disgust. Gag just kept running.

Being stationed in Japan was kind of a vacation after outposts in Afghanistan, Iraq, and Yemen. It was cooler in Japan, and there was so much more to do. Great bars lined the streets outside of the Fleet Activities base in Yokosuka, and many of those bars were tended by gorgeous Japanese women who spoke English and were only too happy to flirt with the Navy boys in exchange for inflated tips.

At twenty-six, Gag wasn't much on hooking up, but he loved to flirt. For him, it was all part of the total package of being a sailor.

Train hard. Fight hard. Play hard.

It was kind of his duty, really, as an ambassador of the USN. These Japanese ladies deserved a good time, didn't they? They were allies, after all.

Gag reached the end of the beach and moved up the sand away from the surf, jogging in place and checking his smartwatch for a heart rate. It was difficult to get his heart pumping after so much training, but a good jog in the water like this could usually get him up to 165 BPM or so. Enough to get the blood pumping.

A message flashed across the watch screen, alerting him to a voicemail.

He'd missed a call sometime while running, which was unusual. All his Navy buddies just texted.

Gag adjusted the wireless headphones in his ears and played the voicemail, starting back the way he'd come. Five seconds into the message, he doubled his pace, breaking into a sprint well above the waterline, a grin breaking across his face.

The call was from command. It was time to go.

13

"How's work?"

Wolfgang looked up from his salad, taking a moment to breathe in a lungful of fragrant spring air. New York was gorgeous in spring—everything was turning vibrant green and lush as the snow finally faded away. It was a fresh start. Hope after the clutches of another brutal winter.

And Wolfgang needed that.

"It's good," he said, smiling and turning his attention to the twenty-one-year-old woman sitting at the end of the picnic table.

Well, she was twenty-one according to her birth certificate. Collins Ward didn't look twenty-one. Not even close. She looked maybe fifteen, frail and small, with a gaunt face and spindly arms. She sat in a motorized chair, pulled to the end of the table with an oxygen bottle strapped to the back, a hose wound around her face and beneath her nose.

That hose kept her alive. After a two-decade battle with cystic fibrosis, Wolfgang's baby sister was finally starting to lose. Many victims of the crushing genetic disorder lived into their late thirties, or even mid-forties. Collins wouldn't make it that far. She'd be lucky to see her late twenties, and that reality tore deeper into Wolfgang's heart than any horror he'd ever witnessed during his lengthy and bloody career.

It was unforgivable. Not just because Collins was innocent and beautiful and helpless. It was unforgivable because Wolfgang promised her he'd find a cure, no matter the cost. He spent years and hundreds of thousands of dollars studying in elite universities and performing his own research. He bought laboratory equipment of his own and invested in every theoretical treatment he could find. He spilled blood to pay for it all, financing the hope of the helpless with the death of the wicked. He gave his own leg while fighting for that hope.

And in the end, here she sat, a little weaker each day, struggling to breathe. Helpless.

"You got fired, didn't you?" Collins asked.

Her smile faded when she said it, and Wolfgang looked away. He wiped his mouth and took a long drink of water, stalling for time.

"What makes you say that?"

"Because I know you. I know what you look like when things aren't going well."

Wolfgang fiddled with an olive in his salad. "I didn't really like teaching," he said. "Turns out I'm not so patient."

He shot Collins a wink as if it were all a big joke.

She smiled weakly. "What are you going to do?"

Good question, Wolfgang thought. What *was* he going to do?

He took the position at the University of Vermont to pay the bills. Prior to losing his leg, Wolfgang worked as an assassin, killing bad people usually for bad people. It was ugly work, but he didn't really have a problem with it because he used the money to advance research for Collins.

All that ended when he lost his leg while working alongside Reed Montgomery during an investigation into organized crime. His killing days were now officially over, leaving him with nothing but a wall of diplomas and no idea how to use them.

So, he took up teaching because somebody told him that's what you did with too much education and no résumé. It was a good idea, but Wolfgang sucked at it. He didn't like college kids and became impatient with their antics. More importantly, he wasn't good at managing the politics faculty were expected to juggle. So, they fired him, and he knew he deserved it. But with a depleted savings account and no place else to turn, it left him up the creek without a paddle. Again.

"I'm thinking about snowboarding," he said, straight-faced. "Tap dancing, maybe. I hear the Bills need a running back."

Collins laughed. "Usually. But apparently, there's a two-leg minimum."

Wolfgang laughed, finally spearing the olive and flicking it at Collins. "You wanna make jokes?"

She giggled in the way she used to, back when she was a kid and Wolfgang was in his early teens. He imagined her sitting on a sagging couch in a dilapidated trailer home, watching cartoons and giggling like that. It made him happy, even if it also made him sad. He loved that Collins found joy in the darkest storms. He hated that she had to.

Wolfgang felt a buzz in his pocket and fished for his phone, figuring that the university was calling about the computer he still hadn't returned. He'd have to get to FedEx and ship it before they sent the dean after him. But the number on the screen wasn't a Vermont area code. It wasn't a New England area code at all. It was a 205 number.

Alabama.

Wolfgang stepped away from the table, wincing as phantom pain shot up his busted leg. The prosthetic groaned, but he made it to the shelter of a nearby oak and hit the green button. "Yeah?" He didn't give his name, but he had a pretty good idea who was calling.

"What's new, Wolf?"

Wolfgang slouched against the tree and indulged in a tired grin. "Montgomery. Been a while."

It had been a while. About nine months, to be exact. Wolfgang hadn't seen Reed Montgomery since losing his leg, but he talked to him the previous summer after President Brandt was killed. Montgomery had partnered with the incoming Trousdale administration to recover the flight recorder from Brandt's downed plane. Wolfgang aided in that mission by conducting stateside research, and he was pretty sure that what he uncovered led to more deaths.

"You still scratching on a chalkboard for a living?" Reed asked.

Wolfgang thought he heard a dull roar in the background and figured he knew why. "Actually, I'm between jobs," Wolfgang said. "Why do I get the feeling that works out for you?"

"Probably because I only call when I need something . . . like a good friend. You want to make some money?"

Wolfgang looked back to Collins. She was dozing off now, her chin resting on her chest, the oxygen hose still wrapped around her face. She looked terrible.

"How much money, and for what?"

"A lot. And for more of what you did before."

"Somebody shoot down Air Force One again?"

"No, thank God. But this could be worse, depending on how it ends. I can't say much over an unsecured line, but let's just say I'm on a plane to Japan. And then I'll be on a boat to someplace else."

Wolfgang's mind raced, clicking through the math quickly. From Japan, Reed could be headed to any number of places, but if he was taking a boat, it wouldn't be far. China, Korea, or Russia made the most sense. None of them were good options.

"What do you need?" Wolfgang asked, still reserved.

"Somebody to watch my back and manage communications. Our friends at the Agency will read you in and provide your equipment. All you have to do is stand between me and them, then cash the check."

"You make it sound easy."

"Easy enough for a man with one leg."

Wolfgang gritted his teeth. He knew Reed was joking, but the comment still stung. It still reminded him what Reed was and he wasn't.

"Who do I call?" Wolfgang said at last. He could stand around and play hard to get, or he could just own the fact that he needed the money.

"They'll call you," Reed said. "Be ready to board a plane."

"Okay."

The line went quiet for a while, and when Reed spoke again, his voice had softened. "How's Collins?"

Wolfgang looked at his little sister in the motorized chair. She was so weak. He felt suddenly choked up. "Been better," he admitted.

"I'm sorry to hear that. Any leads?"

Wolfgang knew Reed was asking about his research. It was probably a polite question, but he still felt two inches tall for admitting defeat. "Not so far." To change the subject, he asked, "How's little man?"

"He's great. Starting to put on some weight. Looks more like his mom every day."

"Well, that's good news."

Reed laughed. "Turk said something similar."

"He's going with you?"

"Yeah."

"Good. You guys watch each other's backs. I've got you covered stateside." Wolfgang hung up, still watching Collins.

She sat up when she heard him walking her way.

He squatted next to her and gently squeezed her hand. "Good news. I got another job."

14

The CIA SAC pilots flew like bats out of hell, burning fuel from Joint Base Andrews and across the country to Edwards Air Force Base in California, where they landed just long enough to top off the tanks. Then they were back in the air and pointed west, a nonstop ride to Japan.

Reed and Turk spent the first half of the flight evaluating their gear, double-checking what the CIA had secured for them. It was pretty much as advertised: crappy Russian rifles matched to Czechoslovakian-designed handguns. Many of the other articles of gear, right down to their socks and boots, were imported or otherwise stripped of any indicator that they were sourced from the United States.

Nothing could lead back to Washington if they were captured. But for his part, Reed didn't plan on being captured. Either their mission would succeed, or he'd eat a 9mm from the sidearm. He wasn't going to be a torture subject for the North Korean regime.

After evaluating his equipment, Reed called Wolfgang to secure his support. It was an easier sell than he expected, and he wondered how bad things had become for the one-legged assassin. After this op, he should get in touch with Wolf. Maybe have a barbecue. Let Wolf meet Davy.

Regardless, Reed felt a lot better about everything with Wolfgang watching their six back in Washington. He may have only one leg, but that didn't mean he'd stand for any funny business from the CIA or the White House.

The flight over the Pacific felt endless, and both Reed and Turk napped in between meals of ham sandwiches and water. Turk did a lot of pushups on the airplane floor between the seats, but Reed just rested. He already worked out four or five times a week and was confident in his physical conditioning.

As the pilot announced their final approach into Kanagawa, Reed took his phone out and flipped through pictures of Banks and Davy. The two of them sat on a park bench near a local playground, and little Davy smiled as Banks cooed to him. His toothless grin was the most adorable thing Reed had ever seen, and even now, it made him feel soppy inside.

He switched to his messaging app and typed a quick note to Banks. His last for a while.

I LOVE YOU MORE ALL THE TIME. TALK IN A FEW DAYS.

He didn't wait for a response. He didn't want to get sucked into a conversation that would only reignite his guilt for leaving her in the first place.

I'm doing this for her. I'm doing it for Davy.

Reed hit the factory reset on the phone, and after the device's memory was wiped, he smashed it over his knee and left it in a cupholder. There was no sense bringing it with him. It would be a liability if things went wrong, and he wasn't going to leave it for the CIA to sniff through, either.

The seatbelt sign clicked on, but Reed didn't bother with the restraint. He looked out the window over the passing coastline and rising mountains of Japan and thought back to a comment Turk had made during their last mission in Turkey.

"Some things do change," Reed said, pointing to the giant American flag flapping in the breeze over the Japanese coast.

Turk leaned across the aisle and took a moment to appreciate Old Glory, then he smiled. "I guess they do."

The jet touched down and taxied immediately into a hangar. Reed and

Turk assembled their gear and waited for the pilots to open the airstair, then they stepped out into Atsugi Navy Base.

It was cold in Japan. Much colder than Alabama, even with the sun beating down from almost directly overhead. Reed pulled his pack closer to one shoulder, and a duffle bag full of ammunition, weapons, and gear swung from his free hand.

The airfield bustled with activity. Men and women dressed in Navy uniforms ran back and forth from hangar to hangar, while F-18 Super Hornet fighter jets lined up at the end of the runway and shot into the sky, one after another. Everything was lost in a constant, endless roar of jet engines, and the smog was so heavy Reed thought the air itself must be flammable.

'Murica.

The two of them stood just outside their hangar for a minute, admiring the rush of the Super Hornets blasting by, and then Reed cast a glance for any sign of a command post or somebody in charge. His inquiry was answered by a skinny guy in plain clothes, bustling toward them, his arms loaded with folded military uniforms.

"Mr. Montgomery?" the guy shouted over the thunder.

"Yeah," Reed said. "Who's in charge around here?"

The guy motioned toward the sheltered side of the hangar, which offered only minimal protection from the next blast of a Super Hornet. They followed him anyway, and he continued to shout.

"I'm Mr. Smith! Welcome to Japan."

Mr. Smith. Of course you are.

Reed and Turk took turns shaking his hand, then he held out the uniforms. "It's important for you to blend in. We got these for you."

Reed accepted the bundle and unfolded the jacket. It was a standard-issue Marine combat utility uniform, printed in woodland green, with his name on a strip over the right breast pocket. Over the left breast pocket, the tape read: "U.S. Marines."

"I can't wear this," Reed said, lowering the jacket.

Smith looked confused, as if he hadn't heard what Reed said. "Huh?"

"I can't wear this!" Reed shouted. "I'm not a Marine."

Smith squinted, then turned to Turk.

Turk put a hand on Reed's arm. "Put it on, man. Once a Marine, always a Marine."

Reed looked back at the uniform, running his thumb across the name tape. It had been a long, long time since he'd worn a military uniform. He still remembered how they felt, sticking to his skin on a hot summer day. He still remembered what it sounded like when those tapes were stripped off in the middle of a courtroom, right before he was hauled off to prison.

Reed gritted his teeth and kicked his shoes off, then commenced to changing right there under the shade of the hangar. Smith seemed flustered and looked away, but Turk followed suit. Within seconds, they were dressed to Marine combat standards, complete with suede leather boots stamped with the Eagle, Globe, and Anchor.

Reed tried not to overthink it and shouted, "When do we leave?"

Smith checked his watch. "Right now! Follow me."

Reed and Turk shouldered their bags and followed Smith across the tarmac, half a mile to a line of Navy planes assembled next to the airstrip, their windshields sparkling under the sun. The nearest plane was a large, twin-prop craft with a black nose and orange tips on its tail rudders. Reed recognized it as a Grumman C-2 Greyhound, most commonly used by the Navy as a COD, or carrier onboard delivery craft. It gave him a pretty good idea of what was coming next.

Smith led them to the open door just behind the cockpit and shot Reed a high-wattage smile. "Hope you enjoyed Japan!"

Turk snorted, but Reed just ignored him. They both boarded the Grumman, hustling up the steps and ducking to slip inside. Two pilots waited in the cockpit, nodding to them but not commenting as Reed and Turk found their seats at the front of a long line of personnel benches. Headsets complete with ear protection waited for them, and Reed slid his on before reaching for the restraining harness. He might be willing to take his chances skipping the seatbelt with a couple of SAC pilots, but there was no way he'd do so on a Navy plane. He'd seen Navy pilots fly. He'd been victim to their depraved sense of humor on many occasions. It was like a badge of honor for a Navy pilot to make his Marine passenger puke, and Reed was grateful for a relatively empty stomach.

"Welcome aboard, Sergeant!" The first officer spoke while the pilot busied himself starting the engines.

Reed glanced down at the chevrons on his sleeves, noting for the first time the rank.

Well, what do you know? I got a promotion.

"Should be a smooth flight today," the first officer continued. "It'll be a minute before we can take off, but there's not a cloud in the sky."

"What's with all the jets?" Turk said as yet another Super Hornet blasted off the runway.

The first officer shrugged. "Exercise."

It was probably Yellin's doing, Reed thought. He probably had the Navy running fighter sorties under the guise of an exercise. If Reed had to guess, the real reason had something to do with intimidating North Korea.

Not a bad idea.

At last, the Grumman's turboprop engines howled, and the plane rolled across the tarmac, taking its place at the head of the runway. The pilot held the brake while talking to the control tower, then pushed the power levers until both engines were screaming and the entire plane shook. When he released the brakes, they bounded forward like the racing dog the plane was named for, hopping only once before leaving the tarmac and pulling into the sky. The pilot laid on the power and nosed up a lot harsher than he needed to, and Reed's stomach flipped a couple times.

Here we go.

When they leveled off, they were high over mainland Japan, but Reed couldn't see anything due to the lack of windows. Only the cockpit's narrow windshield offered him any bearing on their altitude, and all he saw was empty blue sky.

Reed settled back into the seat and smoothed the uniform over his knees. It fit well, and it was comfortable, like an old blanket or a worn pair of shoes. He hadn't worn a uniform in years and forgot how much he missed the feeling.

He thought back to being a Marine. He'd been a good one. Good enough to be selected for Force Recon and to quickly advance through the ranks of the USMC's special forces division. Anything they threw at him, Reed was ready for.

He loved the job. He loved the fight. He just failed to understand the difference between an ISIL insurgent killing his Marines and a fellow American killing his Marines. To him, they were one and the same: the enemy.

But the military court felt differently.

"I'm seeing this chick back in Knoxville," Turk said, shoving gum into his mouth and shouting through the headset.

"Oh yeah?" Reed asked. He realized he hadn't inquired much about Turk's personal life over the past few months, and he felt a pang of guilt.

"Redhead," Turk said with a grin and a wink. Then he made a scooping motion in front of his chest. "*Huge* knockers."

Reed rolled his eyes and held out his hand for a stick of gum. "Cut 'er loose, man," the co-pilot said, joining the conversation. "Redheads are never worth the trouble."

Turk snorted. "Maybe for a Navy guy. This Marine ain't scared of a little fire and fury."

The pilot hit the stick, sending an earthquake-like tremor shooting through the plane. They both slammed into their restraints, and Turk choked on his gum.

"What's that?" the pilot shouted. "I can't hear you!"

Reed laughed, his whole body shaking as he watched Turk swallow hard, his cheeks pale. Man, he missed this.

Turk kept quiet for the duration of the trip, keeping his gum in his pocket and his arms folded.

Reed leaned back, enjoying the drone of the engines and contemplating the upcoming mission. There would be gunfire. A lot at stake. A lot of chances to grit his teeth and push through . . . to find a way. He could barely wait.

"All right, jarheads. Hold on to your panties."

Reed sat up, watching as the bright blue of the Pacific sky turned to the deep blue of the ocean. Far ahead, only visible by a trail of white surf churning in its wake, he made out a speck on the horizon. Only, it wasn't a speck. It was a full-blown warship. The largest warship in service, anywhere in the world.

A US supercarrier.

15

The speck on the horizon grew as the Grumman raced toward it, gusts of wind tearing beneath their wings and rocking the plane as they bled off altitude. The pilot spoke calmly to the air traffic controller aboard the ship, managing the stick with the grace and calm of a practiced professional. But he didn't ease off on the power levers. They plowed straight toward the carrier, the altimeter spinning steadily as they approached the ocean.

Reed cinched his restraints down, noting that Turk followed suit. They both knew what was coming.

The carrier fell out of view as they drew closer and the pilot eased upward on the nose. Reed drew a breath and tried not to overthink the physics of a plane this large hurtling out of the sky and grinding to a stop on a slice of runway barely the length of a Walmart parking lot.

Not my problem.

"Here we go!" the pilot shouted. He eased off power, and the nose ducked. Then they hit. The wheels screamed, and a shock wave ripped through the plane, loud and harsh enough to be mistaken for a land mine. Reed slammed forward against his harness as the arresting cable caught and yanked the plane to a jolting halt. Engines howled, and the pilots laughed as Reed swallowed hard to keep from puking.

Then it was over. The engines died, and he yanked his headset off and covered the mic. "Enough fire and fury for you?"

Turk scowled and unstrapped, pulling a utility cap over his head.

Reed scooped his gear up, sliding an identical cap down over his ears, then waited for the pilots to open the door.

"All joking aside," the first officer said. "Watch your step out there. *Nimitz* is a redhead."

The door groaned and swung open, then Reed followed the pilots out onto the flight deck. It had been years since he walked aboard a US aircraft carrier, and it hadn't been the *Nimitz*, but the smells and rush of noise were all the same. Wind ripped across the deck, and the sun blazed down from overhead, forcing him to squint. Even with the Grumman's engines dead, the perpetual scream of machinery and the blare of orders from loudspeakers was deafening. Everywhere, men scurried back and forth, prepping the Grumman to be secured to the deck and rolling away fire hoses laid out in case of a crash landing.

Two flight deck crewmen in fire-retardant uniforms rushed forward to guide Turk and Reed away from the aircraft and toward the carrier's superstructure. Reed was only too glad to duck through a narrow steel door and shield himself from the chaos outside, but it wasn't much quieter inside. The deck crewmen promptly abandoned them, returning to work and leaving them standing in a narrow hallway.

Turk snorted. "Navy guys."

"Screw like stallions," somebody said.

Both Reed and Turk turned quickly to see a tall man approaching from down the hall, dressed in Navy service khakis. He wore a broad grin beneath thick black hair, and his sleeves bore the twin stripes of a Navy lieutenant—an O-3, equivalent to a Marine captain. But it was the emblem on his chest—a golden eagle resting on an anchor and cradling a trident— that caught Reed's eye.

The badge of a Navy SEAL.

Turk flushed and straightened, but the lieutenant continued to grin.

Instead of saluting, the new guy offered his hand. "Lieutenant Josh Gagliardi. Welcome aboard the *Nimitz*."

Reed accepted his handshake, impressed by a firm but not overbearing grip.

Gagliardi's grin faded into a professional smile, and his gaze swept Reed like a searchlight. Piercing. Curious.

"A pleasure," Reed said. "I'm Montgomery. This is Turk."

The SEAL nodded slowly, his gaze passing over the uniforms and leaving Reed feeling a touch self-conscious.

"Follow me." Gagliardi tilted his head toward the hall, and Reed and Turk scooped up their gear.

He led them deep into the ship, moving down one-way staircases and ducking through narrow doors. The SEAL was a big man by average standards. Six one, maybe six two, with a muscled frame. But he navigated the narrow passages with ease, at home amid the bowels of a warship.

Reed had never felt that way about carriers—or any kind of vessel, for that matter. As a Marine, he'd technically been an amphibious soldier, attached to the Navy and dependent on their support. But precious few of his deployments had anything to do with salt water, and he found himself bunking alongside Army guys far more often than he ever shared a meal with a seaman. Let alone a SEAL.

Gagliardi eventually stopped in front of a narrow metal door and reached for the latch. "We'll brief here, and I'll introduce you to the rest of the guys."

The room on the other side was small, like everything else on the ship, but it was a lot quieter than the bustling halls outside. A narrow table ran the length of it, with bench seats on either side and a pot of coffee on one end.

Three other guys waited along the benches, all dressed like Gagliardi in service khakis. Reed noted the insignias of two E-4s and an E-5, petty officers third class and second class, respectively. They all wore SEAL tridents, and they all stood when Gagliardi entered.

"Gentlemen, meet Sam Rutkins, Jerry Solomon, and Pete Shattler. Guys, this is Montgomery and Turk."

Amid a round of handshakes, Reed noted a lot more aggressive squeezes from Rutkins and Solomon. Younger guys, he figured. More to prove. They both looked to be in their early twenties, while Shattler couldn't have been older than twenty-five.

Man, I'm getting old.

"Have a seat, guys. Coffee?"

"Please." Reed accepted a cup from Gagliardi and waited while the lieutenant poured steaming black coffee into it. Cream and sugar weren't offered, and Reed didn't mind.

At last, Gagliardi leaned against the wall and folded his arms. The perpetual grin of before had vanished, leaving behind intense focus. "All right. Well, I've already briefed my guys on our mission. I understand you've been notified of our planned form of intrusion?"

"SDV," Reed said. "Which means a sub, I guess."

"That's right. You guys comfortable underwater?"

Reed detected the undertone of a dozen questions beneath the pretense of an innocent one, and he decided to give Gagliardi something to work with. For all the SEAL knew, he was about to risk the lives of himself and three of his men, carting two strangers into unfriendly waters. It was fair for him to have questions.

"Turk and I were both Force Recon Marines, serving primarily in the Middle East during the Iraqi civil war. Since that period, our careers have taken us in . . . different directions. We both have experience with scuba and underwater operations. Not on your level, to be sure. But we can handle ourselves if you'll do the driving."

Gagliardi gave Reed a nod, and Reed detected the appreciation in it. The SEAL leader may not have been at liberty to divulge to his men details of Turk and Reed's résumés—he might not have known much himself—but it couldn't hurt for Reed to disclose the basics. He always liked to know something about who he was risking his life alongside.

"The Navy's hooking us up with a chopper at sunset," Gagliardi said. "USS *Louisville* will be our Uber through the Sea of Japan and to our destination, at which point we'll take the SDV and get you ashore. From there, we'll remain on standby and be ready to do the whole dance in reverse when you're ready to exfiltrate. I understand there will be a civilian?"

Reed nodded. "One guy. I doubt he knows anything about diving, but he's motivated to leave."

"Good. It's always easier when they are."

A dull chuckle rang around the room.

"The trickiest part of the next few hours will be boarding *Louisville*," Gagliardi continued. "We'll have to make the transfer after dark to maximize security. *Louisville* is a Los Angeles-class attack sub, and with the SDV on the deck, there's no possible way for the chopper to get in close. You guys ever see *The Hunt for Red October*?"

Reed and Turk grunted.

"It's a lot like that," Gagliardi said. "Being a metal boat, we can't rope down to the deck because of accumulated static electricity. It'll knock your ass out, and it could theoretically even kill you unless it's neutralized, which is difficult. Honestly, there's really only one good option."

"We go swimming," Turk said.

Gagliardi grinned. "Yep. Water shouldn't be too bad. It's typically about sixty degrees Fahrenheit this time of year. The big deal is to not fool around. Once you're in the water, there will be recovery crews from *Louisville* on deck to fish you out. It's important to work quickly. We want to be on the surface for as brief a period as possible." Gagliardi took a seat, producing a deck of cards from his pocket. "My friends call me Gag. You boys play poker?"

16

Gagliardi was well suited to the Navy. He was a shark. Reed wasn't sure if cheating was involved, but by the fourth hand of Texas Hold'em, he was pretty sure the odds were bent against him. He decided to go with it, figuring that the loss of thirty or forty dollars' worth of the CIA's discretionary fund was worth acquiring a little camaraderie.

Turk wasn't as quick on the uptake, calling foul on Solomon twice and doubling down on his bets. The CIA lost a hundred bucks, and Reed slapped him on the back.

"You win some, you lose some, buddy."

They spent the next hour swapping war stories, half of which Reed figured were bald-faced lies, then the phone on the wall rang, and Gag took it. He didn't speak a word as he listened, then hung up and spun his index finger in the air like a whirling blade. His men got up without comment, and Reed and Turk followed, assembling their gear and following the SEALs back onto the flight deck.

It was gorgeous outside. No, *gorgeous* was too weak a word. It was stupendous. The sun was finally sinking toward the Asian mainland, leaving a watercolor of pinks, reds, oranges, and purples to decorate a clear sky. The sea had calmed some, as had the flight deck, and cold wind bore down across Reed's face. He admired the view, breathing in the salty wind and wishing Banks could be there to join him.

He followed Gag and his crew to the waiting chopper near the edge of the flight deck. It was a Sikorsky SH-60 Seahawk, a modified Navy version of what the Army called a Black Hawk. One side door was rolled open, and Reed tossed his gear in before following Turk and the SEALs inside. Prior to leaving *Nimitz*, Gag and his men had changed out of service khakis and into wetsuits with fins slung over their shoulders. They didn't have any wetsuits big enough to fit Reed or Turk, but promised full gear would be available on board *Louisville*. In the meantime, the two former Marines would have to content themselves with goggles and ill-fitting fins.

As the Seahawk's jet engines howled and the chopper left the flight deck, the last of the sun slipped away beneath the horizon. Reed gripped the overhead brace and clung on as the pilot dipped the nose to the left and swung them toward the fading sunlight. Within seconds, the *Nimitz* was just a dot on the horizon, quickly fading away as darkness claimed the sea.

"We call it the Sea of Japan," Gag shouted over the roar of the rotor as he leaned close to Reed. "But the Koreans call it the East Sea."

"You dive here often?" Reed asked.

Gag laughed. "Oh, sure! I was swimming with a megalodon last Wednesday."

Reed ignored the joke and watched the waves rushing by three hundred feet below. He could barely make out the shape of the water in the rapidly dying light and wondered how he was going to find his way on board a jet-black submarine without the aid of any lights.

Maybe a megalodon would lend a hand.

They flew for the better part of an hour, maintaining a steady altitude and riding mostly in silence. Reed enjoyed the wind on his face and the thrash of the rotors overhead, with each passing moment bringing a slight rise to his blood pressure. The unknown lay just around the corner. The next fight. The next struggle. He was ready for it.

At last, the Seahawk slowed and banked left, and Gag smacked Reed on the shoulder. "Look there." He pointed out the open door into the blackness beyond.

Reed squinted and studied the surging water, marking the shadows left by a dim moon.

And then he saw it, all at once, much closer than he thought it would be. USS *Louisville* rose out of the waves like an underwater monster, water breaking across her bow, her sail glinting in the dim light. Everything was painted black aboard the massive attack sub, but Reed detected faint green and red lights marking the bow and stern, with just the hint of a wake surging near the sub's tail.

And behind the conning tower, barely visible as a black silhouette framed against a darkened sky, he saw a long rectangular box bolted to the top of the sub. Like a barn or a garage, waterproof and modular, it housed the SDV that would deliver them into North Korea.

Gag slipped his goggles on and smacked Reed again. "Time to swim, Jarhead!"

The other SEALs moved in unison, assembling their packs and double-checking the straps on their fins. Reed shoved his big feet into the under-sized fins *Nimitz* had provided, cinching the straps down and sliding the goggles over his face. He didn't mind swimming. In fact, he kind of enjoyed it. But ideally, he wouldn't be swimming in sixty-degree water right next to a nuclear-powered submarine with a screw large enough to cut him into sushi. Hopefully, they killed the engine.

The Seahawk rotated in midair, dropping until they were only thirty feet off the black water. Reed could see it clearly now, churned by the rotor wash and torn by waves. The *Louisville* rested just above the surface, fifty yards away, a giant black cigar floating on the waves. He saw sailors dressed in blue rain jackets and orange life vests storming *Louisville*'s decks, life rings and ropes dragged behind them.

Gag moved to the door and steadied himself, that cheesy grin returning beneath his oversized goggles. "Let's roll!"

Solomon went first, swan-diving out of the Seahawk and sliding beneath the waves with barely a ripple. Rutkins and Shattler followed with equal grace, then Gag started shoving gear out.

Reed and Turk's battle bags were waterproof, encasing their electronic gear, weapons, and clothes. Gag had already strapped the bags to orange life vests, and they shot underwater for only a second before bobbing back to the surface for the SEALs to retrieve.

"See you on the other side!"

Gag flipped out, leaving Reed standing in the doorway, his feet aching inside the undersized fins. He looked down at the surging water ten yards below and thought about what it would feel like if he landed on his back or stomach. From that height, that could mean broken ribs or a twisted spine. He almost asked the pilot to drop a little lower, then thought about what the SEALs would say later.

Screw it.

Reed fist-bumped Turk, sucked in a deep breath, and jumped. He opted for a pencil dive instead of a swan dive, pinning his ankles together and falling feet-first.

The water may have been sixty degrees, but it felt like thirty. He dropped a full twenty feet, salty water surging around his face and filling his ears before he even had a chance to kick for the surface. With each stroke, he reached out with both arms, looking up and pushing. There was nothing overhead except more blackness. The icy touch of the water around him cut straight to his bones, and the remaining air in his lungs burned like fire.

Reed just swam. His head broke the surface, and he gasped down air, already conscious of the Seahawk pounding away through a darkened sky. Reed shook his head to clear it and searched for the SEALs, quickly finding them kicking toward the *Louisville*, his gear in tow. They moved like dolphins, ducking in and out of the waves and laughing as they approached the sub.

"Turk?"

"Here."

Reed twisted his back to see Turk treading water ten feet away, a grimace on his face.

"You good?"

Turk mumbled something unintelligible, and Reed kicked toward him.

"Hey. You good?"

"I said I busted my balls!" Turk shouted.

Reed broke into a laugh, then kicked for *Louisville*, Turk not far behind.

The fifty-yard swim passed beneath him with relative ease, the salt water making it easy to float. He reached the side of the sub and caught a line, using it to pull himself in to a rope ladder draped across *Louisville*'s side.

Up close, the attack sub was gargantuan. The sail towered several stories over the waterline, perfectly black against a moonlit sky, while the immense hull lay in the water like a sleeping giant, undisturbed by the waves.

Strong hands grasped Reed's arms as he reached the deck, pulling him on board. He felt unsteady on his feet and spat water back into the sea. Then Gag was there, slapping him on the back, his ever-present grin as bright as a fluorescent light.

"You good, man? You look a little woozy."

Damn SEALs.

The sailors aboard *Louisville* moved with oiled ease, quickly stowing the lines and gathering around a hatch forward of the sail. Reed stripped his fins off and followed them, moving just behind Turk and noting his friend's momentary reluctance to take the steps into the tight confines of the passageway beneath. Turk was no fan of confined spaces, and to Reed's knowledge, he'd never been aboard a sub before.

Tough luck.

Reed gave him a push, and they both clambered through the passageway and into a waiting hall. Soft lights on either side guided their way, and Reed sucked down a deep breath of recycled air. It was filtered with some manner of cheap fragrance—to counteract body odor, he figured —but he still smelled damp steel and salt.

The hatch thudded shut overhead, and one of the sailors spun a wheel to seal it. Then they were ushered down a passageway, led by a short guy wearing sneakers and a blue T-shirt tucked into grey sweatpants.

Sub swag.

"Follow me, sir."

Gag and his SEALs trailed behind, still carrying Reed and Turk's gear, water draining off their wetsuits. Reed's saturated cammies stuck to him, and his teeth chattered, but overall, he felt lucky to have completed the stunt without injury.

Then he heard *Louisville* groan, and he was suddenly aware that they were moving. Someplace far below, amid the guts of the sub, Reed heard metal creaking, and something hissed. He chose to ignore the sounds and followed the sweat suit sailor through a door and into a tight room. It was much like the room on board *Nimitz*, with a narrow table and bench seats, but half as wide and twice as long. At the end, Reed noted four empty bunks, and again he smelled coffee.

"These are your quarters," Sweat Suit said. "Head's down the hall. Dinner at eighteen hundred."

Gag thanked the man, and Sweat Suit cast Reed and Turk a curious look.

Reed could tell he had questions, but the submariner only offered a respectful lift of his chin.

"Welcome aboard the *Louisville*," Sweat Suit said.

17

Minsu could feel the change in the city like a change in the weather. It was dark in Korea, but the sky was pockmarked by sweeping strobe lights and the glow of burning buildings.

At least three structures were on fire—an apartment block and two warehouses. Minsu couldn't imagine why, but the soldiers had to be at fault. The Korean People's Army had taken complete control of the city, boarding up the citizens in their apartments and meager homes while storming from structure to structure and searching each one at gunpoint.

They came to his apartment building, and Minsu dutifully stood amid a long line outside, shaking in the early spring cold while the KPA, led by the Ministry of State Security, turned the building upside down. It took them well over an hour, and when he returned to his tiny unit, the place was a wreck. Half of his rice supply was missing, along with a small roll of local currency he'd been saving for emergencies. That wasn't unusual for a police inspection. Things always went missing. But what *was* unusual was the lack of questioning. The soldiers searched the buildings as though they were looking for something, or somebody, but they didn't bother to interrogate any of the occupants.

Usually, if the MSS wanted to find somebody, they would go to work on anybody suspected of associating with that individual, bludgeoning them in public and threatening a one-way ticket to a prison camp if the victim didn't capitulate.

Of course, capitulation was worse, because then you were definitely headed to a prison camp, almost certainly never to return. But that night, the MSS and their KPA counterparts were skipping the interrogating part and moving straight to ransacking buildings. Meanwhile, the residents were subjected to a speech blared through a loudspeaker, warning them not to venture outside until given further direction.

The orders were ominous and vague, but they incited plenty of fear. Minsu's neighbors were approaching panic as they filed back into their apartments, whispering quietly about what could be happening.

Are the Americans here? Is war coming?

Minsu knew better. Not because he had any clue what the government might be up to, but because he talked with the Americans regularly, and they were just as in the dark about events transpiring in Pyongyang as his neighbors were.

Minsu stood next to his window and peered out into the darkness, using a tiny pair of binoculars supplied to him by the Americans. Binoculars were a contraband item, much like his inhaler camera, all of which he stored beneath a false plank in his dingy apartment. If the police caught him with either, he'd earn a one-way ticket to a concentration camp, no questions asked.

But Minsu didn't care. He'd risked his life for the past three years to feed intelligence out of the hermit kingdom and back to America, and he'd continue to do so for as long as it took. Born on the south side of the 38th parallel, Minsu should've grown up indulging in the riches and comforts of American-style capitalism. He should've attended school and made friends and one day gone off to college. Maybe he would've traveled overseas and become a businessman or an artist.

But none of that was destined to be. Minsu's father was a South Korean native, born to a Korean War veteran, following the war. His mother, however, was a North Korean defector—a rare and precious escapee of the totalitarian regime. While still a teenager, she made the long and perilous trek out of North Korea, through the unprotected border into China, and south to Beijing.

It was a miraculous and life-threatening journey, and reaching China's capital city, while slogging through snow with too little food and nobody to turn to, almost cost her life. But even though she was free of the confines of the DPRK and only a scant five hundred kilometers across the Yellow Sea from Seoul, Minsu's mother was in some ways farther from freedom than ever. China wasn't a safe place for North Korean refugees—not then, and not now, either. If she was caught, his mother would've been promptly deported back to Pyongyang, there to be executed for treason.

So, her journey continued all the way through the core of China, south into the jungles of Laos, and finally to Thailand. It wasn't until she reached the South Korean consulate in Bangkok that she was finally safe. The government in Seoul didn't recognize the existence of a separated Korea, and therefore, in their mind, his mother was as much a South Korean citizen as someone born there. They gave her a passport, a plane ticket into Seoul, and a brand-new start.

She met Minsu's father at a restaurant near the coast, and they fell in love. Minsu was born, and he grew up safe and happy, listening to stories of his mother's harrowing flight from dictatorship. She used to repeat the same tales of her brush with death, over and over, at his request, and then remind him to never forget his brothers and sisters north of the demilitarized zone.

"They're just like you, Minsu. They deserve freedom."

It all became real when the famine struck. It was during the mid-nineties, and Minsu was barely ten years old, but he remembered it well. In spite of a bustling global economy and the celebrated fall of the Soviet Union, disaster struck North Korea like never before seen. In fact, in a way, it was *because* of the Soviet Union's collapse. For decades, the regime in Pyongyang propped up a broken communist economy with subsidies from Moscow. When the USSR tanked, the DPRK wasn't far behind it, and despite the offers of numerous developed countries to send aid, Pyongyang preferred to deny the existence of a problem and let their people starve.

The official death tally North Korea eventually admitted to was somewhere around two hundred thousand. Minsu knew the number to be much closer to three million. He mourned each of those deaths with a special sort of brotherly pain, but it was the death of his mother he mourned the most. The death he would never, ever forgive.

His mother knew about the famine as it was happening. News from north of the parallel was sparse and unreliable, but with so many people dying, of course rumors slipped through. She still had family in North Korea. She knew they were starving. And despite Minsu's father's pleading, she couldn't let that go.

Minsu's mother left them late one night, taking the family car and heading north. She wrote a check at a grocery store outside the city for a trunk load of dry rice and beans. Then she drove to the DMZ and pleaded with the South Korean guards and American Marines to let her through. They wouldn't, so she moved east to a rural checkpoint and tried to force her way through. The Korean People's Army gunned her down like a dog in the street, then torched her car, burning the food with her body.

Minsu would never forget that night. If he lived a thousand years and watched the DPRK collapse a hundred times, it would never be enough. He couldn't stand around and hope for the freedom of his brothers and sisters to the north. He had to help them. He had to accelerate the demise of tyranny, even if it cost his life.

His mother gave as much. How could he give any less?

On his own, Minsu might have become a terrorist. He might have hatched a plot to drive a bus full of explosives through the fences of the DMZ and blow open a hole wide enough to kill a few soldiers and free some of his brethren. But the CIA had better ideas.

They found him during his second year of college. Maybe it was his Google searches that gave him away, or his association with several on-campus freedom groups dedicated to the reunification of the nation. What-ever it was, they made him an offer. An offer he couldn't refuse. Minsu could help the Americans undermine Pyongyang. They would give him everything he needed. All he had to do was cross the border.

They snuck him north on a fishing boat, complete with a fake DPRK identification card and small gadgets that would help him sneak secrets into the outside world. They gave him a handler and a series of targets.

They even paid him, making regular monthly deposits into a checking account in Seoul, waiting for him when the job was done.

That was three years before, and the progress since then had been brutally slow. Minsu soon learned that the CIA was a lot less interested in bringing down Pyongyang than they were in simply managing Pyongyang. They didn't help him plot unrest or blow up government buildings. They just wanted pictures and reports on troop movements and government activities.

It was frustrating. But for Minsu, it was the only path forward. As long as he lived north of the DMZ, he would leverage the CIA's mission into his own mission, learning about the city, scoping out the regime's weaknesses, and dreaming about the day he'd burn it all to the ground. That day felt a lot closer than it had in years. Because whatever was happening throughout the city, it wasn't standard operating procedure. Pieces were moving. Unrest was in motion. And that might mean an opportunity. If the Americans understood how unstable things were becoming, they might be motivated to take action. He just needed to feed them the chaos.

Minsu turned from his window and replaced the binoculars in the cavity beneath the floor, retrieving instead the digital camera disguised as an inhaler. He checked the battery charge and fed in a new memory card, then covered the cavity with the floorboard and slipped into the hall.

The KPA and the MSS might have ordered him to stay put, but Minsu wasn't about to go to bed and sleep this one off. He was going to the heart of the action. He was going to find the Americans whatever they needed to finally make a move.

18

Reed knew they had slipped far beneath the surface. He could feel the pressure change in his ears, and he listened to the groaning of the boat as it elegantly dropped under the waves. He watched the surface of the coffee sitting in front of him as it tilted, like the bubble on a level, marking the angle of their descent.

It was a strange, unsettling feeling, being confined to a small metal room, knowing you were plummeting into the dark, crushing depths of the ocean. Not being able to do anything about it. Not supposed to be concerned about it.

The SEALs certainly weren't concerned. They stripped out of their wetsuits and changed into waiting sweats, then knocked back two pots of coffee before settling around the narrow table. Reed had also stripped out of his saturated cammies, sliding into worn sweatpants and a T-shirt that matched that of the SEALs'. The clothes were too small for him, but they looked absolutely comical on Turk. The sweatshirt looked like a crop top, rising over his stomach and pulled up on his forearms, while the pants hung a full three inches short of his ankles.

"Damn squids," Turk muttered, squeezing onto the bench next to Reed. As if on cue, the sub groaned deeply, and Turk's eyes flicked upward, his lips twitching.

Reed elbowed him in the arm and laughed. "What's wrong, buddy? Not cut out for the silent service?"

"Pride runs *deep*," Solomon barked, smacking his chest with one closed fist.

The SEALs laughed, and Turk just flushed. "Yeah, yeah. Laugh it up. I'd like to see any of you jerks take a tour through Syria."

"Syria?" Rutkins said. "Ain't that where they shipped all those tanning beds for the Corps? Man . . . Must be a tough life!"

"All right, all right," Gagliardi cut in, pouring himself a fresh cup of coffee. "Enough. We've got work to do." He dug through a pack waiting near the end of one bunk and produced an iPad. He laid it on the table where everybody could see and began tapping with a stylus.

Louisville groaned again, and Reed noticed the coffee level off in his cup. He wondered how deep they were and how cold the water was outside. Just the thought sent an involuntary shiver up his spine.

"This will be our last rundown," Gag said. "Montgomery, Turk. Any problems, you sing out. We're here to make this easy for you guys." He flicked across the screen, displaying a map of the Sea of Japan, with the Korean Peninsula stretched across it. He zoomed in, then marked a spot way out in open waters. "We're about here, three hundred nautical miles off the North Korean coast. It'll be sunrise in Korea in a couple hours, but we're cruising at about seventeen knots, so we should arrive around eleven p.m., local time."

Reed double-checked the math in his head. It was good timing. Arriving offshore at eleven gave them time to maneuver the SDV to the coast without rushing, but it still left him and Turk plenty of dark hours to maneuver inland. Good planning on the Navy's part.

"We'll park *Louisville* about four miles off the coast to provide protection against sub nets. Intel suggests North Korea's anti-submarine systems are rudimentary at best, but we don't want to take any chances."

"That little thing can last four miles?" Turk asked.

Reed wasn't sure if he meant to be condescending, but he certainly sounded it. Solomon looked irritated, but Gagliardi took it in stride.

"Sure, no problem. We've gone a lot farther in it. It'll be dark and cold, but you get used to it. Just stay loose and breathe evenly. Worst thing would be for you to hyperventilate or get claustrophobic." Gag looked to Reed as he finished, a clear question on his face.

Reed nodded. "He whines a lot, but he can take it." He threw another elbow into Turk's arm, just to let him know he didn't mean anything by it.

Turk took the hint. "Don't worry about me. I was born to jam big things in tight spaces."

That got a laugh from the SEALs, and Reed gave Gag a nod to continue.

"There's no dry storage on the SDV, but we'll keep your gear in the watertight bags. Once we're about fifty yards out, we'll park it and swim in from there. You guys can go in alone, or we can follow to provide cover. Just in case."

Reed thought about it, trying to imagine what the coastline would look like and if there would be any place to hide or take cover. It would be nice to have four highly trained combat enthusiasts on his tail, ready to emerge from the water and rain hellfire on anything confronting them. But if it came to that, the mission was already lost. He and Turk stood a better chance of slipping in undetected on their own.

"We'll go in alone," Reed said. "Keep it quiet."

Gag nodded, clicking off the iPad. Uncomfortable silence filled the small compartment, everybody avoiding the elephant in the room.

Then Gag cleared his throat. "Look. I don't know why we're doing this. Heck, I don't really even know who you guys are. But whatever you're doing, if it's important enough to sneak two Americans into one of the worst places on Earth, it must be a pretty big deal. So, if you need anything, if things turn sour, we'll be on standby. Just make the call."

Reed met Gag's gaze, weighing the quiet confidence there—evaluating the strength of a soldier, battle-tested and jaded, much like himself. Gagliardi hadn't seen the things Reed had. That was obvious. He hadn't witnessed the ugly underside of the American war machine, and he probably hadn't ever been in a position of choosing between what he believed to be right and what his superiors ordered him to do. But that didn't make him any less a warrior, or any less a brother in arms. He meant every word he said.

"Hoorah, squid," Reed said.

Gag flashed his teeth in a boyish grin. "Hooyah, jarheads."

19

It was the first truly warm day since the previous fall. Maggie left her coat inside the White House and stepped out onto the South Lawn in a simple blue dress, with an American flag pin near one shoulder. She'd let the makeup artists have their way with her this time, subjecting herself to their scrutiny for the better part of an hour before she was sufficiently crafted into an image they were satisfied with.

Maggie hadn't looked into the mirror. She didn't want to shake her own confidence by questioning the face she saw. The next thirty minutes would be all about confidence, strength, and vision. Trite words in Washington, but still meaningful to her.

The podium waiting for her with the South Portico as its backdrop featured a short platform, invisible to the cameras, but significant enough to give her a boost in height. Stratton would be standing next to her during her speech, and analysts advised her that she shouldn't look significantly shorter.

News crews were already gathered around, and staked into the ground next to the podium were the first copies of her brand-new campaign signs:

TROUSDALE – STRATTON
Revive the nation.

Revive was Jill's word. Maggie wasn't sold on it at first, but the more they paired it with possible nouns, the better she liked it. It was a strong word, easy to spell, but also highly flexible. It carried generally positive vibes and positioned her as something of a doctor or a healer—an image almost anybody should be able to get behind.

Stratton shook her hand as she approached the podium and gave her a reassuring smile. "Give 'em hell."

She appreciated his enthusiasm and thought it might come in handy during the long, grueling months of campaigning that lay ahead. Stratton oozed political prowess, which at first encounter, made her nervous. But the more she got to know him, the more of a Boy Scout he became. Her vice president's easy political wit sometimes felt fake only because it was so genuine, and genuine was a rare thing in Washington.

"Ready when you are, ma'am." Her press secretary spoke from one side of the bank of cameras, and Maggie straightened her back, placing both hands on the podium.

And then she smiled. Not because it was time to smile, but because this was a moment she never in her wildest dreams imagined could become a reality, and even though deep tragedy had brought her here, she wasn't going to deny herself the thrill of it.

The press secretary held up a hand. Three . . . Two . . .

"Good morning, my fellow Americans. I hope you're having a brilliant Monday. I'm joining you today alongside Vice President Jordan Stratton to declare my candidacy for election to the office of president of the United States."

The teleprompter rolled slowly, and Maggie followed along with it. She usually scorned teleprompters, but that day, it felt good to just speak the words her speechwriters had prepared and not overthink it—to stand in the sun and drink in this moment.

"It's been a hard twelve months for all of us," Maggie said. "The loss of President Brandt—my friend—has left a scar on our nation that will never be forgotten. But if we're honest with each other, the truth is, our problems date back to far before the tragedy of last August. For decades now, hard-working Americans of every race and creed, from sea to shining sea, have watched the American Dream slowly erode at the hands of corporate, bureaucratic, and governmental corruption. I know because I'm not just another cog in the Washington machine. I'm like you. A dreamer and a visionary, a simple girl from soggy Louisiana swamps. I never aspired to be the leader of the Free World, but I won't deny the call of duty to face the challenges ahead of us, and I will fight for all of you."

Maggie paused there, allowing those words to sink in. Letting America resonate on that message.

"I'm here today to bring you a message of hope. What makes this country great are the things that bring us together—the values we share. Values like honesty, hard work, kindness, sacrifice, family, and an open door for our neighbors. Those values are as vibrant as ever across our heartland, but unfortunately, far too many of you no longer believe that your leaders share them. You don't feel respected in the workplace or by the people you elected to represent you. You feel that divisive, partisan politics are ripping this nation apart, one stitch at a time. I share those concerns, and that's why, against the advice of all the best campaign advisors, I will not be associating my campaign with a party. It's not because there aren't visions I share with both sides of the aisle. It's because I won't answer to *anyone* . . . except you. It's because I, as your president, want to revive integrity in this country. I want to revive the American Dream. Not for one half of the aisle—for all of us. This November, when you head to the polls, I'm asking you to make a choice. I'm asking you to choose integrity. Choose values. Choose the things that made us strongest and will bring us back together again. Vote Trousdale–Stratton!"

There were no cheers to end her speech, just the void of black camera lenses and the quiet attention of two dozen reporters. Maggie was okay with that. She could've delivered her campaign announcement in front of a crowd of supporters, but she wanted to do it there, in front of the White House, to demonstrate that she was already president and could actually win this thing.

Maggie stepped back and allowed Stratton to deliver a brief speech, diving deeper into some of their campaign priorities. When they wrapped up, she joined O'Dell and Jill on a walk back into the White House.

As soon as the doors were closed, Jill snapped her fingers. "You *had* them! No doubt. That's exactly what we needed."

Maggie glanced at Stratton.

He nodded. "I agree. This is gonna make a splash."

Maggie hoped so. She hadn't known if it was a good idea to make the announcement on a Monday, but Jill and some of her advisors recommended that it projected the image of a working woman. Maybe they read too far between the lines.

"We should hit the road soon," Stratton said. "Nothing can replace a handshake and campaign rally. Focus on battleground states, and try to make at least a dozen appearances before the primaries kick in."

Maggie's head already spun with the workload confronting her. This would be the greatest undertaking of her life.

She drew a breath to comment about making an appearance in Louisiana—something to ground her with an existing base—but just then, an aide burst into the room, her heels snapping on the marble like machine-gun fire.

"Madam President, I have general Yellin and Director O'Brien on the phone for you."

Maggie's blood chilled. It was unusual for either man to contact her mid-morning. Both of them together couldn't be good.

"I'll take it in the Map Room," she said, motioning to a door to her left. "Jill, why don't you arrange some lunch for us in the Oval? I'll be right up."

The Map Room was small and quiet, so named because President Franklin Roosevelt used it as a sort of strategic headquarters during World War II, plastering walls and tables with battle maps.

Now it was little more than a spare reception space, with portraits of long-dead presidents and ornate chairs situated beneath a gleaming chandelier. If Maggie was honest, it reminded her of a funeral parlor, but it was quiet, and there was a phone.

"Good morning, gentlemen. Why do I feel like you've got bad news?"

Maggie settled into one of the chairs and crossed her legs, cradling the phone against one ear. It was nice to be alone, however fleeting that moment would be.

General Yellin took the lead. "Morning, ma'am. Congratulations on your campaign announcement. I caught the last half of the speech. Inspiring stuff."

She couldn't tell if he was being genuine, polite, or possibly mocking her. It didn't matter. "Thank you. What's up?"

Silence. Maybe they were trying to decide who would take this one.

Finally, O'Brien filled the gap. "We've received more intelligence out of Pyongyang. It's not good."

"Not good, as in McDonald's discontinued the McRib? Or not good, as in we're about to be at war? Be specific, Mr. Director."

Maggie knew she was punching hard, but she didn't expect her chief of intelligence to beat around the bush.

"The city is in chaos," O'Brien said. "KPA troops are deploying directly into residential districts. They appear to be searching for something, but our asset reported they aren't interrogating anyone. It's strange."

"Why does it concern us?"

"It concerns us because General Jang seems to be leading the charge. We've seen the Ministry of State Security rifle through people's homes a million times before, but we've never seen the army deployed into the city in so much force."

"You said he's conducting searches? Maybe he's using the KPA to help."

"He doesn't need them," O'Brien said. "He's got so many troops on the streets, they can't all fit in the buildings, and he's concentrating them at certain key sectors of the city. Honestly, I don't think he's using them to search at all."

"So, what's he doing?"

"This is pure speculation, but if Jang were staging a coup, this would be the first step. The KPA is loyal to him—probably more so than the MSS. He'd need a pretense to truly take control of the city, but moving troops into position beforehand would be the first step."

"Wouldn't Cho have something to say about this?"

"Cho Jong may be the DPRK's supreme leader, but he doesn't push all the buttons. He relies on accurate and honest information from his closest advisors, just like any leader."

"You think Jang is setting him up?"

"I don't have enough intelligence to express an opinion on that. All I can tell you is what I know, and what I know is that Pyongyang is rapidly descending into martial law under the control of a known radical."

"Instability in Pyongyang bears real consequence to our national security," Yellin said, rejoining the conversation. "If there's even a chance this Jang guy has a shot of taking control, we have to be prepared for immediate military action."

Maggie dropped her face into one hand, thoughts of reviving integrity long lost amid the grit of the actual job.

One day. Just one day without crisis.

"What do you recommend, General?"

Yellin cut straight to the point. "Initially, I thought a show of force might be helpful. We've been running heavy naval air exercises over the Sea of Japan all weekend, just to remind everyone who's boss. But if this thing really is a coup, that may be the wrong move. Rolling out the guns and advancing DEFCON status could put our allies on edge, not to mention Russia and China. For now, I recommend we quietly shift naval assets into strategic positions across the region and increase readiness for all expeditionary forces in Korea and Japan."

Yellin hesitated, as if debating what he was about to say. Then he plowed on. "With your permission, I'd also like to have the War Department formulate a first-strike strategy. Just as an additional precaution."

"And by first-strike strategy, you mean . . ."

"A strategic nuclear attack, ma'am. Designed to neutralize their weapons before they can launch."

My God.

Maggie sat up, her mind spinning. She thought about the note card in her pocket. Nicknamed "The Biscuit," it contained codes used to authenticate herself as POTUS in the event of a nuclear launch order, and she was legally mandated to carry it at all times.

She never expected to actually use it.

"It's only a precaution," Yellin reassured her. "North Korea is a nuclear power, so we have to consider the possibility of a coup leading to nuclear action and prepare accordingly. But that sort of reality is a long way off. There are a lot of tools we can leverage before then."

Maggie appreciated his confidence, but even the mention of nuclear action was chilling. "Director O'Brien, how will we know if things have escalated?"

"That's a good question. A coup of the kind I'm suggesting would be an all-or-nothing play by Jang. Betraying the supreme leader is ultimate treason in North Korea, punishable by death. If I had to guess, Jang is playing a cat-and-mouse game right now, keeping things chaotic to avoid answering hard questions. If I were him, and my eventual goal was to take control of the nation, I'd want to sideline Cho somehow. Get him out of the spotlight and away from communications. As I said, the KPA is loyal to Jang, but they wouldn't follow him if they knew he was committing treason."

"Is there a chance he'll try to assassinate Cho?" Maggie asked.

O'Brien thought a moment. "It's possible, but I don't think so. Cho is one of the more highly protected individuals on the planet, surrounded by an army of personal bodyguards more loyal to him than anyone else. Even for somebody of Jang's rank and influence, getting that near Cho would be next to impossible and would certainly expose him. If I had to guess, he'll find another way to bench Cho. Something more . . . plausible."

"Any ideas on that?"

"Not at the moment, but I'll get some analysts working on it. I have to emphasize, all of this is pure speculation on my part. Jang is a radical, but we don't have proof he's up to anything. This could be exactly what it appears. Some kind of crazed search or simply a show of force for the locals. It's impossible to know."

Maggie leaned back in her chair and rubbed her chin. She thought again about the hypersonic weapon and Reed and Gok. On some level, appearances really didn't matter. It was like having a pistol lying on the floor next to a child. A thousand people could assure you it was unloaded, but you still took action. The risks of disaster, however unlikely, were simply too catastrophic.

"Deploy your naval assets, General," Maggie said. "But keep it quiet. Call it a training exercise. Mr. Director, get those analysts working. If there's even a chance this thing spills out of control, we're gonna cut it off at the knees. Nuclear war isn't an option. Period."

20

USS *Louisville*
Sea of Japan

Reed and Turk spent the seventeen-hour underwater cruise prepping for the mission to come.

The CIA had provided them with an iPad, equipped with a satellite connection that would provide navigation once they landed. This deep beneath the waves, there was no connection, but the preloaded information was still helpful.

Their target, Gok Chin-ho, was described in the CIA's file as small and balding, with dark eyes. They also claimed he was missing two teeth in the upper right-hand side of his mouth, but there was no photograph. The description in the file was taken from a CIA asset code-named Monk—the guy who was apparently now missing and presumed dead.

As for Gok, he resided in the small North Korean village of Anbyŏn—eight miles inland on the far side of the Taebaek mountain range. The nearest city of any significance was Wŏnsan, ten miles northeast of their incursion point.

The CIA had assured them that both their point of incursion and the mountains they would need to cross were both completely unpopulated and desolate—as was much of this portion of North Korea. The first population of any sort they should encounter would be in Anbyŏn, where Gok's house lay on the outskirts and should be easily accessible. From there, they would make a second incursion, leverage a digital translator to speak with his family, and *hope* they found him.

The "hope they found him" part was the bit that bothered both of them the most. Especially since there would be no way to know without exposing themselves to at least a couple locals. But if Gok was unreachable, or dead, they would simply communicate that update to Wolfgang via the secure satellite messenger they'd been sent with, and then they'd extract.

Go home. Get paid. An honest attempt.

After discussing and analyzing the plan in depth for three hours, Turk retreated to his bunk, and Reed spent the next two hours reviewing every item of his gear individually, fully disassembling the AK-74 and CZ pistol and inspecting each part. The weapons were clean and appeared brand-new, drawing curious glances from the SEALs.

Reed would have traded both of them for a single M4A1 with a Trijicon optic, or even a Springfield M1A with a scout scope. Something precise and dependable. The AK-74 was probably reliable to a fault, but it was anything save precise, and he wasn't as comfortable with the manual of arms on an AK as he was a US rifle.

As for the CZ . . . well. He hoped it didn't come to that.

After repacking his gear in the watertight bag, he lay on his back on a bunk and stared up at the metal ceiling, only inches over his face, and thought about Banks. He thought about little Davy. After this job, he'd have enough money to care for them both for a while. Forget renting the house; he could buy one. He could get Banks a clean, dependable car and pay off the medical bills.

But even as his mind raced through the impact this payday would make on their lives, a deeper fire burned someplace in his stomach. Something more primitive and compulsive, ignited by being in the presence of so many service members.

It wasn't just about being paid. In fact, a part of him felt guilty for taking money at all. Diving with the SEALs and joking around with the Navy pilots made him remember what it felt like to be one of them—to wear a uniform with a flag on his arm and wake up every day ready to kill for his country. It was deeper than patriotism. More resonant than simple loyalty. It was . . . meaning. Devotion. Belonging.

It had been years since he'd felt it, and he hadn't realized how much he missed it. There was no chance he'd ever be allowed to go back, and in truth, he didn't want to go back. But knowing Gagliardi's SEALs had his six, and knowing he'd have theirs, gave him a taste of that belonging again.

It felt good.

Reed breathed deeply, forcing the thoughts out of his mind and fixating instead on counting each breath, holding it, and breathing out slowly. It was a technique he used in Iraq to force himself into sleep, even when he wasn't tired. Because when you wore a uniform, you slept whenever you could. You never knew when your next nap might be your last for days.

"Montgomery. Let's roll."

Gag rapped his knuckles against Reed's bunk, and Reed slung his legs out. Turk was already up, just finishing a repack of his gear after completing a full check the way Reed had. The other SEALs were gone, probably already prepping the SDV.

Reed dropped onto the floor and scooped up his bag, Turk falling in behind him as they followed Gag out of the room and back into the passageway outside.

It was deathly quiet in the sub. The grind of machinery and the gentle groan of flexing metal was all gone, and Reed didn't hear any footsteps, either. He noted Gagliardi wearing soft-soled slippers, and the SEAL held a finger over his lips.

"Boat's rigged for ultra-quiet," he said. "We're close."

Gagliardi led them away from the hatch they used to enter, passing half a dozen silent sailors along the way. Everybody walked in the same soft-soled slippers, nodding in way of greeting as they passed.

Reed ducked through the crew's mess, passing long lines of empty metal tables before entering a bunk room, followed by a storage compartment. Gagliardi eased a door open and exposed a blocked-off space with cabinets. Rutkins, Solomon, and Shattler waited inside, already dressed in wetsuits and fitting air tanks onto their backs. They inspected each other's gear and lifted their chins in quiet greeting but said nothing.

Gagliardi pointed to twin wetsuits hanging at the end of a rack, alongside fins, masks, and scuba harnesses. Reed and Turk stripped down, slipping into the wetsuits and quickly inspecting the air tanks and air hoses. Everything was in excellent repair, and much to Reed's relief, fit well. The wetsuit zipped up to his neck, and the fins were much larger than those from the *Nimitz*, leaving plenty of room for his big feet.

They took their time adjusting their scuba harnesses and double-checking each valve and connection, Reed's heart thumping harder with every passing second. It was difficult to truly grasp where he was and what was about to happen. If he closed his eyes, he could just as easily be gearing up in a dive shop, or standing on the sand at Cape May, looking out over a quiet Delaware Bay. But pretty soon, this was about to get real. North Korea was about to get real.

The door eased open, and a tall man with salt-and-pepper hair stepped in. He wore service khakis with captain's bars on his sleeves, but no other pins or ribbons. "Gag, you good?" the captain asked.

"Copy that. We'll be ready in five."

The captain turned to Reed and Turk, surveying them quietly. Reed could see questions on his face. Questions about who they were and why he was driving his boat so deep into unfriendly waters on their behalf.

Reed held out his hand. "Many thanks for the ride," he whispered.

The captain shook once. "I hope it counts."

"Don't worry about that, sir. I guarantee you it will."

The captain pocketed his hands, maybe thinking about what these six men were about to do and thanking God he wasn't one of them. Then he nodded. "All right, Gag. We're going up."

He disappeared back through the door, and Gagliardi flashed another one of his boyish grins. "All right, jarheads. Welcome aboard the SEAL Express."

He led the way across the compartment, and Reed and Turk followed, scooping up their waterproof bags. After squeezing through another door, they were met by a ladder leading straight upward. Gagliardi climbed, his fins slung over one shoulder, then stopped at a closed hatch near the top.

Reed heard *Louisville* groan and noted a slight tilt in the deck. For another five minutes, they stood, nothing but gentle breathing to break the stillness. Then the deck leveled off, and the attack sub became very quiet again.

A dull green light flicked on over Gagliardi's head, and he spun a metal wheel on the hatch. A slight hiss was the only sound to mark the hatch swinging open, and they all squeezed up a long tunnel, one at a time.

Reed knew where they were headed. The steel passing on either side of him was thick, and with every step, the air grew colder. He towed his dry bag between his legs, grasping a strap with one hand while he climbed with the other, just a few rungs below Gag. Turk climbed beneath him, not speaking, but Reed could interpret his rising anxiety level by the shortness of his breaths.

"Stay loose," Reed whispered.

Turk didn't answer, but he took a long breath. Gagliardi eased another hatch open, and a rush of icy air filled the tube. Reed shivered impulsively and looked up to see red lights illuminating a darkened room overhead. Metal walls ran with condensation, and someplace nearby, water dripped.

This would be the so-called dry deck—the watertight compartment bolted to the aft deck of *Louisville* that he had noticed while jumping out of the Seahawk. Inside was housed the famed SDV—SEAL Delivery Vehicle —a mini-submarine about twenty-two feet long, capable of moving six men.

Only, it wasn't a submarine. Not exactly. Because a true submarine was watertight, filled with precious oxygen, and provided a safe compartment for people to ride in. The SDV featured no such luxuries. It was more like an ATV for beneath the waves. It moved you from point A to point B, but conveniences such as oxygen were your problem.

Reed climbed into the dry deck and stood, wiping sweat from his nose, despite the bone-chilling temperature. The SDV rested on a launch rail right in front of him, looming in the red light, its single propeller gleaming only a few feet away. Gagliardi had already moved to the nose of the craft, slipping into his fins and checking something on the dash, like a NASCAR driver prepping his car prior to the big race.

Race of your life.

Turk slid in beside Reed, glancing down the length of the SDV and then impulsively looking toward the giant door at the end of the dry deck. His cheeks turned pale, and he licked sweat off his lip, but he offered a cheesy grin. "Isn't there a TV tower we can jump off of?"

Reed punched his arm, then slipped up beside the SDV and held up his dry bag. Gagliardi pointed to a storage compartment between two seats in the middle of the craft, and Reed tucked the bag in. There was barely enough room for Turk's bag on top, then Solomon and Rutkins climbed into the back of the SDV, squeezing beneath a low metal roof, their goggles and mouthpieces already in place. They shot thumbs-up to Reed and Turk, and Gagliardi motioned to the middle seats.

"There," he whispered.

Reed got in on the right, cramming his oversized frame into the small seat and ducking his head to fit beneath the roof. Turk had an even harder time of it, but made it work, slipping his goggles on and double-checking the pressure on his oxygen before fitting the mouthpiece in and taking a test breath. He moved with perfect calm now, his motions fluid and not wasting any energy.

The warrior had taken over. The battle-tested Force Recon Marine. An SDV dozens of feet beneath the surface may have been well outside Turk's comfort zone, but he was elite. He'd found a way.

Reed checked pressure, sealed his goggles over his face, and sucked in a deep breath from the tank. It tasted stale, but everything operated properly. He and Turk gave a thumbs-up to Gagliardi and Shattler.

The two SEALs returned the gesture, then settled into the nose of the craft. There were twin digital screens there, along with guidance controls for the SDV. Gagliardi took command, using hand signals to communicate with Shattler as they completed some manner of pre-voyage check. It took about thirty seconds, then Shattler looked over his shoulder and gave the others another thumbs-up.

Go time.

Gagliardi pushed a button on the dash. Seconds dripped by, and then the red lights died. In an instant, they were consumed in perfect darkness, surrounded on all sides by cold steel. Reed's heart rate spiked, his body overcome by momentary, natural panic. He regained control, gripping his seat and breathing deeply. He pushed pictures of rushing water and crushing blackness away, focusing instead on an imaginary set of crosshairs overhanging a fictitious backdrop—Iraq or South America; Afghanistan or Iran. It didn't matter.

He pictured imaginary targets as he heard a low hiss, and the air around him grew even colder. He thought about the feeling of a rifle stock pressed close to his jaw and imagined the pressure of a trigger against his finger.

Then he felt the water. It hit his feet first, washing against the wetsuit before quickly climbing up his calves. Reed re-concentrated on the rifle, thinking about the crosshairs and the way they jumped when he breathed too hard.

He calmed himself by picturing a target at five hundred yards. A military-age male, carrying a rifle, pointing the weapon at him. A just kill. A necessary kill.

Reed imagined laying his finger across the trigger as the water climbed to his chest and neared his face. When it reached his neck, he reached up and unzipped the top of his wetsuit, allowing a flood of icy water to surge inside. It was so cold, it drove the air right from his lungs, but he refused to gasp. He remained calm, telling himself that it was all for the best. Soon, the water would be trapped between his suit and skin, and his wetsuit would be warmed by his body heat, providing an insulating barrier between his vital organs and the frigid ocean outside. It was a necessary moment of discomfort.

Reed zipped the suit back up as the water passed his face. He was completely underwater, and he sucked down one long breath, imagining the snap of the trigger. The kick of the rifle. The target hitting the dust.

He opened his eyes and at first saw only blackness. All around him, the water surged, but then someplace ahead was the vague outline of Shattler's shoulder, highlighted by the glow of the digital screens on the SDV's dash. Reed felt a soft buzzing beneath his tailbone, and something shifted. Then a barely noticeable current of water moved past his face as the SDV slipped out of the dry deck and into the blackness beyond.

21

It was perfect silence. Reed thought he'd heard it before, but the stillness he felt as the SDV departed *Louisville* was on another level—like what he imagined astronauts felt while standing on the moon. He lifted his hand and made out the outline of his fingers in front of his face, but he couldn't hear anything, and it was so dark he only knew they were moving based on the faint vibrations beneath him. Even the glow of the instrument panel was muted now, and he relaxed into his seat, choosing to enjoy the otherworldly sensation of drifting through oblivion.

It was beautiful, in a way. Absolute calm. It was only when he remembered how far he must be beneath the surface that anxiety slipped into his mind, but he pushed it back.

It may have been one hour—or three—before Shattler looked back and pointed upward. Reed had lost all track of time, but his eyes adjusted some to the darkness, enough so that he could make out more basic shadows. He wasn't cold anymore, either. The wetsuit was working its magic, and he turned to check Turk.

His battle buddy looked out the open side of the craft and into the endless expanse of water. Reed tapped his arm and held his thumb up. Turk returned the gesture, and Reed looked ahead again.

They had climbed since leaving *Louisville,* very slowly, to prevent a potentially fatal case of decompression sickness should they rise to the surface too quickly. Reed could see little ahead of them, but he could feel the SDV gaining speed. Water moved by his face faster now, and he made out the outline of Gagliardi at the controls, still using hand signals to communicate with Shattler.

They must have done this a thousand times, he thought. Freaking experts.

Then Reed saw something tall and dark just to the right, beneath the SDV. He leaned toward the opening in the craft's hull and peered out but felt a hand on his shoulder. Solomon pulled him back in and shook his head, making a fist with one hand and then throwing it open with drama.

Underwater mine.

Reed could see it now—bulky and round, chained to the seafloor far below like a hot air balloon. A chill rippled down his spine as another mine became visible to their left, and two more just beneath them.

Welcome to North Korea.

He leaned back in the seat and breathed easily, watching as Gagliardi guided them, turning to navigate around another mine, then adjusting a lever and bringing them up to crest the edge of a reef. Reed could now see thirty feet beyond the nose of the SDV. The water was relatively clear and empty, save for the occasional passage of a large fish.

There was a silver light far ahead, and he remembered the nearly full moon overhanging them. The same moon that he and Turk jumped beneath only a few nights previously, now watching over them on the other side of the globe. But maybe it was unfortunate. If he was going to sneak into a hostile nation, he'd just as soon do it in perfect darkness.

Another twenty minutes crept by, the SDV barely moving. The bright gleam of the moon was now strong enough to illuminate the crystal water and the torn surface of the ocean only a few yards overhead, with waves ripping toward the coast.

Gagliardi adjusted a lever, and the buzzing beneath Reed's tailbone ceased altogether. For a full minute, nobody moved and the SDV swiveled, now tugged landward by the tide. Gagliardi looked over his shoulder and gave Reed a clenched fist followed by a thumbs-up.

The "go" signal.

Reed sucked down a lungful of oxygen and slipped his feet into his fins, bending down to latch them in place. The SEALs remained motionless as Reed and Turk ducked through the open sides of the SDV, then tread water next to the craft and reached in for their gear.

The dry bags sagged toward the bottom under the weight of the rifles, but Reed shifted the load to his back, then made eye contact with Gagliardi one last time.

The SEAL sat motionless, his hands resting on the controls, his gaze fixed on Reed. Behind his goggles, Reed made out the strain in his face—a foreboding Reed hadn't seen before.

He hoped he was imagining it.

Reed shot him one last thumbs-up, then turned and kicked for the shore with Turk at his side. Within minutes, he could make out the sandy bottom, and if he tilted his head, he could see the wind-torn crest of white-caps rolling toward the shore.

That was good. Whitecaps made noise.

He reached ahead and kicked, eager to get out of the water and reunite with the rifle before anything could go wrong. The sand rose toward his chest until it scraped his sternum, then Reed dropped his knees, and for the first time in his life, his head broke through the surface into North Korean airspace.

Reed spat the mouthpiece out. Blood churned in his ears as he rose out of the surf like an apparition, breaking for the beach with Turk at his elbow.

The shoreline was dark and desolate. They reached dry ground, and Reed ripped his goggles off, casting a wary glance around the sand dunes rising ahead of him like low mountain peaks. Dry grass swayed in the wind, and a couple crabs scurried near the surf, but all else was quiet.

Empty, just as it should be.

He moved quickly, unstrapping his fins before stripping out of the wetsuit and standing almost nude under the chilling blast of the wind. Then he opened the dry bag, retrieving the rifle first and locking a maga-zine in place. The weapon was equipped with a rudimentary, Russian-designed red dot optic, and select fire with a full-auto option. It was enough to give somebody hell, at least.

Reed laid the rifle next to Turk's and moved to the dry clothes, sliding on black combat pants and matching boots, followed by a black undershirt, a black button-down, and a black operator's jacket. Then came black face paint, a black knit hat, a black chest rig hung with two fragmentation grenades, a smoke grenade, and two extra mags for the AK. Last of all was a belt, preloaded with the CZ pistol and two spare mags of 9mm ammunition, followed by a combat knife. It wasn't a KA-BAR, Reed's preferred edged weapon. The CIA thought the KA-BAR was too American, and they were probably right. This was some Chinese junk, but it would suffice.

Within seconds of leaving the water, they were both fully outfitted and busy repacking their scuba gear. They buried it all behind a sand dune, making note of the spot. The tracks they left in the sand would be mostly washed away by the incoming tide, but Reed took care to conceal them anyway with irregular kicks of his boots. He and Turk knelt in the lee of a dune, and Turk unpacked an iPad and the satellite messaging device from a backpack.

The messenger was small, about the size of an iPhone. A deployable antenna protruded from the back side, enabling a more reliable connection with whatever satellite the device depended on, but when Turk powered it on, the signal was already strong.

Reed took the device and shot off a quick message to the only contact programmed inside.

REACHED THE BEACH. ALL CLEAR. MISSION GO.

He hit send and watched as Turk zoomed in on a digital map of the North Korean coast on the iPad. Turk marked their spot with a silent point of his finger, then traced the outline of their path, nine miles through mountains and rice paddies to Anbyŏn.

Reed checked his watch, tapping a button to adjust to local time. It was five hours to sunrise.

Go time.

22

Everything about Wolfgang's tiny office in the corner of the fifth floor of the George Bush Center for Intelligence said "unwelcome." The desk was small, sat too low to the ground, and had nothing on it other than a cheap lamp, his computer, and a cracked pencil cup with no writing instruments.

The chair was worse, sagging to one side and creaking when he moved. There was no mat on the floor to cover the worn carpet, and the walls were battered and bare. To top it all off, it was cold in the cramped, windowless room, and when Wolfgang inquired about coffee, he was met with a blank stare, as if the existence of any such hot beverage was a secret the Central Intelligence Agency would neither confirm nor deny.

The CIA didn't want him there—that was plain enough. But their open hostility only reinforced his desire to dig in. After receiving Reed's phone call, he found himself irritated by the premise of the situation. The man Wolfgang initially knew as The Prosecutor was a magnet for trouble. Even when life handed him a beautiful wife, a beautiful child, and a chance to break from his violent past, Reed couldn't handle it. He craved conflict like a sled dog craved the run, and that pissed Wolfgang off because he didn't understand it. For Wolfgang, the run had always been a means to an end, not an end unto itself.

Yet, he also understood. In a way, his and Reed's motivations for taking the job weren't so different. Not only because they both needed the money, but also because Wolfgang struggled with the quiet of his rural New York home as much as Reed struggled with security jobs and suburbia. What once had been a fortress of solace and peace had now become an echo chamber of his own thoughts and insecurities—a virtual prison, locking him into endless hours of questioning everything he ever believed in.

But even beyond that, Wolfgang felt a strange loyalty to Reed. It wasn't quite friendship—there were a million people Wolfgang would rather share a Saturday night with, and half of them were dead. It was more . . . an unsettled debt. Unfinished business.

Wolfgang still remembered lying in that darkened room, consumed by fever and wallowing in his own sweat, his busted leg swollen to twice its normal size. Slowly dying. The flesh literally rotted off the bone, so rank he could barely breathe, the pain more real than anything he'd ever imagined.

Pure agony.

After two days, he knew death was coming for him. An infection had set in, seeping through his blood and saturating his body. It would reach his brain soon, and then he would slip away into the great unknown. Probably to Hell. Wolfgang figured that's where people like him were destined to wake up.

But Reed didn't let him go. The Prosecutor could have—probably *should have*—left him to die in that tiny room, imprisoned by a maniacal army of Eastern European mercenaries. But Reed wasn't that kind of man. The Prosecutor rained vengeance on that compound, almost single-handedly burning it to the ground and dragging Wolfgang out under a storm of enemy gunfire. He saved Wolfgang's life.

He had Wolfgang's back.

And now, for some reason, Wolfgang felt that Reed needed somebody to have his. The hostility with which he was greeted in Virginia only served to reinforce those feelings. The CIA didn't want Wolfgang here. They were happy to use Reed and Turk for whatever off-the-books missions they could dream up, but they didn't want a witness back in the States. If things went wrong, they planned to burn The Prosecutor, which was understandable, but Wolfgang wasn't going to stand for it. He owed Reed that much.

A digital chirp erupted from Wolfgang's laptop, signaling an incoming message. He scanned it, then lifted his desk phone from the receiver and hit speed dial 1—straight to the director's office. The CIA might not want Wolfgang around, but that didn't mean he lacked executive access.

"Yes?"

"Green light. Mission is underway."

23

The thermostat on Reed's handheld navigation unit read thirty-five degrees Fahrenheit, much colder than the CIA predicted the weather to be. Not long after he and Turk left the beach and crept across a road into the foothills of the Taebaek Mountains, they encountered a dusting of old snow lying across shallow ravines and under the shelter of low trees. By the way it broke underfoot, leaving jagged icy edges, Reed estimated the snowfall to be a few days old, having partially melted and then refrozen a few times.

Useful information. If it had been cold lately, people might be staying indoors more.

The path the iPad laid out for them led through foothills and across three successive ridges of the Taebaek range before winding down to Anbyŏn. It was a punishing route, requiring a lot of scrabbling over packed dirt and between patches of vegetation encrusted in refrozen snow, but the improvised trail gave Reed and Turk the high ground upon reaching their target, and that was worth some sacrifice.

They jogged without comment, enjoying the rural North Korean countryside. Within an hour, they'd moved almost two miles from the coast and stopped along the mountainside to recheck their bearing and sip water from the bladders built into their packs.

There was nothing obstructing Reed's view of the water, now far below, beyond the busted road. He watched quietly as a lone truck with one headlight bumped along that road, moving slowly from north to south and passing the point where they buried their scuba gear.

It was all surreal. It still hadn't really sunk in where he was or where he was headed.

"Place feels desolate," Turk muttered, wiping water and sweat from his lip and surveying the coast with suspicious intensity.

Reed had thought the same thing. A few miles to the north was the city of Wŏnsan, home to an estimated three or four hundred thousand people. But even this close, there was no hint of city glow rising over the mountains. No taste of smog on the air. He could've pretended he was squatting in the middle of North Dakota, a couple hundred miles from the nearest Walmart. It was eerie.

"Ready?" he said.

They got up again, cradling their AKs and starting into the mountains. Reed's lungs burned, and his calves ached, but something about the familiar weight of the gear was almost comforting.

Back on the warpath.

The next several miles passed without event as they crossed over a snowcapped ridge, moved through a low valley, and started up the next rise. Reed's whole body burned now with the strain, and it was impossible not to breathe harder, but the GPS left them only two miles to go.

They paused again, listening for sounds of approaching traffic, but there were no roads and no signs of life. The mountains felt as empty and forgotten as the surface of the moon, with not even mammals or small birds to observe their passage. It put him on edge. For one of the most isolated, fortified nations on Earth, was it really this easy to sneak in?

Take the luck and keep moving.

The final ridge between the beach and Anbyŏn was the most difficult—steep, with little in the way of vegetation to assist their climb. Chinese-made night-vision goggles illuminated the way forward, but at times, the path disappeared altogether or terminated in a cliff, forcing them to retrace their steps. The crest of the ridge took them by surprise, and they both dropped to their chests to avoid silhouetting against the night sky.

"Binos," Reed whispered, holding out one hand.

Turk passed him a pair of waterproof binoculars from his pack, and Reed squinted into the darkness. One more mile away, nestled in the bottom of a valley along the east bank of the Namdae River, lay the village of Anbyŏn, marked by only a few dozen streetlamps leaning over narrow roads carved between small houses.

The Chinese night vision struggled at this distance, but Reed took his time, slowly sweeping from north to south and immediately noting the shortage of vehicles. He counted only four—all utility vehicles parked next to larger warehouses on the edge of town. There were rail lines, though. One reaching in from the east, connecting Anbyŏn to the coast, a second stretching south out of Wŏnsan, and a third striking westward into the Korean mainland.

Reed passed the binoculars to Turk and lay still, chewing the inside of one cheek and thinking about what he saw. The whole place looked like a movie set, or one of those nuke towns from the fifties, built for the sole purpose of testing the latest atomic weapons.

Everything *looked* real, but something was missing, and it wasn't just people. There was no heartbeat. No life. The village had the visual vibrancy of a graveyard.

"Lovely views," Turk said. "Great school district. Or so I hear."

Reed smirked. He consulted the GPS again and pinpointed Gok's house on the edge of town. Then he reached out for the binoculars again and focused on the spot.

This far away, with this little light, it was almost impossible to make out the home. Reed saw only a shadow sitting at the end of a lonely street. No car out front. The low trees that surrounded the home leaned close to the eaves, and the entire place had a disheveled look, like a rental home on the starter side of town. The kind of place where the tenant might cut the grass once a month but wouldn't do much in the way of intensive upkeep.

Yet, according to the file Reed read while on board *Louisville*, the presence of a house at all was a mark of state privilege. Housing was a governmentally managed resource, like jobs, food, transportation, and pretty much everything else in North Korea. Citizens were assigned places to live, and most often, those places were shabby apartments near the core of town, similar to the high-rises that rose out of the core of Anbyŏn and along the river.

A house was a luxury, even if it was a tiny, outdated thing like Gok's. That meant he was favored by the state and was an important member of the People's Republic. Or he had been, anyway.

Reed lowered the binoculars and thought for a minute, then passed them to Turk to replace in his pack. "Only two hours to sunrise," he said. "The longer we wait, the tougher this gets. I say we take advantage of the dark."

Turk grunted, and the two of them clambered back to their feet and progressed down the face of the ridge. It was a lot easier heading down than it had been coming up, and within minutes, they entered the valley and stepped into dense groves of unmanaged forest, cleared in places for small fields and rice paddies. The snow had melted there, leaving the ground mucky and slick, with underbrush tugging at their pants.

Reed kept the rifle just below his line of sight, safety off, ready to engage. With each step, he was conscious of the sucking sensation of the mud on his boots and the sound it made, but the place was truly desolate. Even a quarter mile from the edge of the village, there was nothing.

No people. No development. No roads, even. Just untamed landscape.

They stopped at the edge of the final forest and knelt in the shadows, surveying the backside of a row of houses only two hundred yards away. Gok's house sat at the end, which left them a sheltered side to circle in from, free of the prying eyes of any neighbors. Reed noted a single spidery electrical line running the length of the street in front of the homes, with thin cable draped to each one, but there were no lights.

They moved north out of the forest until they were even with the end of Gok's street, then they turned west and slowed to a crawl, leapfrogging each other and providing silent cover. Reed kept his finger pressed against the AK's receiver, just above the trigger guard, and thought about what would happen if a fight actually broke out. It was a long way back to the beach, and it would take time for Gagliardi and his underwater charter bus to reach them.

Better not to shoot unless absolutely necessary.

At last, they approached Gok's home, and Reed found the cottage exactly as it had appeared from the mountainside. It was tiny by American standards—maybe a thousand square feet, with narrow, dusty windows. The front door led to a gravel path connecting straight to the street, without any driveway or place to park a car. That didn't seem to matter because no one on the street seemed to own a car. Reed guessed they must all take busses or walk to the train station.

Reed knelt and watched for a while, then turned to Turk and raised his eyebrows in a question. Turk shrugged as if he didn't care, but he didn't look eager to leave the relative shelter of the tall grass, either.

May as well be me.

Reed held up two fingers and gestured toward the house, then motioned to Turk and made a sweeping move with his open hand. Turk crouched lower to the ground, lifting the AK into his shoulder and laying a finger on the trigger.

Reed looked back at the house, scanning the surroundings one last time for the presence of any open windows. Dogs. Pedestrians. Passing cars. There was nothing.

He rose out of the grass like a ghost and broke into a light jog. The ground was hard, and his boots made only light thumping sounds as he quickly crossed the yard and reached the back door in seconds. He immediately pressed his back against the wall next to the door and held the rifle at the ready, the muzzle pointed toward the doorstep.

He reached out and tried the knob. It was locked, but only with a thumb latch.

Reed deployed his lockpicks from a cargo pocket, conscious of Turk covering him from the edge of the rice paddy. The lock was a simple affair, with minimal tumblers and no additional lockout mechanism. He defeated it in under thirty seconds and replaced the picks, then motioned to the rice paddy.

Turk arrived in a crouched run, his rifle held in low-ready. As soon as he reached the house, Reed shifted his AK until the muzzle pointed through the doorway, then he nodded once. Turk put his hand on the doorknob, waited one, then shoved it open.

24

"Don't take the job. You'll never have sex again."

That was the advice of Dr. Sarah Aimes's long-time boss, mentor, and begrudging friend, Chuck Carlisle, when the Agency offered her the position of deputy director of the CIA.

Prior to the Brandt administration, Carlisle served as deputy director, and had for over twenty years, surviving a slew of directors, National Security advisors, and intelligence officials. Carlisle used to joke that deputy directors were like White House staff.

"The bigwigs come and go," he said. "We stay."

But then William J. Brandt was elected, and he promptly replaced every director of every agency in Washington, including that of the CIA. Carlisle's long-time friend, Director Frank Hothburn, was axed and replaced by sitting director Victor O'Brien. A friend of Brandt's.

Carlisle didn't like O'Brien. He didn't trust him, and Aimes thought he probably had good reason not to. Carlisle had made a very long, very profitable career knowing more about the people around him than they knew about him, so if he called into question the ethics, intentions, or integrity of anyone, it was a question worth looking into.

But maybe more than that, Carlisle was just tired. He was old, nearing sixty-five, and ready for less time snooping and more time fishing. He vacated the position of deputy director, and O'Brien—for reasons Sarah Aimes still didn't understand— suggested to the president that she take Carlisle's place.

"I'm telling you, Sarah. Run, don't walk. Take it from an old man . . . That job will kill you."

Aimes knew he was right. She knew he was speaking with her best intentions in mind. But deputy director at only thirty-eight? One step beneath the highest seat in the entire Agency? Who could turn that down?

Not her. She accepted in spite of Carlisle's warning, and she never looked back. But she did miss her love life. That was something Carlisle had been dead right about. She hadn't even dated in nearly two years. Not because men at the bar didn't find CIA officers sexy, and not even because she couldn't willingly advertise her identity. Aimes never went on a date because she never had *time* for a date. She worked twelve to fourteen hours a day, five to seven days a week, and she slept like a rock in between.

Welcome to the CIA.

Aimes lifted her glasses and rubbed bloodshot eyes, wondering whether or not she'd eaten lunch. It was nearing three p.m. in Virginia, and she hadn't left her desk since four that morning, compliments of the off-the-books mission underway.

The Prosecution Force.

That's what the CIA had code-named the trio of washed-up, battered warriors who now operated illegally on a desperate rescue mission to recover Gok Chin-ho from the oppressed confines of the DPRK. Apparently, the name had something to do with Reed Montgomery's underground history as an assassin. Aimes had read his file, of course. She'd read all three of their files, but there were substantial chunks of information missing—especially with concern to Montgomery. The intel wasn't redacted. It simply didn't exist.

Truth be told, the CIA didn't know much about the Prosecution Force. Only that they were somehow deeply connected with the Trousdale Administration and that President Trousdale trusted them. And used them.

It made Aimes nervous on a molecular level. She'd been around long enough to witness a litany of illegal, off-the-books operations and black units before. The CIA was chock-full of them, but such arrangements were something of a revolving door. Asset in, mission accomplished, asset exposed, asset out.

Burn without hesitation. Disown without regret. That was the name of the game.

But never before had she worked so near to a program controlled more by a politician than the Agency, and *that* was what made her nervous. It wasn't because she didn't like Trousdale or believe in what she was attempting to accomplish in Washington. It was because Aimes didn't trust *anybody*. Especially in Washington.

She clicked out of the open digital file for the man called Wolfgang Pierce and cast an impulsive glance toward the corner of the building where they'd left Pierce in a cold, unfriendly room. The man had barely spoken a word to anybody since arriving and didn't seem the least bit perturbed by his unwelcoming accommodations. That only further inflamed her unease. And her curiosity.

The next file on her agenda was another report from *Cortex*, the code name assigned to Minsu Jeong. The South Korean national had proven to be an invaluable asset to the Agency, feeding them an endless stream of images, recordings, and observations from within Pyongyang for the past three years. Minsu was a smart guy—stealthy and aggressive, always willing to push the boundaries to obtain what the Agency needed.

But he was also a time bomb, because while the Agency only wanted a steady flow of intelligence sufficient enough to monitor the regime, Minsu had ambitions of overthrowing it. For now, their interests were aligned enough for a sort of mutualistic harmony to be struck, but that wouldn't last forever. Eventually, Minsu would grow impatient, and when he did . . .

Aimes preferred not to think about that.

She scanned the first two pages of the report, squinting at grainy images Minsu took with one of his disguised cameras, furnished compliments of the Agency. Those pictures displayed increased chaos deep inside Pyongyang, paired with a buildup of KPA troops throughout the core of the city. As of yet, Minsu hadn't reported on any official statements from the core of the DPRK's government, but the increase in tensions was palpable. Striking, even.

She clicked out of the report and opened a file headlined: "POI: Jang, Bon-hwa. General, KPA." Headlining the document was a photograph of a short man with an ugly scowl on his face, dressed in olive drab with stars on his shoulders and a military hat perched on his head. Next to that image was a general breakdown of his identity: parents, estimated date of birth, known medical conditions and associates, and presumed governmental affiliations.

Most of those spaces were left blank. Very little was known about General Jang, other than his increased influence within Pyongyang's innermost governmental circles. The general was a rising star, and it was rumored that he was quickly advancing to become one of the supreme leader's most trusted military advisors. He was somewhere between fifty and sixty years old, single, and relatively healthy. Specifics of his personal life were an enigma.

What *was* known were details of Jang's travels to China and Russia during his period as a sort of military ambassador to both nations. Jang spent time in both Moscow and Beijing during the late nineties and early two thousands, traveling frequently under the guise of political liaison.

His true purpose? Probably negotiating weapons deals on behalf of Pyongyang. North Korea produced almost none of their own munitions during that time. Most of their hardware was purchased from Russia, where they acquired truckloads of cheap, Soviet-era small arms, trucks, and tanks after the fall of the Iron Curtain. When those supplies began to run dry, the DPRK turned to China, where thousands of equally cheap replicas of Soviet designs were churned out of child labor factories.

A good deal. A nice arrangement. And a unique opportunity for somebody like Jang to spend substantial time outside of North Korea.

But what had made him a radical?

Aimes scrolled to details of his psych report, written by Dr. Janet Strickland, the Agency specialist on the DPRK. Most of the report was speculative, of course, progressing through known facts about Jang's attachments within the regime to notes about his supposed desire for nuclear confrontation with the West. It was as well-documented and substantiated as could be expected, given the extreme secrecy of both the KPA and the nation they called home. Copies of emails Jang had sent Pyongyang while serving in China frequently referenced "opportunities" for "ballistic acquisition." The language was vague, but the intention was clear. Jang was very interested in acquiring Chinese nuclear technology for the DPRK.

After returning to his homeland to assume a leading role in the Korean People's Army, what snippets were stolen from Jang's speeches and correspondence reinforced the image of a man thirsty for chaos. He hated America with a passion rivaled only by liberal arts students and Islamic radicals, and he also maintained a sadistic fascination with the concept of total global nuclear war. The end of the ages, he called it. The birth of a new empire, rising from the ashes.

Truly poetic stuff. The ramblings of a madman.

Aimes had read the file before, but she scanned through it twice more, searching between the lines and looking for something she might have missed. Her gaze stopped over a blurry image of Jang standing behind the supreme leader himself, not long after the death of Cho Jong-il. Cho Jong stood behind a mic, his chubby cheeks lifted into a grin as he waved at a crowd of Pyongyang residents. It was one of Jong's first appearances as supreme leader, and General Jang stood not far behind him among a line of military officers, aides, and party officials.

And one woman.

She stood next to Jang with her head held high, dressed in a subdued black coat with a DPRK flag pin affixed to one lapel. Aimes stopped, squinting at the woman and thinking she looked familiar, but she was unable to place her.

Then her gaze slid down the woman's arm, toward her hand. The image blurred there, making it almost impossible to discern details. But was she . . . ? No. Surely not.

Aimes hit the speaker button on her phone and waited for her secretary to pick up.

"Yes, ma'am?"

"Get me Dr. Janet Strickland, Office of East Asian Analysis."

"Yes, ma'am. One moment."

Aimes chewed her lip, studying the blurred spot on the photo again and trying to make sense of the discolored sections. Trying to read between the lines.

"Strickland, East Asia." The woman who answered sounded as tired as Aimes, but her tone cut straight to the point. Aimes liked that.

"Doctor, this is Deputy Director Aimes. Do you have a second?"

"Of course, ma'am."

"I'm reviewing your file on General Jang Bon-hwa. Do you have it handy?"

"I'm pulling it up now. What can I help with?"

"This picture on page four of the general standing behind Cho. Who is the woman standing next to him?"

Aimes heard a mouse click, then Strickland sucked her teeth. "That's Maeng Si-woo. I think. A one-time associate of the Ministry of State Security, thought to be used as a female interrogator. She was publicly executed in 2013 for suspected treason and 'extramarital behavior.'"

"She was married?"

"Maybe. We don't really know."

"What was her relationship to General Jang?"

"Um . . . I don't think they had one."

"You have a file on her?"

"I'm sure we do."

"Please send it, ASAP. Thank you, Doctor."

Aimes hung up and drummed her fingers on the table, still studying that blurry spot. Were their fingers . . . touching?

An email alert chimed, and Aimes hurried to open it. Maeng Si-woo's file was much shorter than Jang's, including a few low-quality images and a rundown of her presumed career as a member of the Ministry of State Security—North Korea's secret police.

The DPRK included precious few women in government. Almost none, in fact, beyond Cho's sister, who was rumored to be a close advisor. But Maeng was an exception. She seemed to have quite the career with the government, beginning with the KPA and trading departments a few times.

Aimes tabbed back to Jang's file and noted the time and place of a deployment. She tabbed back to Maeng, back to Jang, and back again to Maeng.

Then she reached for her phone.

25

Anbyŏn, DPRK

The house was listless, but it wasn't empty. Two women huddled around a low table in the kitchen, immediately on the other side of the door, as Reed entered. They both wore headphones plugged into a radio resting on the table, but they looked up when the man in black stormed in, gun raised.

"Non-coms!" Reed hissed, moving left and covering the living room beyond the kitchen as Turk rushed in behind him.

The two women shrank back, their faces white, their gazes darting to the radio. They seemed confused and disoriented, and then the older one looked ready to scream.

"Quiet!" Turk snapped, kicking the door shut and brandishing his rifle over the two women. "Get down. Get down!"

They both dropped to their knees as Reed moved left down a short hall, quickly clearing two small bedrooms and a bathroom, then returning to the main room and lowering the rifle.

"Clear," he hissed.

He stepped to the table and checked the radio, inspecting for signs of a two-way transmitter or listening device. The unit was battery-powered, still

plugged into a dual set of headphones. He opened the battery compartment and knocked out a row of AAs, then motioned toward the living
room.

"Out of the kitchen! Let's move!"

Turk led the two women into the living room, and Reed checked
between a crack in the curtains to see if their intrusion had aroused any
neighbors or passersby. A quick glance at his watch confirmed it would be
less than an hour before sunrise.

He turned back to the two petrified woman kneeling on the floor, their
hands up. The first was an older woman with greying hair and sagging
cheeks. She wore a simple night-robe, and an anxious tear slipped down
one side of her face.

Reed did a double-take when he looked at the other woman. She was
gorgeous. Early twenties, with smooth, dark hair, and the most perfect olive
complexion he'd ever seen. She wore a night-robe like the other woman,
but it had fallen over one shoulder, draping open over her chest.

Reed looked away, clearing his throat and tilting his head toward Turk.
The big Tennessean scooped a blanket off a chair and passed it to the
young woman. She seemed confused by the gesture and slid closer to the
older woman, murmuring something in frantic Korean.

"Translator," Reed said, holding out a hand. Turk dug past the iPad in
his pack and produced a handheld device. Another gift from the CIA, it was
perhaps the only piece of truly American hardware in their kit, designed to
interpret and translate foreign languages on the fly and equipped with an
aggressive microphone and a digital screen.

Reed flipped the device on and waited for it to power up, then knelt in
front of the women and offered what he hoped was a calming smile. He
couldn't imagine that anything about the black camo paint on his face or
the rifle swinging from a strap around his neck inspired reassurance, but he
couldn't help that. "We're not here to hurt you," he said calmly, speaking
into the device.

He hit the translate button and waited for the device to spit out a
computerized string of Korean. The two women looked confused, and they
shrank closer to the wall.

"Ask about Gok," Turk said.

Reed hit the input button again and spoke into the mic. "We're looking for Gok Chin-ho. Are you his family?"

The device translated, and the women exchanged another look. The older woman began to cry. The younger woman's hands shook, but she seemed to be regaining some of her confidence.

Reed hit the input again.

"Gok Chin-ho," he repeated. "We're looking for—"

"You're from America?" The young woman spoke in clear, heavily accented English.

Reed stopped mid-sentence and looked to Turk. The big man only shrugged.

"Yes," Reed said. "You speak English?"

The young woman nodded. She remained crouched, one protective hand placed over her companion's arm.

Reed set the translator down and lowered himself onto the floor. He unslung the rifle and laid it beside him, pointed away from the women. Then he offered another gentle smile. "We're looking for Gok Chin-ho. Does he live here?"

The women exchanged another glance. The younger one appeared ready to speak, but then the older woman broke into a string of Korean. They seemed to argue, and Reed listened. As long as they weren't attacking him or rushing outside and screaming for help, he could give them time.

Finally, the young woman looked back. She held her chin high now, seeming to have overcome her momentary panic. Iron defiance radiated from her face, mixed with a hint of indignation. "Why are you here?" she said. Again, perfect English, but Reed had to focus to make out the words through her accent.

"We're from America," he said. "We're looking for Gok Chin-ho."

She evaluated that, then repeated her question. "Why?"

Reed hesitated. Whatever he'd expected to find after storming into the house, this hadn't been it. Ideally, he would have found Gok hiding in a closet or something, ready to be swept away to freedom with the schematics he promised.

Next best option would be to find out who these people were.

"You know Gok?" he asked.

The old woman grabbed the younger's arm and burst into stressed Korean again.

The young woman ignored her. "Yes."

"How?"

"You are soldier?" the young woman asked.

Reed grunted. "Something like that."

"From . . . White House?"

"More or less."

The woman tilted her head in confusion.

Turk checked the street through a slit in the curtain, then consulted his watch. "Time . . ."

"Yes," Reed said. "We're soldiers from the White House. We're looking—"

"He's not here," the young woman said.

The old woman continued to claw at her arms, panic filling her lined and saggy face.

"Where is he?" Reed pressed. "We need to find him."

"Why?"

"We're here to help him."

"You here to take him away?"

The question seemed loaded—with what, Reed wasn't sure. Hope? Accusation? Fear?

He decided to roll the dice. "Yes."

Something flashed across her face, confirming his suspicions but not clarifying her intentions. The woman spoke quickly to her companion in hushed Korean. The older woman shook her head a few times, looking in terror at Reed and Turk's weapons, but it was clear the younger woman was now in charge.

"I am Gok Sinju," the young woman said. "I am Chin-ho's daughter. This is my mother, Ye-jun."

Sinju gave her mother's arm a gentle squeeze, and Reed saw tears glimmer on her olive cheeks. "We have prayed you would come."

Reed looked to Turk, and the big man's cheeks flushed.

"Where is Chin-ho?" Reed asked again.

Despite Sinju's flawless complexion and gently brushed hair, she looked exhausted, as if she hadn't slept in days. Reed had seen the look before in Banks's face. Women sometimes disguised strain with careful attention to their appearance, but stress had a way of leaking out.

"Sinju," Reed said. "Please. Where is your father?"

"I . . . I do not know."

Reed's shoulders slumped, a crushing weight moving in from out of nowhere and dragging down on him. This was always a risk, he knew. The chances that Gok's family knew where he was had always been slim. But he still hoped. It still felt like their best shot.

"When did he go missing?" he asked.

"Three . . . four days ago."

"You haven't spoken to him since?"

She shook her head.

Reed breathed a soft curse, then tugged his knit hat off and ran a gloved hand through his hair. "Has the government come? Are they looking for him?"

Sinju shook her head. "No. Nobody come here. My father supposed to be off over week . . . two days."

"Weekend? He was supposed to be off work over the weekend?"

Sinju nodded. Reed thought about the time. They were edging into Tuesday morning. If Gok had bought time for himself by going missing Thursday night or Friday morning, that time was now expiring.

"You take us to America?" Sinju said.

It had been a long time since Reed had seen so much desperation in a person's face. It reminded him of years before, during his early days as a contract assassin. Sometimes his targets saw the proverbial ax coming before it hit them. Sometimes they pleaded with him, face-to-face.

Pure desperation. What he saw in Sinju's eyes felt just as desperate, but he hadn't expected her question, and he wasn't there to recover a family. Just Gok.

"Do you have any idea where Chin-ho could be hiding?" he asked, dodging the question.

Sinju shook her head.

"There must be something," Reed said. "Someplace in the mountains? Someplace he could be safe?"

Sinju didn't answer.

Reed hauled himself to his feet and tilted his head toward the farthest corner of the room, near the front door. Turk followed him, leaving the two women to murmur in strained Korean.

"What now?" Turk muttered.

"She could be lying," Reed said. "I doubt this guy went AWOL three or four days ago and nobody's come looking for him. He's one of their top nuclear scientists. My gut says they're freaking out right now."

"You think she's hiding him?" Turk asked.

Reed looked over his shoulder to watch Sinju cradle her mother, who seemed ready to have a panic attack. Sinju was far calmer, rubbing Ye-jun's back and murmuring platitudes while watching the two Americans.

"Maybe," Reed said. "Or maybe she really doesn't know. There's . . . not really a way to find out."

Turk wiped the back of his hand across his mouth and dropped his gaze uncomfortably. There was absolutely a way to find out. A way they had both employed many times before.

A bloody way.

Reed shook his head. "No. We're not going that route. Let's message Wolfgang a sitrep, then see what more we can get out of them. The CIA may have some other ideas."

Turk retrieved the messaging device, tapping in a note as Reed returned to the women.

He squatted next to them and rested the rifle across his thighs. "We have to find your father," he said, addressing Sinju. "It's very important."

"I already tell you. I do not know where he is."

Reed held up a hand, attempting to calm her. "I know. I'm not accusing you of anything. But I need you to think again. Please. Is there anywhere he could be?"

For a long while, the room was still, the silence punctuated only by the soft click of Turk flipping the messaging device off.

Sinju looked up. "There is place—"

Her words were cut off by a growling outside the front door, growing steadily louder from not far down the street.

Turk rushed to the window and pulled the curtain back a couple inches. A glimpse of the street outside was all it took to identify the sound. "Two vehicles incoming. Guys in uniforms with rifles. We're busted!"

26

Before Reed could stop her, Sinju jumped from the floor, rushing to the window next to Turk and peering out. Her smooth cheeks turned pale, and she grabbed Turk's sleeve, pulling him away from the window and rattling off something in Korean. Her mother got off the floor and rushed back into the kitchen, gathering up the radio and spilled batteries as Sinju waved toward the back of the house.

"Who are they?" Reed demanded, holding his rifle in the low-ready position and already thinking about the network of streets outside—the best route of escape.

"Police!" Sinju said. "Government! Come quickly."

She waved down the hallway, sweat trickling down her face, despite the cold. Turk and Reed followed her past a bathroom to the bedroom farthest from the front door. It was a small room with a narrow mattress on the floor next to a chest. There was one window, also covered in a thick curtain, and a closet door built into the back wall of the house.

Sinju opened the closet and pushed past a row of clothes, beckoning for Reed and Turk to get in. "Hurry!"

A truck ground to a stop outside, and door hinges groaned. It was easy to hear through the thin walls in the dead quiet of the neighborhood, and Reed guessed there were two or three men approaching the house. Then a fist pounded against the front door, and somebody shouted in Korean.

Reed shoved Turk ahead of him into the narrow closet, then packed in behind him. Sinju pulled the clothes in to cover them both, then shut the door and ran down the hall. Reed stood frozen, Turk's hot breath on the back of his neck, his rifle still cradled in his arms. He thought again about the streets outside and wondered what their chances of escaping this house became after piling into the closet.

If somebody opened the door . . .

Voices sounded from the living room, muted by the walls but still audible. They spoke Korean—one angry man making demands of Sinju and Yejun. For a while, there was a back-and-forth, and Gok's name was mentioned at least twice. It wasn't hard to guess what the discussion was about.

Then the demands grew louder as the speakers approached the hallway.

Reed shifted the rifle into his left hand, taking care not to knock the muzzle against the inside wall of the closet. Then he laid a hand on the Chinese fighting knife and wrapped his fingers around the grip. Turk's breathing grew shallower but still rhythmic. Reed was conscious of the muzzle of Turk's CZ pistol resting next to his right thigh, ready for action.

The bedroom door clicked. Reed pressed himself backwards, and he and Turk eased closer to the recesses of the closet. Sinju's clothes hung only inches from Reed's face, shielding his upper torso from view of the closet door, but stopping short of his knees.

The bedroom door swung open, and Reed slipped the knife out of its sheath. Feet tapped the worn floorboards, and someone kicked the mattress, causing the springs to squeak.

The closet doorknob twisted. Reed and Turk froze, not daring to breathe. Reed held the knife against his leg, shielding the shiny blade from any gleam of light.

The door swung open ten inches and stopped. Light spilled in through the gap, and someone in black boots and pants stood just outside of the closet.

Not olive drab. Not KPA.

Reed didn't move, and the man outside didn't poke his head into the closet or shift the clothes back. He just stood with the door open, maybe surveying the row of female clothes or the trio of slippers on the closet floor. Reed was only an inch inside the protective shadow, and if the door swung open just a little farther, light would spill across his boots.

But then the door shut. It clicked closed, and the man thumped across the floor, back to the hall. Reed let out a pent-up breath but remained frozen, listening as the footsteps reached the living room. There was another barked conference in Korean. Reed didn't hear Sinju or her mother this time. It was whatever jerk was interrogating them.

At last, the front door slammed, and the truck rumbled to life again. Reed sheathed the knife and pushed out of the closet, across the room to the window. He slipped the curtain back slightly, watching the truck move up the road under the light of a growing sunrise.

And then it was gone. But the sedan that had accompanied it remained behind, parked down the street and pointed at the house. A lone man sat behind the wheel, watching them.

Reed looked over one shoulder. Turk stood behind him, and both Sinju and her mother peered at them from the hallway. The looks on their faces told him two things: First, they hadn't been lying. They really didn't know where Gok was.

Second, whoever the guys in the truck were, Sinju and Ye-jun were absolutely terrified of them.

27

"Anything else?" O'Brien asked. He sat behind a mahogany desk inside his expansive office, a sixth cup of coffee resting on a coaster next to a picture of his eight-year-old daughter holding the hand of his disembodied ex-wife. After the divorce, he cropped her out of the photo, but he couldn't do much about her damn hand—in the photo and in his bank account. That was the thing about an ugly divorce. It was the gift that just kept costing you.

"That's all," Wolfgang said over the speakerphone, repeating Reed's latest message. "Reached house. Family here. No sign of Gok."

O'Brien ran a hand over his bald head. Both his palm and scalp were sweaty from the strain of another fifteen-hour day. He thought about Gok Chin-ho and the grainy images of the hypersonic missile Gok claimed the North Koreans were testing. For a nation barely able to feed its own people, it seemed highly implausible that a weapon this sophisticated and expensive was under development. More likely, Gok had found another way to obtain the image and was merely using it as a bargaining chip to get out.

But if he wasn't . . .

"I need a next move," Wolfgang said. "The longer they sit there, the more chance they're caught."

Wolfgang's blunt style was a virtue O'Brien would normally appreciate, but from an outsider forced into his agency on behalf of a black ops team he was already uncomfortable with, it just pissed him off.

"I'll let you know when we have a next step," O'Brien snapped. "Tell them to hold tight."

Wolfgang drew breath to object, but O'Brien didn't give him a chance. He hung up just as a sharp tapping rang against the misted glass of his office door. He hit the door unlock button on his desk, and the door swung open, exposing the rosy face of his secretary.

"Deputy Director Aimes to see you, sir."

O'Brien waved, indicating that she should be let in. He pulled a handkerchief from his pocket and swabbed his head. Why wouldn't somebody turn down the AC?

Dr. Sarah Aimes stepped in, her dark hair pulled into a ponytail, her lips pursed in that urgent-business-matter look O'Brien had come to hate. It wasn't that he disliked Aimes. She was good at her job. It seemed she just brought him more problems than solutions.

"Sorry to bother you, sir. We need to talk."

O'Brien flicked his hand irritably toward the door. Aimes shut it, then approached his desk and took a seat without being asked. O'Brien swallowed half a cup of lukewarm coffee, then flinched as Aimes deposited a folder onto his desk with the grace of an elephant taking a dump.

Another problem. A big one, by the look of it.

"What is it?" he said.

"I've been reviewing our files on Jang, and I think I may have found a concerning oversight."

O'Brien's stomach twisted at the name. He wasn't sure why, but Jang Bon-hwa gave him the chills. Not in a fearful way, but more in a dreadful way.

"What?"

Aimes spread printouts across his desk, tapping an enlarged image of a Korean woman dressed in an olive drab uniform.

"Maeng Si-woo, sir. North Korean interrogator and intelligence asset in the KPA. We don't know a lot about her, other than she was deployed multiple times to Pyongyang's field offices in Beijing and Moscow. Possibly as a watchdog—a sort of internal honeypot scheme."

O'Brien lifted the image. It wasn't difficult to guess why Maeng might have been used in a honeypot scheme—a semi-derogatory term for an operation involving the manipulation of a target via sexual means. Maeng was beautiful. Exceptionally so, actually. Curvy and tall, with glowing skin and the kind of eyes a man could get lost in.

"So, they were using her to seduce and expose traitors?" O'Brien asked.

"That's our working theory. She first appeared around 2010 in Moscow, and some of our assets tracked her into 2011. In 2012, she surfaced for six months in Beijing. Then she disappeared . . . Probably back to Pyongyang. As you know, the DPRK doesn't usually trust women, and they are seldom granted positions of leadership or governance. If the Korean People's Army was using her, it's safe to assume it was because of her gender, not in spite of it."

O'Brien grunted. "So, what's Maeng got to do with Jang?"

Aimes flipped through another page, then tapped on a photo. It was a blurry image of the supreme leader giving a speech, Jang standing behind him. And directly next to him stood Maeng.

"She was working him?"

Aimes sat back, folding her arms. "I'm not sure. I went through every file we have on them and noted at least three separate occasions where they shared a duty station outside of Korea. The DPRK deploys very few of their military officials internationally, so it would be rare for two assets to ever cross paths on the outside. To cross paths three times . . . it can't be coincidence."

O'Brien studied the image, focusing on Maeng's stern but radiant features. His gaze traveled down her curvy body . . . and then stopped. "Are they *holding hands*?"

Aimes grunted. "I thought the same thing. I had the image enhanced, and it's impossible to say. I find it extremely unlikely for them to display any sort of affection in a formal public setting such as that. Maybe she just brushed his arm, or . . . I don't know."

O'Brien set the image down. "What's your point?"

"There seem to be only two logical possibilities. Either she was working him, or she was involved with him. The best I can tell, Maeng was assigned to Jang's department during his tenure as overseas advocate to the Russians and Chinese. That could explain why she followed him around. She was some sort of permanent part of his staff. But that seems extremely unlikely. Pyongyang is very untrusting of their own people. They like to cycle out anybody who leaves the nation, making sure to have watchers watching their watchers. To leave two people working together that long . . . it's not like them."

"Unless Pyongyang made an exception and kept her close because they were using her to keep tabs on him."

"That's plausible," Aimes said. "But if they were worried about Jang, why did he go on to advance so high in the government? Maybe she cleared him. But if so, that doesn't explain why they killed her."

"Wait. What?"

"Maeng was executed in 2013, not long after Cho Jong took power."

O'Brien's mind raced, clicking through the mess of pieces strewn across his desk, trying to put a picture together. Nothing quite fit. "I don't understand the relevance," he said at last.

Aimes shifted in her chair.

O'Brien raised an eyebrow. "You didn't truck a load of papers to my desk for nothing. What are you thinking?"

Aimes cleared her throat. "We know Jang is a radical. We know he's nuts about nuclear war. We know he hates America. What we don't know is if that zeal is strong enough to break his loyalty to the Cho regime."

"Right."

"What if . . ." Aimes shrugged. "What if that loyalty is already broken? What if the regime, for whatever reason, executed the woman he loves?"

O'Brien looked at the photo and thought again about his ex-wife and the two thousand dollars of alimony she'd take that next week. He thought about how mad and crazy love had made him and how mad and crazy the fallout of that love still made him. And then he thought about Jang standing behind a nuclear button. "I think it's time we asked the president to brief the National Security Council."

Aimes nodded. "I agree, sir."

28

Anbyŏn, DPRK

Four hours passed, and the sedan sitting fifty yards away didn't move, its nose pointed toward the Gok house. Reed could make out the silhouette of a lone man sitting behind the wheel, upright and alert, monitoring the premises.

It was a problem. If the guy had waited on the front porch, Reed could've jumped him and cut his throat before he knew what was happening. If he parked in front of the house, Reed could've slipped up behind the car and knocked a hole through the glass, breaking his neck long before he reached his pistol or radio.

But sitting in the street, far enough away to detect a potential attacker long before they reached him, but close enough not to miss any comings and goings, there wasn't much Reed could do. Either the guy was smart, or his bosses were smart.

Reed left the window, creeping quietly back into the living room, the AK still swinging from one arm. Turk sat cross-legged on the floor, eating quietly from a bowl of rice that Ye-jun had prepared. The terrified Korean woman hurried from the kitchen as Reed approached, bowing her head and offering him a similar bowl.

"Thank you," Reed said, keeping his voice low. He sat on the floor across from Turk, leaning the rifle against his knee and accepting a pair of metal chopsticks from Sinju.

Gok's daughter looked a lot less scared than her mother. From time to time, she moved to the curtained windows, peeking through to catch a glimpse of the watcher in the car. Reed saw hatred, and maybe bloodthirst, in her eyes. He knew that look. He'd seen it in the mirror more times than he cared to admit.

"What now?" Turk asked.

Reed scooped clumps of sticky rice into his mouth. It was a good meal. Bland, but in Reed's experience, most foreign food was bland compared to oversalted, overprocessed, and oversweetened American cuisine.

"We wait," Reed said, still keeping his voice low. "They won't come back today. Not as long as that guy outside doesn't report anything. It'll give us time to hear from Wolf."

Turk grunted and fumbled with his chopsticks, dumping rice into his lap. Reed shot him a disgusted look and clicked his chopsticks in midair, demonstrating proper technique. Turk still didn't get it.

"I know him," Sinju said, still standing at the window, watching the car.

"He's been here before?" Reed asked.

"He live here," Sinju said. "In Anbyŏn."

Not good.

"Secret police?" Reed asked.

"State security. He go to school with me when I was young." Sinju's mouth twisted into a grimace. "He is dog."

Color crept into her cheeks, and she left the window, moving to the kitchen and putting a pot on the aged stove. When she returned, she carried a tray laden with cups, a teapot, and loose-leaf tea. She knelt on the floor between them and served Ye-jun first, speaking softly to her mother in subdued Korean. Ye-jun took the tea, her hands trembling as she glanced repeatedly at the door. Then she shook her head and handed the cup back before hurrying down the hall. Reed heard a bedroom door click, and all was silent again.

"My mother is very afraid," Sinju said with a shrug, sipping the tea. "She fears a prison camp."

Reed looked toward the window, listening as a bus rattled down the street. Murmured voices were barely audible as the sun crested the mountains and Anbyŏn awoke. The clatter outside gave him some peace of mind, knowing any noises they made would be subdued.

But that shield could only last so long, and eventually, the secret police would return. Ye-jun probably had good reason to be afraid.

"How do you know English?" Reed asked. It wasn't an important detail, but it nagged at him. He hadn't expected any Koreans, oppressed and isolated, to know anything about the outside world, let alone speak an international language.

Sinju smirked. "In his great wisdom, the supreme leader has made it so."

Reed accepted a small teacup. He couldn't tell if Sinju was being sarcastic or not.

"We are taught English in school," she said. "Most do not learn well. My father push me to understand. For future."

Reed sipped the strong, bitter tea, then put it down and looked to Turk. His battle buddy was busy checking the messaging device for the fifteenth time in the past hour. No word yet.

"Does your father speak English?" Reed asked.

Sinju shook her head. "Only little."

Reed got up and moved to the window, slipping back the curtain just long enough to check the car. The watcher was still there, still sitting upright. Alert.

He turned back to Sinju. "I need to know where your father is. I can't leave without him. He's trying to help America prevent a war."

Before Sinju could answer, Ye-jun returned from the bedroom, wringing her hands and looking between the two Americans. She babbled in strained Korean to Sinju, tears slipping down her face. Sinju hurried to soothe her, rubbing her back and cooing until the older woman finally agreed to take a seat. Sinju left her there and subtly beckoned for Reed to follow her into the kitchen.

"My mother does not want you here. If they find you, they kill us."

"We'll leave as soon as we find your father."

"You no understand. If you take my father, they put us in prison. Many beatings, no food. We . . . we die." She fumbled the last words, her lips trembling.

Reed felt a rock in his stomach along with a flush of anger. The CIA hadn't mentioned what would happen to Gok's family after he escaped the country. Stupidly, he hadn't thought to ask, either. It hadn't been top of mind amid infiltration plans.

"Do you know what your father does for the government?" Reed asked. Sinju seemed confused, and he rephrased. "His job. Do you know what he does?"

"My father is smart man. He works on weapons."

"That's right. And weapons are for war. My friend and I are here to stop that."

Sinju wiped her nose with the back of her hand and watched her mother for a while. "I do not know where my father is. I cannot help."

Reed put a gentle hand on her shoulder, pushing until she faced him. He remembered the black camo paint still smeared on his face and wished he'd washed it away, knowing he must look like a night terror. "Sinju, please. It's important. Where would he hide if he were in trouble? With family?"

"No. Not with family. Too much risk."

"Someplace in the countryside, then? In the mountains?"

She thought about that, her gaze drifting to her mother again.

Reed wondered what the dynamic there was and why Sinju seemed to be the parent between the two.

"There is place we go eat. Outside. Good day."

"Good day?"

"Not cold."

"Oh. Nice weather?"

She nodded.

"A picnic place?"

She shrugged, unfamiliar with the word.

"Is it far?"

"Small train ride. In the mountains. My father take us there sometimes. But it is not hiding place."

"Montgomery," Turk hissed from the living room. He held up the messenger, and Reed hurried over.

"Wolf?"

Turk nodded, punching in a quick message on the digital keyboard.

Reed read over his shoulder.

W: SITREP

PF: HOLED UP AT TARGET HOUSE. SURVEILLANCE OUTSIDE. TARGET LOCATION UNKNOWN.

Turk hit send and waited. Wolfgang didn't leave them hanging.

W: SITUATION STABLE?

Turk typed back immediately.

PF: TEMPORARY. REQUEST DATA ON POSSIBLE TARGET LOCATIONS.

W: HOLD ONE.

Turk lowered the device, frustration on his face, and Reed felt more of the same in his gut. An invisible mental clock ticked, louder with each passing minute, warning him that the longer they stayed there, the worse their odds became.

Reed checked on the watcher again. The man had left the driver's seat and was now leaning against the hood, smoking a cigarette. Midday sun beat down on his frame, giving Reed a much better view of him than before. He didn't like what he saw. The soldier was fit, with thick arms and a pistol on one hip. The silhouette of a rifle—probably an AK—was visible in the back seat of the car.

But what bothered Reed the most was something about the way the guy leered at the house.

Reed moved away from the window.

"We can't stay here," Turk said.

"I know."

Turk tilted his chin toward Sinju. "What did she say?"

The young woman knelt next to her mother now, fixing another cup of tea.

"She doesn't know," Reed said. "She mentioned some picnic spot nearby. Sounds like nothing."

The device chirped, and Turk snatched it up.

W: POSSIBLE LOCATION. FORMER CIA COVERT EXCHANGE POINT USED BY

TARGET. POSSIBLE HE WOULD GO THERE TO MAKE CONTACT WITH CIA. SENDING COORDINATES.

Reed dug through Turk's pack and retrieved the iPad, calling up their navigation software. Turk read off the latitude and longitude, and Reed typed them in and waited for the software to load. When it did, he panned around the screen while Turk waited.

"It's a field near a small river," he said. "Some woods. Some kind of abandoned radio tower? I don't know. Nearest building is a small concrete structure. Possibly a bathhouse? I think it's a park."

Reed trailed off, then his head snapped up. He hurried over to Sinju and held the iPad out to her. "Is this the place?" he asked. "The spot where you went to eat?"

Sinju took the iPad and inspected the screen. "I think so. Difficult to tell from above."

Reed took the iPad and turned to Turk. He didn't make it halfway across the room before a harsh knock boomed against the door.

29

They all froze, Reed's hand instinctively dropping to the CZ pistol strapped to his hip. Turk held up a hand, urging the women to be quiet, then retrieved his bag without a sound. Reed sidestepped to the window and held the gun next to his cheek, lifting the edge of the curtain.

The watcher stood at the door. Through the window, Reed saw his boots and half of one hip before his view was obscured by the curtain. A cloud of hazy cigarette smoke drifted toward the window, then the watcher pounded the door again and called out in Korean.

Reed dropped the curtain and retrieved his rifle, holding his finger over his lips to Sinju. She nodded, and he and Turk moved on the balls of their feet down the hallway, back to the bedroom. They eased the door closed, but this time, they didn't retreat to the closet. Turk set the bag down and lifted his rifle into his shoulder, while Reed stood next to the door, keeping it open just a crack, his finger on the heavy trigger of the CZ.

They waited breathlessly as Sinju hid the two extra teacups, then Reed saw her glide to the front door. It opened with a soft whine of hinges, and the watcher launched into an immediate angry outburst.

That was a good sign, Reed thought. He was probably angry for being made to wait, but that also meant he hadn't detected the presence of the two Americans.

Not yet, anyway.

Reed eased the CZ's safety off and thought about the layout of the house. From where he stood, he had a clear shot across half the living room and a portion of the kitchen. If he stormed down the short hallway, he could clear both in mere seconds. But that would cost them their cover. Even if the government had only left one watcher on the house, there might be neighbors at home. People who would rat them out.

No. If this guy was about to die, it wouldn't be with a gunshot.

Reed eased the CZ back into its holster and withdrew the knife again. The watcher was talking now, and his voice had dropped to an almost melodic tone. Reed eased the door open and saw Ye-jun cowering in the back of the room, fixated on the evil unfolding in front of her.

Sinju stood straight-backed in the middle of the living space, blazing defiance at the watcher. He stood in front of her, his back turned to Reed and Turk, his hat gone. Slicked-back hair clung to his scalp, and he was still smoking, filling the room with a cloud as he continued to speak in slow, methodical sentences.

The anger was gone. The demanding body language was gone. Now it looked . . . wrong.

Just about the time the watcher laid a hand on Sinju's shoulder and fingered the top edge of her night-robe, it all made sense. The watcher leaned close to Sinju, and she backed up. He laughed and followed her until her hips collided with the edge of the kitchen counter. She continued to glare defiance at him, and he twisted, pinning her against the counter and exposing his right side to Reed. Then he leaned in, the cigarette dangling from one side of his mouth as he whispered in her ear.

Sinju was perfectly rigid, her fists clenched at her sides. She held her chin up and said nothing as his cheek brushed hers, then his hand returned to her shoulder. He pushed at her robe, easing it down over her arm.

Sinju trembled, but then she said something in a short, demanding sentence, followed by a shove against his chest. The watcher's head rocked back, and the cigarette fell into his mouth. He coughed and spat it out, then backhanded her over the face. Sinju screamed and tried to break free of the counter. The watcher grabbed her arms with both hands, then ripped down on the robe. It tore open, fully exposing her from the waist up as she thrashed to break free.

Reed's heart thundered.

Turk's hand was on his arm, squeezing and pushing him forward. "Montgomery!" Turk hissed.

Reed stood frozen, his grip so tight around the knife that his knuckles turned white. Everything inside of him screamed for him to barge through the door, hurtle down the hallway, grab the watcher by the chin, and twist until his face was pointed at his ass. Break him in half.

But he didn't move. Sinju got in a wide right-hook, knocking the guy in the eye and hurling him back. The robe was tangled around her waist, and blood trickled down her chin from where he hit her. The watcher followed her, taking his time as he kicked aside the teapot and leaned over her. Hungry.

"Take him!" Turk snarled.

Reed put a hand on Turk's chest rig and held him back, growling between his teeth. "If we move now, we blow the whole mission!"

Turk ground his teeth, and Reed saw in that microsecond that his fellow operator was fully prepared to sacrifice the mission. It was what made him such a good soldier—he cared about innocents.

It was also why he wasn't in charge.

Reed moved from the door, pushing Turk back and keeping his voice low. "They have a *bomb*. Do you get me? If these crackpots launch that thing, millions will die."

Turk shook, his fingers clenching and unclenching around the grip of the AK. He pulled away from Reed and faced the wall, breathing deep and long. Sinju screamed a long, nerve-jangling sound, followed by another thud. Ye-jun screamed, too, and glass broke.

Turk just shook like an oak tree in a hurricane.

Reed put his hand on Turk's shoulder and squeezed once, then slowly moved to the door and peered out. Ye-jun lay on the floor, unconscious, bleeding from her temple. The watcher had his pants around his knees, his pistol in one hand, straddling Sinju as she lay on the floor.

He wouldn't use the gun. No way could this guy murder a citizen without approval, even in North Korea. But he could rape her. Nobody would stop that.

Reed concentrated on his breathing, trying not to burst through that door like his own version of unleashed hell. Then something chirped. Reed went rigid, his gaze snapping toward the backpack, but the noise hadn't come from their gear. He heard it again and looked through the crack in the door.

It was the watcher's radio. The man stopped over Sinju and lifted it to his lips, barking a quick reply. A moment passed, and Reed heard a string of garbled Korean. The watcher lowered his radio with a look of disgust and disappointment on his face. He gave Sinju a kick to the hip, then ratcheted his pants up and cinched down the belt. Sinju lay on the floor, covering herself with both arms while he leered down at her.

The watcher hauled her up by one arm, wrenching until she squealed. Then he held her by the neck and pressed a sloppy kiss on her face, one hand pawing at her chest like an animal.

Reed looked away, waiting until he heard the watcher shut the door. He turned to the window and watched through the crack in the curtain as the guy returned to his car and started the engine. The street was quiet, and if anybody had heard the screaming, they weren't willing to intervene.

Dust clouded the air as the watcher pulled a quick U-turn and sped off.

Reed slowly replaced the curtain, then looked to Turk, who had absolute anger in his hard eyes. He was a force of nature, ready to be unleashed, and it was terrifying, even for Reed.

That guy had better not come back.

Reed eased the door open and crept down the hall, replacing the knife in his belt. Sinju had already pulled her robe back on and was now knelt next to her mother, swabbing her head and speaking gently to her as the older woman slowly woke up.

"Are you okay?" Reed said.

He noticed a red spot on her cheek that would soon swell into a bruise. The watcher hit her hard. There were marks on her neck, too, and probably more across her chest.

Pig.

Sinju looked away, murmuring to her mother. Reed felt like an animal himself—a worthless pretender for not taking action. He couldn't explain to Sinju. Either she understood, or she didn't.

Ye-jun got up with her daughter's help, and Sinju led her into the near bedroom, laying her on the bed. The old woman sobbed as Sinju cooed to her.

Turk appeared from the bedroom, the iPad clamped in one hand, his face still dark with restrained fury. He jabbed the device at Reed without a word. There was a GPS map on the screen, outlying the path between the Gok house and the park. It was over thirty miles.

Reed breathed a frustrated curse, then looked up as Sinju appeared from the bedroom. The robe was cinched tight around her waist and she held her head up, proudly and defiantly. Maybe angry at the Americans. Reed couldn't blame her.

She pointed to the iPad. "You are going to park?"

Reed didn't like the idea of giving away his plans to somebody he barely knew, then leaving them behind. It seemed a needless risk.

"We're looking for your father," he said.

Sinju swept dark, sweaty hair behind one ear. The spot on her face had swollen into a welt and looked worse than before. It made Reed want to punch a wall.

"My father is smart man," Sinju said. "He speak with your government? With CIA?"

Reed exchanged a glance with Turk, wondering how a poverty-stricken Korean woman, isolated in the heart of the hermit kingdom, knew anything about the CIA. Turk still seemed consumed with the attempted rape.

"Come with me," Sinju said. "I show you something."

She started toward the hallway, and Reed reluctantly followed her back into the far room—her room. She moved to the closet and knelt next to the short row of shoes. Scooping them to one side, she knocked against the wall. Reed leaned down to see past the clothes, watching as she pulled back a section of drywall, exposing a small cavity inside. Sinju lifted out a box the size of a milk jug, and Reed stepped back as she deposited the contents onto the bedroom floor.

She looked up at the two suspicious Americans. "I may be poor. I am not stupid."

It was nothing like Reed expected. No handgun, roll of banknotes, or covert photographs spilled from the box. Instead, a small DVD player dumped out, followed by a floppy CD case packed with DVDs. There was also a radio—similar to the one he'd seen in the kitchen—headphones, two magazines with glossy pictures of Seoul, and a tiny roll of US dollars.

Reed lowered himself onto the floor next to her, gently picking up the CD case and flipping through the contents. They were pirated movies, their names written with a black marker in English.

Ocean's Eleven. The Proposal. Titanic, an assortment of Reese Witherspoon romantic comedies, and two Tom Clancy–inspired espionage films. Blockbuster Hollywood titles.

Reed looked up. "Where did you get these?"

Sinju held her chin up as she spoke. "People in South Korea send us illegal movies. Magazines. Money. They sneak things into the north to tell us about the outside world. If we are caught with these things, we go to prison. But it is worth risk so we know who is lying, and who is true." She squared her shoulders. "If my father work with CIA, he work to get his family out of Korea. I help you find him. Then you take us to America."

30

"The man you're looking at is General Jang Bon-hwa, high-ranking official within the Korean People's Army, and influential advisor of the North Korean regime."

Maggie sat at the head of the table, while Dr. Sarah Aimes, deputy director of the CIA, addressed her National Security Council. Everyone was present—a full panel of military advisors, her National Security advisor, Nick West, various cabinet heads, and Lisa Gorman, secretary of state. A roomful of high-energy politicians and officials, salivating at the mouth for an opportunity to stand out. After all, in a few short months, Maggie might be out of a job. If they wanted to stick around, they might need to make a name for themselves.

"Our background on General Jang is limited," Aimes continued. "But we know he has traveled extensively for a North Korean official, spending time in both Moscow and Beijing."

Maggie's mind wandered. She couldn't help it. Deputy Director Aimes didn't know it, but she'd already been briefed on Jang. Heavily. She knew all about his background and his radical side. Aimes walked the council through all of the above, discussing in particular Jang's presumed relationship with a woman named Maeng and how that may have impacted his career.

Maggie couldn't help but think about the hypersonic missile rumored to be under construction, only miles outside of Pyongyang. The National Security Council wouldn't know about the missile—she'd already directed O'Brien to keep that quiet. At least for now. But the implications of an unstable radical this close to the seat of power represented a significant threat, regardless.

Aimes finished her presentation and stepped back, ready for questions. For a while, everybody just sat, assimilating the bullet points.

Then National Security Advisor Nick West pulled his glasses off. "Deputy Director. Are you suggesting this clown may instigate a coup?"

Aimes shot O'Brien a glance, probably looking for validation, but she didn't get it. "That's a possibility, sir. The instability we've monitored in Pyongyang over the last few days is of rising concern. Jang is positioning substantial numbers of KPA infantry in key locations across the city, and we still don't know why. It's a case of motivation and opportunity. Too much of one or the other, and we start to get nervous. As I discussed in my presentation, we're still not convinced of Jang's motivation, but the opportunity is there. And growing. That's our chief concern."

West turned to General Yellin. The chairman of the Joint Chiefs sat nearest to Maggie, leaned back with his bullish shoulders bulging beneath his uniform jacket.

"General," West said, "can you comment on the military implications of a Cho displacement?"

Yellin cleared his throat. "It's impossible to say. Barring an invasion of the South, North Korea's principal threat is with regards to a nuclear launch. That seems highly improbable, but even the possibility of nuclear attack carries regional consequences, which is why we have to consider the Chinese and what their position might be."

Maggie noted how the general carefully skirted the topic of the first-strike strategy she had authorized him to prepare. That was just as well. No need to set off alarm bells.

Secretary Gorman was next to speak, addressing the deputy director.

"Dr. Aimes, has your agency prepared a report on Beijing's position with regard to this instability?"

Aimes shook her head. "We're working on it, but as of yet, our assets in Beijing are not reporting on any noise from the Chinese government with regards to Jang."

"But you presume they're monitoring the situation?" Gorman pressed.

Aimes didn't answer immediately. Maggie knew intelligence specialists hated to guess. They hated it more than government oversight and investigative reporting. But nobody moved to intercept the question.

"It's been my experience that China keeps close tabs on Pyongyang in general," Aimes said carefully. "I would assume they are monitoring the situation, but we do not have any intelligence to validate that assumption."

"This may be a stupid question," West said, "but the Cho regime has been a pain in our ass since the Korean War. The DPRK is one of the most despotic, totalitarian governments on the face of the planet. Is a coup such a bad thing?"

The discomfort in the room was palpable. Maggie could always depend on West to voice uncomfortable opinions, but she'd never heard him say something quite like that.

"Are you kidding?" Gorman asked, mild disgust creeping into her tone.

"It's a valid question," Maggie interjected. She motioned to O'Brien. The Director of the CIA had been briefed on an acceptable response, and he stepped right in.

"Cho Jong is a case of 'the devil you know,'" O'Brien said. "His regime is oppressive and fraught with human rights atrocities, but he maintains a relatively stable hold over the region. A guy like Jang—a known advocate of nuclear confrontation with the West—is a loose cannon. With Cho, we know what Monday is gonna look like. With Jang, your guess is as good as mine."

"Also," Gorman snapped, "it is not the foreign policy of this administration to instigate regime change."

Well, Maggie thought. *That depends.*

But she didn't say anything. The purpose of this meeting was to get everybody on the same page, just in case things got out of control.

"Look," O'Brien said. "In all likelihood, Jang is executed next week. If we suspect him of intended treason, it's only a matter of time before Cho does, also. Whatever he's up to in the city, it's a short-term stunt with a long-term consequence. We're just making sure everybody is aware of the situation."

"Be that as it may," Gorman said. "I really must stress the delicate position this places us in with China. Beijing has maintained close diplomatic ties with Pyongyang since the fall of the Soviet Union. Long before military action is on the table, we need to know *exactly* where China stands. It's crucial. We could ignite a world war, here."

Maggie held up a hand. Gorman was getting wound up again, which she seemed to do whenever military measures were mentioned. Maggie's frustrations with the secretary of state began with the Persian Gulf crisis the previous year, and the hostility between the State Department and the Pentagon had now reached a point where Maggie had seriously considered replacing Gorman altogether.

But not yet. Not now.

"We hear you, Secretary," Maggie said. "Please make contact with the Chinese embassy and arrange a meeting with the ambassador. I'll speak with them directly and make sure we're all on the same page."

Gorman ducked her head and made a note on her pad, but she still looked irritable.

"Anybody else?" Maggie asked.

Nobody spoke.

"All right, then. I won't hold you up any further. Thank you for your time."

She didn't get up, but the implication was clear. The NSC slowly stood and gathered their things, moving to the door like a slow parade. Only Director O'Brien and General Yellin remained behind, as prearranged. They sat in silence after the door closed, probably both thinking the same thing but unwilling to comment.

"At what point do we advise the State Department of the presence of a hypersonic nuclear weapon in the DPRK?" Yellin said.

Maggie could hear the blatant disgust dripping off his words, and she sympathized. For a diplomat, Gorman wasted little energy respecting the Pentagon.

"When we know for sure that one is *present*, General. Director O'Brien, where are we with the Prosecution Force?"

O'Brien pushed his glasses up his nose with one spidery finger. "Montgomery made contact with Gok's family, but Gok wasn't present, and they don't know where he is. We sent him the coordinates of a defunct rendezvous point where Gok met with one of our assets for a short time. Maybe Gok went there in an effort to reach us . . . It's really just a guess."

"So, we have no idea where this guy is?"

"No, ma'am. Not exactly."

Maggie tapped her finger on the table, thinking about Jang and trying to get inside his head. Wondering what his next play would be.

Global nuclear war?

"Pull out the stops, Mr. Director. Whatever you have to do. We have to make this work."

31

Anbyŏn, DPRK

"We can't get her out," Reed growled. He stood in the bedroom over the pile of entertainment contraband, Sinju having returned to check on her mother.

Turk stood with his arms crossed, glaring disgust at Reed. It was a level of anger Reed had seen before but never directed at him. He couldn't deny it made him uncomfortable, but that didn't change the ugly realities of their situation.

"Don't make excuses," Turk snapped. "You heard her. If we take Gok and leave the women behind, they'll *die*. That pig will come back and freaking *rape* them to death."

Turk spoke through gritted teeth, and Reed lowered his head. He saw the watcher straddling Sinju again, his pants dropping to his knees, that ugly, salivating grin hanging on his face like a bad joke.

He'd come back, all right. But that was happening regardless of whether or not they found Gok.

"This isn't a humanitarian mission," Reed said, looking up. "We aren't here to play cowboy. We get the guy, and we get out."

"Like *hell* this isn't a humanitarian mission!" Turk closed the distance between them in one short step. "What do you call preventing nuclear war? An investment in the stock market?"

"Exactly. We're here to prevent Armageddon. Save the lives of millions. We take her with us, we jeopardize all of that. Open your eyes, Turk. See the bigger picture."

Turk breathed hard, his arms trembling like a dog pulling at the end of a leash. He turned around and stomped across the room, placing one open hand against the wall and standing for a long time with his back to Reed.

Reed gave him the time, knowing that if Turk decided to force his will on the mission, he would have no choice but to go along with it. He couldn't make it out of North Korea without him, let alone recover Gok.

"Imagine it was Banks," Turk said softly, still facing the wall.

"Excuse me?"

Turk turned. "Imagine it was Banks in that next room. Imagine she was going to die, and look me in the eye and tell me again to see the bigger picture."

Reed didn't move. Despite himself, he couldn't resist the mental image of Banks sprawled on the floor, bleeding and bruised. The watcher leaning over her . . .

He stopped. He couldn't finish the thought. It made him want to rip things apart.

"They won't fit in the SDV." Reed avoided Turk's gaze, already knowing he'd lost the fight.

"So, we find another way," Turk said. "We email Wolf and tell him to have the Navy figure it out. Make it their problem."

"And you think they'll just roll with that?"

"I think we won't give them a choice."

Reed bit back a curse, glaring at the pile of DVDs but not really seeing them. A voice deep in the back of his mind warned him that this was a terrible mistake. Keeping himself and Turk alive while navigating thirty miles across the hostile Korean landscape would be a trick as it was. Finding Gok might prove to be a miracle. Doing it all with a couple of untrained and helpless women in tow was asking to be massacred. Asking to jeopardize the entire operation . . .

Reed stormed through the door and down the hall. "Sinju!"

The young woman appeared from her mother's bedroom, Ye-jun in tow. Reed would have preferred the old woman were still asleep. Even though she didn't speak English, her mental and emotional state of panic wasn't helping.

He beckoned Sinju into the kitchen, Turk not far behind. Once they were safely secreted to the back of the house, he faced her.

"You know this place?"

Sinju nodded.

"You know how to get there?"

This time she looked to her mother. When she spoke, she kept her voice low.

"We no have a car. We use train. But on train, the soldiers see you."

"Right. So . . ."

He waited while Sinju thought it through. Reed couldn't help but notice how composed she appeared, even in the aftermath of a near rape and a good beating. Maybe this wasn't her first such experience.

"I know place to get car," she said. "Not far. I can take you there, then drive to park."

"What about checkpoints?" Reed asked.

Sinju knitted her brows.

"Soldiers," he clarified. "Gates. Roadblocks."

She shook her head. "No soldiers on road. If they pass us, I hide you."

Reed motioned Turk to the corner of the kitchen and lowered his voice to barely a whisper. "I don't like it."

"Which part?" Turk asked.

"Every part. Moving thirty miles across uncharted territory in the daylight. Trusting this chick not to run us into a battalion of secret police. Dragging this thing out another six hours. It's a cocktail of bad decisions."

Turk watched Sinju. She knelt in the living room now, gently cleaning up the shards of a teacup that shattered sometime during her assault. Reed pictured Banks kneeling there and felt a knot in his stomach. Sinju was both strong and innocent like Banks.

"I trust her," Turk said at last. "She's got no reason to screw us."

"You can't possibly know that. Think with your head, Turk."

"What do you *think* I'm thinking with?" Turk snapped. "We just watched one of these assholes beat the piss out of her. You think she's conspiring with them?"

Reed checked his watch. It was barely one p.m., which meant darkness wouldn't fall for another five hours. Precious time to waste sitting around waiting for the secret police to return. But moving during the daylight, exposed, at the mercy of a thousand unknown quantities . . .

"We leave the house now," Turk said. "That way, if they come back, we won't be here. Then we rendezvous with Sinju after dark and move on the park."

Reed studied the floor, pondering the plan and the myriad of ways it could go wrong. Sinju could turn them in. The soldiers could come, and she could sell them out in the hope of better treatment.

But really, Turk's plan was the only plan. Leaving the house mitigated risk. Sinju could betray them, sure. But unless they were going to evac now, they had no choice but to trust her. Those dice were already cast. She already knew too much.

"Sinju," Reed said softly.

The young woman returned from the living room, cradling the shards in one hand. She stood tall, iron defiance in her eyes. A woman destined to be free. He could see that. Whether by escaping this brutal nation, or eventually embracing the inevitable escape of death, she would be free. On her terms.

And that was reason enough to trust her.

"The CIA sent us to help your father. He has documents detailing the development of a new type of nuclear weapon. Do you know anything about that?"

Sinju pondered, fishing through the unfamiliar words. Then she shook her head. "No. But my father is quiet man. He no share these things with me. Not with my mother. He keep us safe."

I'll bet he did.

"We need to get to the park," Reed said. "But not during the daylight. It's too dangerous. You said you have a car?"

She nodded.

"Good. We're going to leave the house and hide, just in case the soldiers return. We'll meet you after dark, down the road, near the river. Then you can drive us. Okay?"

Sinju's face darkened at the mention of them leaving, but she seemed to understand the point. "Okay. I drive you."

A knot formed in Reed's stomach, knowing what he needed to say next. The smart thing would be not to say it and string Sinju along, instead, giving her no reason to betray them. But his conscience wouldn't allow it. She deserved to know the truth.

Reed put a gentle hand on her shoulder, looking into the face of an ironclad woman. A woman who lived in one of the worst possible places on planet Earth but refused to let that break her. "I can't promise to get you out," Reed said. "We'll do everything we can."

Sinju lifted her chin. Despite the growing welt on her cheek and the dishevelment of her hair, she looked beautiful and strong. Again, like Banks.

"You make promise to try?"

Reed nodded.

"That is good enough. I take you to park."

32

Reed and Turk left the house immediately, creeping slowly back to the mountains. It was dangerous moving during broad daylight, this close to so many houses, but the far greater danger would be to stay and risk another invasion of the secret police. At least in the mountains they could keep watch on the house and know if anything happened.

Hidden behind trees a thousand yards away, they settled in for the afternoon, taking turns napping and maintaining surveillance over the house. It was still cool outside, with a steady breeze blowing damp air out of the mountains, but Reed had long ago learned to sleep almost anywhere.

At last, the final rays of the sun disappeared toward China, and the village fell into growing darkness. Local residents returned to their homes in congregation, probably because they all departed the same arriving train, while a few stragglers appeared from their jobs in downtown Anbyŏn.

Still, the watcher hadn't returned, and neither had any other members of North Korea's secret police. Somehow, it made Reed even more nervous. Why would they abandon their best avenue of locating Gok? Logic dictated that if he were in trouble, he'd return to his family. The CIA knew it, and the secret police must, also. So why abandon their post now?

"Maybe they gave up," Turk said.

Or Sinju set us up, Reed thought.

He didn't say it because he and Turk had already agreed to trust her. No use second-guessing now, unless they were gonna call Gagliardi to come get them. And Reed wasn't willing to do that.

"Update Wolf," Reed said, sliding his backpack on.

Turk tapped in a quick message to headquarters and waited for a reply. Wolf shot back a confirmation and wished them luck but didn't provide any further intelligence from the CIA.

Turk stowed the iPad in his pack, retrieved his rifle, and they set off down the mountainside, moving toward the rendezvous point Reed had selected. It took them over half an hour to hike the two miles, but when they crept out of the edge of a rice paddy, they found Sinju waiting, crouched in the ditch, just as she was supposed to be.

"We go now," she whispered. "Two kilometers to car, then drive out to park."

Sinju took the lead, her sneakers squishing through the softer soil as their boots left wide prints. Turk walked just behind her, and Reed trailed them, keeping the rifle held against his shoulder, the safety off.

Ready. Watching.

They moved that way for about half an hour, Sinju leading them in a general northern direction. They crossed the east-west railway line he'd noted on the digital map and skirted along the edge of Namdae River, moving through progressively rural countryside before Sinju stopped at a hilltop and pointed into a valley below.

Fields surrounded some manner of farm depot, consisting of a series of low wooden sheds, several metal silos, and a row of rusted metal farm implements.

Through the gaps in the metal grates that guarded the sheds, he made out the front bumpers of parked tractors—old and rusted, much like the implements. At the end of the line, the dusty hood of a utility van sat behind the gate, its foggy headlamps clouded with age.

"They use it to move fuel, for tractors," Sinju said. "I know where to find the key."

She started forward, but Reed held up a hand. He sat for a while just watching the buildings, checking for signs of life. Even in the darkness, a place had a feel about it when somebody was inside. It was an instinct Reed had honed for years and learned to trust.

But this place was as dead and empty as a graveyard. He gave Sinju the go-ahead, then motioned for Turk to follow him around the low hill to the right, moving into a better vantage point as Sinju crossed into the valley.

"See anything?" Reed whispered.

Turk merely shook his head, his gaze fixed on Sinju as the petite Korean faded into the tall grass. She moved to the end of the vehicle shed, then she slipped elegantly between the bars of a gate and disappeared inside.

"She's slick," Turk muttered.

Reed grunted but didn't comment. He kept the rifle near his shoulder as he crouched in the weeds and waited.

Three minutes passed, then Sinju appeared in front of the van. She unlocked the gate and pushed it back, then got into the vehicle and turned the engine over. It rumbled softly, but the lights remained off. She drove into the yard, got out to close the gate, then headed out toward the highway.

"Let's go," Reed said.

He turned eastward and headed down the far side of the hill, guided through the darkness by nothing more than natural night vision. The moon would rise soon, but thick clouds had moved in from the west and now obscured the stars, intensifying the night around them.

The highway next to the yard wound around the base of the hill, intersecting Reed and Turk's path a quarter mile away in the middle of another field. Sinju waited there, gas fumes gathering beneath the short, black van. It was some make Reed didn't recognize, but he could tell by the general body style that it was old. Probably Soviet, much like the tractors he saw in the shed. The driver's seat was positioned just forward of the front wheels, and the nose of the vehicle was flat with round headlights, similar to a Volkswagen Microbus.

Maybe it was a rip-off of the Microbus. Just like the Chinese ripped things off, the Soviets used to, also. Why reinvent the wheel when capitalism was so busy building great things?

Reed checked the road one last time, then crossed through a soggy ditch and moved to the rear of the van. Windowless double doors blocked his way, and he clicked the latch up. The interior was bare, nothing but an oily metal floor with a few gas cans stacked against one wall. Wheel wells served as the only seats, and Turk settled onto one as Reed eased the door shut.

Sinju shifted into gear with the grind of an aged transmission, then they lurched forward, back onto the road. Reed staggered forward to the vinyl-covered console jammed between the front seats and knelt behind it, the rifle in one hand as he peered through the windshield. Engine heat radiated through the floor, warming his kneecaps and offering some welcome relief from the cold outside.

Fields passed on their left, matched by rising mountains on their right, and Sinju flicked the headlights on. Only one of the headlamps glowed to life, but it was enough light for her to dodge most of the potholes.

All else outside was quiet. It left Reed with a vacant feeling like he'd had before. Like he was standing on the moon.

"Where are all the people?" he asked.

Sinju drove with both hands on the wheel, wrestling the van with brute force around a rut. Reed doubted it featured power steering.

"This part of Korea is . . ." She stopped, searching for the right word.

"Rural?" Reed asked.

Sinju nodded. "Not many people."

Reed already knew that. He remembered it from the maps. South of Wŏnsan, there was almost nothing save fields and mountains, all the way to the DMZ.

Sinju ground to a stop at an intersection and glanced suspiciously to the left, north toward Wŏnsan. Then she turned right and pressed her foot into the gas. The old engine groaned and creaked, and the road turned upward.

For a while, they rode in silence again, then Sinju cast him a sideways glance. "Are you from Big Apple?"

"Big Apple? New York? No, I'm from Alabama."

Sinju frowned, pondering the unfamiliar word. She repeated it quietly, then cocked her head. "Is Sandra Bullock from Alabama?"

Reed grunted a soft laugh. "What?"

"Ryan Reynolds?"

He remembered the bootlegged copy of the rom-com classic, *The*

Proposal, hidden in Sinju's closet. "I don't know where they live," he said. "Hollywood, probably. California. I don't know."

"Is Hollywood close to Alabama?"

"No, not really."

"But you can go there? They let you go there?"

Reed watched as Sinju drove. The tip of her tongue was barely visible, pressed between her lips as she focused. But when he looked in her eyes, he saw a mind a thousand miles away, traveling over paths unknown, to places uncharted. The mystical Free World. America. The Big Apple.

"You can go anywhere you want," Reed said softly.

"Really?"

"Sure."

"Even if they catch you?"

"Nobody is trying to catch you in America. You just . . . live."

She smiled, and Reed felt like she was driving on autopilot.

A soft glow lit her cheeks. "I want to live in Big Apple. Like movie star."

Reed looked away, the uneasiness returning to his stomach. He met Turk's gaze in the rearview mirror and knew they were both thinking the same thing.

It was a long way to New York with a lot of absolute killers standing in their way.

Sinju elbowed Reed. "This is it. We're almost there."

33

The road narrowed as they moved into the mountains, slowly winding their way upward near the same peaks and ridges Reed and Turk had crossed to reach Anbyŏn. But as Reed looked ahead, he saw the path level out, with tall trees guarding the entrance of a narrow meadow. If he looked down the steep mountainside to his right, he saw the railway cutting southwest out of Wŏnsan toward Gok's home and remembered Sinju saying that she and her family visited this place by rail. If the train stopped here, there must be houses nearby, but he didn't see them.

Sinju slowed as she approached the entrance of the meadow, and Reed made out a tower built of metal pipes and soaring skyward, much like the tower he and Turk had jumped from only days prior. Metal guide wires, staked into the meadow, held it upright, and a small radio shack enclosed by a chain-link fence sat at the base.

Strewn about the meadow were a couple benches and a small concrete bathhouse. What North Korea classified as a park, he guessed.

Reed put a hand on Sinju's arm, squeezing softly. "Stop here," he whispered.

Reed directed her to cut the engine, then spent a while just watching the trees outside. A gentle wind stirred them, and a dusting of old snow fell from their limbs and littered the leafy forest floor.

"This is the place?" he said.

Sinju nodded.

"You came here? Often?"

She shrugged. "Last summer. One time every few weeks."

That corresponded to the CIA's timeline of when they used the spot to communicate with Gok. Reed thought about how high the tower was and its rural position relative to the DMZ. At some point it must have served as a transmitter for state-sponsored radio, or else been used by the KPA for some military function. But its location made it an ideal tool for the CIA to leverage in their favor. It was close enough to transmit weak, unobtrusive signals into South Korea and isolated enough to go unnoticed.

A good system, for a while. A logical place for Gok to hide if he were attempting to reconnect with the CIA after losing his handler.

Reed remained behind the console, thinking, the rifle resting in his hands.

"Montgomery?" Turk whispered.

Reed shifted to one side, allowing Turk a view over his shoulder. They let another few moments pass, Sinju waiting patiently, then Reed sighed. It wasn't gonna get any easier.

"I'll take point," he said. "You cover me."

Turk nodded his understanding, and Reed turned to Sinju.

"Stay in the van. If anything goes wrong, I want you to run. Get back to your mother, and don't tell anyone about us. You never saw us, okay?"

She nodded.

Reed shouldered his rifle and turned for the door.

Now or never.

Reed and Turk bailed out of the back, moving quickly into the trees, rifles at the ready.

Reed took the lead, pulling a pair of night-vision goggles on an elastic headband over his skull. Whenever possible, Reed preferred to rely on natural night vision, but the shadows were deep enough and the sky overhead murky with enough clouds that he didn't want to risk it. He'd take whatever advantage he could get.

The clearing was about a hundred yards wide and half as deep, with a rolling meadow filling the space between the trees and the radio shack rising from the middle. Reed and Turk slipped around the anchored bases of a couple guide wires, casting glances up at the tower. It shot up from the mountain ridge, reaching into the black sky without any of the blinking red lights it would've featured in America.

Ten yards from the edge of the tree line, Reed held his fist up, then motioned toward a fallen log. Turk slid into position behind it, resting his AK over the top edge with an identical pair of NV goggles strapped to his head.

Reed slipped up to the last tree blocking his path to the shack and stopped, watching. The chain-link fence surrounding the base of the tower was six feet tall and topped with sloppy curls of barbed wire. A double gate barred the entrance to the protected interior, but as Reed studied the chain, he noted the absence of a lock.

He couldn't see inside the shack. It was windowless, with a plain wooden door, shut tight. Snow dusted the ground outside, free of footprints. If Gok was hidden inside, he'd been here awhile. Days, maybe. Neither the shack nor the meadow around it looked like a very frequented place. He might conceal himself here for weeks without the secret police thinking to check it.

A good plan.

Reed watched a while longer, taking note of the angles around the shack and where he'd dive for cover if something went wrong. There was a shallow depression about halfway between his current position and the tower, which would offer meager protection, should he need it. After that, he would be fully exposed.

"Wanna switch?" Turk whispered.

Reed shot him the bird, then checked his rifle one more time.

Here goes nothing.

He left the cover of the trees and raced into the meadow, running low with the AK held at the ready. He made the depression but skipped it, hurrying instead the final twenty yards to the corner of the fence. His boots made barely a sound in the soft snow but left tracks all the way back to the trees.

Sliding to a stop at the fence, Reed lifted the muzzle of the AK and eased toward the gate. His suspicions were confirmed when he reached the chain and noted the butt of a padlock sticking out of the snow, just inside the fence. Fresh scratches marred some of the chain links, and a soft rut cut through the dirt near where the gate would drag the ground.

Reed bent low and whispered, "Gok Chin-ho?"

Dead silence.

Reed kept his right hand on the grip of the AK and used his left to lift the chain, gently easing it through the gate. The links clinked softly.

"Gok?"

Reed thought he heard a creak from inside the shack, so vague he may have imagined it. He looked back to the tree line and saw no signal from Turk.

The last of the chain slipped through the gate, and Reed pressed the AK into his shoulder and pushed the gate back with his foot. "Gok!" he called again, louder this time.

Now he was sure he heard something from inside the shack. Maybe a small animal burrowed in beneath the sheet-metal walls.

Or maybe a nuclear defector, huddling for warmth.

Reed put his hand on the door and eased it open. The snow at his feet appeared lime green through his night vision, but the shadows inside were driven back. Reed rushed in, sweeping the rifle from right to left in a quick snap, his finger on the trigger. The muzzle of the weapon stopped over a man huddled in one corner, a sharpened stick held out in front of him like a sword, his face stretched into a ghastly grimace of pure terror.

He was small. Balding. Shaking like a leaf, jabbing the stick toward Reed.

Gok Chin-ho.

The man cried out in panicked Korean, and Reed shoved the goggles up. He took a half-step toward Gok, and then the gunfire began.

34

The bombs detonated exactly ninety seconds apart, beginning two hours after sunset and continuing for seven and a half minutes. Four hundred fifty seconds. Five blasts.

Glass exploded from battered apartment buildings, and one complex collapsed altogether. Smoke clogged the sky and dumped into the streets as screams and fire alarms flooded the blackness.

Within seconds, fire trucks operated by Pyongyang's protection department screamed down the street, plowing blindly through the smoke toward each of the five separate blast zones. Hundreds of soldiers deployed, rushing out of the quick response camps organized around the city and wearing both the uniforms of the state-sponsored security department and the olive drab of the Korean People's Army. They brandished Type 88 AK-74 rifles and shouted at civilians, ordering people back into their homes as the screams of the dying rang from the piles of rubble.

More than a few shots were fired. Confused blasts ripped toward the clouds to silence the shouting, or maybe they were mercy shots to put those victims deemed too wounded to survive out of their misery. But even after an hour of surging sirens and increased security presence, the chaos only worsened. Smog clogged the air, horns blared, and guns fired.

Total anarchy.

General Jang Bon-hwa could smell the fear saturating the city as clearly as though it were quality tobacco burning at the tip of a cigar. It rolled over his tongue and filled his lungs, flooding his body with emotions altogether opposite from the Workers' Party officials surrounding him. They felt uncertainty. Terror, maybe.

Jang felt vengeance.

Standing on the rooftop of the Mansudae Assembly Hall, Pyongyang's seat of governance, Jang looked through binoculars and swept the city. Even in the smoke-clogged darkness, he made out flashes of fire and gleams of searchlights, accentuated here and there by the flash of emergency vehicles. It helped him mark the site of each blast, but he didn't really need help with that.

He already knew where the bombs were, even before they detonated.

"General!"

An officer saluted Jang, his face tense. Jang didn't recognize him, but he didn't need to. He identified the insignia on the man's arm as that of the KPA's Special Operation Force, and knew he'd found his man.

"Five bombs in total," the officer said. "Two apartment buildings, three places of work. I do not know how many have died."

Jang continued his survey of the city. There was nothing more to see, but he needed this moment. Not only to sell the situation to the military officers surrounding him, but also for himself. A moment of satisfaction. The moment he laid a noose around the supreme leader's neck and nobody even knew it.

Jang lowered the binoculars and glared at the smoggy skyline. "The Americans have done this. We must secure the supreme leader! Barricade him inside the Ryungsong Residence, and place a guard."

The officer snapped to attention. "Very good, General. What of the party leaders?"

Jang glanced over his shoulder at the cowering officials behind him. North Korea was a totalitarian state. A dictatorship, really. The party leaders hiding in the shadows were mechanisms of the supreme leader's will, not actual decision makers. But they could still be a problem if they were left too close to hand.

"Gather all party leaders and government officials inside the Palace of the Sun, and place an additional guard around them," Jang said. "Nobody leaves."

The officer saluted. "It shall be done, General."

Jang looked back to the city, thinking about the fifty thousand KPA soldiers he'd deployed into strategic locations around Pyongyang over the past five days. Those soldiers were loyal to their supreme leader—both out of genuine reverence, and perhaps more genuine fear. They would fight and die to protect their country, all at the behest of their proudest general.

When the time was right—when the city was in flames and the supreme leader himself lay barricaded in a bunker, hiding from an invisible enemy—they would unleash the ultimate of weapons.

Their own survival be damned.

It was all a matter of perspective.

35

The gunfire erupted from someplace to Reed's right—in the tree line opposite Turk. Reed hit the deck automatically, folding the rifle under his chest and slamming to the floor of the shack as bullets ripped through the sheet-metal walls like they were made of paper.

Gok screamed, and Reed grabbed him by the arm, yanking him down as a fresh blast of fire ventilated the walls just over his head. They lay prone, and Reed fought to raise the AK, but there was nothing to fire at.

Then Turk opened up. The chatter of his rifle snapped from the far side of the meadow and was met by shouts in Korean someplace beyond the shack.

Reed rolled to his feet and smacked the AK's selector switch to full auto, then kicked the door back. "You speak English?" Reed shouted.

Gok lay on the floor, face-down, both hands held over his head. He shook like a leaf in the wind as Reed put a hand on his shoulder and gave it a rough shake.

"Hey! You speak English?"

Gok didn't move, and Reed cursed. He grabbed Gok by the arm and pulled him toward the door as more bullets ripped through the building.

"We're gonna run! You understand? To the van!"

Reed pointed to where the Soviet van sat sheltered by the trees, still out of sight of the shooters. Gok followed his gesture, but the panic in his face was absolute. He shook his head and clawed his way backward into the shed as if it offered some manner of protection.

"Montgomery!" Turk's voice barked over the radio mounted to Reed's chest rig. "You alive?"

"Copy that! Taking fire. Gok won't move."

"Well, put a boot in his ass! You've got five or six tangos moving in from the south, and six or eight more from the west."

Reed shook Gok. "Get up!"

The Korean had returned to his face-down position, trembling with each new blast of gunfire.

Reed was done being polite. He rolled Gok over and smacked him across the face. Gok's eyes rolled back in his head, and he appeared dazed. Then clarity returned to his face, and he seemed to snap out of it.

"We're gonna *run!*" Reed shouted, pointing toward the van.

Gok nodded.

Reed shifted the AK to his left hand, then lifted a grenade from his chest rig and yanked the pin out with his teeth.

"Smoke!" he called into the radio. He moved to the door and flung the grenade in the direction of the incoming bullets.

A soft *pop* resounded from the snow, and a thick grey cloud streamed into the air.

Reed grabbed Gok by the arm and counted to four, squatting next to the door. Then he shoved him ahead. Go! Go!"

Gok ran, staggering over the snow and almost falling. Reed pushed from behind, keeping his head low as Turk's rounds continued to whistle overhead. They made it twenty yards into the meadow, obscured by the cloud of smoke still building behind them. Bullets continued to snap overhead, and two or three struck the ground near Reed. He shifted right and pushed Gok ahead, then they hit the shallow depression Reed noted on his way in.

But Gok didn't see it. He tumbled forward with a scream, and Reed instinctively hit the snow. Gok's cry drew fire like a homing beacon and was quickly followed by another bloodcurdling scream as a heavy thirty-caliber round ripped into his leg.

The Korean rolled over, tears streaming down his face.

Reed held him down and called into the radio. "Gok's hit! Leg shot. Cover fire!"

Automatic fire burst from Turk's position, showering the incoming tangos in a heedless blast of fury.

Reed counted the seconds, knowing Turk would stop at three, then dropped his rifle to swing from its sling and grabbed Gok. The scientist was light in his arms, and Reed hurtled forward.

"Start the van!" Turk shouted, bursting out of the trees.

With Sinju behind the wheel, the old motor coughed and whined, and the headlight flickered as the battery sent a surge of electricity into it.

But the van didn't start.

Reed reached the tree line and dumped Gok, switching the AK back to semiautomatic as he took cover behind a tree. Through the dispersing cloud of smoke, he saw shadows moving through the meadow, marked in places by orange muzzle flash.

Reed swung the rifle easily from target to target, squeezing off shots marked by muted cries and silenced rifles. Turk ground in next to him and took a knee, matching his gunshots one-for-one.

The van coughed and whined behind them, then Reed heard the click of a starter sucking on an empty battery. The sound was repeated a couple times, and Reed looked over his shoulder. The headlight was dead, and as Sinju fought with the key, not even a click resounded from the engine.

"We gotta move!" he called.

Turk backed toward the van, still firing calm shots at the approaching line of soldiers. Reed could hear them now—not just their riles, but their voices, closing in like a noose.

Gok groaned from the ground, a pool of blood gathering around his leg. The shot had penetrated his calf just short of his knee. Reed knew he wouldn't last much longer if the bleeding continued.

Reed scrabbled through the snow to Gok's side, reaching into a cargo pocket for a quick-access tourniquet. Within seconds, he had the wound strapped off and the blood flow cut, but Gok continued to scream like a stuck pig.

"Sinju! Let's go!" Reed called. He scooped Gok over his shoulder. The Korean lay against his back, still crying, and Reed started across the darkened road. Sinju bailed out of the van and ran to join him as Turk covered them from behind.

The storm of bullets snapping around them was constant now, like a cloud of hornets.

Reed made it to the ditch on the far side of the road, taking shelter behind the bulk of the van as glass shattered and tires hissed. Then he heard it. A low rush. A muted shriek screaming through the air from directly behind.

"Hit the deck!" he shouted, slinging himself forward.

It was almost too late. The rocket-propelled grenade slammed into the nose of the van and detonated with an ear-splitting blast. Gok flew off Reed's shoulder and hurtled to the ground. Everything around Reed turned dull and was knocked out of focus, his ears ringing as a shower of van parts rained down in slow motion.

Reed's head buzzed, and he rolled in the snow, coughing and feeling a shaking hand pawing at his body. Then he realized it was his own hand, checking for wounds, and he was overcome by a strange, out-of-body experience, as though he were watching the carnage unfold from ten feet away.

He couldn't hear. He couldn't see anything except black sky and blurry trees. He choked on smoke and instinctively fumbled for his rifle, but all he could find was the muzzle. The weapon was trapped beneath him, and he couldn't tug it out.

"Montgomery!"

Turk's blurry face appeared over him. A rough hand shook his shoulder, calling for him to stand up. Reed blinked hard as his hearing began to return, now flooded with crackling static, like popcorn popping.

No, not popcorn. Gunfire. A lot of it.

"Montgomery!"

Reed rolled to the left, choking and fighting with his rifle, and Turk reached beneath his arms and hauled him up. The world swam around him, and Reed saw Gok lying on the ground, writhing in pain. Sinju lay not

far away, face-up in the dirt, but motionless. Her face was busted and bleeding, and one leg was twisted beneath her. The van burned, and muzzle
flash blazed from the trees.

Turk screamed, "Montgomery! Go!"

Reed felt the hand against his back and knew Turk was right. He knew
the fight was lost. So, he turned into the trees and hurtled forward, stumbling through the snow and fallen limbs as a mass of hot lead ran them
down, only a breath behind.

36

Oval Office
The White House

Maggie didn't know what the reports meant, but her gut told her it wasn't good. She felt the same foreboding she'd felt nine months earlier during the *Air Force One* crisis—a voice calling to her that a death threat was knocking on America's front door, and it was her job to answer it.

O'Brien said there were four bombs, maybe five. They ripped through downtown Pyongyang only hours before, in the middle of the night. US spy satellites caught them as flashes, followed by fire and emergency vehicles. And hundreds of troops. They took control of the city from all angles, deploying from the camps the KPA had established during the previous week under the pretext of hunting down terrorists.

Maybe there *were* terrorists. Some of the bombs went off inside apartment buildings, killing dozens, if not hundreds, of local residents. It certainly looked like terrorism. But it also looked like a convenient excuse to take complete military control of the city, if that's what someone wanted to do.

O'Brien didn't know. He seemed reluctant to draw conclusions. General Yellin wanted to deploy additional forces to the DMZ to brace for further instability in the region, and Secretary Gorman opposed any visible military action. She argued that if the DPRK really was bucking for a fight, it would only make things worse.

Maggie was once again caught in between, agreeing and disagreeing with each of them. And, in the middle of it all, she had China to deal with.

Ambassador Dewei Yang sat across from her on the plush Oval Office couch, his legs crossed casually, a warm smile spread across his sixty-year-old face. Yang had a grandfatherly look about him—soft and gentle. He spoke that way, too. Slowly, in perfect English, with plenty of American slang thrown in.

Gorman warned her it was all a ploy. With constant tensions between Washington and Beijing, Gorman presumed China was being calculative in their selection of ambassador, deliberately sending somebody who was calming and even friendly. Somebody to put the White House at ease, regardless of what Beijing was really up to.

"Madam President," Yang said, folding his hands over one knee and beaming at her like a spotlight. "May I say, what a pleasure it is to finally meet you. My colleagues in Beijing were so excited to hear of your inauguration. You are an American rock star!"

Maggie smiled stiffly and sipped from a China teacup. An identical cup sat on the coffee table in front of Yang, but as of yet, the ambassador didn't seem to notice the irony.

"Likewise, Mr. Ambassador. Thank you for making time to speak with me on such short notice."

Yang bowed and lifted the teacup, sipping softly. He closed his eyes and smiled like a dog lying in the sun on a beautiful day, then he smacked his lips and leaned back. "I always so enjoy White House tea. Your people brew the very best, Madam President. Not too sweet. Now, when I was stationed in London—"

"Mr. Ambassador, what can you tell me about Pyongyang?"

Yang stopped cold, the first glimpse of nervousness edging in behind his facade. He moved to set down the cup. "Well, ma'am. I've never visited. As you know, North Korea is—"

"I'm not asking as a tourist. I'm asking about the bombs. I want to know what's happening north of the DMZ and what your country plans to do about it."

Yang pursed his lips and smoothed the pants over his knees. Then he fussed with his tie. "Madam President, I'm sure I don't know what you're talking about."

Maggie lifted a file folder off the couch next to her, flipping it open and dispensing satellite photos across the table. Yang looked at them without comment.

"Last night, a series of high-explosive blasts were detonated in downtown Pyongyang. The Korean People's Army is deploying in force into the city, and we can't make contact with anyone from inside the government. Maybe you haven't seen the images, but you can't pretend Beijing hasn't been monitoring the situation."

Yang studied the photos. His smile faded, now replaced by a concerned frown, like a grandfather listening to a grandchild telling him about a bully at school. "Honestly, ma'am, this is the first I am hearing of this. Please, tell me your concern."

Maggie resisted snapping at him. Yang's faux innocence was so transparent, she wondered if he intended it to be.

"Mr. Ambassador, please. Tensions with Pyongyang are always a concern for America, and it's no secret that your country maintains open lines of communication with the regime. Let's skip the part where we deny that and cut straight to the chase."

"To the chase?"

"To the *point*, Mr. Ambassador. I'm concerned about military security in the region. I'm concerned that whatever's happening in Pyongyang might boil over. That's a problem for South Korea. It's a problem for Japan. It's a problem for *us*, if it gets out of control."

Yang touched his chin with one index finger, still studying the photographs. "And by *us*, you mean . . . "

Maggie didn't want to say it out loud. The whole world knew China and America were perpetual rivals on good days and adversaries on the worst. But part of the game was to pretend otherwise. To pretend all was well on the far-Eastern front. She wasn't going to let Yang corner her into making a declaration he could later hold against her.

"Look"—Maggie folded her hands in her lap—"I'm not asking your government to take a position on this issue. I just need to be sure we're all on the same page regarding a military escalation in the region."

"What page is America on?"

"We are opposed to it. Absolutely. But our obligations to our Korean and Japanese allies mandate that we take action, if necessary."

Yang pursed his lips. He sat still for a while, perhaps pondering her words and evaluating her body language.

Maggie didn't move. She just waited.

At last, Yang seemed to reach a decision. "I will communicate your concerns and your stated obligations to my government. America can rest assured that China shares your opposition to any military escalation and will most certainly work to ease tensions in the region. But . . ."

He let the sentence hang, and Maggie waited.

"I would be remiss in my duties as ambassador not to advise you that Beijing would be *uncomfortable* with increased American military presence in the region."

Maggie raised both eyebrows. "Uncomfortable?"

"Uncomfortable, Madam President."

Maggie took the hint for what it was, and she rose.

Yang's face melted from concerned diplomat to smiling grandfather in a microsecond, and he accepted her hand with a deep bow. "Thank you for your time, Madam President. Go Tigers!"

Maggie didn't bother to notify him that it wasn't football season and wouldn't be for another four months. She just watched as he left the room, escorted by a Secret Service agent.

Leaving her thinking that *uncomfortable* was a word she better get used to.

37

Kangwŏn Province, DPRK

Reed had no idea how far they'd run before Turk pulled him into a shallow ditch behind a cluster of trees. It took a while for Reed's sense of hearing to return, coupled with a grasp of his surroundings. His head still felt fuzzy, but by the time they huddled into the snow and looked back toward the radio tower, he could feel the ache in his muscles. There was an unidentified bruise on his left arm, too, and somewhere along the way, he cut his cheek.

Turk breathed hard and sucked water from his backpack-mounted bladder. Reed followed suit and listened for pursuers, but the only thing he heard was the whisper of wind. The shouts of the soldiers and chatter of their guns had long ago faded, along with Gok's cries.

"We left a trail," Turk said, tilting his chin toward the track of footprints leading back toward the decimated van.

Reed looked to the sky, hoping that the dark clouds overhead would materialize into a snowfall to cover their tracks.

No such luck.

"If they haven't followed yet, they probably won't," he said. "They probably took Gok and decided to regroup. They don't know who they're dealing with, after all. They might be intimidated."

Turk slurped more water. "I got two or three of them. You?"

Reed shook his head. "I don't know. Maybe a couple. It was too dark to tell."

They sat still, listening for any noises signaling the approach of foot soldiers. Reed felt confident in his assessment, though. If they hadn't been followed yet, they probably wouldn't be until the detachment at the radio tower had been reinforced.

"What happened?" Turk asked.

Reed slipped his pack off and dug into an exterior pouch, fishing for Tylenol. His head pounded, but not so much as to prevent him from unraveling the situation that had just unfolded.

There was only one logical answer to Turk's question. Somebody had sold them out or picked up their trail along the way to the tower and followed them there. Probably to find Gok. And then to exterminate them.

"Sinju," Reed said. "She set us up."

Turk frowned. "You serious?"

"It's the only thing that makes sense. She must've signaled the government somehow. Maybe called them while she was going to get the van, then led us here."

"Why would she do that? One of them tried to rape her."

Reed shook his head. "Think with your head, Turk. How does she know English?"

"She learned it in school. She said so."

"And you believe her? They call this place the hermit kingdom for a reason. Nobody leaves. Nobody visits. The regime has a grip on these people like freaking Stalin. Why would they want people to know English?"

"What about the movies?"

"I'm not sure. It's a good story. They could've been fakes."

"She asked you about Sandra Bullock," Turk snapped, frustration growing in his tone. "She called New York the Big Apple."

"All things a trained operator would be taught to ask," Reed said. "To put me at ease. And I fell for it, too."

Turk looked away, still not willing to agree. Reed let him stew, thinking instead about the situation that now unfolded in front of them. Regardless of Sinju's loyalties, Gok was still an extraction target now held by North Korean secret police. And the longer they sat on this, the more impossible it would be to recover him.

"Get the messenger," he said. "We should send a sitrep."

Turk rolled into a seated position and dug the device out of his pack. Within seconds, he was connected to the satellite and punching out a message to Wolfgang. Reed sat next to him, chewing on a power bar and reading over his arm. He felt like a rag doll run over by a bulldozer, but he was still alive.

PF: SITREP. TARGET LOCATED. UNKNOWN COMBATANTS ENGAGED. TARGET RECOVERED BY COMBATANTS.

It took Wolfgang a few minutes to reply. Reed finished the power bar and crammed the wrapper into his pack. It was a lot colder in the mountains than it had been in Anbyŏn. It seeped through his muddy battle clothes and into his bones, saturating him.

W: TEAM STATUS?

PF: ALIVE, UNINJURED. SAFELY UNDER COVER, FOR NOW.

Reed looked out through the trees toward the distant ocean, still several klicks away. He thought about the soldiers who stormed them and wondered if they were KPA or secret police. The question mattered because who they were might dictate where they took Gok.

"Ask him about nearby prison camps," Reed said.

Turk punched the inquiry into the device and waited.

W: RESEARCHING. HOLD ONE.

Turk lowered the device and sucked down water. He followed Reed's line of sight through the trees and shook his head. "I just don't buy it."

"Which part?"

"Sinju."

"You're thinking with the wrong part of your anatomy."

Turk bristled, but just then, the message device buzzed.

W: NK DETENTION FACILITY, 21 KLICKS NORTHWEST OF YOUR POSITION, OUTSIDE WŎNSAN.

Reed breathed a curse and took the device, punching in a quick reply.

PF: POSSIBILITY OF OTHERS?

W: NEGATIVE. ONLY DETENTION FACILITY THIS SIDE OF MOUNTAIN RANGE.

Of course it is.

He lowered the device and tapped it against his knee, thinking about twenty-one kilometers. Thirteen miles, give or take. Longer with winding roads through the mountains. On foot, it would take four or five hours.

And then what?

He punched out another message.

PF: SAT PHOTO

Wolfgang didn't keep them waiting. He probably already had the images ready. They loaded through the messenger in quick succession, two black-and-white high-level images of the terrain around them.

The detention facility was marked with a red circle, lying in a wide valley south and west of Wŏnsan, nearer to the village of Ch'ilbong-ni. There were a few clusters of houses in the area, but mostly it was desolate, with few roads and not even many fields. A great place to lock people up and forget about them.

The facility was surrounded by a tall fence, complete with twin guard towers, in true prison-camp style. There were long rows of barracks, some parked trucks, and some kind of platform built into the middle near a well. An execution deck? Maybe.

Reed passed the messenger to Turk and let him examine the images in silence.

"A long way," Turk said.

Reed checked his watch. It was nearing nine p.m., which left them no more than nine hours of darkness left. They'd be cutting it close to reach the facility, break Gok out, and then sneak him to the coast without being captured. This entire plan was unraveling, and quickly.

He took the messenger back and began to type.

PF: WILL NAVIGATE TO FACILITY AND ATTEMPT RECOVERY. ADVISE FROGS TO BE ON STANDBY. MAY RECOVER UNDER HEAT.

Frogs referred to Gagliardi and his SEALs, a subtle reference to the SEAL team's heritage as "frogmen."

W: COPY THAT. WILL DO.

Reed moved to switch off the device, but then another message popped in from Wolfgang.

W: Be advised. Instability in Pyongyang. Causes unknown. Heavy military deployments in area.

Reed glanced at Turk. "What does that mean?"

Turk shrugged, and Reed punched out a reply.

PF: Military deployments near east coast?

W: Negative. Concentrations around Pyongyang only.

Reed thought about it a minute, then decided it didn't matter. Pyongyang was ninety miles west of the detention facility on the far side of the country. If the KPA, for whatever reason, was gathering in that region, that only meant there were fewer of them to obstruct their recovery attempt.

PF: Copy that. Signing off.

He flicked the messenger off, then hauled himself to his feet. "Ready to rock?"

Turk was already on his feet, the pack on his back, the AK cradled in his arms. "Born ready. Let's do it."

38

Pyongyang, DPRK

Minsu Jeong was sleeping when the first blast went off. He almost thought it was a figment of his dream, so distant it may have been thunder. By the third blast, he knew it wasn't. He moved to his apartment window and peered through the grimy glass at a collapsing apartment complex two miles away. Smoke poured into the sky, and orange flames burst through shattered windows.

Snatching up his inhaler camera and a coat, he fled his apartment block in a stream of panicked residents. Outside, a column of KPA soldiers wielding AKs surged down the street, shouting at citizens to stand back as they rushed toward the blast. They were accompanied by trucks and even a light tank. The rancid smell of burning insulation and fear hung in the air like a cloud, and Minsu coughed as he fell back into the shadows and watched.

For the first time since being snuck into the DPRK three years prior, he felt a tinge of genuine fear. It was mostly dampened by anger because he knew in his bones that whatever was happening, it wasn't what it seemed. But he still felt a primal unease—an urge in his gut to run.

But Minsu didn't run. He turned toward the core of the smoke and flames and walked straight into it, camera at the ready. Whatever was happening in North Korea's capital city, it mattered. It mattered to him, it would matter to the Americans, and most importantly of all, it mattered to Korea.

It took him two hours to map out a route between blocked streets and columns of soldiers to reach the first blast site. It was a collapsed factory, still burning and surrounded by emergency vehicles. He managed to collect a few snapshots while pretending to suck from the inhaler before a KPA officer saw him standing too close to a barricade and barked for him to return to his home.

There were soldiers everywhere. Thousands of them. They clogged the streets and took control of rooftops and squares. Walls of sandbags were quickly erected to block key passageways, and heavier armor rolled into the city. Ch'ŏnma-ho tanks, built by the DPRK based on the Soviet T-62, were painted in camo with their imposing 115mm cannons jutting toward the sky. Concrete and asphalt caved in as they rumbled past, and KPA machine gunners rode on top of their turrets, still shouting for people to return to their homes.

Chaos. But beneath the smoke and noise, Minsu also detected order. Strategy. Purpose.

He continued through the city, filling a memory card with photos and hiding it in his shoe before inserting a fresh one into the inhaler. After another hour, he found himself lost in a swamp of frightened citizens, corralled into a tight mass and propelled by soldiers into Pyongyang's main square. The buildings surrounding the 75,000-square-meter block were illuminated in bright floodlights and packed with soldiers. Minsu was jostled from behind by a fresh surge of citizens and almost fell. He caught himself in time to see floodlights stream toward the Grand People's Study House, and then a booming voice cut through the chaos.

"Comrades! I call you to attention."

A stillness settled over the crowd, and Minsu's heart pounded as he searched for the source of the voice. He saw nobody, but then the spotlights focused on a giant screen being lowered from a beam in front of the Study House.

Projected onto that screen was a face Minsu had seen before, and not long ago. General Jang Bon-hwa. He stood sharply to attention, probably inside one of the government buildings surrounding the square, KPA officers standing with rifles across their chests on either side of him.

There was no sign of the supreme leader or party officials. Only Jang.

Minsu moved his thumb to the bottom of the inhaler and quickly flicked a tiny switch from "image" to "record." The inhaler was equipped with a microphone the size of a pin head, which wouldn't be strong enough to effectively capture everything, but hopefully it could gather the gist.

"Comrades, it brings me grief to speak to you tonight on the occasion of our nation's saddest moment. You already know that our shining city has been attacked. By brutal and treacherous means, the Americans have bombed many buildings across our homeland and have slain hundreds of our people."

A unified gasp rang through the crowd. Minsu narrowed his eyes.

"I am here to reassure you that our brave and fearless marshal is safe and well, and that the impregnable strength of our armed forces has surrounded him with an invincible wall of protection. He is grieved to tears by the loss of his loyal comrades and is moved to wrath at the evil subjected upon us!"

The crowd was now so perfectly silent, the square so still, one might think it was empty. Minsu waited with bated breath, but he already knew what was coming.

"Comrades! This is our hour. Our adversary, the Americans, have visited upon us an unimaginable evil. The brave people of Korea stand aghast at our loss, but we will not stand still! Return to your homes. Spread word of these horrors to your neighbors. Take shelter, and take heart. In his infinite wisdom, the marshal will lead us to victory!"

A rolling roar erupted from the crowd, and almost in unison, five hundred people threw their hands into the air and fell to their knees. Minsu followed suit compulsively, lowering his head. Chants of "The marshal! The marshal!" echoed from the square, so loud they hurt his ears and shook the ground.

Minsu kept his face down, the inhaler now secured in his pocket and still capturing audio. Proof of the storm that was brewing in Pyongyang.

39

Near Ch'ilbong-ni, DPRK

Reed and Turk reached the prison camp an hour before sunrise. The long march across the rugged Korean landscape was punishing and took a lot longer than Reed had calculated. Endless foothills, mountain ridges, and roads forced them to blaze a trail through uncut forests, slowing their progress.

By the time they neared Ch'ilbong-ni and established an overwatch on a mountain slope, Reed felt ready to drop. He hit the dirt behind a low rise, the sky overhead still roiled with clouds. Sunrise would be soon, and that meant it was time to press ahead. Reed liked to attack in pre-dawn grey. A long history of early morning assaults, ranging from the Battle of Trenton to Pearl Harbor, spoke to their tactical advantage.

It was good to strike your enemy while they were half asleep and disoriented. It gave you an unfair advantage, and right then, Reed would take as many of those as he could get.

"We're getting old," Turk grumbled, sucking again from his water bladder.

"Screw off," Reed said. "I just turned thirty."

"Like I said. Getting old."

Reed punched him in the arm, then rolled onto his stomach and eased up to the crest of the ridge. He dug into his pack and retrieved the night-vision goggles, then pulled them over his head. The valley stretching out before them was wide and flat. Most of the rocky floor was undeveloped, however, with only a couple fields nestled close to the village of Ch'ilbong-ni.

That village lay three or four miles to their right and was marked by only a few streetlamps and the shadowy outlines of low houses. It looked like Anbyŏn, but smaller and shabbier. The prison camp, on the other hand, was lit up like a football stadium. It lay directly ahead, half a mile down the mountainside at the edge of the valley, a block of rocky soil surrounded by high fences, barbed wire, and rows of barracks.

The guard towers were positioned on either end, staffed by armed sentries equipped with high-powered searchlights. Those lights were dark, but both the fence and the interior of the compound were brightly illuminated by security lamps.

"Nice place. Five stars. Would visit with the family," Turk muttered.

Reed lifted a pair of binoculars in front of the NV goggles and took a closer look. There was no sign of Sinju, Gok, or any other prisoners, for that matter. Guards paced the interior of the fence and stood at attention outside the main entrances of each of the rectangular barracks.

On the left-hand side of the facility, a two-story building equipped with a rooftop patio was protected by two more guards and looked somehow better adorned than the rest of the buildings. It seemed to be built of better materials, with clean glass windows and polished steps. The commandant's headquarters, Reed figured. Or whatever the chief asshole was called.

Other than the two-story command post, the rows of barracks, and the guard towers, there was only one other building on the premises, nestled in a back corner to one side of the headquarters building. It was squat and windowless, but there was a metal vent built into the roof.

An interrogation room.

Reed grimaced involuntarily and pivoted the binoculars to the other end of the facility, where a row of trucks were parked. Much like Sinju's van, they looked Soviet in origin, either gifts of the defunct USSR, or perhaps rip-off productions of Soviet designs. Either way, they were old, crude, and looked slow.

Reed passed the binoculars to Turk and allowed him time to make all of the same observations.

"Twelve?" Turk said.

Reed nodded. "Two in each tower, two in front of the headquarters, and six scattered around the grounds. But probably more inside."

Turk lifted his chin toward the back corner of the facility and the windowless building. "Torture shack?"

"I thought so."

Turk dug into his pack and retrieved an infrared optic, flicking it on and sighting toward the buildings. He whispered while making slow passes with the optic. "Big heat blurb from the headquarters building. Internal heat, I guess. The barracks are cold. Trucks are cold . . ." He lowered the optic. "Small heat bubble from the shack."

Reed didn't comment as he computed the data. With twelve men inside the compound, it would be next to impossible to simply storm it. He liked his odds against four or five underfed, undertrained morons with AKs, but the guys in the towers were a real problem. He couldn't depend on getting a clean shot at them, and they would almost certainly have a shot at him.

"What do you think?" Reed asked.

Turk scratched his cheek, then shrugged. "Boom, boom. Breach. Clear and cover. Then take a truck."

Reed grunted. "Yeah, I thought so. You wanna do the sneaking or the covering?"

"I'm better with the explosives than you are. You always use too much. I'll take the towers."

Reed motioned to the backpack. "Check the messenger."

Turk dug the device out and powered it on. After connecting to the satellite, he checked for new messages from Wolfgang. There was nothing.

"All clear," he said.

Turk punched in a quick message, confirming their arrival at the prison camp and preparation to breach. He hit send, then powered off the device.

Reed sat another couple minutes, mapping out the facility, imagining each step and movement through the narrow paths between the barracks and what could go wrong along the way. They were depleted on ammo after the firefight at the radio tower, but all the soldiers in the prison camp would be well equipped with matching ammunition, and they wouldn't complain about losing it. They wouldn't be able to.

"Hoorah, Jarhead." Reed held out a clenched fist.

Turk pounded it. "Let's get some."

40

"Masyal! Masyal! Masyal!"

The video turned black as the camera dropped into a jacket pocket, but the audio was still clear. All around the square, the people fell on their faces, hands up, and chanted the same word, over and over.

O'Brien clicked a button on a remote, ending the clip.

"What does it mean?" Maggie said.

Deputy Director Aimes sat near the end of the table, just beneath the screen, a pile of notes between her arms. "*The marshal*," she said. "It's one of Cho's many titles, and one of the most frequently used by state media and propaganda. It basically refers to his status as supreme commander of the Korean People's Army."

Maggie's shoulders dropped. "So they're calling for war."

O'Brien grunted. "They're being prompted. But yes. That's the gist."

General Yellin's giant head pivoted on his non-existent neck, but he didn't comment. He didn't need to. Maggie already knew what he was thinking.

"What's the worst-case scenario, here?" Maggie asked.

"Nuclear launch," Yellin said. "It'll take them time to fuel their missiles and choose targets. And it's unlikely they would take action without at least notifying Beijing and Moscow. But that's the next step."

General Albert Porter, Chief of Staff of the Air Force, spoke next. "We can prepare a strategic nuclear response to counter North Korean action, but you should know that our intelligence indicates their ballistic capabilities to be limited at best. They might hit Alaska, or possibly Seattle, but they can't reach the heartland, and we're confident in our ability to bring down their rockets in flight."

Maggie glanced sideways at Yellin. The chairman of the Joint Chiefs said nothing, but again, she knew what he was thinking.

Not if they have a hypersonic, you can't.

Maggie addressed Gorman. "Secretary?"

For a change, the secretary of state had reserved her thoughts and waited to be asked.

"We need to attempt diplomatic contact," Gorman said. "Not just with Pyongyang—with all our allies. It won't be long before the DPRK publicly accuses us of . . . whatever happened. We need to get in front of it. Deny and rally."

Maggie nodded. "I agree. Make contact with London, Paris, Berlin, Tokyo, and Seoul. Make sure they understand our position, and reinforce our dedication to security in the region. Whatever happens, nuclear launch is the very last option. Period. Make sure that's clear."

Maggie stood. "Thank you for your time. Mr. Director, General Yellin . . . join me in the Oval, please."

The short walk through the West Wing to the presidential office was already so familiar, Maggie could've done it blindfolded. She walked with her head down, the virtual pressure weighing on her shoulders feeling like an actual bag of rocks on her back. She brushed hair behind one ear, conscious of new streaks of grey joining the dirty blonde.

This job was killing her. Literally.

Once safely inside the secluded confines of the office, Maggie walked to the window and watched a gardener trimming a bush in the rose garden. It was hot and muggy in Washington, and the gardener sweated and was covered in dirt, but Maggie still would've traded jobs with him in a heartbeat.

"What now?" she said.

Yellin spoke first. "I've already ordered additional ballistic assets into the regions. General Porter is correct. If they sling some outdated Soviet crap at us, we can bring it down over the Pacific. But should they have something nastier at hand, we'll need to hit them first."

"You mean a first strike," Maggie said.

"Yes, ma'am."

She turned from the window. "What does that look like?"

"You don't pull punches with nukes, ma'am," Yellin said. "The world is watching. If we launch at all . . . well . . ."

"We wipe them out," Maggie said.

"Yes, ma'am."

Maggie shook her head. "There are twenty-five million innocent civilians up there. They didn't pick this fight."

Yellin hesitated. "We could be more tactical. Target military bases, missile silos, Navy bases."

"And the fallout will still kill millions."

The general didn't answer.

Maggie pivoted to O'Brien. "Be blunt. Is this guy for real?"

O'Brien removed his glasses and polished them with his tie. He took a while answering, choosing his words carefully. Maggie used to appreciate that sort of consideration. Now it just felt like political maneuvering.

"Our intelligence on Jang is limited," O'Brien said. "But it's useful to consider the predicament he's placed himself in. Obviously, we didn't bomb Pyongyang. We presume he did. If that's true, it's only a matter of time before the truth comes out. Jang wields a lot of power in the KPA, but like Dr. Aimes said, he's not the supreme commander. So whatever happens next, he's running on borrowed time. He's locked Cho away in the name of protection, which more likely is an effort to simply isolate him. But that's a short-term strategy. If Jang *isn't* for real, well, he's not long for this world."

Maggie had thought the same thing. Jang might be a faker, but if he was, he was also an idiot. You don't go all in unless you have cards to play.

"So, this is legit," Maggie said. "Where does that leave us?"

O'Brien made a noncommittal tilt of his head. "We could give him a few days. Give Cho time to retake control of his government and execute Jang. Or give the Chinese time to step in, which could leave them with dangerous levels of control in the region."

"Or?"

O'Brien replaced his glasses. "Or we could take him out."

Yellin growled. "Take him out?"

O'Brien made a squeezing motion with his trigger finger. "Right."

"How would we do that?" Yellin pressed.

"We already have assets in place. It's my understanding the Prosecution Force has experience eliminating people. We realign their mission. Send them to Pyongyang."

Maggie shook her head. "They're on the other side of the country, still hunting Gok. We need that guy."

"Not if they plan to launch this sucker," O'Brien said. "Gok was only useful before things spun out of control. At this point, we can't play chicken with the existence of a hypersonic weapon. We need to assume they have one and take action accordingly."

Maggie thought about Reed and the job he signed on for. She didn't feel any particular loyalty to The Prosecutor. They served each other's purposes on occasion, and that was that. Business. But she couldn't help thinking of his newborn baby. His young wife, waiting for him in Birmingham. Reed's chances of surviving North Korea were already slim. Shifting him into the heart of the storm cut those chances in half.

But if Jang launched a missile, would that matter?

"I agree with the director," Yellin said. "It's a long shot, but if it fails, or if Reed is discovered, we can still disavow him."

"And if he succeeds, everything rocks back to normal," O'Brien said.

"You mean, we reinstall a totalitarian dictatorship," Maggie countered.

O'Brien only blinked behind his glasses.

Maggie looked back to the rose garden. The gardener now knelt in the soil, gently arranging mulch around the base of a bush. He wore a gentle smile, the sweat running down his nose not seeming to distract him from the joy of the work at hand.

Rosebushes. What ordinary things, really. But the ordinary things brought joy. The simple, daily life. A life that would be annihilated if the world went nuclear.

"Get Wolfgang on the phone," she said. "Let's make it happen."

41

Langley, Virginia

The CIA's headquarters was busy, even in early evening, but Wolfgang barely noticed. He sat behind his desk in the cramped office and read the latest message from Reed and Turk.

PF: Reached prison camp. Preparing to breach. Will update after.

Wolfgang typed out a quick reply, but he doubted it mattered. Reed and Turk were already in battle mode, narrowing in on their target and zoning the rest of the world out. They were going in alone, with nothing save Wolfgang and his worthless computer for backup.

Screw the CIA.

Wolfgang clicked out of the messenger and into a satellite software linked directly to one of the CIA's numerous, specially equipped spy satellites. The imagery it offered was several hours old, taken during the daylight. A live feed was available, of course, but it wasn't much to look at.

He zoomed in on the prison camp and mapped out the premises, taking note of the two-story command center, the barracks, and the guard towers. He could only see two guards, both standing just outside the headquarters building, but he knew there were more. Probably many more.

Wolfgang sat back, feeling nauseous. He wasn't sure why, but this mission put him on edge in a way that many more personally dangerous operations he'd engaged in over the years hadn't. Maybe it was something about sitting detached, watching it unfold, and knowing there was nothing he could do to help if things fell apart.

Wolfgang ran a hand through long, dirty hair and let out a tired sigh. For the first time in a long time, his mind wandered back to almost a decade previously, when he was on the other end of this scenario—the operator, not the controller. The man behind the computer back then had been a scrawny tech wiz named Lyle, and the company they both worked for was called SPIRE.

Together, with three other operators, they served as a sort of mercenary special operations unit—more espionage focused than combat. Missions in France, Egypt, Russia, Brazil, Japan, and Australia hallmarked that short and bloody period of Wolfgang's career. By the time it was over, he and Lyle were the only two surviving members of the team.

He hadn't talked to Lyle in years. Wolfgang didn't even know where he lived anymore. But thinking about him now brought a smile to his face. Lyle would be impressed with the CIA's satellite, but not by Wolfgang's access. For Lyle, access to pretty much anything was just a matter of patience and coding.

Wolfgang thought he should give his old friend a call. Maybe get together for dinner. Or maybe not. It wasn't like they had a lot to talk about besides painful memories of bygone days.

The phone on his desk buzzed, and Wolfgang hit the speaker button without checking the caller ID. Only one person ever called him.

"Sitrep?" O'Brien said. His voice was dry and already sounded half pissed off.

"They just reached the prison. Breaching now."

"Call it off."

Wolfgang sat up. "Excuse me?"

"Call off the breach. The mission has changed."

Wolfgang picked up the phone, flipping it off speaker. "What do you mean, the mission has changed?"

O'Brien was quiet, then the phone clicked and a female voice joined the line.

"Wolf? It's Maggie."

Wolfgang didn't say anything. A dull irritation burned in the back of his mind, despite himself. He hadn't expected Maggie to take the line. He didn't ever expect to speak to the president. And for some reason, he didn't think he wanted to now.

"Is it too late to call them off?" Maggie asked.

Wolfgang looked at his computer. There was no reply to his confirmation message. That probably meant they'd turned off the device to conserve battery.

"I don't know," he said. "Probably."

A pause. Then O'Brien jutted in.

"Send the message anyway."

Wolfgang twisted in his creaky, uncomfortable chair, dragging his prosthetic leg across the floor. It hurt in the cold and sent dull aches up what remained of his leg.

"I think you better tell me just what the heck is going on," he said. "I just had my guys force-march twenty klicks through hostile mountains, and now you want me to pull the plug?"

An email alert dinged on Wolfgang's computer, and he opened the software to find a note from O'Brien, with a single file attached.

"I just sent you something."

Wolfgang clicked the message open and scanned the top page. A color photograph of a Korean People's Army officer headlined the document. He was small and ugly with gold stars on his shoulders.

"You're looking at General Jang Bon-hwa," O'Brien said. "He's a leading official inside the Korean People's Army, and we believe he's just taken control of the country."

Wolfgang breezed through the document, noting details of Jang's affiliations with DPRK governance and control of the KPA.

"What's this got to do with Gok?" he asked.

"We deployed Reed and Turk to recover Gok *because* of Jang," Maggie said. "He's a radical inside the KPA and a known advocate of nuclear confrontation with the West. Gok's warnings about a hypersonic weapon were concerning, but Jang is the catalyst that converts that concern into an emergency."

"Okay . . . so?"

"So, Jang just set off a series of bombs inside Pyongyang," O'Brien said. "And he's blaming them on us."

The reality of where this conversation was headed sank over Wolfgang like a ton of bricks. He turned away from the computer. "What did you mean when you said the mission has changed?"

"We need this guy eliminated," Maggie said. "Before things spin out of control. I need Reed to take care of it."

Wolfgang's hands turned cold. "Excuse me?"

"You heard the president," O'Brien said. "We're reassigning Reed and Turk to move to Pyongyang and eliminate Jang."

"Pyongyang? Are you kidding me? They're ninety miles from Pyongyang! There are a few hundred thousand Korean soldiers standing in their way. You told me so yourself!"

Maggie took over again. "Wolfgang. Listen. I know what we're asking is unreasonable, but please, think of the consequences. If this guy obtains control of North Korea's nuclear capabilities, and they *do* have a hypersonic weapon, what would that look like? He could hit us anywhere in the country and we couldn't stop it. New York City. Washington. Los Angeles. Millions would die."

"That's why you need Gok," Wolfgang snapped. "That's what this whole mission was about!"

"No. Getting Gok was all about intelligence gathering. Figuring out what was happening on the inside so we could make a plan. Things have moved far beyond that. We need a solution, *now*, before Jang is able to launch."

"And you think capping this guy is a solution?"

"You got a better one?" O'Brien said.

Wolfgang didn't. He ran a hand through his hair again, thinking about the mess this would make and watching Reed and Turk's chances of survival shrink from fifty-fifty to something like the odds of him making it into the NBA with one leg. "Pyongyang is on the west coast," Wolfgang said. "How do you plan to extract them? You can't expect them to march all the way across the country."

"We don't," a new, gruffer voice said. "Son, this is General John David

Yellin, chairman of the Joint Chiefs. I've already given orders for USS *Louisville* to maneuver around the southern tip of the Korean Peninsula and into the Yellow Sea. She can hug the western shore of South Korea while moving north to minimize detection by Chinese naval assets, then go deep before circling toward Pyongyang. When your boys are ready to get out, we'll be there for them."

Wolfgang called up a map of the region on his computer. The Yellow Sea lay between the Korean Peninsula and the Chinese mainland—a body of water barely a hundred and ten miles wide at its narrowest point, and at no point wider than two fifty after moving north of the DMZ.

A death trap. A zone sure to be chock-full of Chinese ships, mines, and detection devices, to say nothing of North Korean naval assets.

"Are you for real?" Wolfgang said. "You'd send a sub in *there*?"

"I'm asking you to risk your people," Yellin said. "It's fair for me to reciprocate."

Wolfgang studied the map again and thought about Jang and nuclear war and the ninety miles that lay between Reed and Pyongyang. And he realized it probably didn't matter whether *Louisville* made it deep into the Yellow Sea or not. Reed would never survive that long.

"I'll ask," Wolfgang said.

"*Ask?*" O'Brien said.

"You heard me, genius. I'll *ask*. I'm not the one risking my hide, and I don't give orders. I'll ask."

O'Brien blustered again, but Maggie cut him off. "That's all we need, Wolf. But please make sure they know this isn't coming from the White House. This is coming from America."

42

Near Ch'ilbong-ni, DPRK

Reed and Turk moved together down the mountainside, sticking to the shadows and leveraging whatever scant cover they could find on their way to the valley floor. The guards in the towers seemed preoccupied with staying awake, and whenever they did make a show of monitoring anything, they focused on the interior of the camp.

Apparently, whatever troops had been involved in capturing Gok and Sinju hadn't advised the camp of the possibility of a rescue mission. Probably because the thought of two men marching twenty klicks inland to stage a desperate prison break was stupendous.

Reed had to agree.

A hundred yards from the fence line, they knelt in the grass to don night vision. The sky was turning gradually greyer, but it was still too dark to see clearly. Reed double-checked his rifle, then helped Turk unpack the tiny stock of C4 plastic explosives they'd brought with them. It wasn't a lot, but properly placed, it would be more than enough to deal with those towers.

Once the explosives were divided into equal amounts and Turk had dispensed the detonators, they started toward the camp again.

Turk motioned right with two fingers, marking the guard tower adjacent to the gate. There was no gatehouse, but with a majority of guards gathered around the entrance, it would be the most difficult place to sneak the closer they drew toward sunrise.

Better to deal with it first.

Reed hid behind a low shrub as Turk crept forward on his own. He glided on his elbows and knees, his stomach barely clearing the ground as he advanced toward the tower.

Reed watched, switching his gaze from the top of the tower to the fence line and keeping a lookout for passing foot patrols. There were still enough shadows cast by the tower itself and the fence posts to create a mottled field of yellow and black patches, suitable for Turk to sneak through if he took his time.

Turk did take his time, creeping so slowly that Reed might have lost him were it not for the night vision. Minutes ticked by, and Reed watched a guard at the top of the tower light a cigarette. Reed's mouth watered, and he imagined what the nicotine would taste like, rolling over his tongue. He hadn't enjoyed a cigarette since leaving America.

Turk cleared the final ten yards to the base of the tower and rose into a low crouch, moving to one corner of the four-legged structure and affixing a small wad of C4. There was no need to blow all four legs. If two were taken out, the tower would collapse on one side, then gravity would do the rest.

Turk moved to an adjacent leg and worked quietly, then shrank down. Reed's head pivoted just in time to catch a pacing guard walking the interior of the fence. He wore combat fatigues and carried an AK on a sling, hung low around his stomach.

Reed watched him shuffling along, moving toward the tower. Turk squatted at the base of the structure, only inches from the fence and barely concealed by shadow. Hardly enough to guarantee his cover.

The guard walked onward, his eyes drooping. He yawned and stopped at the base of the tower, barely a yard from Turk, then he craned his head back and called in Korean to the guys above him. A joke was exchanged, and the guys laughed. Then something small and white fluttered downward from the top.

A cigarette.

It hit the dirt, and the sleepy guy scooped it up, ducking his head and grinding a lighter. He turned his back to Turk as he inhaled, then started forward again. He passed by Turk with barely twelve inches to spare but never looked down. Seconds later, he reached the corner and turned into the compound.

Reed breathed out, relief washing over his body. He beckoned, and Turk returned with that same slow crawl, reaching him five minutes later.

"Top notch security," Turk whispered. "I felt safe while staying here."

Reed resisted a chuckle, and the two of them moved down the south side of the fence line, keeping far enough into the shadows to avoid exposure to the security lights.

As they passed the back ends of long barracks buildings, Reed noticed the thin walls coated in flaking paint, with cracks near the corners. There was no snow on the ground, but he imagined that during the winter, icy blasts must tear right inside the sleeping quarters, slowly freezing the occupants.

The blatant difference in the headquarters building was striking—thick glass, brick coated in fresh paint, and a heavy electrical cable feeding energy to the structure. An HVAC unit surrounded by a low fence purred near the back, pumping the interior full of waves of warm air, and Reed remembered the patio built on the roof—a place to eat on nice days and watch your guards beat political prisoners to death.

They moved toward the second tower. It was a lot darker there, with only sparse lights. Turk secured the two explosive packs in half the time as before, then crept back to join Reed.

"We could trigger an alarm," he whispered. "Flush everybody out."

Reed shook his head. "They might have automatic locks on the barracks. It's not worth the risk."

"Does this look like the kind of place that would have automatic locks?"

It didn't, but Reed still didn't like the idea of tipping his hand. Sometimes triggering an alarm triggered a panic with it, offering an opportunity to storm in and seize the initiative. Other times, it resulted in instant and effective action from your adversary, making the mission needlessly complicated.

It all depended on how well trained the soldiers inside the camp were, and that wasn't a risk Reed was willing to take. He much preferred the opportunity to knock half a dozen of them off before they even realized what was happening.

"We stick to the plan," he said. "On three, we breach. You take the truck. I'll take the barracks."

Turk readied his weapon, and Reed double-checked his own AK.

Then the alarm went off.

A loud shrieking flooded the compound, accompanied by lights from inside the barracks and flashing from the guard towers. Soldiers jogged toward the interior of the camp, weapons brandished.

Turk jerked his rifle into his shoulder, but Reed put a hand on his arm. Something about the proceedings inside the camp felt wrong. They were urgent but not panicked. Both the lights and the soldiers were focused on the parade ground—not the exterior of the camp where a threat might originate.

He checked his watch. It was five a.m. on the dot, local time.

"Wake-up call," he whispered, one hand still on Turk's arm.

Reed breathed a curse, wishing he'd thought of that. Breaching before the wake-up call, while most of the soldiers were still sleepy and maybe not yet armed, would've been preferable. Nothing for it now.

The doors of all six barracks buildings burst open, and sleepy prisoners stumbled out while guards screamed in harsh Korean. The prisoners were mostly barefoot, wearing threadbare clothes patched in places with scraps of cloth and even plastic.

They were bone-skinny and small, all Korean, all dirty and malnourished, but they moved quickly into two long columns over the parade ground—maybe a hundred and fifty people—all crowded together as the guards berated them and randomly struck out with the hard stocks of AKs.

A woman fell, crying out as she landed in cold mud. The guard behind her drove his foot between her legs with a raucous laugh, then grabbed her by the hair and hauled her up. She sobbed and limped but made her way into line.

Then Reed felt Turk's hand on his arm, his fingers digging in through the black fabric of Reed's jacket. Turk's gaze was fixed on the end of one

line, where the last of the prisoners were stumbling out of the final
barracks building.

Reed traced his line of sight and stopped. It was Sinju, still wearing the
subdued clothes she'd put on before leaving Anbyŏn, but they were now
torn and dirty. Her face was a bloody mess, and she held one arm over her
chest to cover herself where the shirt was ripped. She was barefoot and
stumbling, flailing with her free arm as the guard prodded her with the
muzzle of his AK.

When she reached her place in line, the guards closed in around her,
jeering and pulling at her shirt. Sinju sobbed and tried to ward them off,
but they weren't in a hurry. They laughed, then a tall man in a black
uniform barged through and ordered them back with a harsh burst of
Korean. It was the watcher from Anbyŏn. Reed recognized his smug face
and hungry eyes. He approached Sinju with a sultry sneer, then lifted her
chin and grinned.

Sinju scowled and spit, blasting his face with saliva. He struck her in the
face so hard that Reed winced. She fell to the ground, and the watcher
commenced to kicking her in the stomach to the cheers of the soldiers.
Sinju writhed and cried out, begging for mercy. None of the other prisoners
moved.

Turk snarled. "Still think she sold us out?"

The watcher stopped kicking and leaned over Sinju, leering at her.
Reed saw him reaching for his belt, slowly unlatching it.

Enough.

Reed held up three fingers. Dropped one. Turk raised his rifle. Dropped
two. Turk flipped the safety off with a sharp click.

Dropped three.

43

Reed hit the detonator the same moment Turk opened fire. Four simultaneous blasts drowned out the crack of the AK as shards of metal exploded from the base of the towers, and the watcher's head burst apart like a dropped watermelon.

Shouts erupted from the prison, and both towers shrieked and crumbled to the ground, tearing wide holes in the fences as they fell. Reed smacked Turk on the shoulder and flicked his own safety off, then they burst through the fence. Turk went straight ahead, driving toward the parade ground and Sinju, while Reed circled left behind the headquarters building.

The first soldier who appeared in his path went down without a sound, simply collapsing under a trio of hot slugs from Reed's AK. The next two followed suit, only one of them managing to squeeze off an errant shot that flew into the sky as Reed ran him over. Then Reed was in the back corner of the compound, listening to gunfire from the parade ground as Turk waged a one-man war against Sinju's captors.

A door smacked open behind Reed, and he whirled in time to dump his magazine into the exposed entrance to the headquarters building. Three KPA soldiers collapsed over each other in a bloody heap, and a siren screamed from inside the building. Reed ignored it and rushed the windowless building in the corner of the compound.

The torture shack.

There was no reason to believe Gok Chin-ho would be secured with the rest of the prisoners. They hadn't seen him in the lineup at the parade ground, and besides, Gok wasn't the target of the regular ground-pounders who worked this facility. He was the prize of the Ministry of State Security —the black-suited secret police, like the watcher. And those guys would waste no time going to work on him for his treason.

Reed reached the door and pivoted to one side, banging twice on it with one fist. The door was made of solid metal, with no window or vent, and it was warm to his touch. A lock rattled, then the door swung back, and a hatless man in a black uniform stuck his head out. Reed wasted him before he even knew what was happening, grabbing him by the collar and jerking his lifeless body across the threshold to block the door. Then he pivoted, leading with the AK, and faced the interior.

The building consisted of only one room about twenty feet deep and ten across, with a wooden chair bolted to the floor in the middle and a variety of torture implements lining the walls. Blowtorches, electrical probes, knives, pliers . . . Old-school stuff for a nation that hadn't evolved beyond the early twentieth century.

Gok Chin-ho sat tied to a chair, his gunshot leg bandaged, but that small mercy seemed irrelevant in the context of a bloody mess of cuts and welts across his face and chest. All of his fingernails were missing, and two of his fingers were sawed off near the palm, then cauterized with a blowtorch that still burned in the hand of another black-suited secret policeman.

Reed could smell the burned flesh and see the agony on Gok's face.

It was hell on Earth.

He hit the trigger and cut down the two remaining men in a storm of well-placed lead. They fell with barely a cry, then Reed was inside, sliding to a stop next to the chair.

Gok was barely conscious. His head rolled to one side, trails of blood running down his neck. Reed checked for a pulse and couldn't be sure if he felt one, but there was no reason for the secret police to have killed Gok. He couldn't talk if he was dead.

Two quick slashes of Reed's combat knife freed Gok's arms, and two more took care of his feet, then Reed dropped the AK's mag and refreshed it with a full magazine from a fallen secret policeman.

Thirty rounds. Fully automatic. Time to roll.

Reed scooped Gok's frail frame up with his left arm, rolling him onto his shoulder, then turned to the door, leading with the AK. He was almost too late. A KPA soldier stood in the doorway, raising his rifle as Reed faced him. Reed was quicker on the draw, firing from the hip with the AK and showering him with a blast of slugs that sent him reeling backward. Then Reed hurtled out of the shack.

Time to go.

He ran to the left, moving behind the barracks as the gunfire continued from the parade ground. There were more screams and no shortage of alarms, but the number of rifles engaged in the fight seemed to be a lot less than only seconds previously.

Hello, Turk.

Reed skidded to a stop at the last barrack and surveyed the line of trucks. There were four, and they were all backed in with their noses pointed toward the gate. As he watched, he saw Turk hurtle in from the parade ground, his back slamming into the end of the barrack, Sinju supported by his free arm.

The Korean woman hit the dirt in an exhausted heap, slumping against the wall as Turk pivoted around the corner and emptied his mag.

"Change!" Turk shouted, catching sight of Reed as he set Gok on the ground and moved to join him.

Reed slid to his knees adjacent Turk and unleashed on the parade ground as Turk dropped his mag. Bodies of dead and dying KPA soldiers littered the open portion of the compound like flies, but the majority of the prisoners had retreated into the barracks and were now out of sight. There were two or three shooters on the roof of the command building, and several more dug in around the compound's perimeter. But none were advancing. They knew better.

"Roll out!" Reed shouted.

He backed away from the corner, motioning with his elbow for Sinju to help her father. She could barely stand and clutched her stomach like she was about to puke, but she struggled to lift the unconscious man as tears streamed down her face.

"Which one?" Turk shouted.

"Nearest!"

Turk left the Goks in Reed's hands, moving instead to the line of trucks. Reed heard a series of quick, successive shots, signaling the flattening of tires on the remaining three vehicles. Then a diesel engine groaned and rolled over lazily.

"Let's go!" Reed shouted to Sinju, leaving the corner and stooping to help her lift Gok. They ran to the back of Turk's truck as the motor grumbled to life, and reached it as fresh gunfire roared from the headquarters building. A bullet ricocheted off the metal tailgate of the truck, and several more tore through the soft canvas top. Reed yanked the pins out of the gate and lifted Sinju in, then reached for Gok.

Something caught his eye from the right, storming into the alleyway between the fences and the barracks that he'd used only moments before. Two KPA soldiers filled the gap at the far end of the compound, fifty yards away, and raised their rifles.

Reed hit the dirt, swinging his rifle into his shoulder. Bullets whistled over his head, and he engaged, dropping them in quick succession, but then he heard the truck's transmission grind into gear.

No way I'm staying here.

Reed grabbed Gok one-handed and hauled his frail body up, reaching for the truck with the other. Sinju's petite hands closed around her father's arms, and she pulled, then both Gok and Reed rolled into the bed of the truck.

"Go! Go! Go!" Reed shouted.

The truck lurched forward. A continued hail of lead pinged off the metal bed walls, and a long hiss indicated that one of the rear tires was blown out, but the truck was a dually and still had a tire to spare on that side.

Turk swung hard left, grinding through the gears and exposing the open rear of the truck to incoming fire. Reed rolled in the bed and grabbed one of the tailgate chains, yanking the gate shut just as bullets smacked against it and whistled off into the darkness.

"Hold this!" Reed shouted, passing the chain to Sinju. He tore the mag out of the bottom of his rifle and replaced it with a full one.

"Brace!" Turk shouted from the cab.

Reed shoved his feet against the sidewall and grabbed the outside edge of the truck bed as they hurtled through the gate. Wire and fence posts banged and scraped against the truck walls, and the diesel roared.

Then they were through. Reed rolled into a kneel and unleashed through the back of the truck, spraying their pursuers with a deluge of steel-core bullets. One of them went down with a leg wound, and the rest took cover.

And then, as soon as it began, it ended. The truck tore across the valley toward Ch'ilbong-ni, and early morning sunrays broke through the clouds.

They were free. For now.

44

Turk drove like a maniac, leaving the road and plowing straight through the countryside. The heavy truck slogged through rice paddies and across rocky fields, heading deep into the undeveloped regions of the valley farthest from the prison camp and Ch'ilbong-ni.

Reed and Sinju hung on, doing their best to stabilize Gok as the unconscious man tumbled across the steel bed. He bled from a busted nose and cut face, but he was still alive.

After ten minutes, Turk stopped the truck at the edge of a heavily forested mountain ridge and piled out. He circled to the rear and pulled the tailgate open, beckoning for them to bail out. "Time to run!"

Reed hit the dirt, feeling like he'd been dragged by the truck more than carried by it. Sinju was just behind him, and then they lifted Gok out.

Tears gleamed on Sinju's cheeks as she knelt next to her father, cradling his mutilated hands and whispering to him in Korean. Gok didn't answer, but his pulse was strong and he breathed softly. Reed passed Turk his rifle and lifted the Korean in his big arms.

Within moments, they were lost inside the dense forest, but they didn't stop running for half an hour. Sinju kept up well, even in bare feet. Her heels and shins bled, and she still had to hold one hand at her shoulder to keep her blouse on, but she didn't complain.

At last, Turk called a halt, and they collapsed into a small clearing. Overhead, a cloudy sky was barely visible between the tangled limbs of trees, and the earth floor was damp with the runoff of melted snow from farther up the mountains.

But to Reed, it felt amazing just to stop. He leaned against a tree and sucked from his water bladder. There was so much adrenaline in his system, his whole body felt numb and buzzing, as if he'd just knocked back a six-pack of beers. He really wasn't sure what hurt and what didn't.

But he was alive, and that was good enough. He passed Sinju the mouthpiece, watching as she gulped it down and trying not to think about his depleted water supply.

Time to get out of here.

Turk was busy leaning over Gok, bandaging his wounds from the first aid kit they brought with them and doing the best he could about the bleeding nose. It was smashed—probably from colliding with the metal floor of the truck bed as Turk hurtled over a pothole.

Reed moved to the Korean's side and checked his pulse. Still strong. They propped him up against a tree, and Reed squeezed water over a cloth before mopping Gok's head with it. The blood washed away in a torrent, running down his face and neck like a waterfall.

Sinju returned to her father's side and held his hand, tears streaming down her face again. Reed squatted and checked his watch, noting that a full hour had passed since they breached the compound. It was fifteen miles back to the eastern coast, and they still had to connect with Gagliardi and his guys about a way to bring Sinju back.

And Ye-jun.

Reed remembered Gok's wife and cursed under his breath. Ye-jun might have to stay behind. It was simply too hot to return to Anbyŏn.

Gok stirred, his blood-crusted eyelids flickering. Sinju leaned in and continued to speak softly to him, and for a while, Gok only sat there, his eyelids half-open, a dazed and disoriented look on his face. Turk fed him water from his own supply, and Gok lifted his head.

Sinju asked him something, and Gok muttered a pain-filled reply, then seemed to notice the two Americans for the first time. He recoiled, probably noting their black clothes and associating them with the Ministry of State Security.

Reed held up a hand, and Sinju chattered a quick reassurance. Gok's eyes watered, and he listened as Sinju explained. Reed noted that she repeated herself a lot—using the phrase "migug salam" over and over.

American, he thought. Or something to that effect. At last, Gok seemed to understand, and he sat up, looking from Reed to Turk.

Reed kept his voice low. "Tell him we were sent by the CIA to get him out. Tell him we've come to learn about the missiles."

Sinju translated, and Gok began to cry. Sinju pulled him into a hug and patted his back, and again, Reed marveled at her quiet strength. She had as much reason—or more—to panic as anybody, but she wouldn't allow herself. It was admirable.

"My father says he is very grateful. Six days ago, he try to reach America through CIA, and the secret police come. He has been in hiding ever since."

Reed grunted. The CIA had presumed as much, but it was still good to confirm with a third party.

"Ask him about the missiles," Reed said.

Sinju spoke again, and Gok seemed hesitant to answer, looking between Reed and Turk and running a swollen tongue over busted lips.

"It's important," Reed said. "We're not leaving until he talks."

Sinju pressed Gok. At last, the old man acquiesced, ducking his head and motioning toward Turk's water hose again.

He drank a lot, and Turk didn't complain. Gok leaned back against the tree and spoke slowly. Sinju translated in chunks, giving her father time to sort through his mental inventory.

"He say he buried documents in woods near radio tower. But he remembers about the weapons . . ." Sinju listened for a bit, then turned to Reed. "There are two missiles in building outside Pyongyang, near military base. The government is building them, but they got idea from China. Design is from China."

"Are the weapons ready for launch?"

Sinju asked, and Gok shook his head and mumbled on.

"My father say they are not ready, but soon. He does not know if they will work. There is much . . ." She tilted her head, trying to think of the right English word. "There is much guess. Much doubt."

"They're rigging it," Reed said.

Sinju shrugged and asked Gok to clarify.

"He say they do not understand about heat. They are afraid the missiles will fall apart in the sky."

That made sense. Reed didn't know much about hypersonic weapons, but he knew that anything moving that fast generated a ton of heat from air friction alone. It must be a trick not to melt your weapon while in flight. The Koreans might not know how to deal with that problem, but depending on how much engineering expertise they'd ripped off from the Chinese, they might figure it out. And regardless, if they had a warhead attached to this thing, it was a problem for South Korea, and probably Japan.

At least Pyongyang wasn't holding two complete, Chinese-built weapons.

"How long until the missiles are operational?" Reed asked.

Gok listened to the inquiry, and his answer was brief.

"He does not know," Sinju said. "Maybe weeks. Maybe days."

Too soon.

Reed turned to Turk and motioned to the pack. "Update Wolfgang. Time to haul out."

Turk retrieved the device and retreated a few feet into the trees to find a signal. Reed offered Gok a piece of a power bar, but Gok shook his head.

"His mouth hurts," Sinju explained, her voice faltering. "They take his teeth."

Reed thought he'd noticed blood dripping from Gok's lips, but he didn't know if they'd pulled additional teeth or if they had simply bludgeoned his face.

He offered Gok more water. "Tell him we're taking him to America."

Sinju didn't translate immediately, watching Reed instead. A question hung on her face as clear as a billboard.

"You too," Reed said softly.

She still didn't turn away. "My mother?"

Before Reed could answer, Turk returned with the device. His face was flushed, and he gritted his teeth, jamming the messenger at Reed. "You're not gonna believe this."

45

Wolfgang sat behind his creaking metal desk, messaging Reed and Turk. After sending the initial request for a change in mission, he hadn't received a response. But he knew they were still online. The connection bars at the top of his screen assured him that their mobile device was still linked with the satellite.

PF: ARE YOU FREAKING KIDDING?

Wolfgang let out a strained sigh and lowered his face into his hands. He hadn't slept more than six hours in the past forty-eight, and the exhaustion was starting to show. But he refused to leave the computer for any length of time. He refused to trust monitoring the chat box to some disconnected CIA analyst.

W: POTUS BELIEVES JANG TO REPRESENT NUCLEAR THREAT. PYONGYANG GOVERNANCE UNCERTAIN. INTEL SUGGEST CHO REGIME MAY BE DEPOSED.

The reply was almost instant.

PF: GOOD RIDDANCE

Wolfgang expected the sentiment and was ready with a reply.

W: CHO GOVERNMENT EVIL BUT STABLE. JANG GOVERNMENT EVIL AND UNSTABLE. POSSIBILITY OF CATASTROPHIC WAR GREATLY INCREASED WITH JANG.

No reply.

Wolfgang held a hand over his mouth and watched the cursor blink. Knowing what he was asking. Knowing that Reed and Turk were ready to throttle him right now.

And also knowing that they were going to say yes. It was that last fact that hurt him the most. Because at the end of the day, if it was the right thing to do, the Prosecution Force would run off a cliff.

PF: WHERE IS HE?

W: PYONGYANG

Wolfgang expected cursing after this message. He didn't get it. Instead, a quick question popped up.

PF: WHERE IN PYONGYANG?

Good question.

Wolfgang typed a note asking them to hold, then snatched up his phone. "Get me Deputy Director Aimes."

"Uh, sir . . . I'm under orders to direct your calls straight to Director—"

"Shut up," Wolfgang snapped. "And get me Aimes."

The line went silent.

Wolfgang tapped his fingers on the table. His heart rate was up, and all he thought about was Reed and Turk, alone in North Korea, with an impossible mission at hand.

"Dr. Pierce?"

It was Aimes. She sounded surprised to take his call.

"I understand you're in charge of assets in North Korea," Wolfgang said without prelude.

"Um . . . sure. Okay. What do you need?"

"Where's Jang?"

"Pyongyang. We think."

"You *think*? Let's get something very clear, Deputy Director. I'm not sending my people in on a *think*. I need you to *know*. And Pyongyang isn't good enough. I need to know what building. What floor. What room."

Aimes was quiet for a while.

Wolfgang heard clicking, and he switched back to the computer, but there wasn't a new message from Reed and Turk.

"I don't have an exact location," Aimes said. "But—"

"Then I'm pulling my people out," Wolfgang said. "Sorry."

"*But.*" Aimes stressed the word, making no effort to disguise her annoyance. "We have an asset in Pyongyang who has proved reliable over the past few days. He's our primary source for most of our updates inside the city. I can ask him to look if you'll get your people headed that way."

Wolfgang gritted his teeth. He didn't curse. Hadn't cursed in years, as a matter of principle. But working in Langley brought him a lot closer than he'd ever been before.

"It's *ninety miles* to Pyongyang," he snapped. "Do you understand that? The farther inland they move, the harder it'll be for them to cut bait and get out if things hit the fan. I'm not marching them west until we know—"

"Dr. Pierce, allow me to be blunt. I realize you care about your people. I respect that. But let me tell you what *I* care about. I care about the ten *million* Americans, Japanese, and or South Koreans who will die if this nutcase unleashes nuclear holocaust. I care about children and the elderly and innocent civilians. Do you get me? Your buddies are *soldiers*, and soldiers are paid to protect those people. So, I need you to trust that I will do everything in my power to get them out alive, and freaking work with me."

Aimes finished the tirade, and Wolfgang remained quiet for a long time, one hand still resting over his mouth. Then he sat up.

"Okay. You get me a precise location, ASAP. I'll have them move to Pyongyang."

Without another word, he hung up and returned to the keyboard. He hovered his fingers over it, unsure. Or maybe unwilling.

Then he punched in the order.

W: Precise location unknown. Working on it. Proceed to Pyongyang and await further.

Almost a full minute slipped by. Wolfgang rested his face in his hands, feeling like a backstabbing traitor for what he was asking. But this was the job. Aimes was right about that much.

PF: How?

Wolfgang's head snapped up, and he reached for the keys. This was a question he was ready for. He'd spent the last four hours devising a plan for Reed and Turk to sneak from eastern Korea to Pyongyang. It wasn't a perfect plan. In some ways, it was pure lunacy. But it was the best plan, given limited resources. And he thought Reed would understand that.

Wolfgang typed in his reply and hit send.

46

Reed stepped away from Gok and Sinju, moving into the trees with Turk at his side as Wolfgang's next message popped in.

W: PRECISE LOCATION UNKNOWN. WORKING ON IT. PROCEED TO PYONGYANG AND AWAIT FURTHER.

"I could tear that one-legged SOB in half," Turk snarled.

Reed's blood surged. He'd seen red ever since Wolfgang's first message about Jang appeared on the screen, but he chose not to join in Turk's tirade, simply shaking his head instead.

"It's not Wolf. It's the CIA. And Trousdale. They cooked this crap up."

They stood quietly, avoiding the inevitable. Reed tapped the device against his hand, then looked back to Sinju and Gok. She cradled her father and spoke softly to him, mopping his face with the damp cloth.

One heck of a daughter, he thought. A good woman.

"It's ninety miles," Turk said.

Reed said nothing.

"We're on foot."

Reed chewed his lip, then looked back to the messenger. He thought about telling Wolfgang, the CIA, and POTUS to screw off. He thought about ordering their ride to rendezvous at the coast, and then hightailing it that way.

But as badly as he wanted to tell Washington to shove it, he knew he never would. From the moment the rationale was explained, he knew Trousdale and the CIA were right.

Jang had to be stopped. The risk was simply too great.

"We don't have a choice," Reed said. "If there's even a chance this guy is gonna launch something, he has to be terminated. You heard Gok. Those missiles may be ready to fly."

"And they might fall apart, midair."

"Or they might not. They might hit Seoul or Tokyo. And then what?"

Turk looked away, and Reed gave him time. He knew his battle buddy had already reached the same conclusion he had, but it was unfair to force him.

"Ninety miles," Turk repeated. "Any bright ideas on how we're going to play the invisible man for ninety miles?"

Reed had no idea, but there was no reason for him and Turk to figure it out on their own. He lifted the messenger and tapped in a single word.

PF: How?

Wolfgang's reply was quick, almost as if he had been waiting for that very question.

W: TRACKING CONVOYS OF MILITARY TRUCKS FROM WŎNSAN TO PYONGYANG. RECOMMEND YOU HITCH A RIDE.

"Is he freaking kidding?"

Reed held up a hand, his mind already moving ahead of Turk's. Wolfgang's scheme, at first glance, was beyond insane. Sneaking in *closer* to the KPA in an effort to avoid them sounded like pure stupidity.

But beneath the madness, there was a method. If he and Turk were able to seclude themselves aboard a truck—especially a materials truck without any troops aboard—they would pass undetected all the way to Pyongyang, gliding through checkpoints and slipping right to the heart of their target.

Once they arrived, they would have to deal with the headache of being trapped inside a swarm of troops. But with so many soldiers already flooding the city, they'd have to deal with that anyway.

"It's not a bad idea," Reed said.

"Not a bad idea?" Turk spluttered. "Have you lost your mind?"

"*Think*, Turk. The sun is up. It won't be dark for another twelve hours. How are we going to sneak ninety miles, in broad daylight, across a country full of checkpoints and soldiers? And not only that, but neither one of us has slept since yesterday. Even if we could hoof it part of the way there, then steal a car to finish the job, how worthless would we be by the time we arrived?"

Turk said nothing.

Reed gave him more time, but he was running out of patience. "Look. This is going to suck, no matter which way you slice it. It's a crap sandwich, and there's nothing to do but eat it. Now, you can go back to the beach—"

"Shut up," Turk snapped. "I'm not going to any beach."

"Okay, then. Got a better idea?"

Turk wiped his nose with the back of one hand. "What about extraction? The plan was to use the SDV on the east coast. They can't seriously intend for us to hike it all the way back to the Sea of Japan."

Fair question.

Reed punched a new message in.

PF: EXTRACTION?

Another immediate reply.

W: USS LOUISVILLE EN ROUTE TO YELLOW SEA. WILL PICK UP OUTSIDE PYONGYANG.

Turk saw the message and grunted in surprise.

"No kidding . . ."

"Those squids have some balls," Reed said. "I'll give them that."

PF: WE HAVE COMPANY. GOK, PLUS FAMILY. TWO WOMEN.

W: YOU WANT THEM OUT?

PF: YES. NONNEGOTIABLE.

A long pause. Reed bit down on his lip, and Turk just watched.

Then Wolfgang replied.

W: OKAY. I'LL FIGURE IT OUT.

Reed lowered the iPad and looked back to Sinju. He thought about the long drive across the Korean Peninsula into one of the most fortified, militarized cities on planet Earth. All so they could kill one of the most protected men on planet Earth.

It probably didn't matter if Wolfgang could figure it out or not. They probably wouldn't make it that far. Either way, it wasn't something he and Turk could worry about. Sinju would have to dig deep and find a way.

"Okay," Turk said. "If we've got to eat this thing, let's eat it. What's the plan?"

Reed looked over at his dusty battle buddy and felt a reassurance deep in his core he hadn't felt in years. Not since fighting insurgents alongside him during the Iraqi civil war. It was reassurance that he wasn't standing alone.

"We'll send Sinju and Gok back to Anbyŏn to retrieve Ye-jun. Then they can meet us near the west coast after we deal with Jang."

"You don't think the secret police will be watching their house?"

"Maybe. Probably. But that's their problem. We can't fix everything."

"So, how do we reconnect with them after?"

"We won't tell them where we're going. We'll just pick a spot to rendezvous. Then we take a convoy into the city."

Turk grunted, absently chewing the edge of one thumbnail.

Reed noticed the nervous tic and shook his head. "Man, I'd kill for a cigarette right now."

"Yeah. I don't wanna be that guy, but . . . this is beyond the job description."

"Well beyond."

Reed started back to Sinju and knelt in the leaves. He checked his watch again. Almost half an hour had passed since they hid in the forest. Time to move again.

"I need to talk to you," Reed said.

Sinju looked up from her father, glancing from Reed to Turk. She must've seen something in their faces because a shadow fell across her own.

Reed led her a few feet into the trees. "Plans have changed," he said. "We're going to get your family out, but not here."

Sinju frowned. "I don't understand."

Turk pulled the iPad out of his backpack and panned across the peninsula to the coast, just south of Pyongyang. Sinju recognized the spot, and her face turned white.

"We cannot go there. Too many soldiers!"

Reed held a hand up. "I need you to trust us, okay? Can you trust me?"

She stared up at him, her wide brown eyes flooded with tension and fear. He saw a wall behind those eyes—a levee built inside of her to stem the flow of fear. He'd seen a similar dam inside Banks and loved her for it. It was the mark of a strong woman. But that levee was under strain now. Sinju had been arrested, beaten, and almost raped. She had to be ready to break.

"We're going to get you out," Reed said, lowering his voice. "I need you to return home and get your mother. Then find a car and make it to this spot."

Reed tapped the iPad, and Sinju peered at it. He put a gentle finger beneath her chin and lifted her face. "Look at me. We're going to get you out, okay? Get your family to that spot by this time tomorrow, and we'll be there. I promise."

A tear slipped down Sinju's swollen cheek, then without preamble, she ran a hand behind Reed's neck, pulled him in, and kissed him.

Reed stood rigid, still holding the iPad, unsure what to do.

Sinju's soft mouth pressed harder against his, and he gently pushed her away.

She stepped back, confusion crossing her face.

Reed offered an apologetic shrug. "I'm married, Sinju."

She flushed scarlet and ducked her head, stepping back.

"I am so sorry. So sorry." She turned and rushed to her father, leaving the two of them standing awkwardly amid the trees.

Turk grunted irritably. "Well, I'm not."

Reed wiped his mouth and shot him a sideways look. "What happened to the redhead with big knockers?"

Turk rolled his eyes. "Get your head out of your ass. I *obviously* made that up."

Reed cut loose with a low chuckle and smacked Turk on the back. "Well, take a breath, Jarhead. Save the planet from nuclear annihilation, and you'll never go home alone again."

47

Pyongyang, DPRK

Minsu returned to his apartment not long after Jang's televised speech from the Grand People's Study House. He was tired and strained and couldn't wait to download the photos and video and sneak them off to the CIA via the microcomputer connected to the satellite internet they gave him to hide in his apartment.

That was four hours ago, and he still hadn't left the building. Outside, the KPA had established complete martial law across the city, seizing control of streets, squares, and intersections, to say nothing of major buildings. As the sun rose over North Korea's capital city, smoke from the bombed-out buildings flooded the sky. When Minsu opened his window, he could smell that smoke mixed with the diesel fumes of the passing trucks and tanks, and all he heard was the rattle and clap of military machinery.

Almost overnight, Pyongyang had transformed into a true police state, and it sank deeper terror into him than anything he'd seen in North Korea to date. *What* was happening? Minsu didn't believe the Americans had bombed those buildings. And not just because the CIA had already denied it to him, but because it made no sense. Why would the CIA want to bomb apartments in Pyongyang? There was no strategic advantage. No tactical purpose.

Bombing apartments was a terrorist's move, not the play of a global superpower. But for whatever reason, the North Korean government had decided to propagate that lie, and it was certainly having an effect. Minsu could feel the fear—and desperation—seeping through the city like an invisible wave. It drenched the buildings and crept into his lungs until even *he* felt desperate. Until even *he* thought about getting out.

Was it time to ask the CIA to extract him? Had his mission north of the DMZ crashed toward a final, miserable end?

Minsu paced the apartment floor, rubbing his face, his stomach a knot of nausea. He was usually hungry since moving to North Korea. Even in the capital city, there was never enough to eat, and he remained skinny. But right then, he couldn't have eaten a feast if it were steaming on a tray right in front of him. The anxiety that saturated him was too real. Too pressing.

A soft ding rang from the bed, and Minsu's face pivoted toward the computer. He impulsively checked the door to ensure it was locked, then knelt next to the bed and checked his messages. There was a new message from his anonymous handler on the other side of the world. The man Minsu knew only as "Joe."

J: UPDATE?

Minsu hesitated, caught off guard by the question. Update on what? He'd already sent the photos and the video hours before.

M: NONE. AT HOME. CITY UNDER COMPLETE MILITARY LOCKDOWN.

Joe didn't reply for a while, and Minsu returned to the window. He pulled a thin curtain back and peered out. Three Ch'ŏnma-ho tanks rattled down the street, their cannons pointed to the sky, loaded machine guns pivoting above their turrets.

For what? There were no Americans there. No invading foreign army. Why the show of force?

The computer dinged again. Minsu raced back.

J: SPECIAL MISSION. WE NEED YOU TO LOCATE GENERAL JANG.

A fresh wave of anxiety washed over Minsu. He shook his head as if they could see him, and he typed back.

M: CANNOT LEAVE APARTMENT. TOO MANY SOLDIERS.

J: This is very important. Jang is planning a war. We must stop it.

Minsu's blood boiled. In an instant, all of the growing resentment he'd felt against the Americans for years bubbled to the surface—all his doubts about their integrity and any real desire they may have to secure freedom for North Koreans.

They'd used him. For all these years, they'd used him. Not to advance freedom for all Koreans, but simply to preserve the status quo.

Minsu shot a message back before he could stop himself.

M: Maybe a war is good. Maybe a war will finally free Korea.

Minsu's fingers felt numb. Part of him regretted the message, and part of him kicked himself for biting the hand that fed him—the only hand that could ever get him out of there.

But another part of him was proud. He'd finally called their bluff.

J: If Jang launches missiles at the United States, America will be forced to respond. A war will kill millions of Koreans. Please do not let that happen.

Minsu sat back, his blood running cold. Missiles? As in . . . nuclear missiles? Did the CIA think Jang was staging a coup?

That was why they wanted to find him. They were going to kill him.

Minsu looked back at the computer and rubbed his palms against the bed to wipe away sweat. It was cold in the apartment, but his body didn't seem to know.

Another message popped in.

J: Find Jang, and we will get you out.

So that was it. The ultimatum. They were ready to pull him.

Minsu lowered his face into his hands and let out a sob. The crushing weight of his failure rested heavy on his mind. He came to North Korea to fight for the freedom of millions of oppressed countrymen—people who were no different than him other than their geographic location north of an arbitrary line. He came here to fight for the people his mother loved. The people she died to feed.

And he'd failed. The CIA was going to pull him out or cut him off. They never intended to free Korea.

He looked to the window again as a shout rang out from the street and then a gun fired. Minsu ran to pull back the curtain and looked down to see a small crowd of soldiers beating a woman on the sidewalk. A dead man lay next to her, shot through the chest. Their offense wasn't immediately clear, but Minsu could guess: they violated the stay-at-home orders. They contradicted the soldiers in a time of national emergency.

Except it *wasn't* an emergency. It was all fake.

Minsu ground his teeth and felt his fingers shake. He thought about the hundreds of Koreans who died the previous night as Jang's bombs went off. Maybe the Americans had lied to him or misled him. Maybe they'd used him. But Jang was killing his own people, and if what the CIA said was true, he was about to do much worse.

Minsu couldn't turn back the clock and save Korea from the grip of totalitarianism. The CIA would never help him free his countrymen. But he could do something about Jang. He could weaponize the CIA to fix at least this problem. Or he could die trying.

It was enough.

Minsu returned to the computer one more time.

M: I'LL DO IT.

48

90 Miles East of Pyongyang, DPRK

Something had changed in the air when Reed and Turk parted ways with Sinju and her father and left the forest. Reed could feel it in his very bones. There was a sort of oppression in the atmosphere—like the calm before a hurricane makes landfall.

Part of it had to do with the actual weather. The clouds he'd noticed earlier that day were now building across the horizon, signaling a coming thunderstorm. But deeper than that, he felt something sinister in the works. The promise of another kind of storm, just around the corner.

He and Turk left Sinju with instructions to collect her mother and sneak to the western coast. Gok was awake, if weak, but Sinju said she knew where to find another van. It was going to be a perilous trip for the Gok family, and Reed doubted whether any of them would survive. Part of him wished he could stick with her and increase her chances.

But at this point, his own chances of survival had shrunk to almost zero. For that matter, the world's chances weren't a lot better. Not if nuclear war erupted. Reed could already envision how it would play out in his head:

Jang would launch on the United States or one of its allies. America would strike back, deploying enough firepower to wipe North Korea out of existence. And then the moment of truth would come. Would China join the fight, launching missiles to defend their authoritarian ally? Would Russia? If so, that was the end. For everybody and everything.

It was times like this when Reed wished he understood God. He'd always known about God, and he thought he believed, but he wished he understood. He wished he could ask why.

Reed stood at a tree line at the base of a mountain ridge and shielded his eyes with one hand. Far below them, a smooth basin filled what remained of the Wŏnsan valley, and through it ran the empty blacktop of the Pyongyang-Wŏnsan Tourist Motorway—a fancy name for a crappy road.

To the east was the prison camp, probably still in chaos. But from where they stood in the heart of the Taebaek Mountains, there was nobody to see. This was one of the more rural parts of the hermit kingdom, with only sparse villages scattered around the region. A great place to hide. And if Wolfgang was to be believed, a great place to catch a ride.

After departing Sinju and Gok, Turk had collected GPS coordinates from Wolfgang, who traced the progress of a military convoy moving west, out of a depot near Wŏnsan and toward Pyongyang. Wolfgang was tracking it via satellite and informed them that it consisted of fourteen vehicles in total. Two tanks headed the column, which reduced the speed of the entire convoy to maybe thirty miles per hour.

Following them were twelve Soviet-style trucks, similar to the one they'd stolen from the prison camp—large, with canvas-covered beds. They were the kind of trucks an army might use to transport troops or gear, but long experience with military convoys told Reed they would be transporting both. Not just because troops seldom moved without stores of ammunition, water, and food close to hand, but mostly because tanks *never* moved without mechanical support in tow—especially old, outdated junk, like whatever Soviet rip-off North Korea used.

On a road like the Pyongyang-Wŏnsan Tourist Motorway, which was mostly concrete but also contained sustained patches of dirt, the troops would follow directly behind the tanks, and the mechanical gear, supplies, and ammunition would trail the rear of the column. It was the dustiest position by far, and therefore reserved for trucks carrying the fewest personnel.

All he and Turk would need to do was lie low next to the highway, and then as the column rolled by, jump up and climb aboard the last truck. A simple plan, in theory, but theory almost never resulted in reality.

"Look." Turk pointed eastward toward Wŏnsan.

A faint column of dust rose from the landscape. Reed dug his binoculars out and focused on the spot, adjusting the focus until the vague outline of an imposing green vehicle appeared on the horizon. A tank. Some old, Soviet-looking thing, just as he figured. Another tank appeared, and then a truck, still several miles out but clearly visible.

"That's it," he said, passing the binoculars to Turk.

Turk studied the column and grunted an agreement. "For the record . . . this is a terrible plan."

"Record so noted. Let's move."

The hike into the bottom of the valley was punishing, and they had to move quickly. Reed wanted to reach the road well ahead of the trucks, giving them a place to hide and confirm that the vehicles were carrying hardware, not troops.

It was also a lot farther than it looked to the motorway. Reed led the way, jogging with his depleted backpack smacking against his spine and his rifle held across his chest. As soon as they left the mountainside, they lost sight of the column of dust marking the convoy, but that also meant the convoy wouldn't see them, offering some freedom of movement.

It was now nearing nine a.m., and Reed figured that if they boarded the trucks by nine thirty, they could make the outskirts of Pyongyang just after lunch. With tanks in the lead, progress would be slow, and it might slow even further if something broke down. But they weren't really in a hurry, anyway. Reaching Pyongyang without knowing Jang's precise location would be pointless.

"What if he's barricaded in some kind of government facility?" Turk asked, breathing evenly as he jogged behind Reed.

"Well," Reed said, pausing to sip water. "We could nuke it."

That brought a dry smile across Turk's face, but it didn't last as the roadbed appeared a hundred yards ahead and dust rose to their right.

Reed increased his jog to a run, Turk on his heels as they rushed the final stretch. A shallow ditch ran along the southern side of the roadway, lined on its outside edge by scrub brush. A light breeze drifted across the barren landscape, drying the sweat on Reed's face as he slowed to a walk and searched for a place to hide.

The column of dust was only a half mile away now, and he could clearly hear the rough growl of the heavy-duty engines. If he looked eastward, he could see the black soot of diesel exhaust mixing with the dry cloud of dirt kicked up by the tires, but he still couldn't see the column. A slight rise in the road obscured the vehicles for another precious few seconds.

"Here!" Turk marked a depression in the landscape, just behind the line of light brush.

Reed drew the Chinese knife and quickly cut through several swaths of the scrub as Turk fell face-down into the depression. It took two trips to cover the big man, then Reed cut a third armful for himself.

Just as he dropped into the depression, he felt the familiar grumble of a heavy diesel engine shaking the ground, and then the lead tanked topped the rise. Reed lay on his stomach and flicked the brush over his back, twisting his feet to lay them flat against the dirt. He couldn't be sure he was covered. The dry grass growing around his face was only about ten inches tall and did little to conceal his full frame.

But it would have to do. Movement now would hurt him as much as exposure. Luckily, visibility inside a tank was next to nothing, and the trucks following would be clouded by dust.

Reed lay perfectly still as the tanks churned onward, and he rolled his head to one side to leave his right eye with a glimpse of the road. Wheels and tracks squeaked, and the earth under his head shook, vibrating into his skull. He could smell the stench of diesel, now saturating the air. The grind and pop of tires across the dirty asphalt and loose gravel was so close it sounded like soft gunshots, and he suddenly felt the very real sensation that he was about to be flattened.

The column rolled onward. Dirt clogged his nostrils. The crunch and grind of the motors flooded his ears, and all he felt was the artificial earth-quake of dozens of tons of mechanized steel rolling onward, unstoppable.

At last, the lead tank crossed into his obstructed field of view, rumbling across the rough road. It moved relatively slowly, just as he expected, about thirty miles per hour with its giant cannon pointed skyward.

The second tank moved much the same, a single soldier riding behind a machine gun mounted to the turret's top. He looked sleepy or bored and didn't so much as glance toward the ditch.

Then the trucks came. The first truck lumbered toward them with clouded windows, the canvas that covered its beds swaying in the wind. Reed twisted his head to catch a view of the back side as it passed. It was full of troops.

Reed remained perfectly still, watching as the second truck passed. He saw more of the same—green-clad KPA soldiers cradling AKs between their knees. Then it was the same with the third and the fourth.

A lot of firepower.

Reed breathed easily and counted the trucks. He guessed that the first eight would be loaded with troops and the last four filled with supplies and equipment. He was right. The ninth truck passed, and he saw crates of gear heaped up near the canvas, hastily strapped down with rope. Ten looked the same, as did eleven.

Time to move.

Reed twisted his head to the right, risking a subtle movement. The final truck rolled near them, the driver barely visible behind a filthy windshield. Reed waited until the cab was roaring past them, then he shot his elbow into Turk's ribs. The two of them leapt up and dashed straight for the truck. It rushed past in a blast of popping tires and diesel fumes, moving a lot quicker up close than it had looked from a distance.

But Reed reached the rear, grabbing onto the tailgate, his feet scraping across the dirt. Turk was right beside him, hanging on to the bumper. Reed managed to hook his arm over the tailgate and pull himself up, grabbing a toe-hold over the bumper. Then, for the first time, he looked inside, and a wave of relief passed over him as he saw stacks of ammunition crates housed within. But there were no soldiers. Reed's gamble had paid off.

He yanked himself up like he was boarding a canoe after falling off.

Throwing one leg over the gate, he rolled into a small gap between the columns of boxes and the open back—left there to prevent exposure to the elements, should it rain. As soon as he hit the floor, Reed turned to haul Turk in, the rifle hanging around Turk's neck clattering against the tailgate as he fell inside, coughing.

Reed wiped dirt from his face, coming away with a smear of black camo paint. He'd forgotten he was wearing it.

Turk spat dirt out and pulled himself into a sitting position, taking inventory of his torn pants legs and skinned boots. Then he glanced around the interior of the truck and rested against a column of ammo crates to catch his breath.

Reed followed suit, looking out the open back to the empty road behind them. Already, they had moved over a slight rise and out of sight of their hiding place, now well on their way to Pyongyang.

49

Gagliardi was sleeping when Solomon tapped him on the shoulder.

"Captain wants to see you."

Gag rubbed the blur of boredom out of his eyes and dropped his feet off the narrow bunk. Inside the SEAL quarters aboard *Louisville*, the past thirty-six hours had been a grind of hurry-up-and-wait. He expected to be back inside the SDV, headed to pick up Montgomery and Turkman by then, and with each hour that dripped slowly by, his anxiety about their mission grew.

Gagliardi had been around awhile and seen more than his share of combat missions go sour or just blow up in his face. In his experience, a protracted timeline was almost never a good sign. "Hand me a water, would ya?"

Solomon passed him a bottle, and Gag drained half of it, running a hand over his face and reaching for a shirt. Then he hit the floor and ducked out into the hallway outside.

Louisville was quiet, and it had been since they returned the SDV back to the dry deck and the captain took the attack boat down to wait in the depths. With little to do and no drills to run while keeping quiet, the crew were spread across the cramped interior, playing cards and video games, cooking lunch, and watching movies. Submariner life at its best.

Gagliardi hated it.

He found Captain Ramirez at the bridge, leaned over a digital chart with the XO—executive officer, or first mate, in civilian terms. They held a whispered conference, and Gagliardi caught them marking the screen with short tick marks, mapping out a path . . . south.

South? Why south?

Gag waited patiently until Ramirez looked up. *Louisville's* commander also appeared tired. And strained. But alert.

"Sorry to wake you, Lieutenant. Need a coffee?"

"I'm good, sir. Thank you."

Ramirez tilted his head to a secluded corner of the bridge, and Gagliardi followed. When they reached the corner, the captain scooped a printout off a desk and passed it to Gag without comment.

Gag accepted it and scanned the first few lines. Then he stopped, read them again, and looked up. "Are they serious?"

Ramirez nodded. "As a heart attack."

Gag started at the top and read to the bottom, his heart rate accelerating. He wasn't sleepy anymore. Thoughts of boredom and concern for Montgomery and Turkman were now replaced by calculating strain and confusion.

"Can you even do that?" he asked.

Ramirez shrugged. "It won't be easy. We can hug the South Korean coast, moving around the peninsula. When we reach the DMZ on the west side, that's where things will get hairy."

"So we go deep?"

"Have to. And slow. But the real problem is right here." The captain tapped the bottom half of the page, where the note that most concerned Gag was typed.

Two additional passengers to be extracted.

What did that mean? Two in addition to Montgomery and Turkman, or two in addition to Montgomery, Turkman, and the guy they came here to snatch? Five people?

"I can't get that many people on the SDV," Gagliardi said. "Not even assuming they were all capable divers who could control themselves underwater."

"I know," Ramirez said. "And they won't be. They're civilians."

Gag lowered the paper and wanted to curse every action film ever made featuring camo-clad action heroes wielding assault rifles. Hollywood made Washington believe that people like him were miracle workers—freaking Captain America.

Or maybe they didn't think that. Maybe they just didn't care whether he and his guys came back alive.

Ramirez lowered his voice. "This is off the record."

"Okay . . ."

"I've been advised by fleet command that two of our boomers are moving into position off the Korean coast, and naval and air bases in Japan are moving to full alert."

"What? Why? Because of Montgomery?"

"No. Something else is going on. Something in Pyongyang. I don't have details, but we both know what it means if they're moving boomers that close to the coast."

"First strike," Gag said.

"Exactly. I'm too far down the food chain to know why. But if Washington is shifting nuclear chess pieces, and they *still* want these people out . . . it must be important."

Gag scratched his cheek again, feeling stubble. He stared absently at a control panel across the room, where a young ensign monitored a screen. He thought about the cold North Korean coastline, only a precious few miles across the Yellow Sea from China.

They would need to be stealthy, but also fast. Stealthy *and* fast? Opposites in most universes. But not his. There had to be a way.

"We could use a zodiac," Gag said. "It would be big enough to get us in and them out. Not too loud."

"Not too fast, either," Ramirez said. "If you're under pursuit, we can't remain on the surface."

"Right . . ." Gag stroked his chin, still watching the ensign.

The guy leaned back, absently twirling a pen in one hand like a blade. Around and around . . .

Gag looked up. "I think I may have something."

50

Pyongyang-Wŏnsan Tourist Motorway, DPRK

It didn't take long for Reed and Turk to settle in for the ride. They carved out a space near the middle of the truck, surrounded by boxes of ammo just in case a stop was made and somebody happened to check inside the cargo bed. Then they cracked a box open and helped themselves to a fresh loadout while the heavy truck ground into the mountains.

The bed walls were made of steel and stood about eighteen inches high. But above them, the truck was covered with nothing save steel arches and dark canvas. Reed used his knife to cut a slit in one side of the canvas, allowing him to monitor the passing terrain outside, but there wasn't much to see besides desolate farmland and rising and falling mountain ridges. The occasional ramshackle village sat next to the highway like a forgotten soda can—just litter for the KPA, gathering dust as they rolled on past.

"There's no joy," Reed said.

"What?"

Reed pulled away from the wall and leaned against a stack of ammo crates, cradling his rifle. "I've been trying to put my finger on what's wrong with this place. It's a feeling I got when we first arrived but couldn't narrow down. Just this . . . sort of emptiness. A graveyard thing. I think it's because there's no joy. No hope. It's like people are already dead."

"Not a lot to be joyful about when your government is throwing people in prison camps and beating them to death," Turk grumbled.

Reed shifted, struggling for a more comfortable position relative to the crates. It was impossible to be comfortable in the back of the truck. Every pothole sent a jolt up his spine, and even on smooth sections of road, the vibration of the stiff suspension made his teeth rattle.

Turk scooped the iPad out of his pack and checked their position. They were crossing through the main mountain ranges stretching through the core of the Korean Peninsula. Reed figured that on the western side of those ranges, the little villages would grow in both size and frequency as they approached Pyongyang. There was a reason the Koreans chose to place their capital city on the western coast so many centuries ago. Probably something to do with more fertile farmland, coupled with a better water supply and the presence of building materials.

He studied the map over Turk's shoulder and nodded his agreement when Turk tapped a spot a few miles southeast of the city in a narrow patch of forest alongside the highway.

"Ditch here?" Turk said.

"Yeah. Then wait for dark."

Reed checked his watch. It would only be around one or two in the afternoon when they reached the city, meaning they would have hours to go until dark. He didn't like sitting on his hands with a job to do, but this mission was already nearing suicidal. Attempting it during daylight hours, with thousands of troops around, would make it pure kamikaze. And besides, they still didn't know where to find Jang.

He let his head fall back, and he closed his eyes. He hadn't slept since he and Turk took turns resting on the mountainside outside the Gok home the previous day. The rough and cold metal of the truck was no sort of bed, but it would have to do.

Sleep today. Die tonight.

Reed pictured Banks back at home, cradling little Davy and reading him a nursery rhyme as he drifted off to sleep. He saw their cozy rental house in Mountain Brook and thought of the Sonic across town where he and Banks shared cheeseburgers and listened to the radio. He thought of the old Camaro—his father's car—and how he dreamed of restoring it. He pictured taking Davy to school and watching him play baseball in junior high. He thought about growing old next to the same woman, raking leaves in the fall, and grilling hot dogs for the Fourth of July.

He thought about everything he ever dreamed of for a peaceful, happy life. And he prayed to God that life wasn't about to end for everyone.

The truck stopped with a jolt. It was the next thing Reed remembered, and as he sat bolt upright, he realized he'd slept a lot harder than he intended.

Turk was next to him, holding up a finger. Reed smelled diesel fumes and heard a soft rattle against the canvas overhead. Something cold touched his elbow, and he pulled it back to find the sleeve of his jacket wet.

It was raining, and water had run in through the slit he cut in the canvas wall.

Reed snatched his rifle up and squatted next to Turk, listening. There were voices outside, shouting at each other in Korean, and those voices approached the rear of the convoy.

Reed and Turk crouched behind the barricade of ammo boxes, and Reed cursed himself for sleeping at all. A quick inspection of his watch confirmed that only an hour had passed since he drifted off, but that was at least forty minutes too long.

Fool.

"Where are we?" he mouthed.

Turk only shook his head, confirming what Reed had already calculated. They hadn't reached Pyongyang yet. They couldn't have.

More voices joined those around the rear of the truck. Reed sniffed the familiar odor of cigarette smoke on the air, and his mouth watered. He leaned left and peered between a crack in the ammo crates, spotting a knot of KPA soldiers dressed in raincoats and gathered near the tail of the truck. They smoked cigarettes and exchanged muted small talk but didn't move. It was as though they were waiting for something.

Reed twisted left and used his finger to push back the slit in the canvas, risking a peek. He saw a chain-link fence outside and rows of metal ship-ping containers. Tank tracks ran through the mud outside the truck, but he didn't see a tank. Then he realized he didn't hear any engines, either. The entire convoy had stopped.

Reed held out his hand, motioning to the pack, and Turk dug out the iPad. The display loaded slowly and blurred each time Reed zoomed the map, but the feed was live—compliments of a CIA-sponsored spy satellite.

He squinted at the spot and bit back a curse. They hadn't reached Pyongyang. They were still about four miles south of the city, parked in a field at the intersection of the Pyongany-Wonson Highway and the Pyongyang-Kaesong Highway, which ran from North Korea's capital city all the way to the DMZ, about a hundred miles south.

And that field was full of military hardware: trucks, tanks, jeeps, tents, and even a couple helicopters parked to one side. It was some kind of depot, and Reed was one hundred percent certain that it *hadn't* been there when he and Turk surveyed Pyongyang previously.

Reed passed Turk the iPad. His buddy surveyed the field and shook his head, probably thinking what Reed was thinking. The trucks hadn't paused. They had stopped. Reed and Turk should've jumped ship twenty minutes before.

Turk replaced the device in his pack. Reed checked the gap between the boxes again and noted to his disgust that the KPA soldiers were still gath-ered out back, having a grand old time with another round of smokes. The gathering rain didn't seem to faze them.

"What now?" Turk whispered.

Reed held up a finger, conscious of more voices outside the truck. He returned to the slit in the canvas and felt his stomach tighten as two figures, dressed in black, neared the back of the truck. More Ministry of State Secu-rity officers.

They reached the smoking soldiers and held a brief conference, passing around a soggy document pinned to a clipboard. Reed squinted through the crack, then gritted his teeth when he caught a glimpse of Gok's face printed on the sheet.

So, the Koreans were looking for him. Word of the prison break mattered, even in context of whatever intensive military buildup was underway. Gok's intel about the missiles must be good, then—critical, in some way. Reed wasn't sure what that meant for him other than adding urgency to his current predicament.

Thunder rolled overhead, loud and close, and the rain intensified. The water running down the canvas and through the slit was now a steady stream, puddling in the bottom of the truck bed around Reed's boots. He ignored it, focusing on the soldiers and hoping the rain would drive them inside.

But it didn't. After the black-suited secret police departed, the KPA soldiers dropped their smokes in the mud, and then Reed heard a sound that sent a jolt through his body.

The pins of the tailgate being drawn.

He eased his finger through the trigger guard of the AK. The tailgate dropped, and two soldiers hopped into the truck and began shifting crates of ammunition toward the open rear. Two more rows, and Reed and Turk would be exposed. Reed tucked the rifle's stock into his arm and readied himself to blast out of the truck like his own version of hell.

Then Turk shifted his leg, kicking a column of ammo boxes. Reed flinched and almost raised the rifle, but Turk held up a finger, and kicked the boxes again.

The column of crates slammed into the next one, and like a row of dominos, the momentum carried to the tailgate where a precariously placed column toppled into the mud. Two crates burst open, and loose ammunition spilled out, resulting in Korean shouts and a cluster of focus around the mess.

"Canvas!" Turk hissed, tilting his head left. Reed drew the Chinese knife as the two unloaders jumped from the tailgate to help rescue the ammo, unaware of the Americans still hiding in the front of the truck. The sharp blade of the knife widened the canvas slit into a hole, and Reed dove through.

The rain outside had intensified into a downpour. Reed landed in a puddle and was instantly covered in mud as he completed a roll and returned to his feet. The soldiers were still clustered behind the truck, and no other troops were visible on that side of the convoy. To the left was a parking lot crammed with military vehicles and surrounded by muddy ditches, all obscured by growing rain. To the right were the shipping containers and the voices of more soldiers. Reed chose left, breaking into a sprint for cover behind a tank thirty yards away.

As he hit the mud and rolled between the tracks of the war machine, he caught sight of KPA soldiers rushing for cover beneath tents and inside shipping containers. The downpour was rapidly increasing into a deluge, and already, rivers of water ran between the parked trucks and dumped into the ditches. It was bitter cold, and Reed's breath clouded beneath the tank. He and Turk were concealed from the soldiers, but that moment wouldn't last—especially if the rain stopped.

"Come on," he hissed. "Now or never."

He led the way out from under the tank, still holding his rifle, then broke into another run between the parked vehicles and turned north, toward Pyongyang.

51

Pyongyang

The building was over one thousand feet high, reaching far above the city with each of its three wings shooting out to form the footprint of a triangle before rising into a point at the building's top. It was like a pyramid, built of concrete, covered in glass, and even after thirty-five years of construction, still incomplete.

In the mind of General Jang Bon-hwa, the Ryugyong Hotel represented everything that was wrong with North Korea. It was commissioned by the eternal leader himself, Cho Il-sung, and was meant to be a symbol of North Korea's industrial might and influence over a new world order. As the founder of the Democratic People's Republic, Il-sung was a god among men—a historic revolutionary to stand among the likes of Joseph Stalin and Mao Zedong. He successfully led the DPRK's war against the imperialist tyranny waged by the Americans and founded what Jang himself considered to be the premier society on the planet.

The Ryugyong would seize the title of the world's tallest and grandest hotel, and demonstrate once and for all that North Korea was *the* Korea. The project began in 1987 and was due to be complete in 1992, in time for Il-sung's eightieth birthday.

A monolith of Korean glory.

But then the Soviet Union collapsed, and those dreams were washed down the drain. Without Soviet subsidies, upon which the workers' paradise heavily depended, the DPRK's economy quickly collapsed, and the Ryugyong remained unfinished. For decades, the eternal leader's son, and then grandson, would fight to finish the project. Glass would be added to the exterior, and even LED lights would display proud visions of Korean potential across the sprawling triangular wings of the building.

But the interior would never be complete. The floors would remain empty, all 108 of them. The Ryugyong wasn't a glowing emblem of Korean glory. It was a bad joke—polished on the outside, empty and hollow on the inside, just like the rest of the Republic.

And that was why Jang chose to make the failed hotel the headquarters of his own revolution—because the eternal leader's vision was a good one. It was what Korea *should* have become. Would have become.

If only his son and grandson had the stones to see that vision through.

Jang stood on the top level of the hotel, looking out through a wide window at the stormy landscape of the mighty city, and all he saw was a sham. Wind and rain blasted the hotel, coating the glass exterior in rivers of water and keeping the interior frigid and uncomfortable. Even in a heavy coat, Jang shivered, but he didn't care. He wanted this moment. The last moment before the real storm. The final storm. The storm that would bring the birth of a new empire or the ultimate destruction of an old one. Jang didn't care which. It was better to die in glory than to live in shame.

And shame was all North Korea had become. Oh, sure. The party officials in Pyongyang could brag about the glory of their empire. They could launch rockets and make threats at the West. The supreme leader could snap selfies with dictators in China and Russia and brag about how things were better than ever north of the DMZ.

The whole world knew the truth—that Pyongyang was broke, and their people were starving, and their prison camps were overflowing. Even the people themselves knew that. The supreme leader could lock them down and outlaw foreign media all he wanted. He could arrest people for watching movies and wearing blue jeans. He could beat their families and execute their children.

It wouldn't matter. The world was changing, and the supreme leader was either too stupid or too conceited to see it.

Jang saw it. He saw it on his trips to Moscow and later to Beijing, on late nights in fancy restaurants, surrounded by people with cell phones smarter than the computers in Cho's rockets, or wandering the streets in the arms of his only lover, Maeng Si-woo. Jang saw that North Korea was being rapidly left behind—an afterthought of a cold war now faded into a dead one.

There was only one way to revive the dream. It required a nuclear burst —a blast of the ultimate weapon against the ultimate enemy. And after that, fate would have her way. The DPRK would rise from the ashes, or she wouldn't. Regardless, the Cho Dynasty would end.

The supreme leader would pay for the death of Maeng.

Jang took two steps closer to the window and looked down. The sleek glass walls of the Ryugyong glistened with running water, all the way to the wide streets far below. Tanks rolled down those streets, their cannons hung with North Korean flags as a symbol of Cho's Korea.

A symbol of wasted potential.

Jang then looked across the skyline toward the supreme leader's palace, several miles outside of town. The dictator was now confined to the premises, surrounded by a full battalion of the KPA, unaware that he was a prisoner of his own system. The panic Jang had injected into the city was real, the emergency so convincing that Cho ran to his palace, willingly. He demanded additional security. He handed Jang the controls of the KPA without a second thought.

So much for the unmatched wisdom of the marshal.

Jang huddled deeper into his coat. The unheated interior of the Ryugyong was icy cold, but the cold fueled him, just like the blast of rockets would fuel a war only a few short hours from now.

The weapons Jang had manufactured right under the supreme leader's nose, based on stolen Chinese plans, were unlike anything the world had ever seen before, capable of flying far faster than any missile-defense system the West boasted, but only needing to complete a short trip.

Because Jang wasn't firing at America. Why bother? Seoul was a scant one hundred twenty miles away. Tokyo, only eight hundred. There was no need to hit the US, when their allies were so close and helpless.

Jang would get his war, either way. And once it was started, North Korea didn't have to win. They just had to stand back and watch while nuclear holocaust slowly brought the planet to its knees.

Would the DPRK rise like a phoenix?

Perhaps.

Perhaps not.

Jang would let fate decide.

52

The cabinet room was full long before Maggie arrived. Everybody stood when she entered, and she remained behind her chair, looking down the long lines of strained faces surrounding the conference table. Thirty-five people in total. A full panel of her National Security Council, bolstered by intelligence advisors and every member of the Joint Chiefs of Staff.

A war party.

The military officials dressed in the proud colors of their respective branches stood tall and fearless, projecting confidence. But in the faces of the politicians—the secretaries, advisors, and aides—Maggie saw fear. This was a meeting they prayed would never happen.

Maggie nodded to O'Dell, and he shut the door, remaining just inside. She took her seat and waited for the Security Council to settle in, but she didn't speak. An instinct deep beneath her own strain warned her that it was more important to say the right thing than the quick thing. The people surrounding this table would involuntarily project the feelings they left this meeting with into the various governmental branches they represented. Fear could spread like wildfire. But

so could courage. It was up to her to set the tone for her entire administration.

"Thank you for joining me on short notice," she said at last, sitting up
straight and holding her head high. "I called this emergency session of the
National Security Council to address growing concerns with instability in
North Korea. Many of you already know that sometime yesterday—
midnight, local time—a series of explosions detonated in downtown
Pyongyang, and the regime is blaming America for acts of terrorism."

The military officials blazed anger, while the younger and less senior
advisors radiated panic.

"North Korea is now a nuclear state, and what happens in Pyongyang
will carry global consequences. Obviously, America is not responsible for
these bombings, but the implication that we are is both serious and potentially deadly. Let me be perfectly clear. No matter what happens next, it's up
to us to maintain control. The United States leads the Free World, without
exception. We will not cower to the bullying tactics of an evil regime. We
will do whatever is necessary to protect ourselves and our allies—no matter
the cost. These points are nonnegotiable."

Maggie surveyed the crowd, making eye contact and holding it while
projecting confidence. Projecting control.

Then she nodded to CIA Deputy Director Aimes.

Dr. Aimes rose from the end of the table and clicked a projector on with
a remote, displaying a graphic of North Korea with the DMZ highlighted in
red. "You're looking at the DPRK—the Democratic People's Republic of
Korea, commonly known as North Korea. The hot red line along the
bottom marks the demilitarized border between North and South, where
North Korean, South Korean, and US troops maintain constant patrol."

Aimes clicked the remote, and a series of red flags populated across the
map, concentrating around Pyongyang. "These flags represent troop movements of the Korean People's Army—North Korea's principal military force.
Beginning just prior to the explosion and ramping up over the last twelve
hours, we've seen over a quarter million infantry, bolstered by armored
units and air forces, deploy across the nation. Principally concentrating
around Pyongyang and north of the DMZ, they're assuming defensive
postures, but the heavy armor accompanying the infantry indicates an

offensive capability. South Korean military units have been placed on high alert, and troops are gathering south of the DMZ, where US Marine detachments are serving in an advisory role."

Aimes lowered the remote and looked to Maggie.

"What Dr. Aimes is about to share does *not* leave this room," Maggie said, emphasizing the point by tapping on the table.

The deputy director clicked the remote one last time. The final image was one Maggie had seen too many times over the past few days—a face she was growing to detest.

"The activities within the KPA over the last five days are startling, but we do not believe they're at the behest of the regime. The Agency . . ." She hesitated, then seemed to commit.

"The Agency has reason to believe that the Korean People's Army, the state of North Korea, and the nuclear arsenal housed within, may now be under the control of a rogue actor. Assets deep within Pyongyang report that this man, General Jang Bon-hwa, a high-ranking military official, may have staged these explosions and isolated Cho for the purpose of establishing a coup and instigating nuclear war in the region."

A soft gasp rang around the room, and a couple of the aides covered their mouths. The military officials remained stoic while Dr. Aimes ducked her head and returned to her seat, leaving the image of Jang plastered across the screen.

Maggie let the moment sink in. It was better for people to let the fear resonate now, within the confines of the West Wing, than to let it slip out in front of a news camera.

When soft murmurs and whispered conferences began around the table, Maggie took control again by signaling Yellin to make his statement.

The old general leaned forward with a gruff clearing of his throat. "While the CIA works to confirm this intelligence, there is no reason to fear immediate military action from Pyongyang. Even if they intend to launch, it will take time to prep their missiles. All military installations in South Korea, Japan, and the west coast are now operating at full alert, and we've shifted assets in the Seventh Fleet to launch airstrikes, if necessary. Meanwhile"—Yellin sat up—"to ensure our national security and prevent any possibility of a surprise attack, I have advised the president to advance the

Pentagon to DEFCON Two, establishing protocols to prepare for imminent nuclear action."

There was another muted gasp, and Maggie held up a hand. "Stay calm. Your job is to maintain control. Am I clear?"

Nobody challenged her.

Yellin continued.

"At DEFCON Two, the full force of our military will be ready to deploy and engage in under six hours. Our timeframe for a nuclear response, if necessary, is much shorter. Our nuclear monitoring programs and anti-missile defense systems are also on full alert and will maintain constant open communication with the White House. There is no reason to think, even if the KPA were to launch an attack, that we would be unable to defeat it."

Secretary Gorman was the next to speak. "Per the directions of the president, I have instructed the State Department to make contact with our allies in both the Far East and Europe, and to advise them of our defense readiness and the situation in North Korea. Following protocols preempting the possible use of nuclear force, the State Department is also in contact with NATO, and we will maintain open lines of communication with the United Nations, as well. Attempts to contact Pyongyang for a direct line of diplomacy have thus far failed, but we will continue to reach out in hope that members of the government or military officials will speak to us. Unless, and until, a direct attack is made, the president has asked me to continue pursuing all routes of diplomacy."

Gorman leaned back in her chair, and everyone pivoted toward Maggie. She saw the concern in their faces.

A person could know something might happen their entire life, but it still hit them in the face like a baseball bat when it did—like being diagnosed with terminal cancer or losing control of a car on the highway. It happened to other people. Not them.

Maggie knew how they felt, but she also knew they couldn't afford to embrace the feeling.

"Let me be perfectly clear. The United States is not at war. We will do everything in our power to avoid a conflict, and in the event of aggression from the North, a nuclear option will always be the *last* option. But we won't be caught with our pants down. Communicate with your departments, branches, and reports. Tell your people that the nation now requires their *very best*. And be brave. Whatever happens, we will not be cowed. It's not an option."

The meeting wound down after a series of additional reports from various military aides and Steven Kline, the secretary of defense. Maggie stood and followed Jill out. Her chief of staff had a pair of statements prepared for corresponding national addresses—one to give in the event things escalated, and another to give if any attack were to be made. Maggie prayed she wouldn't need either one, but she still wanted to review them.

O'Dell opened the door, and they were immediately confronted by Secret Service Agent Jenkins—the head of Maggie's protection detail—and a tall man in a blue uniform with a heavy brown satchel clutched in one hand. A pair of handcuffs connected the handle of that satchel to his wrist, and as Maggie approached, he delivered a sharp salute with his free hand.

"Madam President, I'm Major Sullivan with the United States Air Force. I have orders to remain at your side while we're at DEFCON Two."

Maggie's gaze settled on the satchel, and a dull chill ran up her spine. She'd seen it before, of course. Whenever she left the White House, a military aide carrying this famed briefcase wasn't far behind and always within reach. Colloquially known as *the football*, that satchel represented the most dangerous piece of luggage known to man. A mobile command device used to authorize the launch of nuclear weapons.

Maggie just nodded. "Very well, Major." She turned to continue down the hall, but Jenkins stepped in her path.

"I'm sorry, ma'am, but I need a moment of your time."

Maggie cocked her head. "For what?"

Jenkins looked uneasy. "Protocol, ma'am. We need to discuss what will happen if . . ." He hesitated, and Maggie suddenly wondered if he'd ever given this speech. "If we have to evacuate the city."

Thoughts of the speeches in her arm evaporated in an instant as Maggie imagined a red flash and a mushroom cloud rising over DC. A brick dropped into her stomach.

It was going to be a long night.

53

Outskirts of Pyongyang

Roiled clouds poured in from the west, and the rain beat down. Within minutes of creeping out of the army depot south of the city, Reed and Turk were soaked to the bone. Windswept torrents washed out the shallow ditches on either side of the road and quickly filled small creeks, raising the water level to the bottoms of shabby bridges. Mud clung to their boots, and the bite of the early April wind cut straight to the bone, but in one way, the rain was a blessing. It drove the KPA under cover and provided a screen for their advance into the city.

Reed and Turk left the roads and moved instead through patches of forest and soggy fields, leaning close to the ground and taking turns covering each other as they leapfrogged from one concealment to the next. Reed ditched his heavy pack, keeping only his body armor and weapons. Whatever happened next, he'd rather scrounge for food than risk being hampered by the pack, and there was no shortage of water falling from the heavens.

The landscape south of the city was almost completely barren. They moved cautiously, always on the lookout for civilians who might sound an alarm, but there was nobody. All the houses were clustered at the edges of the fields, their windows blacked out, the citizens locked inside. As for the military, a steady column of them poured south along the Pyongyang-Kaesong Motorway, headed for the DMZ, but they didn't leave the road. It was easy enough to remain out of sight by simply skirting the rural edges of the fields, but as soon as they approached the shadow of the city, everything became a lot harder.

The houses closed in on all sides, and the wide fields they'd relied on for open movement shrank out of existence. The pounding rain that shielded them from view at one or two hundred yards distance now did nothing to provide cover against the rows of houses only a stone's throw away, and the roads they'd easily avoided only a half mile back now wound and overlapped around them like the strands of a spiderweb.

And there were soldiers everywhere, marching through the rain as though it didn't exist. They invaded the small houses, forcing themselves upon unwilling hosts while their tanks and trucks clogged the roadways outside.

Reed and Turk took cover in a low ditch overhung by a row of bushes and watched as a detachment of KPA soldiers descended on a village, beating the doors down and packing in to escape the rain. Some of the villagers protested and were promptly struck in the ribs with the hard butts of rifle stocks. Most of them simply acquiesced without comment, standing back as the soldiers ravaged their kitchens and devoured their meager food stocks.

Reed clawed his binoculars out of his pocket. It was still a couple hours until sunset, and low fog hung near the ground, further obscuring the terrain and making it more difficult to find cover.

"How far?" Reed whispered.

Turk fought with the navigation app on their iPad, the screen slick with rainwater. "We're two miles south of downtown."

"Any word from Wolf?"

Turk checked the messenger. It was slow to load and struggled to connect with the CIA satellite orbiting overhead.

"Negative."

Reed thought about the expanse of city stretching out in front of them and the million places their target could be hiding. It would be impossible to find him in this mess. Impossible to navigate around the hordes of troops choking the city streets, and even more impossible to remain concealed if the rain broke.

Without the messenger, this mission was already as good as dead.

"We need to get the hardware out of the rain," Turk warned.

Reed crept back into the ditch. The current of water running along its bottom was now knee-deep, but there was no one to block their path as he moved upstream alongside a washed-out dirt road to a small farm situated three hundred yards away. There was a barn out back with a caved-in roof that rendered it undesirable for the passing soldiers.

It would do.

They crept in, shifting debris aside and crawling beneath the collapsed roof. It was a tight fit, and the dirt sheltered beneath rotting roof timbers was still slick, but the bulk of the storm was now deflected from their gear.

Reed folded himself into the narrow space next to Turk and leaned against a partial stone wall. Water drained off his hair, and his legs cramped, but it was good to be sheltered from the brunt of the storm.

"Try it again," Reed said.

Turk wiped rain droplets off the face of the messenger and hit the power button. The device was supposedly waterproof, but no touch-screen electronic functioned well in inclement weather.

The messenger powered up slowly, displaying a low battery signal. Then a heartbeat-style monitor pulsated across the middle of the screen, signaling an attempted connection to the satellite.

Nothing.

Reed watched as Turk adjusted the connection settings and waited another thirty seconds, then powered the device off.

"It's the cloud cover," Turk said. "We can't waste the battery."

Reed peered beneath the edge of the fallen roof. He could still see the soldiers clustered around the subdivision and rifling through houses. They seemed to be having a good time, but they were there for a reason.

"We'll give it an hour," he said. "Then we have to make a call."

54

Pyongyang

Minsu spent seven hours creeping through the North Korean capital, hiding in the shadows from passing troops and risking his life should he be caught, and he still hadn't found Jang.

The militarization of the DPRK was complete, and even though Minsu had spent years witnessing endless demonstrations of the KPA's power and potential, he was still shocked by the sheer number of soldiers flooding the streets. Maybe well over a hundred thousand of them, all crowded into private homes and apartment buildings to shelter from the rain, their tanks and trucks parked out front. They controlled every bridge and major inter-section, blocked out every large market, and filled every square, polluting the city with a pervasive fog of diesel fumes and clamor.

The orders were clear: All Pyongyang residents were to take cover in their houses, making room for soldiers wherever required. Moving through the streets or into the public squares was strictly forbidden, and an arrest-on-sight order was in place.

Minsu didn't care. The brutal crush of martial law on the city was merely the cherry on top of a bloody sundae of oppression and abuse. And the fact that all these measures were being made without any statements from the supreme leader only reinforced his instincts that the Americans were correct. Something very unusual was going on, and with this large of a military force permeating the city, it couldn't be good.

Minsu crouched in the shadows of a narrow alley, soaked to the bone and shivering as the thunderstorm persisted. He long ago gave up any hope of feeling comfortable or staying dry, embracing the cold and wet as just another punishing force in this hostile land.

Outside the alley and down the street, the bulk of Cho Il-sung Square was clogged with soldiers and a row of tanks, obscured by the driving rain, but still an impressive show of force. They blocked out the face of the Grand People's Study House, milling about and sheltering under hastily erected tents, but not moving, not headed anywhere, and not really seeming to prepare for anything.

They were just ... there. And Jang was nowhere in sight.

None of it made sense. There were half a dozen probable locations Jang might be holed up in, and all of them were nearly impenetrable. He could be housed inside the Kumsusan Palace of the Sun, or barricaded within the Mansudae Assembly Hall—the headquarters of North Korean government.

It would be impossible for Minsu to sneak inside any of those places, but he didn't really need to. The CIA had taught him how to look for envoy vehicles and official transport coming and going from a place, to help him identify the presence of military leaders hiding within. No such vehicles or personnel had come or gone from either the Palace or the Assembly Hall in the hour he'd spent monitoring each. In fact, even though both buildings were heavily guarded by detachments of the KPA, they didn't seem to be any sort of headquarters for military operations. No military commanders were present, and nobody came or left.

It was like those buildings were on lockdown.

Minsu watched the square, puzzling over the horde of soldiers. Had Jang left the city altogether? It made sense that he might. Maybe he would retreat to the outskirts, or seclude himself in a military base deep in the mountains—someplace safe and isolated enough to protect him from an American attack.

But secluding himself so far from the action would reduce his ability to control the city, and if Jang really were staging a coup like the CIA thought, he'd need all the control he could get. He'd need to be *here*, in the thick of things, keeping the fires of fear burning hot.

So why hadn't Minsu detected any of Jang's entourage? Why hadn't he seen the general's envoys and commanding officers coming and going from a command center, carrying orders for the detachments of soldiers scattered around the city? Had Jang cut bait and simply left? Given up on the coup?

Minsu turned down the alley, walking through ankle-deep puddles, his heart racing with frustration and fear. He couldn't stay out much longer. He should've already been back in his apartment, reporting to the CIA. Preparing for extraction. Isolating himself from the soldiers who might stand in his way.

Isolating himself.

Minsu stopped mid-stride, frozen in the middle of a puddle. Suddenly, it all made sense. Of course, Jang wouldn't be operating from the midst of standard North Korean government buildings. It was too great a risk. There were too many party officials and government leaders to stand in his way as he moved to escalate the emergency. Too many people to question him.

The heavy detachments of soldiers gathered around the Assembly Hall and the Palace weren't there to protect Jang. They were there to seal off the premises. To *isolate* those party officials while maintaining the illusion of an imminent American attack. Jang would be somewhere else. Someplace close enough to maintain control, but out of the way enough to provide a level of personal security.

Someplace unexpected.

Minsu's gaze snapped up, a thought crossing his mind. He jogged to the end of the alley, glancing up at a darkening sky still clogged with black clouds. The rain poured down harder than ever, with occasional blasts of lightning illuminating the otherwise darkened city.

He stopped at the end of the alley, glancing both ways down the streets behind, searching for soldiers. He could hear laughs and jeers from a nearby apartment block, where a few dozen troops had descended like vultures, but nobody stood guard on the streets outside.

Turning left, Minsu broke into a run along a busted sidewalk, away from the Taedong River. Now he moved northwest, weaving carefully among towering government buildings and tiny parks, dodging encampments of soldiers and using parked military vehicles for cover.

It took him fifteen minutes to reach the Potong Gate—an ancient pagoda-like building guarding the north side of downtown. It sat in the middle of a giant roundabout, now empty of traffic save for two parked tanks, both symbolically blocking the bridge across the Potong River to the north region of the city.

Minsu left the shadows of a low-hanging tree and dashed through the rain to the rear of the nearest tank, dropping beneath it and crawling quickly between its tracks. A river of water ran over his arms and splashed his face, but for the moment, he was sheltered from the rain.

Minsu crawled to the front of the war machine, peering between the tracks directly northward, across the bridge, down the length of a wide, empty avenue, to a section of the city conspicuously uncluttered by KPA presence.

Fourteen hundred meters away, the glistening mass of the Ryugyong Hotel punched skyward like a tri-bladed arrowhead. An unfinished monolith of the Cho Il-sung era, it was a glass-encased marker of dictatorship and poverty and things left undone. The South Koreans called it the Hotel of Doom. A bad joke from the outside. A symbol of failure from the inside. Just another eyesore for starving North Koreans—yet another thing more important to their supreme leader than their own sustenance or survival.

And for a radical like Jang, ready to push his nation over the brink, it was the perfect place for a hidden command post.

Minsu crawled to the front of the tank and looked both ways, checking for troops or surveillance. Then he returned to his feet and started across the bridge.

Because it wasn't enough to suspect Jang's location.

The Americans needed to *know*.

55

The hour drained by in slow motion. The city faded from grey to black, now only illuminated by underpowered streetlamps and what little light leaked from high-rise apartment buildings. And still, the rain persisted, now approaching a flood. The floor of the caved-in barn was filled with so much water that Reed and Turk were both kneeling in a soup of mud and rotten hay. But they didn't leave. They still hadn't received word from Wolf.

Every ten minutes, Turk checked for new messages, but the device only connected to the satellite about half the time, and the battery had slipped down beneath ten percent. They had a backup battery, of course, but it had become waterlogged sometime after leaving the truck and was now useless.

From inside the barn, Reed watched the encampment of KPA soldiers two hundred yards away and listened to what little he could hear between claps of thunder. Voices were muted, but what sounds he gathered weren't representative of a panicked army standing on the brink of a nuclear conflict. Instead he heard laughs. Jeers. The cries of women, punctuated by occasional breaking glass.

Thugs.

"Down to eight percent," Turk said.

Reed didn't comment. He was already working through a mental checklist of next steps. If Wolfgang didn't message them before the device died, they would have to preemptively message him, then move directly to the coast, with or without the Jang situation resolved. Otherwise, they risked becoming permanent residents of the hermit kingdom.

Reed pulled his arms closer to his chest, involuntary shivers racking his body. The temperature had dropped precipitously over the last six hours, but at least it helped to keep him awake. He thought of Banks and their home in Mountain Brook, and he wondered how little Davy was. Did he miss his father? Did he even notice the absence?

Reed envisioned his family vaporized in an instant under a radioactive blast. Or maybe spared an instant death in favor of a slow and agonizing one—slowly eaten alive by radiation poisoning as nuclear fallout swept the nation. Either way, the end of humanity.

Reed adjusted his protocol. If Wolfgang didn't message in the next half hour, he would call for *Louisville* to send in the SEALs. But not to rescue him. He would send Turk back while he himself pressed farther into the city to find Jang, regardless of the cost.

The thought of never again holding his wife and small child sent waves of pain radiating through him deeper than anything he'd ever felt, but the thought of surrendering their fate to nuclear holocaust was insufferable.

"Sinju likes you," Reed muttered, just to say something.

"Huh?" Turk looked up a little too quickly, feigning confusion.

Reed knew better. "Oh, yeah. Hunky American guy kicking ass and saving hers? Who could blame her?"

"Dude. She kissed you."

Reed's face snapped toward him. "No, she didn't. And that's the last of that."

Turk held up an empty palm. "Right. Got it."

The persistent river of muck continued washing past their legs, and Reed's saturated feet were so cold he could no longer feel his toes. But he ignored the sensation and just kept thinking about Banks. He thought about Davy playing little league and getting into his first fistfight.

He bet his son would be good at fistfights.

"You really think so?"

Reed blinked away the daydream. "Think what?"

Turk looked away, his cheeks flushing.

"Oh," Reed said. "About Sinju? Yeah, dude."

"Did she say something?"

Reed shrugged. "She asked if you were involved. I said there was a redhead."

Turk flushed again, fussing with the device.

"You should ask her out, man. When we get home, take her to get some Korean barbecue."

Turk looked up again, a little too quickly. "Seriously?"

"Of course not." Reed rolled his eyes. "Wake up, Turk. I'm yanking your chain."

Turk muttered a curse, fixating on the device.

Reed felt a grin coming on as he watched his buddy awkwardly avoiding the elephant in the room, and he decided to push the envelope. "She did ask about that redhead, though."

Turk reached for a shard of fallen brick, and Reed raised his hands to deflect it, but it never came. The piece of brick dropped into the water with a soft *klunk*, and Turk snatched up the messenger.

A bright green "New Message" bubble flashed across the screen, and Reed leaned in.

Turk unlocked the device with his thumbprint, and the message box appeared.

W: Positive location confirmed. 39.0368° N, 125.7309° E. Ryugyong hotel.

Reed dug the iPad out and powered it on, quickly opening the navigation app and plugging in the coordinates. The satellite signal was weak, but the navigation finally loaded, slowly revealing a satellite image of the city, a red dot marking the location of Wolfgang's coordinates.

It may have been a hotel, but it was unlike any building Reed had ever seen before. Looking straight down from space, it was impossible to tell how tall the structure was, but he could clearly mark out the triangular footprint of three separate wings shooting out from a round core, like the fins of a spaceship.

Dark glass encased the building, and a wide complex of concrete buildings and paved parking lots surrounded its base. It was north of downtown, across both the Taedong and Potong rivers, mostly isolated from the governmental district. An odd place for a military command post.

"I don't get it," Reed said. "Are we certain?"

Turk tapped on the messenger.

PF: CONFIRM CERTAINTY?

W: ASSET IS 90%.

Ninety percent certain.

Reed gritted his teeth. Ninety percent was a strong feeling, not certainty.

"What floor?"

Again, Turk tapped on the messenger.

Wolfgang's reply was immediate.

W: UNSURE. PROBABLY TOP FLOOR.

Reed took the messenger, noting a battery supply of only five percent as he input his next question.

PF: SECURITY?

W: INFANTRY AROUND BASE. HOTEL IS INCOMPLETE INSIDE. CONCRETE FLOORS AND STAIRCASES. POSSIBLE ELEVATOR. NO ROOMS OR FINISHED SPACES. ADDITIONAL SECURITY MAY BE INSIDE.

PF: ACCESS POINTS?

W: ASSET IS UNSURE.

Reed lowered the messenger and thought about crossing through the bulk of Pyongyang in the darkness, dodging large encampments of troops, navigating around roadblocks, and infiltrating the Ryugyong without any knowledge of its interior layout.

And with nothing but a rifle.

Reed typed one more message.

PF: PROBABILITY OF NUCLEAR ATTACK?

The cursor in the message block blinked, and he waited.

W: PENTAGON AT DEFCON 2. WASHINGTON READY FOR LAUNCH.

Again Reed imagined a flash of red, followed by absolute silence. The end of the ages.

But not today. Not while he still drew breath.

He checked his watch. It was nearly nine p.m., local time. He figured it would take two hours to reach the Ryugyong, a half hour to infiltrate, and maybe another hour to reach the rendezvous point on the coast.

The math was crude, but deep inside, Reed knew it didn't matter. His chances of making that rendezvous point were near zero anyway.

PF: Be advised, battery almost dead. Backup failed. Will proceed with mission. Meet at rendezvous point in T minus 3.5 hrs.

W: Copy. Good hunting, Prosecutor.

Reed switched the messenger off, then handed it to Turk.

"Okay. Here's the plan. You'll move south to meet up with Sinju, then—"

"Like hell I will. I'm not going anywhere except that hotel."

Reed held Turk's steady gaze and saw no bravado. Turk packed the messenger away, then retrieved his rifle.

"There's no point in two of us getting killed," Reed said. "We both know that's how this ends."

"Maybe. But look at it another way. Two guns doubles our odds of taking this guy out."

Crude math. But not wrong.

Reed nodded slowly, then held out his hand. Turk's waterlogged combat glove closed around his, and the big man squeezed. Reed felt iron in his grip. Resolve.

Maybe enough to stop a madman.

56

Reed moved bent over, his AK held into one shoulder, the safety off. Turk followed six feet back and to one side, ready to cover him as they crossed the last soggy field and then entered the city. The rain beat down in a steady shower, but the deluge of an hour previously had slackened considerably. Now the inclement weather only served to assist their advance into North Korea's heart.

Reed no longer made note of the passing landscape or paused to consider the scars of dictatorship and economic hardship around him. Now every thought, every move, was simply about making his way from one concealment to the next, staying buried in the shadows and avoiding encampments of KPA soldiers gathered around houses and apartment complexes.

In a way, the KPA occupation actually made things easier. With Pyongyang locked tight under martial law, there were no citizens out and about, or even street cops on patrol to accost them. Restaurants, markets, and parks all lay deathly still and empty, or else were full of KPA infantry all huddling under makeshift tents to avoid the storm.

For two former Force Recon Marines, both trained extensively in the art of slipping deep behind enemy lines and remaining hidden in the shadows, the first part of the incursion was almost too easy. The KPA didn't expect enemy intrusion this deep inside their hermit kingdom. They probably weren't expecting armed conflict or unrest of any sort.

Not this soon. Not with America so far away.

South Pyongyang was largely residential, with expanses of battered houses packed together amid narrow streets, and occasional high-rise apartment complexes built of weathered block rising amid them. The closer they drew to the Taedong River, though, the more those houses were replaced by tall apartment towers, and the tighter everything was crammed together. Deep shadows drenched the saturated streets, broken only by the bright lights of KPA encampments clogging every square and intersection. Reed and Turk moved away from those main avenues, choosing instead the narrower, untraveled alleys and backstreets.

Reed couldn't help but marvel at how clean everything was. It wasn't free of dirt—everything was dirty, dingy, and caked in peeling paint—but there was no trash. No stray paper, empty soda cans, abandoned glass bottles, or cardboard boxes blocked their path. The wires that fed electricity into select buildings were stretched between skinny poles, overhanging bare concrete and flooded gutters.

There were also no newspaper dispensers, vending machines, storefronts, or even park benches. And no ads, either. None of the bright and gaudy billboards, flyers, and displays Reed was accustomed to lined the streets. Instead, there was state-sponsored propaganda. Loads of it, printed in Korean, with bold and flashy letters and no shortage of glossy images of the supreme leader himself, flanked by ranks of the KPA.

Typical dictatorship crap.

Reed ignored the posters and focused on the pinpoints of light leaking through curtained windows or from the gaps in KPA tents. Most of the soldiers had forced themselves upon the locals, taking cover inside their meager homes to wait out the rain. Any shift in light or shadow could indicate somebody moving past a window or through a doorway.

The Taedong River served as their first serious roadblock. Ranging between five to over seven hundred yards wide, it curved through the heart of the city, blocking off the residential districts from downtown. Reed and

Turk knelt in the shadows of an alley and used the iPad to survey the spot, identifying six separate bridges that crossed the river along a five-mile stretch. The two primary bridges lay directly ahead, one crossing near the Ssuk Islet, and the other crossing directly over the Yanggakdo Islet—both small islands in the midst of the river.

Neither bridge was an option. Both were guarded at either end by KPA checkpoints, tanks, and sandbags. Near the governmental heart of the city, the military concentration grew even worse, with thousands of soldiers clogging the streets. Even through the continued rain shower, Reed could make out individual figures marching along sidewalks and occasional tanks rolling down wide and empty streets.

It had been easy to penetrate the outskirts, but even if they managed to cross the bridge, downtown was going to be impossible.

And the Ryugyong Hotel still lay three miles north of the river.

Turk pointed out of the shadows. "What's that?"

Reed squinted at a dark outline crossing Yanggakdo Islet. At first, he thought it was simply the distorted shadow of the bridge, obscured by rain, but now that he studied closer, he could make out the outline of a completely separate bridge running parallel to the first.

Reed unzipped Turk's pack and dug out a night-vision optic, flipping it on and knocking water off the lens. A quick adjustment of the zoom brought the city into focus, and he settled over Yanggakdo.

"Train bridge," Reed said, pivoting right to trace the rusty superstructure of this second bridge back to the south side of the city. As he did, a soft rumble echoed through the streets, followed almost immediately by the blare of a horn.

"Check the map!" Reed snapped.

Turk flicked the iPad on and zoomed in on the spot. The imagery from the CIA's spy satellite was no longer live, but now it didn't need to be. Turk traced the outline of train tracks moving out of Pyongyang's southernmost districts, across the Taedong River, and deep into downtown. As he ran his finger along the railway, he marked a spot where the tracks passed within six hundred yards of the Ryugyong.

And then Reed saw the train.

It may have been a passenger railway, but the engine rattling toward the Yanggakdo bridge wasn't pulling civilian coaches—it pulled flatbeds. A long line of them, loaded with military equipment shrouded in heavy tarps, bound for the city.

"That's it," Reed said, smacking Turk on the shoulder. "Let's go!"

Reed led the way out of the alley, jogging along the southern bank of the riverbed and hurtling toward the train tracks half a mile away. The train hit the bridge and began to clatter across, lighting the path ahead of its iron nose with a powerful headlamp. It was impossible to judge from this distance, but Reed guessed it to be moving at about twenty miles per hour, dragging a long trail of flatbeds behind it.

Reed broke into a run, abandoning the jog and risking an open dash past a riverside industrial district packed with warehouses and boat docks. Mucky water lapped at the bank, and slick mud squished beneath him, but there wasn't time to sneak anymore. If a civilian saw them at a distance, they would likely assume them to be KPA soldiers. Anyone close enough to notice their ethnicity would be a problem, but the area next to the river was dark and abandoned while the dockside workers were sequestered in their homes.

The train tracks loomed ahead, now only a few hundred yards away. Reed breathed easily and slogged out of the mud, moving up the bank and toward a row of apartments all packed together right next to the railway. He could see the end of the train now, rattling toward the bridge at what appeared to be breakneck speed. Reed selected the most direct path between the buildings to the railway, conscious of a large encampment of KPA troops on the other side of the train, and he sprinted.

He reached the tracks just as the next-to-last flatbed rattled past and grabbed a tie-down strap securing an artillery piece to the deck. Hurling the AK onto the flatbed, he threw one leg up and jumped without bothering to see if Turk was still behind him.

Reed's right arm slammed onto the deck of the flatbed, and he rolled into the side of the artillery piece. Metal bit into his back, and loose tarpaulin flapped next to his face. The train was slick with water and oil, both running off the tarp and across the flatbed, making it difficult to hold on. Reed looked back to see Turk clinging to the end of the car, latched on to a tie-down strap, much the way Reed was. Then he felt the snapping of metal against metal as the train hit the bridge.

Lights flashed on the far side of the train, shining across the flatbed and gleaming off the artillery pieces. Reed rolled beneath the edge of the tarp, dragging the AK with him and landing on his back. The car jolted and shrieked, and icy wind tore across his face.

But they hurtled onward, across the Taedong River bridge, and into the heart of Pyongyang.

Reed peered beneath the edge of the tarp to inspect the passing cityscape. Parked military vehicles, industrial buildings, and groups of KPA infantry passed on his left side, all oblivious to the two Americans concealed on the train. Reed noticed that the rain was slackening, and he looked down the flatbed to catch sight of Turk.

His battle buddy was obscured by the tarps. Without the iPad, Reed had no idea how much farther lay between them and the hotel, but he remained still and tried to envision the map in his head, counting the seconds and estimating speed.

The train clacked on, deeper into the city. Outside, the buildings became more visible as the storm finally began to clear, exposing tall towers shrouded in mist and plastered with state propaganda. Everywhere he looked, Reed saw more soldiers, but none of them moved to engage the train as it rushed by.

Then Reed heard another shriek of metal on metal and felt the car jerk. He watched light poles pass outside, and thought he felt the train slow.

Not good.

Reed wrapped his hand around the grip of the AK and wormed his way out beneath the edge of the tarpaulin. A wide gravel ditch ran along the left side of the train. When he looked forward, Reed saw the bright lights of another depot racing toward them only a half mile away, and gathered around that depot were yet more soldiers. A lot more.

Reed slid his legs out over the edge and looked back to see Turk following suit. Then the two of them dropped off the train and into the ditch, rolling across rough gravel as the train shrieked on. In mere seconds,

Reed reached the bottom and rolled back to his feet, pulling the rifle up and sweeping the area around him for potential combatants.

There was no one, and only empty railway blocked their path. Beyond it, rising like a mountain out of the blackened Pyongyang skyline, was the thousand-foot mass of the Ryugyong Hotel.

57

The hotel was lit up like a Jumbotron—every square inch of the glass exterior covered in LED lights. Each of the three blade-like wings that shot out from the base and gathered toward a point at the hotel's top were engulfed by the blue, white, and red colors of the North Korean flag, with its single star gliding back and forth across the glass as if it were fluttering in the wind.

Reed felt his natural night vision melting away as he squinted into the light. The so-called Hotel of Doom was immense, dominating a full city block at its base and piercing the sky at its top, where the three wings culminated into a rounded point. From his angle, Reed couldn't see the building's base, but he guessed it to be clogged by even more KPA infantry.

"Let's try the back," Turk hissed.

They stormed out of the ditch and across the train tracks, reaching an empty asphalt road on the far side. More business buildings and apartments stood between them and the base of the hotel, and they resumed their earlier leapfrog creep through the darkness, leveraging the shadows to remain out of sight.

Reed's heartbeat quickened as they reached the edge of the hotel complex—a wide garden area packed with unmanaged trees and shrubbery, all glistening with colored refractions of the flashing LEDs. Kneeling next to a stooped tree, Reed quickly identified fifty or so infantry gathered around the base of the building, bolstered by a tank and a couple trucks, then patrols orbiting the courtyard at the main entrance.

But no one was guarding the unmanaged garden. Reed timed the flap of the digital flag, noting the moments when the LEDs were darkest and cast the least illumination, then he broke to the left.

Turk followed, and they moved around the building to the darkened back side. Reed located the door almost immediately. It was built into the base, some kind of executive entrance with a semi-circular drive leading up to it. Four KPA guards lounged beneath a concrete awning, smoking cigarettes and talking quietly. Now that the deluge of rain had finally slackened, Reed felt as though his hearing was sharpened, and he could make out fragments of sentences. Not that he understood them.

"Left or right?" Turk whispered.

"I'll take left. Keep it quiet."

Reed slipped the AK sling over his neck and drew his combat knife.

Turk crept straight toward the secluded entrance while Reed swung wide to the left and moved in from the opposing direction. The grass was waterlogged and slick but didn't make any noise as he circled to the far side of the entrance, then knelt in the shadows and waited.

The KPA soldiers stood twenty feet away, sleepy-eyed and bored. One of them flipped through a magazine while two others held a conversation and the fourth smoked. None were alert, but all four stiffened when the glass broke. Reed heard the sound from Turk's position, twenty yards from the hotel's entrance.

A quick conference was followed by brandished weapons and a shout from one of the soldiers. Reed held the knife ready in his right hand and slipped out of the darkness, moving toward the soldiers' exposed backs. Another crash of glass rang out, and two of the soldiers broke free of the others, jogging toward the noise and leaving their companions alone with their backs turned to Reed.

Just as he expected.

Reed grabbed the first guy by the top of his head and cut his throat before he even knew what was happening. The second guy choked on a shout and fumbled with his rifle, but long before he reached the trigger,

Reed was on him, kicking the gun aside and thrusting upward with the knife. The blade went up through his mouth and into his brain.

The guy went limp, and Reed let him fall. He was conscious of a scuffling noise from Turk's position, then the big man appeared from the darkness like a wraith, his black clothes still sopping with water and now speckled with blood.

Turk wiped his knife across his thigh, then sheathed it and lifted the AK. "All clear."

The door was made of glass and metal, unlocked and now unguarded. They pushed straight through, finding an empty hallway on the other side.

Reed took point, moving quickly without any idea what lay ahead. His boots thumped against bare and unfinished concrete, and all around him stood more of the same.

There was no electricity, no climate control, and no sign of further security. The hallway ahead shot straight into the darkness as far as Reed could see, and the only thing he heard was their footsteps. After fifty yards, the passageway was still desolate. But as they drew toward the core of the massive complex, Reed thought he heard grumbling voices.

He held up a fist as they neared an intersecting hallway, and they listened, rifles at the ready. Reed was now sure he heard voices, and he saw flickering light, too.

More KPA.

Reed crept forward, the AK held at eye level, his back pressed near the wall. Turk followed, taking the other side, and they moved another fifty yards. Then the hallway abruptly terminated, and Reed looked out into the main atrium of the Ryugyong. The hotel was built with a cavernous, hollow interior, soaring upward before the walls closed in to create a roof.

Reed easily traced the voices to soldiers gathered around a long bank of tables laden with electronics and weapons. Cigarette smoke clouded the air around their heads, and occasional laughter broke from their ranks. Reed thought he saw playing cards spread between ammunition crates and the occasional bottle of hard liquor.

A real party.

He scanned the hallways leading out of the hotel in search of a stairwell. It would be a long hike to the top, but without any visible elevator in view, he didn't see a choice.

"Stairs, nine o'clock," Turk hissed from across the hall.

Reed pivoted his attention in that direction, and he identified the spot Turk had marked. Unguarded steps rose upward into the dark, but to reach them, they'd need to cross the open atrium, fully exposed to the soldiers. Reed was busy deliberating when a loud pop resounded from high above them, someplace buried in the ceiling. At the same moment, the flickering LEDs froze, and the soldiers went silent. Then a shouting voice, so amplified it shook the glass panels, boomed over the city.

58

The CIA sent Minsu coordinates to rendezvous with an extraction team west of the city, but his mission was still incomplete. First, they wanted him to monitor events in and around the Ryugyong, and Minsu accordingly crept into a vacant factory building one mile west of the glowing Hotel of Doom, where he watched from a broken window.

The building was dank, and Minsu was still soaked from sneaking through the city during the rainstorm. Every breath of wind tearing through the shattered glass cut to the bone, but it was how he felt inside that truly chilled him.

Minsu had failed. He knew it in his blood, in his very being. He had sacrificed so much to live in North Korea and work for the Americans. He'd put his very life on the line. Now he wondered what it all meant and if the CIA really had deployed assets into Pyongyang to assassinate Jang.

Maybe they were about to launch rockets. Maybe they only wanted him this close to the Ryugyong to ensure that when the first bomb went off, he would be vaporized by the blast. No witnesses that way. No loose ends.

Minsu watched the flashing LEDs of the Ryugyong glowing across the city in a digital representation of a giant North Korean flag flapping in the breeze.

What a fake.

Like everything else North Korea ever did. A blatant lie. Empty and hollow. Just like the hotel.

Minsu checked his watch. It was nearing ten thirty. He wasn't sure how much longer he should wait. His last communication from the CIA directed him to rendezvous with the extraction team around midnight, on the coast. But should he really wait that long? How were they going to extract him in the Yellow Sea, anyway? Were they mad? Or were they setting him up?

Minsu began to pace, fingering the inhaler camera in his pocket. The remainder of his gear, including his messenger, leaned against a wall, housed inside his backpack. He'd abandoned his apartment, now convinced that whatever happened that night, he wouldn't be going home. He'd either flee North Korea or die here.

Outside on the streets, a short convoy of KPA trucks ground by. There were so many soldiers clogging the city, even as Minsu could still smell the smoldering ruins of the bombed-out buildings from only days before. The Americans had reason to be afraid, but if Jang really was planning to trigger a war, what was he waiting for?

He had control of the army. He had the citizens convinced that a grave threat lay at their door, ready to devour them.

But that would only last so long. If he wanted the army to launch missiles at America, he would need something more. Something to realign their loyalties from the supreme leader to Jang himself. But what?

Something caught the corner of Minsu's eye, and he returned to the window. Squinting out, he tried to decipher what had changed. The city looked the same—murky dark, overhung by smog, only lit up by street-lamps and the blaze of the Ryugyong.

But the LEDs on the hotel had stopped moving. The digital flag was now plastered across the face of the glass, frozen in place.

A shriek rang from the light-post-mounted loudspeakers bolted to every corner. Minsu covered his ears from the shrill cry, stepping back as a voice, loud but controlled, boomed across the city.

59

On the top floor of the Ryugyong, General Jang Bon-hwa stood with a microphone clasped in one hand. His lieutenants—the only three men he trusted to understand the true objective of his plans—waited in the shadows.

Eager. Nervous.

Jang had them freeze the LED lights plastered beneath the glass of the Ryugyong. He wanted the flag to stop, held motionless in time as a symbol of this moment. The moment the heartbeat of Pyongyang stopped. The moment the trajectory of a nation ground to a halt, preparing to change forever. The moment the fate of the globe itself hung from his finger.

It wasn't about symbolism. Not really. It was about gratification. A moment of silence for Jang to relish the power he held. A moment to remember beautiful Maeng Si-woo and dream about the life they may have shared together. A moment to appreciate how easily he had seized control of the world's fourth largest military and isolated that military's marshal.

All it took was a little fear and misdirection. A manipulation of security measures already in place to protect the supreme leader in the event of an attack. The trickiest part was severing communications to the dictator's bunker, but Jang's lieutenants helped with that. They severed communications after a flash signal to the supreme leader that an imminent South Korean invasion was underway.

The ruse would only last so long, of course. But Jang didn't need much longer. After successfully marooning the dictator inside his own country, the next step was simply to convince the nation that the unthinkable had happened. That nothing short of total nuclear retaliation could ever avenge the injustice waged against them.

Jang stepped closer to the window, allowing him an open and unobstructed view of the city a thousand feet below. Lights marked the skyline and highlighted each of his key military camps, along with all the outposts scattered in between.

His men weren't alarmed—not nearly so much as they should be. They partied in small houses, drank, and gambled. They thought themselves invincible and couldn't imagine open war raging against them. Maybe they would feel differently as Seoul and Tokyo burned. Or maybe it wouldn't matter by then.

Jang would let fate decide.

He nodded to a lieutenant, then lifted the mic to his lips. Amid the streets, the Cold War–era loudspeaker system came to life with a scream, and a hush seemed to fall over the city.

Jang spoke loud and clear. "Comrades! This is General Jang. I speak to you tonight to bring word of a dark and heinous tragedy which has befallen our beloved homeland." Jang stopped, sniffing loud enough for the mic to catch the sound, and hocking up snot to make his next words sound choked and strained. "Our supreme leader, the wise and fearless marshal . . . has been murdered by treacherous American assassins!"

Jang shouted into the mic, "The evil of this unprovoked act tears deeply into the heart of our nation! My soul is crushed under the weight of my grief. I . . . I am broken and lost. A man without a leader. A man without the marshal!" Jang lowered the mic and spat sideways across the concrete. He waited, listening to the city and noting every subtle sound.

Then he heard it. Soft and vague at first, carried a long way from deep inside the residential districts, but growing rapidly louder and building in momentum and desperation. A gut-wrenching wail. The sounds of hundreds of thousands of people joining together in desperate cries, throwing themselves on the floor and clawing at the stones and carpet, retching and writhing and grieving the loss of their beloved leader.

A slow smile crept across Jang's face. The longer the wail continued, the louder it became, until the city reverberated with the sound. The glass walls of the Ryugyong gleamed with the flag, and the voice of agony flooded the air.

A unified desperation. Horrific pain. Unanimous outrage.

Jang lifted the mic. "Comrades! The anger that rages within me is beyond all words! America will *pay* for the evil they have visited upon our land. We will deliver to them death and devastation like never before seen on the face of the Earth! I call upon our brave army to stand ready at our borders. Lock down our streets, and surround our golden city. Ready our rockets to rain hellfire and vengeance from the skies!"

His voice boomed loud above the wails, echoing between the buildings, and slowly, the mournful cries changed, mixing with bitter screams of rage. A voice of vengeance and bloodthirst. A voice of war.

Jang just smiled.

60

Maggie lay up to her neck in hot bathwater, her face surrounded by bubbles. The executive bathroom inside the White House residence wasn't the fanciest she'd ever seen. Five-star hotels and resorts were far more ornate, but the home of America's leader was a mansion, not a palace. It was comfortable and spacious, not opulent.

And just now, Maggie wouldn't have noticed if she were bathing in the Taj Mahal. The deep strain eating away at her mind, gnawing at her stomach, and sending tense waves of pain down her spine was too real for any amount of luxury to assuage.

The hot bath—her first such indulgence since becoming president—helped ease her muscles, but it couldn't take away the reality of the precipice the Free World teetered on. Or the knowledge of how little a push it would require for everyone and everything to simply topple over the edge.

Maggie rested her head against the edge of the tub, eyes closed. She drew a deep breath, then simply slipped beneath the surface. Warm water engulfed her face and saturated her hair, blocking out the soft noises of the house around her.

Her heart thumped and she felt a lightness in her head as the oxygen she held in her lungs slowly burned away. But all she saw was a wasteland, stretching from sea to shining sea. Grey ash and the twisted remains of tall towers and giant football stadiums. Shadows on the concrete where people once stood. Empty craters ripping through the land where lakes and rivers once lay. Evaporated. Gone, in the blink of an eye.

The price the world would pay if she failed.

A shrill ringing sound echoed from someplace far away, and Maggie surfaced with a gasp. The phone lying on the table next to the tub rang, almost buzzing onto the floor, and at the same moment, a fist pounded against the bathroom door.

"Ma'am! We have to get you to the bunker."

Maggie ignored the phone, lurching out of the tub, grabbing a bathrobe, and knotting it around her waist. She rushed for the door, but she remembered the Biscuit lying on the counter next to her dirty clothes and snatched it up.

O'Dell stood outside, his posture stiff with strain. Jenkins and Major Sullivan burst into the room right behind him, two Secret Service agents on their heels.

"Ma'am, come with us."

O'Dell fell in behind her, but Maggie didn't wait for them to push. She ran from the room and down the hallway, finding the bunker elevator waiting and open. The doors rolled shut, and they rocketed downward, nothing but tense breathing filling the small space.

"Is it happening?" Maggie said, her voice low.

O'Dell spoke softly. "I don't know."

The car slammed to a stop at the bottom of the elevator shaft, and the doors rolled back. Maggie ran with the others down a now-familiar route to the Presidential Emergency Operations Center, or PEOC—a nuclear-proof bunker built far beneath the White House for the worst emergency situations.

The giant steel door hung open, two Marines armed with assault rifles standing at attention next to it. Maggie rushed past them and into the bunker, hearing Jenkins shout into his throat mic as the door swung shut.

"Saint is secure! Repeat, Saint has reached PEOC."

Maggie ran a hand through her saturated hair, then felt a nudge at her elbow. Jill stood there, her face chalk white but her chin held high. She still wore her pantsuit from earlier that day, and Maggie realized she'd probably never left the White House.

In her outstretched hand, Jill held a folded pair of jeans and a royal blue sweatshirt with the presidential seal embroidered over the chest. Maggie accepted the clothes gratefully, then ducked into the nearest bathroom to change. Ten seconds later, she was back in the hallway, rushing along with Jenkins, O'Dell, Jill, and Major Sullivan to the main conference room. The big Air Force officer walked smoothly, the nuclear football swinging from one arm.

Calm and collected. Ready for war.

Inside the PEOC's primary conference room, a panel of military advisors in various stages of casual dress crowded around the table. They stood when she entered, and Maggie swept their faces.

General Albert Porter, chief of staff for the Air Force.

Admiral Dan Turley, chief of naval operations.

Steven Kline, secretary of defense.

And General John David Yellin, chairman of the Joint Chiefs.

The doomsday squad, joined by Deputy Director Aimes and a smattering of lower-ranking military and DOD advisors.

"The remaining Joint Chiefs will be here shortly, ma'am," Yellin said.

Maggie settled into her seat. "Where's Lisa?"

"She's on her way," Jill said, taking the seat to her left. "Ten minutes out."

Maggie ran another hand through her hair. Water drained over her back, and the sweatshirt clung to her damp skin. She suddenly felt hot and closed in.

"Can we get some air in here?" She directed the question to an aide in one corner, then turned to Kline. "All right, Steven. What's happening?"

Kline flicked the display screen on. Maggie expected a map or some kind of nuclear alert software. Instead, it was a grainy video pointed toward a darkened skyline.

"We just received this video from the CIA's asset inside Pyongyang,"

Kline said. "I can play it, but the summary is that Jang has taken complete control of the city and is threatening imminent nuclear launch."

"Why?"

Kline set the remote down. "He claims we killed Cho."

"What?"

Dr. Aimes broke in. "I just got off the phone with Director O'Brien. We have no intelligence to indicate Cho is dead, but he's been offline and invisible for the past thirty-six hours. It's very likely Jang has simply isolated him in a palace or bunker and cut off communications."

"There's no chance he staged an assassination?" Maggie asked.

Aimes shook her head. "Cho is one of the most secure people on the planet. Even with the assistance of co-conspirators, it's extremely unlikely that Jang could get away with killing him. And if he tried, the army might turn on him. Cho is like a god to these people—they're unbelievably loyal. It's much more likely that Jang sidelined him and is now claiming his death."

"Where does that leave us?"

"In one hell of a corner," Yellin said, scooping up the remote. He flicked the screen to a satellite display of North Korea, the DMZ marked in a bold yellow line with little red flags highlighting key cities and military installations. One of those installations was circled and lay northwest of Pyongyang.

"This is Sino-ri, an unpopulated mountainous region about fifty miles north of the capital. The DOD has been gathering evidence since 2014, indicating that a secret ICBM base is on-site here, probably including nuclear-tipped missiles. If Jang is going to launch a strike, Sino-ri is the most likely source."

"Is this their only missile base?" Maggie asked.

Yellin shook his head. "No, ma'am. They maintain at least four more, but Sino-ri is by far the closest to Pyongyang, and the most logical for a strike. If Jang is gonna hit us, he'll need to hit quickly before Cho's death is discovered to be a hoax."

"Unless it's not a hoax," Maggie said.

"He'll still need to move quickly. Outrage and fear will fuel the KPA for now, but once that initial shock fades, they may resist the prospect of instigating nuclear war. Jang will strike while the iron's hot."

Maggie picked at the edge of the conference table with her thumbnail. Yellin hadn't said it aloud yet, but she knew what he was thinking and what he was about to ask for. And she knew it had little to do with Sino-ri or any number of traditional intercontinental ballistic missiles the DPRK might hold. It had a lot more to do with the possible presence of Gok's hypersonic weapons and the targets they might reach.

They could hit Sino-ri with a non-nuclear strike, but could they guarantee all nuclear weapons would be neutralized? No.

"Probable targets?" Maggie asked.

General Porter took that one. "Our analysis indicates Seoul, Tokyo, and Yokohama would be the most likely targets. American military installations in those regions would be devastated by even a moderate nuclear weapon, and flight time would be short enough to inhibit our ability to deflect."

"How much of the Seventh Fleet is at anchor in Yokohama?" Maggie asked.

"Barely a third," Admiral Turley said. "We've steamed most of our Seventh Fleet assets into the Sea of Japan to stage air strikes, if necessary."

So, this is it. The big decision.

"Will we have any warning?" Maggie asked, already knowing she was priming Yellin for what he needed to ask.

"Twenty to forty-five minutes from launch," Yellin said. "Depending on targets and payload. But if the missiles leave the silos, our chances of preventing effective hits are dramatically reduced."

The general's burley shoulders bulged, and he cleared his throat. "Ma'am, by far, our best option is to hit them before they hit us. We have ballistic missile submarines in position to initiate a first strike protocol, specifically targeting their missile facilities and military bases. Civilian casualties will be minimal if we launch on our terms."

Maggie thought about everything she knew of nuclear weapons and what happened after they detonated. Radiation flung into the air like invisible confetti, caught by the atmosphere and swept by weather patterns around the globe.

Yellin was speaking as a soldier, making recommendations based on a soldier's priorities. But Maggie didn't kid herself for a moment. If any nuclear weapon was launched, however small, civilian casualties would be catastrophic.

"How will we know if they plan to launch?"

"We'll have some warning," General Porter said. "They'll need to fuel their missiles and open the tubes. If we see either of those things happening, we'll know they plan to launch."

"But I need the order to prep first strike *now*," Yellin said. "We need our finger on the trigger long before they reach for a gun."

Maggie swallowed hard and looked to Jill. Her chief of staff's face was still chalky white, but she sat upright and said nothing.

The door behind them smacked open, and two Secret Service agents escorted Secretary Gorman and Vice President Stratton in. Lisa wore jogging sweats, but Stratton looked as he always looked—polished and clean, dressed in a jet-black suit with a red power tie.

They both stopped cold as they entered the room, feeling the tension in the air.

Maggie looked to Yellin. "You have my authorization."

Both Stratton and Gorman hurried to the table, questions on their faces. Maggie brushed them aside and lifted the phone off her table, hitting zero for the operator. She named the person she wanted to speak to and waited calmly for him to pick up. It didn't take long.

"Hello?"

"Wolfgang, it's Maggie. Tell Reed he's running out of time."

61

Pyongyang

Reed didn't know what the speaker at the top of the hotel had said, but the gut-wrenching wail that enveloped the city shortly after told him enough.

"Go!" Reed snapped.

The soldiers encircling the tables at the far end of the room stood in shock, seemingly disoriented by whatever they had heard. As Reed and Turk broke out of the shadows and stormed toward the stairs, they stood dumbfounded, wasting a precious second in confusion before fumbling for weapons.

A hail of bullets from Reed's AK tore down the first three men while the fourth scrambled for his gun. Two more rounds struck the fourth guy and knocked him backwards across the table before a stray bullet blew out glass and extinguished LEDs behind him.

Turk had finished with the other half and swapped his mag before racing to follow Reed up the stairs. The continued whine outside the Ryugyong was so loud that Reed doubted if anyone had heard the shots, but he wasn't going to wait around to find out. If Jang was at the top of the hotel, he was boxed in.

The concrete steps built into the nearest wall were wide and shallow.

Reed took two at a time up to the second level, where a terrified soldier crouched around a corner and showered the landing with random lead.

"Frag out!" Reed shouted, yanking a grenade from his chest rig and flinging it around the corner. It detonated in a cloud of concrete dust, and the soldier's gun fell quiet.

They took the landing in tandem, Reed moving ahead and Turk covering him from behind. Two more soldiers confronted them at the next stairwell but never stood a chance. Reed took the left one, and Turk took the right, flowing automatically without need for communication.

Then they were back on the stairs, racing up the next eight floors without encountering any resistance. Empty hallways and hollow rooms littered with abandoned construction materials were all that greeted them.

Reed began to wheeze by the twelfth floor. By eighteen, his legs burned, but he kept climbing, Turk on his tail. The Ryugyong's walls had closed in now, merging over the atrium and forming a solid building still entirely constructed of concrete. It felt like a parking garage, with every step echoing around the hollow rooms. And still, there was no sign of Jang or his soldiers.

At the twenty-first floor, Reed skidded to a stop, sweeping the muzzle of the AK around the landing. "How high up was that voice?" he gasped.

Turk shook his head. "Couldn't tell. It was amplified. Top, maybe?"

How many floors? At a thousand feet, it had to be at least a hundred, and it would take half an hour to climb that far.

Reed dug a flashlight out of his belt and clicked it on, scanning the floor. Footprints he'd seen winding up the stairway had vanished, and now only dust coated the steps moving forward. There was so much water on the floor, he and Turk were leaving a sloppy trail across the rough concrete. If Jang had climbed these steps, he should've left one, too. Especially with an entourage in tow.

Reed left the stairwell and searched the floor. Cavernous hallways and empty rooms struck out in every direction, moving into each of the three wings of the structure. But he saw no footprints.

"What's that?" Turk whispered.

Reed held his breath, listening carefully. The wail of the city outside was now joined by a clamor of honking horns, blaring sirens, and chanting voices, making anything else difficult to hear, even on this side of the glass. But as he waited in the darkness, he thought he heard something else. A soft whirring.

An elevator.

Reed signaled with two fingers, and he and Turk split off, each moving in opposite directions from the stairwell and deeper into the floor. The core of the Ryugyong was blocky and round, consuming the stairwell and the empty shafts where future elevators were destined to be constructed. But someplace else, deeper in the darkness, the whirring grew louder.

Reed's steps quickened, leading him toward the sound. He rounded a corner, and the flash of blue and red LEDs blazed across his face from the end of a glass-capped hallway.

He turned left, and in the back of the Ryugyong's core stood a service elevator shaft. Rusted elevator cables squeaked and smacked against the wall under the tension of a car above, and Reed rushed to the shaft and flashed his light, shining it on the metal bottom of a large service car five or six floors up. Reed heard the grind of a motor, along with muted voices, and he snatched his head back to shout for Turk. "Here!"

Turk stormed around the corner, gun raised, and Reed stepped back from the door.

"Four or five floors," he warned.

The cables rushed by, still smacking against the wall every time the car passed a landing.

Three. Two.

The bottom of the car slid into view, and they both opened fire. A hail of lead ripped through the steel mesh of the car's door and ventilated the interior, dropping the three men housed inside like cattle. But the car kept dropping.

"Down!" Reed shouted, rushing back for the stairs.

Turk followed on his heels as they raced down three flights in an open run. Reed listened for the snap of the cables against the wall, but the man at the top of the hotel had begun shouting into his loudspeaker again, and it was all Reed could hear.

They left the stairwell three floors down and rushed for the elevator, reaching the shaft just as the bottom of the car slid into view. This time they didn't wait for it to pass. Reed lunged forward and grabbed the latch of the metal gate, yanking it open just in time for it to catch against the floor. The car snapped to a halt, and the cables went rigid as a motor ground overhead.

Turk rushed past him and jumped into the car, grabbing the control module and flicking the switch from the down position to the stop position.

The motor shut down, and Reed wiped sweat from his forehead, still wheezing. He looked down at the bodies crumpled on the floor and identified the ornate patches of KPA officers, their uniforms now drenched with blood. Turk kicked their legs aside to make room for his feet, and Reed hurried in.

The gate clanged shut, and the latch dropped. Then Turk flipped the switch into the upward position, and the motor restarted.

A split second later, they were rising through the empty hotel, crawling toward the top and whatever lay waiting for them.

62

"Conn, Radio. Receiving flash traffic!"

Captain Reece O'Hara scooped up the radio handset and braced himself against an overhead rail. He already knew there was better than a fifty-fifty chance of what the radio officer was about to say.

"Radio, Conn. Aye."

"Conn, radio traffic is emergency action message. Recommend alert one."

O'Hara's heart skipped, but he didn't hesitate. He depressed the call button and spoke calmly into the mic. "Radio, Conn. Aye."

O'Hara exchanged a glance with Commander Jim Lampier, his executive officer. The look on Lampier's face told O'Hara they were sharing the same feelings.

This can't be happening.

But again, O'Hara didn't hesitate. "Chief of the watch! Sound general alarm. Man battle stations missile. Set condition 1SQ."

"Man battle stations missile, aye, sir. Setting condition 1SQ."

The flurry of action around the command hub of *Nebraska* was both instant and fluid. Officers raced to battle stations. Seamen took their seats behind controls. Lampier snapped orders for a sonar sweep around their current position.

O'Hara moved with the rest, stepping out of the conn and into a narrow ante room, where the emergency action message would be authenticated. Lampier joined him, followed by the weapons officer. Together, the three of them moved mechanically, retrieving order authentication codes from a safe and spreading them across a table next to the EAM. O'Hara stood back, waiting while Lampier and the weapon's officer compared their codes to the code listed on the message from Washington. It took only seconds, then Lampier looked up.

"Captain, the message authenticates."

"I concur, Captain," the weapons officer said.

O'Hara looked down at the authentication card in his hand, double-checking even though he already knew the digits matched. He nodded. "I concur. The message is authentic."

O'Hara scooped the printout off the table, moving past the authentication codes to the core of the directive. A momentary wash of relief passed over him when he completed the message, but that relief was short-lived.

Washington hadn't given the order to fire. But they wanted his finger on the trigger.

O'Hara passed the printout to Lampier, then swung through the low door back into the conn. The buzz of activity had subsided as the highly trained sailors around him completed their preemptive tasks and now awaited further orders.

O'Hara placed his hand on the overhead railing again and spoke calmly and professionally, a proud sailor of the finest Navy in the world. "Officer of the deck, proceed to launch depth, and prepare to hover."

63

Pyongyang

The elevator moved upward at one floor every two seconds, and Reed stood tense behind the gate, cradling his rifle. The blood saturating the floor had filled the bottom of the car and now puddled around his boots, flooding the small space with a metallic stench.

Reed watched each floor pass and saw nothing but more empty landings and hallways. Overhead, Jang was still busy shouting from the loudspeakers, his voice growing steadily louder the farther they climbed. Reed didn't understand the Korean, but he thought the maddened voice was repeating the same phrases again and again.

A call for war.

In the back of his mind, Reed knew Washington must be aware of the madness. Maybe their asset inside the city had alerted them of Jang's tirade and the outrage it had unleashed. Maybe even now ballistic missile submarines were preparing a first strike launch off the Korean Peninsula. Reed couldn't afford to care. The only thing that mattered was reaching the top of the Ryugyong in time.

"Twenty more floors," Turk muttered.

Lock and load.

Each floor passed in a steady blur, and Reed counted down in his mind, breathing evenly, ready to hurl himself through the gate and unleash hell on whatever lay in his path.

A full magazine was locked into the rifle, and one more remained in his chest rig, along with two grenades.

Enough.

The elevator began to slow. Turk put his thumb on the stop switch, then the car reached the next-to-last floor and came to an unexpected stop. Reed dropped to his knees, brandishing the rifle, then he grabbed the latch and hurled the door open.

The landing outside the car was paved in concrete, like everything else. But this high into the gathering point of the pyramid, the walls on every side had narrowed to a space barely fifty feet wide. As he hurtled out of the car, he saw half a dozen soldiers scattered around the room and standing near the windows with rifles slouched against their legs.

Reed opened fire, pressing his body against the elevator core to shield himself from being shot in the back. Next to him, Turk's boots slung a spray of blood across the floor as his AK joined the fight. Glass shattered, and LEDs went dark as four of the soldiers hit the floor in bullet-ridden heaps.

The last two were quicker. Instead of reaching for weapons, they opted to dive for cover behind padded chairs and upturned tables. Reed stitched a path of hot lead through windowpanes and across the furniture, chasing his target as the man disappeared behind a table. The pop of a handgun sounded from behind the table's edge, and Reed was forced to seek his own cover on the far side of the elevator shaft. He met Turk on the back side and kicked an empty magazine out of the rifle, loading in his final one.

"Find Jang!" Turk shouted. "I'll deal with this."

Reed ratcheted the AK's charged handle back to load a new round, then swung to the left. He'd already marked a stairwell, and just as he turned, another KPA soldier spilled down the steps. Reed cut him down and leapt over his body, racing to the top of the stairs and turning the corner just in time to gun down another two soldiers. Jang's voice had long since gone silent, and Reed detected shouting through ringing ears. He reached the floor above, where he was greeted by silence.

Unlike the previous floor, the room Reed found himself in wasn't triangular to match the footprint of the Ryugyong. Instead, it was circular, like a giant donut orbiting around the stairwell he just exited. The windows on the outside were curved to match the outline of the donut, moving in at an angle to meet a ceiling that was slightly smaller in diameter than the floor.

A rotating restaurant, Reed thought. Like the Space Needle. Only this one was unfinished, like everything else about the hotel.

And it was also empty. Jang wasn't there.

Reed stooped to retrieve a fresh magazine from one of the dead soldiers, then shouldered the rifle and jogged around the donut. The entrance to another set of stairs faced him on the far side of the donut's core, but long before he reached for the next step, a storm of automatic gunfire showered the floor. Reed jerked back, bracing himself against the wall as chunks of lead blasted across the floor in an endless hail. There were at least three rifles, maybe more.

Reed shifted the AK to his left hand, pulling another grenade from his chest rig and jerking the pin with his teeth. He released the spoon and counted to three, then flung the device up the stairwell as hard as he could.

The grenade detonated with a clap of thunder, and the gunfire abruptly ceased. A single scream flooded the stairwell, but Reed didn't wait for the soldiers to regroup. He raced up the stairs past a waterfall of blood, orbiting the corner and clamping down on the AK's trigger without waiting to see who stood in his path.

Two soldiers lay across the steps, blown down by the grenade. A third scrambled across the floor, one arm limp, the other fumbling for a pistol. Reed put him down, then crossed into the next level of the hotel.

The floor was another donut, but slightly smaller than the first. Guns popped to Reed's left. He ducked back into the stairwell and pulled his final grenade, yanking the pin and flinging it toward the sound of panicked shouts. The weapon detonated with an ear-splitting blast, and glass shattered. A roar of wind ripped into the room, and Reed left the stairwell, orbiting left and already opening fire.

Two bodies lay next to a shattered glass panel. Reed stepped across the bodies to confront the last two men in the room. One was almost as tall as Reed, a hat sliding off the back of a bald head. His face gleamed with sweat and fear as he brandished a pistol, popping off crazed shots at the American marching toward him.

Reed fired from the hip, spraying his chest with slugs. The man collapsed, dropping the handgun, and leaving only the final figure backing away from Reed, his outstretched palms held up in panicked fear.

General Jang Bon-hwa. Reed recognized him in an instant from the mugshot. He was short, almost petite, with greying hair and a fat, flabby face. He wore a KPA uniform that matched those of the dead men surrounding him, but his was decorated with red ribbons and gold stars.

Tacky glamour marking his rank.

Reed lowered the gun and stepped across the final body, kicking the pistol away. Jang scrambled into a run, but as he reached the backside of the donut, he slammed face-first into the hulking form of Rufus Turkman.

Turk grabbed him by the collar and raked him across the face with a lightning left hook. Jang screamed, and blood sprayed from his nose as his head snapped back. Reed reached him and drove the butt of his AK into Jang's right kidney, hard enough to break bone. Jang crumpled. Reed caught him by the collar and dragged him, kicking and screaming, back to the table laden with radio equipment.

"Watch the door," Reed said, throwing Jang to the ground at the foot of the table. Turk assumed a position at the top of the stairs and lifted his rifle while Reed placed a boot onto Jang's chest and pressed down until something snapped and the general thrashed in pain.

Reed grabbed the nearest radio handset off the table and dropped it next to Jang's head. "Call your people off! Cancel the launch!"

Jang babbled in Korean, his hands flailing in a desperate attempt to dislodge Reed's boot, but it was a useless gesture.

Reed pressed down again, and Jang howled.

"I *know* you speak English, you scum! You worked in Beijing. Moscow. You wanna pretend you don't speak half a dozen languages?"

Jang continued to babble and flail.

Reed kicked him in the ribs and pointed to the radio with the muzzle of his AK. "Call off the launch!"

After more babbling and tears, Reed lost patience. He drove his boot into Jang's chin, hard enough to stun him, then laid the AK on the table and dropped to his knees. In seconds, he yanked Jang's uniform belt from around his waist, then looped it around his left ankle and held the long end. Jang's head rolled. He seemed dazed and disoriented, but as soon as Reed grabbed him by the shoulder and dragged him toward the shattered window, he got the picture.

"No! Don't drop me!" Jang screamed, suddenly speaking English.

Reed ignored him, shoving the radio into his hand and hauling him all the way to the window frame. Shards of broken glass tore into Jang's back as Reed pushed him out, still clutching the long end of the belt.

Jang fought like hell, his arms overhanging the precipice. He scrambled to grab onto something, but there was nothing but more razor-sharp glass.

Reed put his boot between Jang's legs and pushed. Jang flopped outside, then slammed hard against the panel directly beneath the window.

"Talk!" Reed screamed, gripping the belt with one hand. "Give the order!"

Jang dropped the radio handset, and it slid down the sloping side of the first floor donut glass before vanishing into the darkness. A thousand feet below, Reed saw military truck headlights as the KPA mobilized throughout the city. Sirens screamed, and a pair of jets tore through the sky overhead.

And he saw fire—the rise of a mushroom cloud.

His son, vaporized in a second at the hands of a madman.

Reed held out his hand. "Radio!"

Turk scrambled to pass him a new handset. Reed hit the key to make sure it worked and was rewarded by an electronic chirp, followed by a Korean voice asking a question.

"You drop this, I drop you!" Reed shouted. He tossed the radio toward Jang. The general floundered to catch it, his body rigid with panic. It almost fell through his hands, and the belt slid a couple inches between Reed's fingers.

"No!" Jang screamed. "Don't drop me!"

"You've got three seconds! Call off the missiles, now!"

Jang's hands shook, but he found the call key and depressed it. The radio chirped. The guy on the other end repeated his question.

Jang screamed in Korean, a series of panicked, repeated sentences.

Reed looked to Turk. The big soldier stood next to him, glancing between the mouth of the stairwell and the pocket translator the CIA had given them.

"We didn't hear you!" Reed shouted, voluntarily releasing another four inches of the belt.

Jang thrashed and cried. He shouted another three sentences into the radio.

The translator blinked, then loaded a crude translation.

Turk nodded.

Reed dropped the belt.

Jang screamed all the way down, sliding off the edge of the donut before free-falling a thousand feet between two spread wings of the hotel. Reed stood in the roaring wind and watched him flail and flop in slow motion, fading in the darkness, and then finding the ground.

Reed wiped rainwater from his nose and took a step back. His left hand was cut and bleeding from the belt, and his body was charged with adrenaline, but one way or the other, it was done.

"Message Wolf," Reed said.

Turk was already digging through his backpack, retrieving the messenger. He hit the button to turn it on, pressing with his thumb and waiting. The device didn't power on, and instead, a red light flashed across the screen in the shape of a battery.

Turk looked up, his face washing white. "It's dead."

64

The phone on Wolfgang's desk had rung five times in the last eight minutes, but he didn't have an answer for the voice on the other end. The Prosecution Force had gone dark, leaving him with nothing but a crushing feeling of doom weighing down on his mind. Their last message still gleamed on the screen, offering an explanation for their silence but doing nothing to assuage his anxiety.

PF: BE ADVISED. BATTERY ALMOST DEAD. BACKUP FAILED.

Wolfgang slammed his fist against the metal desk, then he chewed absently on one knuckle, leaning back in the chair and willing a message to pop through. The phone rang, but Wolfgang ignored it, just staring. Pleading. Even contemplating lying to the person on the phone.

But he couldn't. The risk was too great.

Wolfgang snatched up the receiver. "What?"

"Any update?" CIA Director O'Brien's voice was ice cold and collected as always, but it still made Wolfgang want to put his fist through the wall.

"No," he snapped. "Nothing."

"Wolfgang." O'Brien's tone dropped a notch, somehow also dropping in temperature. "I'm about to brief the president. Do you know where she is?"

"Of course not."

"She's sitting at a desk next to the nuclear football. Do you know what that means?"

Wolfgang slammed his palm against the desk. "No, you listen to me, O'Brien. You tell her to *chill* out. They'll get it done. You hear me? They'll get it done!"

"That's not your call, Dr. Pierce. You've got five more minutes."

O'Brien hung up, and Wolfgang laid his fingers on the keyboard. He shot off one last panicked message and prayed that it found its way to Reed and Turk.

W: US NUCLEAR STRIKE IMMINENT. HAUL ASS.

65

Maggie watched the screen on the wall in morbid fascination as it displayed a satellite image of the missile-launch site north of Pyongyang. She could clearly make out the heat signatures of trucks moving toward the site. In the deeper shadows sheltered by the curvature of the mountains, she thought she saw a series of low humps in the ground—launch silos ready to spit nuclear annihilation into the atmosphere.

"Ma'am, we need a deadline," Yellin said. "We've got two boomers hovering at launch depth, but it will take time to spin up their missiles. If those trucks reach the silos—"

Maggie held up a hand. She'd already decided for herself that the moment those forces reached the launch site, she would have to make a decision. There wouldn't be another option.

Two miles. Maybe three. The short convoy moved quickly through the mountains, doubtlessly carrying orders from Jang. Maybe about to take the silo by force, if the soldiers waiting there protested. And then it would be done. A launch would be inevitable.

A part of her wondered why Jang had made his intentions for nuclear war so obvious, but in a way, it made sense. He was a madman. He didn't really care so much about the victory as he did the fight. He wanted it bloody.

The trucks ground closer to the silos.

Major Sullivan stood at attention at her elbow, and a single tear slipped down Jill's face. It was like watching a train wreck in slow motion, knowing what was about to happen and having nothing to do to stop it.

The trucks closed to within a mile of the silo, and Maggie swallowed over a dry throat. The Biscuit stuck to her sweaty palm. She had never laid it down after giving the order for the Pentagon to prepare the strike.

Somewhere on the other side of the globe, two ballistic missile submarines hovered just beneath the surface, only minutes away from punching before they were punched.

And then . . . what? How would Russia respond? How would China?

The trucks now closed to within a quarter mile, gaining speed.

Maggie slowly turned to Sullivan. She licked her lips and opened her mouth to speak.

And then a flash of orange illuminated the screen, and the silos simply vanished.

66

Admiral James Sandfort stood at the bridge and stared across a black sky toward the distant, invisible Korean Peninsula. The storm that had raged for the past six hours across the ocean had blasted his flight deck with rainwater, ravaging the launching aircraft with gusts of wind so strong it was almost unsafe to launch at all. Visibility was so poor Sandfort could barely see the bow of the mighty carrier, and the waves crashing against its hull were strong enough to send tremors through the bridge.

But Sandfort and the crowd of officers surrounding him were unmoved. They'd spent the last decade training for a moment like this, and they knew exactly what to do. *Nimitz* pointed directly into the wind, its nuclear-powered engines churning just strong enough to hold them in place as wave after wave of F/A-18E Super Hornet fighters screamed into the air and established flight patrols along the North Korean coast.

Under normal circumstances, an operation like this would be called a show of force. An intimidation technique. But at DEFCON 2, with the United States only a breath away from advancing to DEFCON 1 and nuclear war, it was no exercise. Having those jets in the air was all about ensuring that the moment North Korean bombers headed south toward Seoul, or east toward Japan, they were blown out of the sky like piñatas.

"Admiral! I've got conventional missile strikes north of Pyongyang."

Sandfort's head snapped away from the glass, toward the radio deck where a half dozen of the most highly trained radar, sonar, and communication specialists in the world crowded around banks of multi-million-dollar equipment. He moved quickly through the ranks of officers, reaching the lieutenant at the end of the line.

The man pulled his headset off and pointed to the screen. "Multiple strikes across the Korean west coast, sir, including Sino-ri missile base. Somebody's wiping them out!"

Sandfort squinted at the screen. "What the hell?"

The signatures on the radar weren't lying. Some manner of massive air strike was underway, and it wasn't American. It wasn't South Korean, either. Sandfort would be advised of any South Korean military activity.

"Do we have any aircraft on display?"

"Negative, sir. Just strikes."

No aircraft.

Then it might not be an air strike at all. It might be a missile strike. But not a nuclear one, which meant . . .

"Air Boss!" Sandfort snapped, moving back to the front of the bridge. "Call back those fighters! I want all of our planes to stand down."

67

Pyongyang

Reed saw the flash of light from the top of the Ryugyong—far to the north, hazy through the light rain. The sky glowed faintly orange, but the spot was so distant he couldn't be sure what he was seeing. A nuclear hit?

Turk saw it, too, but there was no time to wait around and find out. If nuclear warheads were headed for Pyongyang, he and Turk would never escape in time. But they still had to try.

"Let's move!" Reed snatched up a fresh magazine from one of the fallen KPA soldiers as he raced around the donut and took the stairs two at a time.

Turk followed, leaping bodies and rushing all the way to the first level of the rotating restaurant, where the service elevator waited. Reed flicked the switch to the down position as Turk slammed the gate closed. The elevator dropped quickly, clacking with every passing floor.

"How long to the pickup?" Reed said.

Turk consulted the iPad, brushing away a low battery warning. Reed saw the alert.

"Thirty-six miles," Turk said. "Pickup in sixty minutes."

Reed checked his watch.

Sixty minutes. That was assuming *Louisville* had successfully navigated this far into the Yellow Sea without being blown away. Assuming Gagliardi and his crew had arranged a way to pick them up safely. Assuming the entire idiotic extraction request hadn't been called off by Washington, leaving them there to rot.

And they still had to rendezvous with Gok, Sinju, and Ye-jun.

"We'll take a military truck," Reed said. "Pedal to the metal and pray."

Turk flipped the iPad off. Without the messenger, they had no way of knowing whether Gag and his men would be there or not. They just had to trust and roll the dice.

Floors continued to flash by, and Reed set his watch to countdown from sixty minutes. He double-checked the AK one more time and thought about the chaos he'd heard from outside the Ryugyong. The KPA forces clogging the city were in a state of panic and outrage, but Reed hadn't detected a whole lot of order in their deployments or behavior. He figured Jang had clogged the city streets with soldiers, precisely to cause chaos and disorder, which meant the KPA wouldn't be in the best position to block their escape. Disguised in a military truck, they might be okay if they could only escape the city.

The elevator clanged to a stop, and Reed and Turk burst out to take the stairs. As they approached the wide atrium, Reed could hear the desperate screams outside mixed with blaring sirens. It sounded like total chaos, and when they stormed out of the stairwell and into the bloody lobby, his suspicions were confirmed.

The bodies he and Turk had gunned down only half an hour previously still lay strewn around busted bottles and scattered playing cards. Through the long hallways leading to open doors, feet pounded on pavement and desperate screams reached toward the sky. It was as though the entire city was engulfed in explosive grief, overlaid by the blare of air-raid sirens.

Riots, he thought. A blessing and a curse.

"Out back!" Reed shouted.

They broke into a run down the same hall they'd entered from, Turk favoring his left leg as the bullet wound from the previous year ignited under strain. Reed put one arm on his back and pushed him forward.

The AK swung from Reed's left hand, and he pushed Turk harder with his right. Sweat dripped down his face, and the AK slammed against his ribcage as it hung from its sling, but the burn in his lungs fueled him.

Faster. Move now.

They reached the doors and stopped, Turk wheezing as Reed swept the patio outside for signs of the KPA. The four men they'd killed while infiltrating still lay in puddles of red, but no other soldiers had come to take their place. The noise flooding the city was overwhelming. Women screamed. Soldiers shouted. Random gunshots snapped. And still, the sirens persisted.

Complete chaos.

"Find a truck!" Reed shouted.

He and Turk moved automatically to the left, toward the nearest street. Once they burst through the low trees and hedges, absolute anarchy greeted them. The building across the street burned, and a wrecked car was plowed against a light pole, the radiator still steaming. Half a block away, a cluster of citizens knelt on the ground, sobbing and raising their hands to the sky.

"What the . . ." Turk breathed.

Reed jabbed his rifle to the right. They broke into another run, clearing the block and turning left. In the distance were authoritative shouts of what Reed presumed to be soldiers, and he could only hope they found a truck before those troops found them.

Skidding to a stop near the next corner, they both raised their rifles and moved in unison, Reed clearing left and Turk clearing right.

The soldiers crowded around the face of an apartment block fired guns into the air as they shouted at the sobbing citizens on the sidewalk. There seemed to be some effort underway to corral the locals back into their homes, but nobody was moving, and the soldiers' commands were obscured by the sirens.

Reed noted it all, but his attention moved almost immediately to the truck parked twenty yards beyond the crowd, its engine running, diesel fumes clouding the air.

"There!" Reed shouted, breaking into a run.

Turk followed him, still brandishing his rifle as they charged down the sidewalk. The KPA had their backs turned, but one of the sobbing civilians saw them and cried out in panicked Korean.

The soldiers turned straight into a wall of lead, dropping like bowling pins as Reed and Turk continued to run. The last of them hit the dirt next to the sidewalk, and the desperate locals turned to run, fleeing into their homes.

Reed rushed right by them, leaping the bodies and grabbing the driver's door. The truck was old, and its bed was covered in canvas. Reed folded his big frame behind the wheel of the cramped cab and stomped on the clutch, finding first gear and lurching forward.

Turk rode in the passenger seat. He fumbled with the window crank, then gave up and knocked the glass out with the butt of his rifle before shoving the weapon's muzzle through the hole.

"Navigate!" Reed called, moving away from downtown and onto an open street.

Smoke flooded his path from the burning building they'd passed earlier, and he plowed over an unidentified object, keeping his foot on the accelerator the entire time.

"Next left!" Turk called, fumbling with the iPad. "Take the highway."

At the intersection ahead were signs printed in Korean and another cluster of soldiers. Reed didn't bother braking, pulling the truck through the turn and into a light flow of traffic. Other military trucks joined by a smattering of aged sedans slammed on their brakes as he rammed through.

"Next right! Pulgun Street!"

Turk could've saved the street name. Reed wasn't bothering with signs. A stopped truck blocked his path at the next intersection, and he jerked the wheel, hopping up onto the sidewalk. The corner of the truck shredded through bushes and obliterated a park bench, then Reed turned again. He screamed past the parked truck and onto Pulgun. Tires bit the pavement, and the truck lurched as he left the curb. Turk held onto the dash and dropped the iPad.

"What next?" Reed shouted.

Turk ducked to retrieve the device. The highway ahead lay mostly clear, with a few cars pulled to the side of the road where more civilians knelt on the sidewalk with their hands in the air.

"Bear right after the bridge!" Turk called.

Reed saw the bridge, but also the line of military trucks headed toward them in the opposing lane. As they drew closer, the driver behind the lead truck shouted and pointed, then grabbed the wheel.

"Take him out!" Reed called.

Turk sprayed the oncoming truck with lead. The front left tire blew open even as the driver fought to turn and cut off their path, then a string of bullets shattered the windshield, and the driver collapsed over the steering wheel.

The truck had crossed the middle of the road and now blocked half of their path. Reed hugged the side wall of the bridge and downshifted, stomping on the gas. The truck roared forward, and Turk braced against the dash again.

Then they hit the bottleneck, their right fender slamming into the bridge wall while the left tore past the stopped truck. Gunshots pinged off their front bumper, but by the time the disoriented soldiers in the convoy took aim, Reed and Turk had already passed them.

Reed left the bridge, taking an exit and shifting up again. "How far?"

"Fifteen miles to rendezvous. Twenty-five to the beach."

Reed checked his watch.

Forty minutes.

68

Gagliardi stood near the bow of the submarine. The three other SEALs around him were dressed in full-black with black camouflage paint on their faces. They busied themselves double-checking gear and loading extra magazines full of steel-core, green-tipped ammunition.

No hint of fear marred their fluid movements, but Gag could feel the tension in the air. They'd be fools not to feel it. This extraction would be unlike anything they'd attempted before.

The door at the end of the room groaned open, and Captain Ramirez appeared. He surveyed the working men, then tilted his head to one side.

Gagliardi stepped to a darkened corner, a set of night-vision goggles in his hand, his fingers busy adjusting the strap.

Ramirez spoke quietly. "You sure about this?"

Gag looked back at his men. Truth be told, he wasn't sure. His hare-brained scheme to rush five passengers off the Korean coast was dicey on a good day. At DEFCON 2, it felt more like madness.

But he couldn't leave Reed and Turk behind, even if he didn't really know them. Even if he highly suspected that both men worked closer to the black side of black ops than he might be comfortable with. He had seen the gleam of a warrior's courage in their eyes, and he couldn't leave them to die.

"Positive."

Ramirez nodded softly, pursing his lips and still watching the others. Then he faced Gag. "Twenty minutes. That's all I can give you. Then we dive—one way or the other."

"I understand."

Ramirez smacked him on the arm. "Good luck, Gag."

He disappeared back toward the conn, leaving Gagliardi standing in the cramped room and looking down at the night vision, thinking he'd need all the luck he could get.

69

"What was that?"

Maggie was the first to challenge the flash of orange light, quickly followed by successive blasts rippling across the screen. A flutter of activity rippled around the room, with military aides reaching for phones and officers shouting orders.

"Was that us?" Maggie demanded.

Yellin didn't answer immediately. He dialed a phone and held an abrupt conversation, then slammed the receiver home. "It wasn't us. Somebody hit multiple military installations with a barrage of cruise missiles."

"Somebody? *Who*?"

Yellin only shook his head, then returned to the phone. Maggie gnawed her thumbnail and watched as the screen zoomed out, still orbiting around the general Pyongyang area. Whatever had hit the missile site, it wasn't nuclear, but it had made a mess.

"Did the South Koreans launch a strike?" Jill demanded, her squeaky voice assuming an authoritative lilt.

"Not possible," General Porter said. "They'd need our authorization."

"What about Japan?"

"Same problem," Porter said. "Plus, we would've detected the launch. Whoever hit that missile base was close."

Yellin slammed the phone down and snapped his fingers. "Quiet! Everybody."

He hit a button on the display remote and switched to a view of his laptop screen.

Maggie was looking at another satellite map with heat signatures marking a column of vehicles moving south along a highway, but she couldn't tell where. "What am I looking at?"

Yellin looked up from the laptop. "It's a highway just north of Dangdon, China, right on the Chinese/North Korean border. And you're looking at a column of Chinese troops moving south."

It was the last thing Maggie expected. "Lisa!" she snapped. "Get me Ambassador—" Her voice was cut off by the sharp ring of a phone.

Gorman lifted the receiver and spoke quietly. Her back stiffened, and she hit the mute button. "Ma'am, it's President Chen."

70

Not long after leaving the outskirts of Pyongyang, the highway became eerily empty. Reed had expected a fight leaving the capital city, and he almost got one. But only a few kilometers west of downtown, desolation consumed the landscape, with only occasional cars passing them on the lonely highway.

Every one of those cars—more battered sedans and a couple government vehicles—raced by without so much as pausing to challenge them. Reed thought the military truck had something to do with that, but he couldn't deny that he had drastically underestimated the panic that had swept the city following whatever announcement Jang had made.

"I think Cho's dead," Reed said. "Or at least, they think he's dead."

"What? Why?"

Reed shook his head. "I remember seeing a news story years ago when Cho Jong-il passed away. This is how they reacted. Total panic. Grief. Chaos. Except, a madman wasn't screaming at them from the top of a hotel. I can only imagine this is worse."

Turk looked over his shoulder, back toward the city. "Madness . . ."

"Their dictator is their god. How would you feel if your god died?"

"If he can die, he isn't a god."

Reed didn't argue the point. He pressed harder on the gas and watched as the speedometer bobbed around the 100 kilometers per hour mark. It was as fast as the old truck would go, and the fuel gauge was slipping dangerously close to empty.

"How much farther?"

Turk checked the iPad. "Five or six miles."

"If they aren't there, we'll give them five minutes," Reed said. "Then we're out. All right?"

He met Turk's gaze and saw the frustration there, but his battle buddy didn't argue. He just nodded.

The highway wound on, and the urban sprawl of only minutes before was now fully replaced by fields and rural neighborhoods. Reed couldn't hear anything over the roar of the truck, but in the distance, smoke rose over a small village, and there were silhouettes of people gathered on the ground between the houses.

Word travels fast.

At last, Turk pointed to a dark spot sheltered by a grove of trees, and Reed pulled off. He kept the motor running and surveyed the area through the shattered windshield. The rain had now ceased altogether, replaced by wind that tore at tall grass and pulled against tree limbs.

Reed had a bad feeling. He couldn't put his finger on it, but something in his gut made him uneasy. He kept one hand on the gearshift and the other on the wheel, then checked his watch. Twenty-five minutes remaining and still ten miles to go.

Turk reached for the door, and Reed put a hand on his arm. "Two minutes."

Turk climbed out of the truck with his rifle in tow. He stood next to the road and peered into the shadows, then offered a soft whistle.

Nothing happened. The uneasiness in the back of Reed's mind grew. He placed his hand on the CZ pistol still holstered on his hip and slipped the safety catch off.

Turk whistled again. The grass moved against the wind, and a dark head popped out between the brush. Reed's fingers tightened, but as the silhouette moved out of the shrubs, he recognized Sinju. The beautiful

Korean woman was battered, her face still swollen from the prison camp beatings. Her shirt was torn, and one forearm was bandaged. But as she stepped toward Turk, she beckoned to the grass, and Gok Chin-ho moved out of the shadows, followed quickly by Ye-jun.

Reed relaxed, releasing the CZ. Turk called for them to hurry, then raced around to the back of the truck. Reed waited while his passengers clambered aboard, then he heard a stiff pounding on the truck's cab.

He shifted into gear and dumped the clutch, lurching ahead again. The iPad in the seat next to him guided him forward with a blue line leading straight to the coast, but there were no more turns to make. It was all ahead full to the ocean.

He worked the truck back up to top speed, watching the fuel needle flick around the empty mark. There might be fifty miles left in the tank, or only five. It was impossible to say.

Reed chose not to think about it, focusing on the road ahead. For the first time in hours, he allowed himself to think about Banks and little Davy and the house in the hills, surrounded by peaceful streets. About being home.

Almost there.

He pushed his foot harder against the gas and checked the iPad. Seven more miles.

The uneasiness returned to Reed's mind, and a thought, elusive and vague, fluttered through the back of his head. Like remembering a melody but forgetting the name of a song. Or seeing an actress in a movie and knowing you'd seen her before but having no idea where.

Something was off. Something didn't add up.

Reed laid the AK across his lap and weaved around a rut. The engine coughed as he hurtled down a hill, and again he saw the fuel needle jump. The suspension creaked, and the hard seat slammed into his tailbone with every bump.

And still, the voice in the back of his head persisted.

I'm exhausted. Paranoid. It's nothing.

At last, the black horizon ahead fell away, and the truck started down a final hill. Far ahead, Reed thought he could make out the coast, but with the thick cloud cover overhead, he wasn't sure. The iPad indicated he had another mile to go, but just then, the engine choked, rumbled, and died.

Reed cursed and shifted into neutral, releasing the brake and allowing the truck to coast. He hit the ignition and listened to another grumble, followed by a series of coughs, but the motor wouldn't start.

The truck rolled on, carried by gravity toward the bottom of the hill. Ahead, the road leveled out, and low heaps of sand covered in grass were lined up next to the asphalt. They were close.

The truck coasted to a stop with half a mile to go. Reed checked his watch and saw six minutes remaining on the clock. He kicked the door open and jumped out, carrying the iPad in one hand and the AK in the other. Turk met him at the back, confusion clouding his face.

"Out of gas," Reed said. "Let's move!"

Turk dropped the truck's tailgate and beckoned to the Goks. The family moved cautiously.

"Move!" Reed grabbed Sinju's hand and helped her out, then beckoned toward the beach. "Run! Let's go."

It was impossible for the Goks to run. Sinju forced a wounded hobble, and Gok staggered along supported by Turk, but Ye-jun managed little better than a fast walk. She kept looking over her shoulder, back up the road, her face flooded with terror.

Reed figured she had reason to be afraid. The KPA might be a disorganized, leaderless mess, but that still left the secret police—or a nuclear blast—to worry about.

"Move!" Reed hissed. "Let's go!"

He pushed with an open palm, glancing down at the iPad to catch a last glimpse of the rendezvous point before the screen blinked and went black.

Dead battery.

Reed shoved the device into the small of his back, then broke into a run. He left Turk to shepherd the Goks and followed the navigation path by memory. Two hundred yards away, the white crest of a wave crashed toward the shore. The road twisted and ran along the coastline, leaving him to fight through tangled weeds and low sand dunes toward the Yellow Sea.

The rendezvous rested in a shallow cove, surrounded on both sides by sandy fingers and scrub brush. To the best of Reed's memory, that spot lay ahead and to the right, but without the iPad, he couldn't be sure. They would have to reach the coast and search it out on foot.

Reed's watch beeped, and he looked down to see 00:00 displayed across the screen. Turk and the Goks were still fifty yards behind, fighting along the narrow makeshift trail he'd blazed through the sand. Reed gave them time to catch up, then gestured along the coast.

"This way! We're looking for a cove."

Reed took point, craning his neck to see over sand dunes and waving columns of grass. But that feeling in the back of his mind had returned, dragging him back. It was too vague to identify, but too persistent to ignore.

He looked back over the long column, tracing past Gok's exhausted face, to Sinju's swollen cheeks, to Ye-jun, looking over her shoulder again, her hands twisting knots into the tail of her shirt.

And then it finally clicked.

"Down! Down!" Reed shouted.

They hit the sand the same moment gunfire erupted from fifty yards back.

71

Sand exploded into the air as Reed huddled behind a low dune, crouched in with Sinju at his side. Gok and Turk lay ten feet away in a similar depression, with Ye-jun rolled into a fetal position at their feet.

Reed heard shouts in Korean between the shots, and he risked a swing to the left to return fire. Managing only six or eight rounds before being forced back into cover by another string of automatic fire, he huddled in place and called to Turk. "Grenade!"

"I'm out!" Turk shouted back, pressing his rifle over the top of the dune and firing blindly at the enemy position.

Ye-jun moved on her hands and knees, tears streaming down her face as she approached the gap between their two dunes. She made eye contact with Reed, and hatred glared at him as harsh as the gunfire ripping through the air.

Then Ye-jun stood.

"No!" Reed shouted.

It was too late. Ye-jun raised both hands and waved toward the soldiers, shouting out in Korean. She stepped out from behind the sand dune, her voice pleading, her arms up.

For just a second, the gunfire paused, almost as though the shooters were hesitating or changing mags. Reed watched as Ye-jun walked out, almost in slow motion, and he knew . . .

He knew the voice in the back of his head had been right and that he had been a fool.

But so had Ye-jun.

A fresh storm of lead erupted from the entrenched Koreans, and Ye-jun was cut down in the blink of an eye. A dozen rounds shredded her torso and knocked her back as though she'd been hit by a sledgehammer. Blood soaked the sand, and Sinju screamed. Gok scrambled over the dunes toward his wife and almost immediately caught a round in the shoulder, hurling him down. Turk grabbed him by the leg and pulled him back as the endless blast of lead continued.

Reed couldn't see anything. A dust storm filled the air, mixed with shouts from the advancing soldiers and the irrefutable reality that they were all about to die, right there on the beach. Seconds away from extraction.

Reed gritted his teeth and swapped in his last mag. He rammed a fresh round into the chamber and braced himself, ready to roll left and let them have it, taking as many of them with him as he could.

He made eye contact with Turk, and his battle buddy nodded once, then tucked the stock of his AK into his shoulder and prepared to roll also. But then there was another sound, sharper and more surgical than the blare of the AKs, though every bit as persistent. It was a sound Reed knew well. The voice of NATO caliber 5.56.

The SEALs had arrived.

Moving from over the dunes, the four American warriors slid into the depression around Reed and Turk, rifles raised, their faces obscured by night-vision goggles. M4A1 rifles against their shoulders blazed hellfire and fury toward the Korean position, cutting them down like cornstalks amid screams and silenced AKs.

Reed recognized the bold jawline of Gagliardi just as the SEAL leader reached for the grenade launcher mounted beneath his rifle's barrel and shouted to his team.

"Frag out!"

The launcher popped, and a concussive explosion detonated from the

ranks of the Koreans. Most of the rifles fell silent, and two of the other
SEALs shouted in unison as they flung hand grenades. "Smoke!"

Gagliardi knelt next to Reed and shook his shoulder. "You good, man?"

Disoriented, Reed stretched his mouth open to clear his ringing ears,
and he nodded. "Nice of you to show up!"

Gag hauled him up by the arm.

"The old man is wounded," Reed said. "Woman is dead."

"Copy that. Solomon, get the old guy. Leave the body. Let's roll!"

Sinju shouted and rushed toward her mother's body. Turk caught her
and shook his head, urging her to stay calm. The column of SEALs gathered Gok's body and headed back through the sand. Turk pulled a sobbing
Sinju along with him, and Reed closed in to cover their rear.

Behind him were the shouts of dying Koreans and the continued pops
of desperate gunfire, but the fight was over.

Reed ran to catch up, slogging through the sand and over a hill. They
moved only a hundred yards before Gagliardi led his men down a slope to a
cove. Reed's vision was blurred by dirt and strain, but he thought he saw a
zodiac inflatable boat pulled up onto the beach, a strange metal superstructure built over the top.

"Montgomery!" Gag called. "Haul ass, man!"

Reed sprinted the last twenty yards, throwing himself into the boat just
as Rutkins pulled the cord on the tiller motor.

It roared to life, and Shattler shoved off, jumping into the bow and spinning his finger in the air. "Let's move!"

Reed settled into the middle of the small craft, looking up at the superstructure. Four steel legs bolted to the rigid frame of the craft before
meeting five or six feet over his head and attaching to a giant metal loop
about five feet across. The entire system looked to be improvised, with
rough metal work and hasty welds, but Reed had a pretty good idea what
the design was intended for, and he didn't like it.

Rutkins cranked the motor to full throttle, and the zodiac's nose lifted
toward the sky. Sinju and Gok lay in the bottom of the boat, the young
woman cradling her father. Despite the bruises on her cheeks, it was her
eyes that held the most pain. Pain and loss. And Reed knew why. He had
been a fool not to see it from the start. It had been Ye-jun, not Sinju, who

sold them out at the radio tower. Sometime while they were lying low at Gok's house, she'd contacted the Ministry of State Security and turned them in.

But the MMS hadn't rushed to capture the two Americans. They'd waited, biding their time and even calling the watcher off to give Reed and Turk time to slip away and then lead them right to Gok. Ye-jun had probably acted in fear, trusting her own government more than two unknown Americans. So, even after they rescued Sinju and Gok from the prison camp, Ye-jun sold them out a second time, arranging the ambush at the beach and dying for it.

Reed should've seen it all along, but after he was convinced of Sinju's loyalty, he had been too preoccupied with the Jang mission to think again about the watcher or the ambush at the radio tower.

Stupid.

His thoughts were shattered by white light flashing across the zodiac. Over the whine of the vessel's motor, a deeper roar reached his ears, and he traced the source of the spotlight to the bow of a patrol boat rocketing toward them, only two hundred yards away and closing.

Gagliardi and Solomon responded automatically, lifting their rifles and unleashing a quick burst at the craft. The spotlight shattered and went dark, but the patrol boat roared on, and then the chatter of machine-gun fire split the air.

Rutkins jerked the tiller, and the zodiac swung hard to the left, almost slinging Turk out of the bow. He grabbed onto the metal superstructure as Gagliardi shouted into a radio.

"Any day now!"

Reed caught himself on the edge of the boat and fumbled with his AK. Water exploded only a few yards away as a blast of the patrol boat's machine gun opened up again. The zodiac hit a wave and shot upward, then nosed down and raced into a trough.

"Gag!" Reed shouted. "Tell me you've got a plan here!"

Gag looked back from the bow, most of his face still obscured by goggles, but Reed saw his lips rise into a crazy grin, and that's when he heard the chopper.

The Seahawk rushed downward like a diving eagle, a heavy machine gun unleashing on the patrol craft. The pursuing boat turned hard right to avoid the blast, and the Seahawk continued its plunge toward the water.

Reed saw the tow hook bolted to the bottom of the chopper, and his fears about the rigged superstructure were confirmed. Rutkins killed the motor, and the four SEALs reached for something to hold on to.

Gagliardi shouted, "Hang tight, jarheads!"

Then the Seahawk struck. The expert pilot sitting behind the controls guided the big chopper in with the grace and ease of a retiree parking his Corvette in the back of a grocery store parking lot. The tow hook slid through the giant loop, and Gagliardi shouted into his radio. Then the boat beneath them snatched upward, and they hurtled into the sky amid a roar of rotor wash.

72

The Seahawk lifted the zodiac as though it were made of paper, and in a split second, they were racing out to sea at over a hundred miles per hour. The force of the wind beating down on them drove Reed into the bottom of the boat as the SEALs clung to the superstructure and howled like drunk frat boys on a Friday night. Horizon and water blended together, and Reed just lay there and breathed, happy to be alive.

Within minutes of leaving the water, the Seahawk was setting them down again, the pilot sliding the tow hook free with just as much grace and efficiency as he had snagged it. Then the chopper turned and raced toward South Korea at full throttle, rushing back to safety before a Chinese or North Korean aircraft could say otherwise.

Reed sat up in the bottom of the zodiac and looked over the torn and tossing water, searching for *Louisville*. The attack sub was nowhere to be seen, but the SEALs were busy starting the motor again. They sat for about twenty seconds, then Reed saw something immense split the waves fifty yards ahead.

The hulking bulk of USS *Louisville* broke through like a soda bottle bobbing to the surface, water washing off its bow, not a light to be seen anywhere on the hull. Rutkins cranked the throttle, and the zodiac raced toward the sub, breaking over waves and not slowing until the rubber bow hit the curved nose of the submarine and they slid right onto the deck.

"Let's go!" Gagliardi shouted.

Reed scrambled to his feet, tossing the AK into the ocean and helping Sinju onto the slick, steel deck. A hatch popped open just forward of the conning tower, and a sailor beckoned urgently.

Reed looked over his shoulder in time to watch the SEALs kick the zodiac back into the water, then unloaded on it with their rifles. In mere seconds, it began to sink, leaving its passengers to rush for the hatch.

Sliding down the ladder, Reed wasn't even conscious of slipping back into a confined space. His sopping boots hit a metal hallway, and the hatch overhead cranked closed. Sailors rushed by, and Sinju lay crumpled on the floor next to her father.

Reed breathed hard and leaned against the wall, then slowly sank to the floor as the *Louisville* groaned and he imagined it diving beneath the waves again.

Turk slumped down next to him, wheezing hard, his face and hair saturated with salt spray. For a while, they sat across from each other, too exhausted and relieved to move, just drinking in the surreal moment of still being alive. Still being in one piece.

"So"—Turk wheezed—"about the BASE jumping . . . I think I'm good on thrills for a while."

Reed indulged in a dry grin. "How do you feel about golf?"

73

The White House
48 Hours Later

Another bright April day broke over DC, bringing with it the fragrant smell of the cherry blossoms along the National Mall. Maggie stood in the Oval Office with the windows open, the sun on her face, the ache in her bones.

An unbelievable, inexpressible relief in her soul.

She watched the wind play with the trees outside, blowing stray leaves from the previous autumn across the South Lawn and washing her world in scents too rich to be manufactured. It was so good to be alive. It was so good to know her country was safe. At least for a little longer.

There was a soft tap on the door, and Maggie invited the knocker in without looking to see who it was. She already knew. Only Jill tapped with the strength of a mouse and the spirit of a dinosaur.

"Good morning," Maggie said, still not turning from the window.

Jill shut the door and moved to the desk, smart enough to maintain the silence for a few precious minutes longer. She stood next to Maggie with her arms crossed, an elegant, sky-blue dress hanging from her shoulders, her chin held high.

Maggie thought the world may have faced crisis, but at least she still had a chief of staff at her side after the smoke settled. That was an improvement over last summer.

"Get much sleep?" Jill asked.

Maggie chuckled. "Not for a couple years now."

Jill joined in the laugh, then helped herself to a cup of coffee from the tray nearby. She settled onto one of the couches in the middle of the room, and Maggie sat across from her, leaning back and enjoying the soft cushion. All the little things felt a little more vibrant, a little more real in the face of near total destruction. The funny part about it, of course, was that most of the planet would never know how close they came to extinction.

"Secretary Gorman called," Jill said. "She's arranged a meeting with Ambassador Yang next week. I expect it to be a lengthy conversation."

No joke, Maggie thought.

Following her phone call with President Chen, in which the executive leader of the People's Republic of China disclosed his military as the authors of the missile strike against North Korea, Maggie spent a few minutes in a mental tailspin, confused and taken off guard.

Grateful, despite herself.

But it didn't take long for reality to set in and for her to realize she should've seen it coming. China was North Korea's closest—and in many ways, *only*—ally. Of course, Beijing had sources buried in Pyongyang—probably far more than America ever dreamed of. Those assets would've reported Jang's intentions to President Chen. When the bombs went off in Pyongyang, China would've known America had nothing to do with it.

Beijing wouldn't have been in a hurry to defend its Western rival, but that didn't mean the Chinese were eager to embrace nuclear war, either. Not on these terms, anyway.

So, as Jang's insurrection gained steam and an imminent nuclear attack seemed inevitable, Chen made the call to launch a conventional missile strike against the DPRK's most operational missile bases. Unlike Washington, Beijing probably had a clear picture of which missile bases were truly a threat and which were just for show. While the US couldn't risk implementing anything short of a full nuclear strike, China could leverage a cruise missile barrage against key targets and then invade from the north.

Well, not invade—not in an aggressive way. China was only there on a "peace-keeping mission," of course. A humanitarian operation. The fifty thousand soldiers they deployed in under twelve hours hadn't been secretly staged on the North Korean border in preparation for a dive into the Korean Peninsula—they just *happened* to be conducting training exercises in that region and were prepped to take action when their ally needed them most.

It was complete crap, all of it, and Maggie smelled it from across the globe. Sure, Beijing did restore relative stability to the DPRK, and they even found a way to miraculously raise Cho from the dead—a feat that sent a shockwave of euphoria across North Korea. But Maggie saw through the charade.

It was far too advantageous a move on China's part for her to believe it was strictly an act of humanitarian compassion. Chinese forces now held a strategic foothold only miles north of the DMZ, and unless Maggie was a far greater fool than she thought herself to be, she never expected them to leave. Cho would be a puppet leader now, and the People's Republic of China would take one step closer to global dominance.

Meanwhile, the US would remain at DEFCON 2 for a few days longer, just to remind China that not everything was hunky-dory. Eventually, the Pentagon would migrate back to level 3, then 4. Now that whatever hypersonic missiles North Korea possessed were under Chinese control, their threat was no greater than those housed in Beijing.

But even though a restoration of the relative status quo was on the horizon, in some ways, things had changed forever for Maggie. Just for a second, she'd seen the ugly scepter of potential world war raise its head out of the murk, and even as that scepter sank into the shadows again, she couldn't unsee it.

And nor should she.

"I guess . . . the world wasn't ready for nuclear war," Jill said, trying to be cheerful, though her words were tarnished by the ugly truth of it all.

"No," Maggie said. "I guess not." She looked out at the rose garden and thought, but didn't say . . .

At least not yet.

74

Edwards Air Force Base
Kern County, California

The CIA SAC Gulfstream taxied off the end of the runway and turned toward a secure hangar, a few hundred yards away. Reed sat in a chair near the tail, only half awake, basking in the bright California sun.

After four days of bleak weather in Korea, followed by two days of creeping slowly out of the Yellow Sea on board *Louisville*, he felt like he could soak in the sun forever.

It took almost a week to get back to the States. After reaching Japan and bidding farewell to Gagliardi and his men, Reed and Turk were isolated, along with Gok and Sinju, in a windowless building at the edge of a Navy installation.

Gok was treated for his numerous injuries, Sinju for her extensive beatings, and Reed and Turk were left to sleep for twenty hours straight. While the military remained on full alert in the face of a Chinese advance into North Korea, it took some time for the CIA to send a jet to pick them up.

Reed wouldn't have minded much, but he wasn't allowed to make any phone calls, and he knew Banks would be stressed out of her mind. He worried about her, but he was so glad to be headed home that he didn't complain much.

Turk seemed to have completely forgotten about his imaginary busty redhead, instead investing extensive amounts of time looking after Sinju and caring for her every need. He bribed their courtesy officer—or jailer, depending on your point of view—to bring them a stack of American board games, and he spent days teaching Sinju how to play checkers, Parcheesi, and Clue. She struggled with Monopoly the most, unable to wrap her mind around the concept of owning property or building wealth. But she laughed a lot when she was with Turk, and he looked at her in a way Reed had never seen the big Tennessean look at anything.

Reed figured that was okay.

As the Gulfstream parked in the hangar and the doors rolled closed, the pilots gave them permission to depart. Gok went first, and Turk was close behind with Sinju's arm hooked in his. Reed let them slip out, then lazily found his way to the bottom of the stairs.

A row of black-suited men in sunglasses waited for them, hurrying to greet Gok as he set foot on American soil for the first time. Somebody spoke to him in Korean, translating for a guy who introduced himself as "Mr. Smith."

Reed just smirked.

"Welcome home, sir," somebody said.

Reed turned to see an Air Force captain standing behind him, offering his hand. Reed shook it, and he saw something in the guy's eyes that told him the captain had a vague idea who he was talking to.

Word gets around.

"Thanks," Reed said.

"We've got accommodations arranged for you overnight. We can put you on a plane first thing in the morning, if that works for you."

Reed looked out the narrow crack in the hangar door, toward an auburn sky. He drank in the warmth and thanked God it was the setting sun—not a bomb. "If it's all the same to you, Captain, I'll take that plane tonight."

"Uh . . . I mean, I guess I could make some calls."

"Please do. I just want to go home."

75

Minsu was back in his apartment, overlooking the city, the inhaler camera in one hand. His shoulders sagged, and almost every part of him hurt. It had been a week since he'd enjoyed a full night's sleep, and per usual, he was hungry.

The strain and terror that wore on his mind during the Jang insurrection was unlike any of the fear he encountered since infiltrating North Korea. It was primal. Unearthly. It let him know just how ugly a place the world could really be.

Outside his window, Chinese soldiers marched down the street, leading a unit of KPA toward downtown. In a lot of ways, the Chinese troops looked like their Korean counterparts. They were outfitted in dark uniforms, wore angry looks on their faces, and were harsh with the local civilians. But what set them apart was the tone of their presence. It was obvious to Minsu, and obvious to the world, the Chinese were in charge.

The elation that washed over the city upon the news of Cho Jong's survival—or resurrection, depending on who you asked—was unlike anything Minsu had witnessed before. It was as vibrant as the desperation and fear of only days prior, and no less loud. The supreme leader lived. The world was no longer ending. Hope was in the air.

But not for Minsu. He wasn't fooled by the Chinese soldiers flooding the city or the humanitarian intentions they claimed. He also wasn't fooled by Cho's disappearance or the Americans' hand in Jang's unfortunate fall from the Ryugyong.

In Minsu's mind, it was all part of a chess match. The players were the big dogs, Washington and Beijing. Korea and Koreans were just pawns—the same as they had always been.

Minsu stepped away from the window and settled onto his bed. He rolled the inhaler in his hand, then lay back and stared up at the ceiling. He thought he could sleep that night.

The CIA had kept their promise to extract him. Shortly after the supreme leader returned to power, the Agency reached out to arrange an exfiltration. But Minsu declined. As the fear faded and the reality of North Korea's new situation sank in, he knew he could never leave—as badly as he wanted to. And as much as he knew the Americans were simply using him.

He would stay.

Not because he really believed anything would ever change or because he believed his work mattered to Korea. He would stay because it would make his mother proud. Because she had sacrificed her life for her people, and in her memory, he was ready to do the same.

Minsu slid the inhaler under his pillow and closed his eyes, breathing slowly. Yes, he could sleep tonight. And then tomorrow, he would go back to work, fighting for his people.

76

Mountain Brook, Alabama

Reed tipped the Uber driver in cash, then hauled his aching body out of the car. He knew Banks would've picked him up at the terminal, but he didn't want her to have to strap little Davy into the back of the Camaro and rattle across town on her own.

He took the short ride from Birmingham-Shuttlesworth International Airport to his rental home in the hills, drinking in the gorgeous spring landscape. After shouldering his backpack and stepping to the end of the driveway, he took a moment to admire the little house. It may not have been his—not really—but to him, it felt like a palace. The best address on planet Earth.

Passing by the mailbox, he saw a copy of the *Birmingham News* sticking out, along with a wad of envelopes, and he stopped to collect them. Banks didn't like to check the mail. Maybe because there was always only ever bills and bad news waiting for her.

There were, in fact, plenty of bills. Reed shuffled through a stack of medical, phone, and utility invoices before a plain white envelope fell into his hand. It was addressed to him in simple black type, with a Washington, DC, return address printed in the top left corner.

Reed held the bills and newspaper under one arm and tore the envelope open. A single document was housed within—a check, folded into a paystub. He flipped it open, and his heart skipped a beat as his gaze fell over the amount, printed in neat and tidy text.

Two hundred fifty thousand dollars, made payable to Reed David Montgomery.

Reed's eyes stung. At the top of the check was the name of the CIA's phony law firm—Hughe, Long and Crawley—and as his gaze settled over the memo line, a soft smile tugged at his cheeks.

FOR PROSECUTION SERVICES RENDERED.

Reed looked up to Heaven and breathed a soft prayer. Not so much for the check, but for all of it: His happy little family. His cozy little home. His wonderful life, protected for the moment from annihilation.

It was more than enough.

He walked up to the porch and pulled out his key to unlock the door. When he walked in, he smelled poopy diapers and a grungy old bulldog. Reed smiled again.

It was good to be home.

ELECTION DAY
THE PROSECUTION FORCE THRILLERS Book 3

In less than a week, America will select her new president.
Three candidates are tied in a dead heat.
But one of them is about to step into a lethal trap.

From twenty-four hundred yards, an invisible shooter takes an impossible shot. As the gun smoke clears and panic erupts, the Free World is once again threatened with the prospect of chaos.

Pulled out of a blissful family vacation, Reed Montgomery watches the carnage unfold on cable news, as helpless as any other American.

But then the phone rings and Reed's Prosecution Force is called into action.

Because the shooter is still out there, and he's already picked his next target.

Unless Reed acts quickly, he's going to strike again.

Get your copy today at
severnriverbooks.com/series/the-prosecution-force

ABOUT THE AUTHOR

Logan Ryles was born in small town USA and knew from an early age he wanted to be a writer. After working as a pizza delivery driver, sawmill operator, and banker, he finally embraced the dream and has been writing ever since. With a passion for action-packed and mystery-laced stories, Logan's work has ranged from global-scale political thrillers to small town vigilante hero fiction.

Beyond writing, Logan enjoys saltwater fishing, road trips, sports, and fast cars. He lives with his wife and three fun-loving dogs in Alabama.

Sign up for Logan Ryles's reader list at
severnriverbooks.com/authors/logan-ryles

Printed in the United States
by Baker & Taylor Publisher Services